THE DON NOVELS OF
MIKHAIL SHOLOKHOV

AND QUIET FLOWS THE DON

THE DON FLOWS HOME TO THE SEA

SEEDS OF TOMORROW *

HARVEST ON THE DON *

* Published together in the original Russian under the title
Virgin Soil Upturned

These are BORZOI BOOKS, *published by*
ALFRED A. KNOPF *in New York*

HARVEST ON

THE DON

Harvest

ON

THE DON

By MIKHAIL SHOLOKHOV

TRANSLATED FROM THE RUSSIAN BY
H. C. STEVENS

ALFRED A. KNOPF : NEW YORK

1 9   6 1

L. C. catalog card number: 60–14767

THIS IS A BORZOI BOOK,
PUBLISHED BY ALFRED A. KNOPF, INC.

Manufactured in the United States of America.

FIRST AMERICAN EDITION

THE PEOPLE AT GREMYACHY LOG

ARZHANOV, IVAN, elderly collective farmer.

ATAMANCHUKOV, VASILI, member of Gremyachy collective farm, but secretly a member of the Polovtsiev conspiracy.

BESKHLEBNOV, AKIM, collective farmer (called "the Older" to distinguish him from his son).

BESKHLEBNOV, AKIM (called "the Younger").

BOIKO-GLUKHOV, POLIKARP PETROVICH, a G.P.U. officer.

DAMASKOV, TIMOFEI, nicknamed "the Ragged," anti-Red, Lukeria Nagulnova's lover.

DAVIDOV, SIEMION, a Communist metal worker, a sailor during the civil war. One of 25,000 workers mobilized by the Soviet Communist Party in 1930 to organize collective farms. Chairman of Gremyachy Log collective farm.

DIEMID, a poor Cossack, nicknamed "the Silent."

DUBTSIEV, AGAFON, collective farmer; in charge of second brigade of field workers.

KHARLAMOVA, VARIA, a girl of seventeen, working in second brigade.

KHIZHNAK, G.P.U. officer; assistant to Boiko-Glukhov.

KUPRIANOVNA, DARIA, cook to second brigade.

LIUBISHKIN, PAVEL, collective farmer; in charge of the third brigade.

LYATIEVSKY, VATSLAV AUGUSTOVICH, formerly a lieutenant in the Russian Imperial Army; now an organizer of an anti-Soviet conspiracy.

MAIDANNIKOV, KONDRAT, collective farmer; member of second brigade.

NAGULNOV, MAKAR, secretary to Gremyachy Communist group; parted from his wife, Lukeria, on ideological grounds, but still secretly in love with her.

NAGULNOVA, LUKERIA (Lushka), Nagulnov's wife; having an affair with Davidov, but in love with Timofei Damaskov.

NAIDIONOV, IVAN, a young Communist.

NECHAYEV, ALEXANDER, collective farmer; member of third brigade.

NESTERENKO, IVAN, secretary to district Communist Party, Don area.

OSIETROV, TIKHON GORDEICH, collective farmer; member of third brigade.

OSTROVNOV, YAKOV LUKICH, formerly a medium-rich Cossack; now manager of Gremyachy collective farm, but secretly working against the Soviets.

POLOVTSIEV, ALEXANDER ANISIMOVICH, formerly a captain in the Russian Imperial Army; now organizer of an anti-Soviet conspiracy.

POLYANITSA, NIKIFOR, one of 25,000 workers mobilized to organize collectivization; chairman of Tubyanskoe collective farm.

POPOVA, LIUDMILA SERGEEVNA, young teacher in Gremyachy village school.

PRYANISHNIKOV, collective farmer; member of second brigade.

RAZMIOTNOV, ANDREI, a Communist; chairman of Gremyachy village Soviet.

RIKALIN, USTIN, collective farmer; member of third brigade.

SHALY, IPPOLIT SIDOROVICH, the Gremyachy blacksmith.

SHCHUKAR, an old man; worker in Gremyachy collective farm.

USHAKOV, DIEMKA, collective farmer; in charge of the first brigade.

HARVEST ON

THE DON

HARVEST ON THE DON

Chapter 1

AFTER the rain the earth was swollen with moisture, and when the wind scattered the clouds, it languished in the dazzling sunlight and steamed with a dove-grey haze. Of a morning, a mist arose from the stream and the swampy, muddy leas. It billowed over Gremyachy Log, hastened towards the steppe uplands, and there melted, dissolving imperceptibly into a delicate turquoise haze. As late as noonday a leaden-heavy, copious dew lay like shot scattered over the leaves of the trees, over the reed-thatched roofs of the houses and sheds, and pressed down the grasses.

Over the steppe the quitch-grass rose above the knee. Beyond the pasture lands the melilot was in blossom. In the late afternoon its honeyed scent spread all through the village, filling the girls' hearts with a fretting languor. The winter wheat extended right to the horizon in a solid dark-green wall; the spring grain rejoiced the eye with its unusually close-sprouting shoots; on the slopes of the hillocks and the dry hollows the more recently sown millet was pricking through the ground. The sandier patches were thickly brushed with the spikes of young maize.

Towards the middle of June a spell of settled weather began;

not a cloud was to be seen in the sky; and beneath the sun the blossoming, rain-washed steppe was marvellously coloured. Now it was like a young mother feeding her child at the breast: unusually beautiful, tranquil, a little weary, and beaming with the fine, pure, and happy smile of motherhood.

Every morning Yakov Lukich was up and away before sunrise; flinging an old canvas coat round his shoulders he walked out of the village to rejoice in the sight of the grain. He remained standing a long time by the furrow marking the bound of the fields of winter wheat, which sparkled with dewdrops. He stood motionless, his head sunk on to his chest, like an old, weary horse, meditating: "If the south-east wind doesn't blow from the Kalmik steppe while it's ripening, if the wheat isn't scorched by drought, the collective farm will have more grain than it will know what to do with, damn and blast it! The bloody Soviet government is in luck. Think of all the years we lived as individual farmers and never once did the rain come in season. But this year it's poured down in bucketfuls. And if there's a good harvest and the collective farmers do well with their labour days, what chance will we have of turning them against the Soviets? Not on your life! A hungry man's like a wolf in the forest, he'll go where you like; but a full man's like a pig at the trough, you can't shift him. And what is Mr. Polovtsiev thinking about? I can't make out what they're waiting for. This would be just the moment to shake the Soviets; but they've cooled right off. . . ."

Yakov Lukich had grown tired of waiting for Polovtsiev's promised rising, and these thoughts only reflected his spiteful reaction. He knew well enough that Polovtsiev hadn't cooled off at all, but was waiting for some definite news. Almost every night messengers made their way from distant villages and district centres along the ravine which ran from the hills up to Yakov's garden. Doubtless they left their horses at the wooded head of the ravine and continued their journey on foot. At the quiet knock which was the agreed signal, Yakov Lukich opened the door to them without lighting the lamp, and led them in to Polovtsiev in the best room. Here the shutters of the two windows looking out on the yard were shut fast day and night, and

on the inside they were closely covered with thick grey woollen rugs. Even on a sunny day the room was as dark as a cellar, and, just like a cellar, it smelt of mildew, dampness, and the fusty air of a house rarely opened up. During the day neither Polovtsiev nor Lyatievsky went out of the house. A galvanized iron bucket underneath a hole left by a broken floorboard met the voluntary prisoners' needs.

As he struck a match in the passage, Yakov ran his eye hurriedly over each of the men who stole up to the house by night; but none of the faces he saw was familiar. They were all strangers and appeared to have come a long way. Once he ventured to ask one of these messengers: "Where've you come from, friend?"

The flickering light of the match lit up the bearded, apparently good-natured face of an elderly Cossack beneath the cowl of a peasant coat, and Yakov Lukich saw his narrowed eyes and teeth gleaming in a smile.

"From the other world, friend," the man answered, adding imperatively: "Take me to him quick, and don't be so nosy."

Two nights later the same bearded Cossack came again, accompanied by another, younger Cossack. They carried something heavy into the passage, but they moved quietly—almost noiselessly. Yakov struck a match and saw that the bearded man was carrying two officers' saddles, and bridles with silver ornamentation were flung across his shoulders; the other man had some kind of long and shapeless bundle wrapped in a shaggy black cloak over his shoulder.

The bearded Cossack winked at Yakov Lukich as at an old friend, and asked: "Are they both at home?" Without waiting for an answer he made his way to the best room.

The match burned down and scorched Lukich's fingers. In the darkness the Cossack knocked against something and swore under his breath.

"Wait, I'll give you a light," Yakov Lukich said, taking a match out of the box with his clumsy fingers.

Polovtsiev himself opened the door, and said quietly: "Come in. Oh, do come in, what are you playing at out there? You come in too, Yakov Lukich: I need you. Not so much noise; I'll light the light in a moment."

He lit a hurricane lamp, but covered its top with his jacket, leaving only a narrow beam of light which fell slantwise over the ochred floorboards.

The visitors greeted him respectfully, and put down the things they had brought beside the door. The bearded man stepped two paces forward, clicked his heels together, and held out a packet which he took from his inside breast pocket.

Polovtsiev tore the envelope open, swiftly read the letter, holding it close to the lamp, and said: "Tell Grey Hair I thank him. There's no answer. I expect news from him not later than the twelfth. You can go. Dawn won't find you still on the road, will it?"

"Not at all. We'll make it. We've got good horses," the bearded Cossack answered.

"Well, off with you. Thank you for your service."

"Glad to help!"

They both turned as one man, clicked their heels, and went out. Yakov Lukich thought admiringly: "Now, that's what I call trained! They went through the old school, you can tell that by their bearing."

Polovtsiev came over to him and laid a heavy hand on his shoulder. Lukich involuntarily drew himself up, straightened his back, and brought his hands to attention down his trouser seams.

"You saw those eagles?" Polovtsiev said, laughing quietly. "They won't fail us. They'll follow me through fire and water, not like certain scoundrels and doubting Thomases of Voiskovoi village. Now let's see what they've brought. . . ."

Going down on one knee, he expertly untied the white rawhide thongs wound tightly round the cloak, unwrapped it, and took out the parts of a dismantled hand machine gun and four shining machine-gun discs wrapped in greasy sacking. Then he carefully unwrapped two sabres. One of them was quite plain —a Cossack sabre in a worn scabbard that had seen better days; the other was an officer's weapon with a deeply engraved silver hilt and a faded sword-knot in the colours of the St. George's Cross ribbon. The scabbard was ornamented with anelloe silver and was attached to a black Cossack sword-belt.

Dropping down on both knees, he held out the officer's sword on the palms of his outstretched hands, throwing his head back,

as though admiring the tarnished gleam of the silver. Then he pressed it to his chest and said in a shaking voice: "My darling, my beauty! My faithful old friend! You'll serve me yet in faith and truth."

His massive lower jaw quivered; tears of rage and rapture came to his eyes. But he took himself in hand and, turning his pale, contorted face to Yakov Lukich, asked him in a ringing tone: "Do you recognize it, Lukich?"

Yakov Lukich swallowed convulsively and nodded without speaking: he certainly did recognize that sabre. The first time he had ever seen it was in 1915, when the young and daring ensign Polovtsiev wore it during the war on the Austrian front.

Lyatievsky, who had been lying silent and unconcerned on the bed, sat up, letting his bare feet dangle. Stretching himself till his joints cracked, he flashed his one eye moodily. "A touching sight!" he said hoarsely. "Truly idyllic, so to speak. But I'm not fond of these sentimental scenes with their touch of the idiotically *pathétique*."

"Stop that!" Polovtsiev said sharply.

Lyatievsky shrugged his shoulders. "Why should I? And in any case, what have I got to stop?"

"Stop it, I ask you," Polovtsiev said quietly, rising to his feet and making for the bed at a slow, almost stealthy pace.

He held the sabre in his trembling left hand; his right hand unbuttoned and tore at the collar of his grey Tolstoyan shirt. Yakov Lukich noted with alarm that in his frenzy Polovtsiev's eyes had converged at the bridge of his nose, and his usually bloated face had gone as grey as his shirt.

Lyatievsky calmly and deliberately lay back on the bed and put his hands under his head. "A theatrical gesture," he said, smiling derisively, gazing with his one eye at the ceiling. "I've seen it all before, and all too often, in lousy provincial theatres. I've had enough of it."

Polovtsiev halted two paces away from the bed, raised one hand with a weary gesture, and wiped the sweat from his brow; then the hand, feeble and limp, dropped again. "My nerves," he said, stammering and incoherent, like a man with paralysis; his face twisted sideways with a long grimace that remotely resembled a smile.

"I've heard that too, more than once. Oh, stop behaving like a woman, Polovtsiev. Take yourself in hand."

"My nerves . . ." Polovtsiev bellowed. "My nerves are playing me up. And I've just about had enough of this darkness, this grave . . ."

"Darkness is the friend of the wise. It encourages philosophical meditations on life, while in practice only anaemic pimple-faced virgins and ladies suffering from breach of promise and migraine have nerves. Nerves are a shame and dishonour to an officer. And you're only pretending, Polovtsiev; you haven't any nerves really: that's all nonsense. I don't believe you. I give you my honest word as an officer, I don't believe you."

"You're no officer, you're a brute."

"I've heard that from you more than once too. But I shan't challenge you to a duel: you can go to the devil! Duelling's obsolete and out of place: we've got more important things to do. Besides, as you know, officers with any feeling of self-respect only use swords, not policemen's carvers like that specimen which you pressed so touchingly and tenderly to your chest. As an old artillery-man I despise that sort of cold filigree work. And there's one other objection to challenging you to a duel: by origin and blood you're a plebeian, and I'm from one of the oldest families of the Polish aristocracy, which—"

"Now listen here, you aristocrat!" Polovtsiev interrupted roughly, and his voice surprisingly recovered its normal firmness and metallic, imperative tone. "Are you scoffing at my George sword? Say another word and I'll cut you down like a dog."

Lyatievsky half rose on the bed. No trace of his ironic smile remained on his lips. He said quite seriously and simply: "Now that I *do* believe. Your voice betrays your sincere and kindly intentions, and so Ill shut up."

"I'll kill you all the same," Polovtsiev asserted obstinately, putting his head down like a bull as he stood beside the bed. "With this very same blade I'll turn one lordly brute into two. And d'you know when I'll do it? As soon as we've overthrown the Soviet regime in the Don."

"Well, then I shall live quietly to a great old age, and I may even live for ever," Lyatievsky said with a laugh. He swore violently and turned his face to the wall.

Yakov Lukich stood at the door, hopping from foot to foot as though on hot coals. More than once he started for the door, but Polovtsiev stopped him with a gesture. At last he could stand no more, and he implored: "Let me go: do release me, your excellency. It'll be dawn soon, and I've got to drive out to the fields early."

Polovtsiev sat down on a chair, laid the sword across his knees, and, resting his hands on it, bent his heavy, massive body almost double. He remained seated thus for some time without uttering a word. The only sounds to be heard were his heavy, wheezy breathing and the tick of his large pocket watch lying on the table. Yakov Lukich thought he must have dozed off, but he suddenly started up from the chair and said: "Pick up the saddle, Lukich, and I'll bring the rest. We'll go and hide all this in a safe and dry spot. How about the shed where you store your dung-briquettes, eh?"

"That's suitable: let's go," Yakov Lukich willingly agreed, for he had not hoped to get out of the room so quickly.

He stooped to pick up one of the saddles; but Lyatievsky jumped out of the bed as though scalded, and hissed, his one eye flashing furiously:

"What are you doing? I ask you, what d'you think you're doing?"

Polovtsiev, who was bent over the cloak, straightened up and said coldly: "Well, what's the matter? What's upset you now?"

"D'you mean to say you don't understand? Hide the saddles and all that scrap metal if you wish, but leave the machine gun and the discs. You're not staying in a friend's country house, and we may have need of the machine gun any moment. Surely you realize that?"

Polovtsiev thought for a moment, and then agreed. "Maybe you're right, you Radzivill mongrel. So let it remain here. Go to bed, Lukich: you're not wanted any more."

How deeply his old service habits were still ingrained in Lukich! Before he had time to think, his bare feet involuntarily did a "left turn," and his toil-worn heels knocked against each other with a dry, almost inaudible patter. Polovtsiev smiled as he noticed the movement. But as soon as Yakov was outside he realized what he had done, coughed with embarrassment, and

thought: "That bearded devil has got me all tied up with his military bearing."

He did not sleep a wink until daybreak. The hopes he had had that their rising would be successful turned to fears that it would collapse, and he felt belated regrets that he had bound up his fate so imprudently with such hopeless individuals as Polovtsiev and Lyatievsky. "I was in too much of a hurry; I rushed in like a chicken into the soup," he thought mournfully. "You should have waited, you old fool; you shouldn't have invited them here. Then if they'd got the upper hand over the Communists, I could have joined them. But now it's clear enough that they're leading me right up the garden, like a blind man. And yet if I was to stand aside, and others like me, then what would happen? Carry the Soviets on our backs for ever? That wouldn't do either. But it's a sure thing they'll never get off our backs by themselves, not on your life! Anything rather than that. Polovtsiev promises that there'll be an invasion from abroad and we'll be helped by the Kuban Cossacks. He offers a soft bed. But what sort of sleep shall we have? The Lord only knows. And supposing the Allies don't land on our soil? What then? They'll send us English overcoats just like they did in 1919, but they themselves will stay at home drinking coffee and having a good time with their wives. And what will we do with their overcoats? All we'll do with them is wipe our bloody noses with the edges—that's all. The Bolsheviks will smash us, God knows they will. They're used to it. The Don country will go up in smoke."

Such thoughts made him feel melancholy and almost tearfully sorry for himself. He groaned and coughed, crossed himself, muttered prayer after prayer, and then his importunate thoughts returned to worldly matters. "But what Alexander Anisimovich won't do with that crooked Pole! Why are they always quarrelling? They've got a great task before them, and they live like two dogs in one kennel. That one-eyed fellow's getting more and more bad-tempered, he's always putting in his spoke and bragging. He's a rogue, I don't trust him a bit. The proverb says aright: 'Don't trust a crooked man, a hunchback, or your wife.' Alexander Anisimovich will kill him; sure to God he will. Well, let him ! He's not of our faith anyway."

And with these reassuring thoughts he dropped off into a brief and oppressive sleep.

Chapter 2

He awoke after sunrise. In that short hour or so of sleep he had had many dreams, and all of them unpleasant.

When he woke up he sat a long time on his bed, staring idiotically with terror-stricken eyes. "Such filthy dreams don't bode any good. There's some misfortune on the way," he decided, feeling an unpleasant weight on his heart and spitting with disgust at the very memory of his dreams.

He dressed in the gloomiest of moods, kicking away the cat which rubbed itself against his legs; at breakfast he called his wife a "little fool" for no reason whatever, and when his daughter-in-law ineptly joined in the farm talk at the table, he even waved his spoon at her as if she were not a grown woman but a little girl. Siemion was highly amused at his father's lack of control: he pulled a stupid, terrified face and winked at his wife, who shook with silent laughter. That put Yakov Lukich right out of humour: he flung his spoon down on the table and shouted in a voice quivering with rage:

"You're grinning now, but before long you may be crying."

To make things worse, as he demonstratively left the table without finishing his breakfast he put his hand down on the edge of his plate and sent his unfinished, hot beetroot soup over his trousers. His daughter-in-law hid her face with both hands and flew into the passage. Siemion remained seated at the table, his head in his hands; but his muscular back shook and his broad shoulders rose and fell with his laughter. Even Yakov's everlastingly straight-faced wife could not help laughing.

"What's the matter with you today, Father?" she asked. "Did you get out of bed with your left foot first, or have you had a bad dream?"

"What d'you want to know for, you old hag?" he shouted frenziedly, and stamped away from the table.

At the kitchen door he caught his sleeve in a protruding nail and tore his new satin shirt right to the elbow. He returned to his room to look for another shirt and leaned the lid of the chest rather carelessly against the wall; it fell and gave him a resounding crack on the back of his head.

"Oh, damn you! This is one hell of a day!" he exclaimed angrily, helplessly sitting down on a stool and tenderly feeling the healthy bump already rising on his head.

Somehow he managed to change his torn shirt and stained trousers; but as he was very agitated and in a great hurry he forgot to do up his fly. In this indecent state he walked almost all the way to the collective-farm office, noting with surprise that the women who greeted him smiled mysteriously and hurriedly turned their eyes away. His bewilderment was unceremoniously dispelled by old Shchukar, who came trotting towards him.

"Growing old, my dear Yakov Lukich?" he asked sympathetically, coming to a halt.

"Well, are you growing any younger? I can't see any sign of it. Your eyes are as red as a rabbit's and full of tears."

"My eyes are streaming because I read at night. In my old age I'm reading a lot and taking all sorts of higher educational courses. All the same, I do keep myself decent, but you've grown so forgetful you might be a very old man."

"What do you mean?"

"You've forgotten to shut the wicket gate at home; you'll have all your cattle wandering off. . . ."

"Siemion will shut it," Lukich said abstractedly.

"Siemion won't shut that gate. . . ."

Struck by an unpleasant supposition, Yakov Lukich looked down; he groaned and set his fingers quickly to work. To complete the toll of the misfortunes which had descended on him this luckless morning, he stepped on a mouldy potato in the office yard, squashed it, and, slipping over, fell headlong.

That was the last straw: obviously so much couldn't happen by chance. The superstitous Lukich was profoundly convinced that some great misfortune was about to fall on him. With pale face and quivering lips he went into Davidov's room and said: "I'm

not feeling at all well, Comrade Davidov. May I go home? The storekeeper will take my place."

"You certainly do look queer, Lukich," Davidov replied sympathetically. "Go and rest up a bit. Will you drop in to see the doctor yourself, or shall we send him to see you at home?"

Yakov Lukich waved the idea off hopelessly. "He can't help me. I'll lie up and it'll pass off. . . ."

When he returned home he ordered the shutters to be closed, undressed, and lay on the bed, patiently waiting for the misfortune which was about to fall on him. "It's all this damnable Soviet regime!" he thought. "There's no peace from it day or night. In bed I dream stupid dreams such as I never had in the old days, and during the day one misery after another drags around with me as though tied by a rope. Under this regime I shan't live out my allotted span. I shall give up the ghost before my time."

However, his anxious expectations proved unjustified that day; the misfortune failed to arrive, and it came upon him only three days later.

To give himself courage, before going to bed he drank a glass of vodka; he slept through the night peacefully, without one dream. Next morning he felt better, and thought joyfully: "It's gone." He spent Saturday in his usual bustle of activity. But on Sunday evening, noticing that his wife appeared to have something on her mind, he asked: "You don't seem quite your usual self, Mother. Has the cow fallen sick? I noticed she came back from the pasture not very bright yesterday."

His wife turned to their son. "Siemion, leave the room for a bit; I've got to have a talk with your father."

Siemion, combing his hair before the mirror, answered in a disgruntled tone: "What are you all playing at with your secrets? There are those friends of father's in the best room; the devil has hung them round our necks. They sit whispering day and night. And now you've started. Before long life at home won't be worth living with your secrets. It's not a home, it's a convent: nothing but whispering and muttering everywhere. . . ."

"In any case it's nothing your sheep's brains need concern themselves with," Lukich said angrily. "You've been told to go out, now go out. You're grown very talkative lately. . . . Tuck your

tongue in, I tell you, or you'll get it bitten off before very long."

Siemion flared up, turned to his father, and said thickly: "You'd better be a little less free with your threats, my dear father. There aren't any timid or little ones in our family. And if we start threatening one another it might be the worse for all of us."

He went out, slamming the door behind him.

"Well, you can be proud of your darling son. What a hero he's turning out, the son of a bitch!" Yakov Lukich exclaimed bitterly.

His wife never entered into argument with him, but now she said measuredly: "Well, you think it over, Lukich: these idle guests of yours don't bring us much joy. With them around we have to watch our step so much it makes me sick. One of these days the village authorities will search the house, and then we'll be done for. I don't call this life, it's relapsing fever; you're afraid of every knock, every rustle. God forbid that anyone should have to live such a life. I'm worried to death over you and our Siemion too. If they find out about our visitors they'll take them away and you men as well. And then what will we women do? Wander through the world with a sack over our shoulders?"

"That's enough!" he interrupted her. "I know what I'm doing without needing you and Siemion to tell me. What is it you want to talk about? Out with it!"

He closed both doors and sat down beside his wife. At first he listened to her without revealing the anxiety which slowly took possession of him. But towards the end he lost his self-control, jumped up from the bench, and hurried about the room, muttering disconsolately: "We're done for! My own mother's ruined me. She's as good as chopped off my head."

When he calmed down a little he drank two large mugs of water one after the other and then sat down gloomily on the bench to think things out.

"What will you do now, Father?" his wife asked.

He did not answer. He didn't even hear the question.

His wife had told him that a day or two previously four old women had come to the house and insistently demanded to be taken to the officer gentlemen. They were all terribly anxious to know when the officers, with the help of Yakov Lukich and

other Cossacks in the village, would start the rising and overthrow the impious Soviet regime. His wife vainly assured them that there were no officers whatever in the house. One bowed and surly old woman angrily told her: "You're young to lie to me, Mother. Your own mother-in-law has told us officers have been living in your best room ever since the winter. We know they're living in secret from the people, but of course we shan't tell anyone about them. Take us to the senior officer; his name is Alexander Anisimovich."

As he went to tell Polovtsiev the news, Yakov Lukich felt all his usual anxious uncertainty. He was sure the officers would fly into a frenzy and give him a hiding. And he waited for his punishment humbly, trembling like a dog. But when, stammering and choking with agitation, he repeated all his wife had told him, Polovtsiev only smiled.

"I must say you make fine conspirators. . . . Well, it was only to be expected. So your mother's given us away, Lukich? Now what do you think we should do?"

"I think you must leave here, Alexander Anisimovich," Lukich said resolutely, growing bold at this reception of his news.

"When?"

"The sooner the better. There isn't time to think it over."

"I know that without your telling me. But where to?"

"I can't say. But where's your comrade? . . . I . . . Please forgive me for using that word. Where's Mr. Lyatievsky?"

"He's gone off. He'll be back tonight, and you'll meet him out in your orchard tomorrow. How about Atamanchukov—does he live on the outskirts too? I'll pass the rest of the time waiting there. Take me to him."

They made their way stealthily to Atamanchukov's house. Before they parted, Polovtsiev said to Lukich in a significant tone:

"Well, good-bye, Lukich. You think over what to do with your mother. She may spoil our game. Think it over carefully. Meet Lyatievsky and tell him where I've gone to."

He put his arms round Yakov Lukich, touched his dry and rough, unshaven cheeks with his own dry lips, and vanished as though he had merged into the dirty whitewash of the house-wall.

Yakov Lukich went back home and, as he got into bed, roughly

turned his wife to the wall and said: "Listen now . . . you're not
to give Mother any more food, and no water either. . . . After
all, she's got to die some time or other."

His wife, whose married life with Yakov had been long and
difficult, only groaned: "Yakov dear! Lukich! But you're her son."

In answer, almost for the first time in their life together, he
raised his hand and struck his elderly wife violently, saying in a
thick, hoarse voice: "Hold your tongue. She's putting us to a lot of
expense. Keep quiet! D'you want to be sent into exile?"

He rose heavily, unlocked the small padlock on the family
chest, cautiously crept into the warm passage, and padlocked
the door of his mother's room.

The old woman heard his footsteps. She had long since learnt
to recognize him by his tread. Once, over fifty years ago, she had
been a young and beautiful Cossack girl, starting up from her
domestic chores or her cooking, and listening with a beatific
smile as the little bare feet of her first-born uncertainly slapped
over the floor of the next room. Her beloved little Yakov was just
learning to toddle. Later she recognized his feet trotting and
jumping along the veranda as he returned from school. In those
days he was as merry and lively as a little goat. She could not recall that he ever walked, he always ran; or, rather, he did not
run so much as take a succession of little jumps, like a goat. Life
dragged on, as it does with all living things, rich in prolonged
sorrows and brief happinesses, and the time came when, as an elderly mother, she listened discontentedly at night to Yasha's light,
stealthy step as he came home. Now he was a smart and energetic youth, and secretly she was proud of him. When he returned late from his fun in the village his boots hardly seemed to
touch the ground, so light and impetuous was his step. So, without her realizing the change, he grew into a mature, staid family
man. His gait acquired a heavy assurance. And now the master's
steps had sounded about the house for many years. He was almost an old man; but he was still her little Yakov, and in her
dreams she often saw him as a small, flaxen-haired, nimble ur-
chin.

So when she heard his footsteps outside the door she asked in
her cracked, aged voice: "Is that you, Yakov?"

He did not reply. He stood by the door for a moment, then

went out into the yard, hurrying as though he had a purpose. As she dozed the old woman thought: "I bore a good Cossack; and a good farmer, thank God, has come of him. Everybody else is in bed and alseep, but he's gone out into the yard to see to the cattle." And a proud, maternal smile touched her faded, withered lips.

From that night there was a heavy atmosphere about the house. Though very feeble, the old woman clung to life. She pleaded to be given at least a scrap of bread, at least a sip of water; and as Yakov Lukich stole past her room he heard her stifled almost inaudible whisper:

"My dear, my little Yakov! My own little son. What are you doing this to me for? Do let me have some water at any rate."

The rest of the family hardly entered the house. Siemion and his wife spent day and night out of doors, and when her household duties forced Yakov's wife to stay at home she came out shaking with sobs. When, towards the close of the second day, as they were sitting at supper, Yakov Lukich said after a long silence: "We'll live in the summer kitchen for the time being," Siemion shuddered, rose from the table, and went out, staggering as though someone had pushed him.

On the fourth day the house grew very still. Yakov removed the padlock with trembling fingers, and he and his wife entered his mother's room. She was lying on the floor close to the door; beside her lay an old leather glove which by chance had been left on her bed since the winter. She had gnawed it with her toothless gums. It seemed that she had managed to assuage her thirst; a fine drizzle of rain had found its way through the shutter onto the windowsill, and possibly some dew too, for the nights were misty.

The dead woman's friends washed her whithered, wrinkled body, performed the due rites, and wept over her; but at the funeral none wept more bitterly and disconsolately than Yakov Lukich. The pain and remorse, and the burden of the loss he had suffered, lay heavily on his soul that day.

Chapter 3

Siemion Davidov, the Soviet-farm chairman, was oppressed by
an irresistible longing to do some physical labour. All his strong,
healthy body cried out for work: for work which by the end of
the day would make all his muscles ache with heavy yet pleasant weariness, and ensure easy, dreamless sleep.

One day he went along to the smithy to see how the repair of
the communal harvesting implements was progressing. The acrid,
bitter scent of heated iron and burning coal, the ringing song of
the anvil and the hoarse, complaining wheezes of the ancient
bellows made his heart beat violently. He stood for several minutes in the twilit forge with his eyes closed beatifically, silently, almost painfully, enjoying smells he had known since
childhood. Then he could not resist the temptation any longer:
he picked up a sledge-hammer. For two days he worked from
dawn to dusk, and did not leave the smithy. The smith's wife
brought him his dinner. But how could he do good work when
he was called away every few minutes? The shoe went blue and
cold in the tongs, the old smith, Sidorovich, grumbled, and his
apprentice openly grinned as he noticed that Davidov's hand,
weary with the physical strain, wrote absurdly twisted squiggles
instead of letters on the official documents brought out to him,
and sometimes even dropped the pencil on the earthen floor.

Davidov hated working in such conditions, and, to avoid being
a hindrance to the smith, swearing as juicily as any bo'sun, he
went back in a foul temper to his seat in the collective-farm
office.

There were times when he spent all day deciding everyday
but important problems of husbandry, checking reports and innumerable summaries drawn up by the book-keeper; listening
to the reports of the brigadiers; sorting out the collective farmers' applications; sitting in production conferences, busily attending to all those things without which it is impossible to run a
large collective husbandry, but which he regarded as the least
satisfying of all labour.

He began to sleep badly, invariably woke up with a headache, took his food wherever and however he could, and a feeling he had never known before, a feeling of incomprehensible lassitude, was with him all day. Without being aware of it he began to lose heart, grew irritable as never before, and looked by no means so young and well-nourished as when he had first arrived at Gremyachy Log. To add to his anxieties there was Lukeria Nagulnova and his constant thoughts of her . . . all kinds of thoughts. It hadn't been a good day for him when that blasted little hussy crossed his path.

Staring with derisively narrowed eyes at Davidov's sunken features, Razmiotnov, the village-Soviet chairman, said one day: "You're getting thinner and thinner, Siemion. You look just like an old bull after a bad winter; you'll be lying down in your tracks before long; you've gone all shabby and chicken-faced. Are you moulting? You shouldn't have your eyes on our girls so much, especially wives who're parted from their husbands. It's terrible bad for your health."

"You can go to the devil with your stupid advice."

"Now, don't get angry. I'm advising you because I like you."

Davidov flushed slowly but heavily. He was unable to conceal his embarrassment, and he tried to talk disjointedly of some trivial matter. But Razmiotnov was not to be put off.

"Did they teach you to flush like that in the fleet or in the factory? Not just on your face, but right down your neck? I wonder if you go red all over? Take your shirt off and let me have a look."

Not until he saw the angry light in Davidov's glazed eyes did Razmiotnov swiftly change the subject. Yawning as though bored, he began to talk of the haymow, gazed through half-closed lids with a pretence of sleepiness, but either could not or just would not suppress the impudent smile beneath his flaxen whiskers.

Had he guessed at Davidov's relations with Lukeria, or did he know about them? Most probably he knew. Of course he knew! How could the liaison be kept secret when the shameless woman not only had no intention of concealing it, but even deliberately flaunted it in public? Evidently she was flattered in her cheap self-esteem by the thought that she, the discarded wife of the

Party secretary, had hooked not an ordinary rank-and-file collective farmer but the chairman himself; and he had not repulsed her.

Despite the strict Cossack customs, she often left the office together with Davidov, taking him by the arm and even gently pressing her shoulder against his. His eyes darted from side to side like those of a hunted animal, for he was afraid of falling in with Makar Nagulnov; but he did not remove his arm, and adjusted his pace to hers, taking short steps like a hobbled horse. He stumbled again and again without cause. The cocky village lads—always merciless to lovers—ran after them, making faces and shouting in their thin voices:

"From sour dough made,
Bridegroom and bride."

They had highly inventive minds, and endlessly varied their clumsy couplet. While Davidov, wet with sweat, was walking with Lukeria past two blocks, inwardly cursing the boys, the woman, and his own feeble character, the "sour dough" was successively turned into heavy, unleavened, rich, sweet, and so on. At last he was unable to stand any more: he gently removed Lukeria's swarthy fingers from his elbow, said: "Excuse me, I'm in a hurry," and went on ahead with great strides. But it wasn't so easy to escape those boys. They split into two groups: one group followed Lukeria, the other accompanied Davidov. There was only one sure way of dealing with them: he went across to the nearest wattle fence, and made as though to break off a switch. Then they vanished as if the wind had blown them away, and the collective-farm chairman remained the lord and master of the street.

Not long before, in the dead of night he and Lukeria had run into the watchman of the windmill in the steppe outside the village. The watchman, an old farmer named Vershinin, was lying under his overcoat beside the hillock of an abandoned marmot run. Seeing two people coming straight towards him, he suddenly rose to his full height and called sternly, in military fashion:

"Halt! Who goes there?" He raised his ancient firearm (which was not even loaded) and levelled it.

"Friends! It's me, Vershinin!" Davidov answered somewhat re-

luctantly. He turned sharply on his heel, dragging Lushka after him. But the watchman ran after them and implored:

"Comrade Davidov, you don't happen to have tobacco on you for a cigarette, do you? I'm simply dying for a smoke."

Lushka did not turn away, step to one side, or even cover her face with her kerchief. She watched unconcernedly as Da· vidov hurriedly poured some tobacco out of his pouch, and then remarked as unconcernedly: "Come on, Siemion. As for you, Daddy, you'd be better employed looking out for thieves, not for lovers walking over the steppe. Bad men aren't the only ones who go out at night."

Vershinin laughed curtly, and slapped her familiarly on the shoulder. "But, my dear Lushka, deeds done at night are dark whether they're love-making or robbing other people. It's my job to act as watchman and challenge everybody. I'm guarding the windmill because it hasn't dung-briquettes but collective-farm grain inside. Well, thank you for the tobacco. Have a good walk! And the best of luck!"

"What the hell did you start talking to him for? You ought to have stepped aside; then he mightn't have recognized you," Da· vidov said as soon as they were alone, making no attempt to conceal his irration.

"I'm not sixteen, I'm not a girl to feel shy in front of any old fool," she curtly answered.

"But all the same . . ."

"What all the same?"

"You don't need to make a show of it, do you?"

"Why, is he my father or father-in-law?"

"I don't follow . . ."

"You try a bit harder and you will."

He could not see her face in the darkness, but the tone of her voice suggested that she was smiling. Furious at her unconcern for her own reputation and contempt for the decencies, he warmly exclaimed: "Can't you get it into your head that I'm anxious about you, little fool?"

She replied still more curtly: "Then don't bother. I can look after myself. You keep your anxiety for yourself."

"I am anxious about myself too."

She stopped at once and pressed right up against him. A note of

spiteful pleasure sounded in her voice. "You should have said so in the first place, my dear little man. You are only anxious about yourself, and you're only annoyed because you've been seen out in the steppe with a woman in the dark. But Daddy Nikolai doesn't care the least bit who you go playing about with in the dark."

"What d'you mean by 'playing about'?" he demanded angrily.

"Well, what else would you call it? Daddy Nikolai's spent quite a long time in this world, and he knows you and I haven't come out here by night to gather blueberries. So you're afraid of what the good people, the honest collective farmers of our village, think of you? Is that the trouble? You don't care a damn for me. If you didn't go roaming over the steppe with me you'd be doing it with some other woman. But you like to sin in the cellar; you want to hide in the shade, so that nobody knows of your fornicating. That's the sort of worm you are! But, my dear child, life isn't like that; you can't always hide away in a cool cellar. Pah, and you were a sailor, too! How did you get this way? I'm not afraid, but you are! I must be the man and you the woman."

She spoke more in jesting than truculent mood, but she was clearly stung by her lover's behaviour. She stood silent for a few moments, giving him contemptuous looks; then she swiftly took off her black satin skirt and said in a hectoring tone: "Undress!"

"You're crazy! Now what are you up to?"

"Put on my skirt and I'll wear your trousers. That'll only be just. Anyone who behaves like you in this pleasant world should wear what suits him. Now, get a move on!"

He laughed out loud, though he was affronted by her remarks and the proposed exchange. Doing his best to control his growing irritation, he said quietly: "Stop playing about, Lushka. Put on your skirt and come along."

Slowly and reluctantly she put on her skirt, tidied the hair which was breaking loose from under her kerchief, and said unexpectedly in a tone of deep dejection: "How you bore me, you sailor mattress!"

They walked all the way back to the village without exchanging another word. Outside her house they parted as silently. He nodded curtly; she hardly even nodded, and slipped through the

wicket gate as though she had melted into the deep shadow of
an old maple.

They did not see each other again for several days. But one
morning she walked into the collective-farm office and waited
patiently in the passage for the last caller to go. Davidov was
about to shut the door to his room when he noticed her. She was
sitting on the bench with her feet planted wide apart, masculine
fashion, her skirt drawn tightly across her knees. She smiled
serenely as she cracked a sunflower seed.

"Would you like some seeds, Chairman?" she asked in a low,
jesting tone. Her fine eyebrows quivered a little; she stared at
him with open insolence.

"Why aren't you out weeding?" he asked.

"I'm just off. You can see I'm in my working clothes. I just
dropped in to tell you: when it's dark come along to the pasture.
I'll wait for you by the Leonovs' threshing floor. D'you know it?"

"Yes."

"Will you be there?"

He nodded without speaking, and shut the door. He sat for
some time in gloomy meditation at his table, his cheeks supported on his fists, his eyes gazing into vacancy. He had much to
think about!

Even before their quarrel on the steppe she had come to his
room more than once as dusk was falling, had sat in the room for
a little while, and then said in a loud voice: "See me home, Siemion. It's getting dark, and I'm afraid to go alone. It's terrible how
nervous I am. I've always been nervous ever since I was a child;
I've always been frightened of the dark."

He pulled a fearful face and glanced at the board dividing the
room. On the other side the housekeeper, an old and pious
woman, sniffed indignantly, like a cat, and rattled the dishes noisily as she prepared her husband's and Davidov's supper. Lukeria's keen ears clearly caught her hissing whisper: "So she's
frightened, is she! She's not a woman, she's a devil. Why, even
when she gets to the next world she'll make her way through the
darkness to some young devil, and won't wait for him to take pity
on her. It's a great sinner I am for saying such things, forgive me,
Lord. But she: frightened! Oh yes, you're frightened of the dark
all right, you evil spirit! I should say!"

Lushka only smiled as she listened to this far from flattering description of her character. She was not the sort of woman to be influenced by the slanders of some God-fearing old hag. She felt like spitting at the everlastingly slobbering hypocrite and sniveller. During her brief spell as a married woman she had never found it necessary to impose any constraint on herself or to let any of the village women walk over her. She heard the housewife muttering under her breath on the farther side of the partition, calling her a wanton and a loose hussy. But such comparatively innocuous abuse was nothing to what she had had to listen to or had herself resorted to when she clashed with other women, when they started to quarrel with her, assuming in their blind naïveté that they were the only women entitled to love their husbands. She was quite able to stand up for herself and always gave as good as she got. There wasn't one jealous woman in the whole of the village who could have made a fool of Lushka, or have torn the kerchief off her head. None the less, she was determined to give this old hag a lesson; she always acted on the rule that she, Lushka, must have the last word.

The next time she visited Davidov she stopped for a moment in the housewife's room, letting Davidov go on to the front door. When she heard him hurrying down the creaking steps of the veranda she turned to the old woman with an innocent look on her face. The housewife hastily licked her moist lips and said all in one breath:

"You're absolutely shameless, Lushka, I've never met anyone like you before."

Lukeria half closed her eyes and put on a look of utmost modesty, standing in the middle of the room as though sunk in remorseful meditation. She had very long black lashes which seemed almost as though they had been pencilled in, and when she lowered her eyelids a deep shadow fell over her pale cheeks.

Taken in by this pretence of humility, the old woman whispered more gently: "Just think, woman: is it wise for you, married as you are, even though you are parted from your husband, to come to a single man's room, and in the dark too? Don't you think you ought to have more shame in front of people, ah? Come to your senses, have some sense of decency, for the love of Christ."

Lushka replied just as quietly and unctuously, mimicking the old woman's tone: "When the almighty God, our universal support and Saviour . . ." She paused, then raised her eyes, which glittered unpleasantly in the twilight. At the mention of God the devout old woman bowed her head and hurriedly crossed herself. But Lushka continued in an exultant, masculinely coarse and rough voice:

"When God handed out conscience to human beings He gave it to the good children. But I didn't happen to be at home: I was out on the spree, roaming with the boys, kissing and loving. And so you see I didn't get the tiniest scrap of conscience in the share-out. Well, what are you gaping at me for? Why don't you shut your mouth? And I tell you this: so long as your lodger hasn't come home, so long as he's making himself miserable over me, you can pray for us sinful ones, you old bitch!"

She swept out majestically, without one contemptuous glance back at the bewildered, dumbfounded woman. She found Davidov waiting for her outside. He asked her anxiously:

"Now what have you been up to, Lushka?"

"Chiefly talking about godly matters," she replied, quietly laughing and pressing close to him; she had picked up her former husband's trick of evading awkward questions with a joke.

"But seriously, what have you been whispering about? She hasn't upset you, has she?"

"She couldn't upset me, she wouldn't know how. She hissed at me out of jealousy. She's jealous of my freckled face," she joked again.

"She's got her suspicions of us, and that's a fact." He shook his head mournfully. "You shouldn't have come to my room, that's the trouble."

"Are you afraid of the old girl?"

"Why on earth should I be?"

"Well, if you're such a brave young fellow there's no need to waste breath on the subject."

It was difficult to get the self-willed and flighty Lushka to see reason about anything. But Davidov was completely bowled over by his feeling for her and was thinking seriously of speaking to Nagulnov, her former husband, and marrying her in order to ex-

tricate himself from his false position and to stop the village gossip. "I'll re-educate her. She won't lead me such a dance, and she'll give up her goings on. I'll get her into doing social work and persuade her, or make her, go in for self-education. Some good will come of her, and that's a fact. She's no fool, and I'll cure her of her fiery temper. I'm not Makar Nagulnov. She and he were like a scythe trying to cut a stone. But I'm different: I'll find a way of winning her." So he presumptuously thought, grossly overestimating both his own and Lukeria's potentialities.

The day they arranged to meet by the Leonovs' threshing floor he started looking at his watch quite early in the afternoon. Great was his amazement and fury when, an hour before the agreed time, he recognized her light step on the veranda outside, and then heard her ringing voice:

"Is Comrade Davidov at home?"

Neither the old woman nor her husband, who also happened to be in, made any reply. Davidov snatched up his cap, rushed to the door, and ran right into the smiling Lukeria. They went out through the wicket gate without speaking.

"I don't like this game," he said then, panting with anger and clenching his fists. "What did you come along here for? Where did we agree to meet? Answer me, damn you!"

"Who are you shouting at? D'you think I'm your wife or your coachman?" she asked with perfect self-control.

"None of that! I'm not shouting, I'm only asking."

She shrugged her shoulders and said with derisory calm: "Oh well, if you're asking without shouting, that's different. I felt bored so I came along early. I hope you're pleased and satisfied?"

"Why the hell should I be satisfied? Now my landlady will go wagging her tongue all over the village. What did you say to her last time you came that now she won't even look at me, but only cackles away and feeds me on all sorts of muck instead of decent cabbage soup? So you talked about godly matters, did you? It must have been a wonderful godly talk, seeing your name's only got to be mentioned for her to choke and go as blue as a drowned man. That's a fact, I tell you."

She laughed so youthfully and merrily that his heart involuntarily softened towards her. But in reality he was not feeling at

all inclined to laugh. Her smiling eyes wet with tears, she asked him:

"So she chokes and turns blue, does she? So she should, the pious old crone! Let her keep her nose out of other people's business. Just imagine: she's started to watch over my behaviour!"

But he interrupted her coldly. "You don't care what tales she spreads about us in the village, do you?"

"So long as she finds that occupation good for her health," Lushka answered unconcernedly.

"It may not matter to you, but it matters very much to me, and that's a fact! You've done enough playing the little fool and letting everybody see us together. I propose to have a talk with Makar tomorrow, and then you and I will either get married, or . . . glass against glass, and good-bye to you. I can't live with everybody pointing their finger at me—'there goes the chairman, Lushka's admirer.' You're undermining my authority by your brazen behaviour, get that?"

She pushed him away violently, and said through her teeth: "So you've found a groom for me, have you? What the devil do I need you for, you dribbling coward? If I take you for a husband you must open your pocket wider. You're ashamed to walk through the village with me, and yet you say: 'Let's get married.' He's afraid of everything, he looks round at everybody, even the children, and shies off like a half-wit. Well, you can take your authority out beyond the Leonovs' threshing floor to the pasturage and roll in the grass by yourself, you miserable Russian! I thought you were a bit of a man, but you're just like my Makar: all you think about is the world revolution and your authority! Why, with you around, any woman would be left to die of longing."

She was silent for a moment or two, then abruptly said in an unexpectedly kindly voice that quivered with emotion:

"Good-bye, my dear Siemion!"

Her white kerchief flashed like a spark round a corner and faded in the darkness. Passing his hand over his burning face, Davidov stood stock still, smiling with embarrassment and thinking: "Well, my boy, you chose a fine moment to propose! And now you're married, all right, you old stick, and that's a fact!"

The tiff proved to be anything but a small matter. In fact it
was not a tiff or even a quarrel—but rather a complete break.
Lukeria obstinately avoided him. He changed his lodging shortly
after, but although she must have heard of the move it did not
induce her to seek a reconciliation.

"Well, then, damn her, if she's so hysterical," he thought angrily, when he finally lost all hope of seeing her anywhere alone.
But the thought was a very bitter pill, and he grew gloomy and
unsettled, like a rainy October day.

True, this break had its good side: to begin with, there was no
longer any need for him to have a serious talk with Makar Nagulnov; and, second, there was now no threat to his strict authority, which had been undermined by his behaviour. But such
considerations were very little comfort to him. The moment he
found himself alone he began to drift into contemplating the
past with unseeing eyes, smiling with pensive melancholy, recalling the scent of her always dry, quivering lips, the constantly
changing expression of her burning eyes.

She certainly had amazing eyes. When she looked at you
from under her eyebrows there was something touching about
her glance, almost childlike in its helplessness, and she seemed
more like a young girl in her teens than a woman with much
experience of life and the pleasures of love. But the next minute, adjusting her always spotlessly clean, faintly blued kerchief
with a gentle touch of her fingers, she would throw up her head,
gaze at you with a challenging, bantering look, and there was an
openly cynical and knowing look in her glittering, unpleasant
eyes.

She had not had to study to learn this gift for sudden changes
of expression and mood; it was natural to her. So at least Davidov
thought. Smitten with the blindness of love, he did not realize
that in fact she was excessively self-confident and in love with
herself.

On one occasion, after kissing her lightly rouged cheek, in an
access of lyrical ardour he had remarked: "My darling Lushka,
you're like a little flower. Even your freckles are scented, that's a
fact. D'you know what they smell like?"

"Well, what?" she asked, interestedly rising on her elbow.

"Of something fresh, like dew, for instance. . . . Or . . . I've

got it: like snowdrops; a scent you'd hardly notice, but good. . . ."

"That's how it should be with me," she declared with dignity and the utmost gravity.

Unpleasantly surprised by her self-satisfaction, he made no comment for a moment. But then he asked: "But why should it?"

"Because I'm beautiful."

"Why, do you think all beauties have scent?"

"I can't speak for everybody; I don't know. I haven't sniffed at other women. And in any case I'm not very interested in them. I'm talking about myself, you queer man. Not all beauties have freckles. And freckles are may-flies: they ought to smell of snowdrops."

"You've got a good opinion of yourself," he said, rather peeved. "If you wish to know, your cheeks don't smell of snowdrops but radish with onion and vegetable oil."

"Then why do you come making up to me with your kisses?"

"I like radishes with onion . . ."

"You do talk a lot of nonsense, Siemion. You're just like a child," she said discontentedly.

"A man talks wisdom to the wise, don't you know that?"

"A wise man's wise even to a fool; but a fool with a wise man still remains a fool," she retorted.

Then, too, they had quarrelled over nothing, but it had been a passing tiff, and they had made it up again completely a few minutes later. But this time there was no reconciliation. Now all his experiences with Lushka seemed wonderful but irrevocable, a long time past. Despairing of seeing her alone to have an explanation and to discover what their relations were to be in the future, he began to grieve in earnest. He handed over the collective-farm administration to Razmiotnov to manage in addition to his own work as Soviet chairman, and went off to the second brigade for an indefinite period, to help turn over the fallow land in one of the more distant parts of the farm.

His departure was not the result of any practical considerations; it was the shameful flight of a man who both looked forward to and was afraid of the crisis developing in his love affair. He saw that quite well, for he did at times examine himself, as

it were, from outside. But the strain had completely exhausted him, so he decided to clear out of the village as the easiest solution. At least he would no longer be seeing Lushka, and would get a few days of comparative peace.

Chapter 4

At the beginning of that June, rain fell with a frequency unusual in summer, but it was gentle, autumnally light, without storm or wind. Each morning an ashen-grey cloud crept over the sky from the west, over the distant rises. It swelled and broadened until it filled half the sky; its dark underwings whitened ominously, and then it dropped till its lower fringes, as translucent as muslin, clung to the ricks standing in the steppe, to the burial mounds, to the windmills; thunder rolled somewhere very high, and good-naturedly, quietly; and a copious rain began to fall.

The rain fell plentifully, as warm as fresh milk, on the earth waiting in the misty stillness. The drops danced in white bubbles on the foaming puddles, and so gentle and peaceable was the summer shower that it did not bow the heads of the flowers. Even the chickens in the yards did not shelter from it. They went on fussing busily around the sheds and the damp, blackened wattle fences in search of food, and, taking no notice of the rain, the cocks crowed their long-drawn-out calls. Their brave voices blended with the chattering of the sparrows boldly bathing in the puddles, and with the whistle of the swallows as they dropped down in vehement flight to the graciously welcoming earth with its smell of rain and dust.

The village cocks produced an amazing variety of crows. The Liubishkins' cock was the first to wake up, beginning the interchange at midnight. He crowed in a cheerful, flowing tenor tone, like a young and enthusiastic commander; the cock in Agafon Dubtsiev's yard answered him in a solid baritone like a colonel; then for a good five minutes the whole village echoed and re-echoed with incessant crowing. Last of all, the Maidannikovs'

rufous and corpulent cock opened up, first muttering sleepily, strongly beating his wings as he squatted, then in a general's hoarse bass, with a commanding croak. He was the oldest cock in the village.

Except for any villagers in love or seriously ill, which to Maker Nagulnov's way of thinking were almost the same thing, he was the last person to go to bed. He was diligently studying English, making good use of his evening leisure. A linen towel hung over the back of the chair in his room, a ewer of cold well-water stood in one corner. He found study hard going. With his shirt collar unbuttoned, his hair tousled and wet with sweat, he sat at his table by the open window, wiped the sweat from his face, his armpits, his chest, and his back with the towel, and from time to time hung out of the window, poured water from the ewer over his head, and growled with pleasure.

The paraffin lamp burned dimly; the moths knocked against the newspaper lamp-shade. In the next room his old landlady snored peacefully, while word by word he mastered the terribly difficult, but, for him, terribly necessary language. One night, just about midnight, he broke off and sat on the window sill to smoke; and then for the first time he heard the cock chorus properly. Listening attentively, he exclaimed in delight: "Why, they might all be on parade, it's just like a divisional review. It's marvellous, there's no other word for it."

From then on he began to wait for the cock reveille each night, and enthused over the commanding tones of the nocturnal choir, thinking scornfully of the nightingale's lyrical gurgles and trills. He was especially pleased with the bass tones of Maidannikov's old cock which came as a coda to the general chorus. But one night the order of the calls, to which he had grown accustomed and which he mentally approved, was violated by a completely unexpected and hooligan intervention: that powerful bass was followed, quite close at hand, in the next-door yard, by some lousy and obviously young cockerel who called in a childish, devil-may-care alto, cackled away like a hen for some time and finished up with a disgusting belch. In the ensuing silence Makar clearly heard the wretched little bird fussing in the chicken run, treading, flapping its wings, evidently afraid of falling off its perch as the result of its effort.

This escapade was a clear violation of discipline and displayed an utter contempt for superior officers. In Makar's view it was just as though, after a full-blown general had spoken, some gaunt and lonely subaltern began to correct him, stuttering into the bargain. He was indignant to his very soul; he could not endure such monstrous conduct. He shouted into the darkness: "Stop that!" and banged the window shut, cursing under his breath.

Next night the incident was repeated, and the third night too. Twice more Makar shouted "Stop that!" into the darkness, disturbing and frightening his landlady. The strict harmony of the nocturnal cock crows, with the voices and times of entry seeming almost determined by rank, was hopelessly destroyed. He began to go to bed immediately after midnight. He could not study any longer, nor could he remember the words he had learnt. His thoughts were concentrated on that insolent cockerel, and he angrily reflected that it must be just as stupid and empty-headed as its owner. He mentally called the innocent fowl a scoundrel, a parasite, a parvenu. This cock which had dared to give voice after Maidannikov's quite upset Makar's equanimity; his ability to learn English declined rapidly; his mood grew worse with every day. It was high time to put an end to such disorder!

On the morning of the fourth day he went to his neighbour's yard, greeted him laconically, and asked: "Here, let me see that cock of yours."

"What d'you want to see it for?"

"I'm curious to know what it looks like."

"What the hell are you interested in its looks for?"

"Come on, fetch it out! I haven't time to waste arguing with you," Makar said irritably.

While he stood rolling a cigarette, Arkashka got a switch and, after some difficulty, drove a mixed lot of chickens out from under the granary. Makar's supposition proved quite right: among the dozen or so of brightly plumaged, frivolous, and coquettish hens a small, half-moulting, mouse-coloured, and quite unimpressive cockerel went wriggling about like bindweed. Suppressing his contempt, Makar ran his eye over the bird. Then, turning to Arkashka, he advised him:

"Wring the neck of that abortion."

"But why should I?"

"To make soup," Makar answered curtly.

"For what reason? He's the only one I've got and he's a rare one for the hens."

Makar twisted his lips into an ironic smile. "Is that the only thing that matters: he's fond of the hens! Very important, I must say. But not all that clever!"

"But that's all we want him for. I'm not intending to plough up the garden with him, he couldn't even draw a single-share plough. . . ."

"None of your sarcasm. I can be funny too if I like."

"But what has my little cockerel done to you?" Arkashka asked impatiently. "Has he crossed your road, or what?"

"He's just a fool, he knows nothing about good order."

"What are you getting at? Does he fly into your landlady's orchard, or something?"

"No, he doesn't: it's just that he's generally . . ."

Makar found it difficult to explain what disorder the cockerel was causing. He stood for a moment thinking, his feet planted wide apart, shooting murderous glances at the bird; then he had a bright idea.

"I tell you what, neighbour," he said more cheerfully. "Let's swap cocks."

"But where's your cock? You haven't any horses in your yard." Arkashka began to show some interest.

"I'll find one, and it won't be such a ragged-looking specimen as yours."

"All right, take it. We'll swap if your cock's suitable. I'm not all that fond of mine."

Less than half an hour later Makar dropped casually into the yard of Akim Beskhlebnov, who kept a lot of chickens. He talked to Akim about various unimportant matters, scrutinizing his chickens the while, and listening to the cocks' chatter. All Beskhlebnov's cocks were prize specimens, full grown and with magnificent plumage, but, above all, they were staid and restrained in their vocalization. As he was about to say good-bye Makar suggested:

"D'you know what, master? Sell me one of your cocks?"

"Excuse me for saying so, Comrade Nagulnov, but hens make

the sweeter soup. Choose which you like: the old woman's got more than enough."

"No, I only want a cock. Lend me a sack to put it in."

A few minutes later Makar was back in Arkashka's yard, untying the sack. Arkashka, who, as everybody knew, was passionately fond of swapping anything, rubbed his hands with satisfaction in anticipation of the coming exchange, and said:

"Let's see what sort of trump you've got. We may have to ask for something to make up the value. Untie the sack quick. I'll catch my little cock this minute, and then we'll set them fighting each other. The one whose cock wins can wet his whistle at the other's expense. By God, let's get on with it or I shan't swap. What's yours like to look at? Well grown?"

"He's a guardsman," Makar barked; then he got his teeth to work on the knot which fastened the cord round the sack.

Holding his trousers to keep them from slipping as he ran, Arkashka hurried to the fowl-house. There was a wild cackle of hens. But when he returned with the scared, panting cockerel pressed to his chest, he found Makar standing over the untied sack, scratching his head in perplexity: the "guardsman" was lying with outspread wings on the sack, and its round orange eyes rolled in mortal extremity.

"What's the matter with him?" Arkashka asked in amazement.

"Misfire!"

"Was he sick?"

"I tell you it's a misfire."

"But how can a cock be a misfire? You do say queer things."

"Not the cock, you fool, but me: I've had a misfire. As I brought him along I thought he might crow a bit in the sack just to shame me in front of everybody—it was close to the office—so I just twisted his head a little to one side. . . . Only a little, but look what's happened. Bring an ax quick, or he'll die without good reason."

Makar flung the beheaded cock over the wattle fence to his landlady, who was busy below the veranda. "Hey, Mother! Pluck him while he's still warm and make some chicken-noodle soup tomorrow."

Without a word more to Arkashka he went back to Beskhlebnov. At first he refused to let him have another, saying: "If you

go on like this you'll widow all my hens." But in the end he sold
Makar a second cock. This time the exchange was successful,
and a few minutes later Arkashka's beheaded cockerel flew
across the wattle fence. Makar, as pleased as punch, shouted
across to his landlady:

"Pick up that plague, Mother! Pluck him, the undisciplined
devil, and put him into the pot."

He went out into the street with the air of a man who has done
a very important and necessary job. Arkashka's wife watched
him go, shaking her head at the sanguinary slaughter Makar had
performed in her yard. In reply to her curt question Arkashka
put his finger to his forehead, twisted it round and round, and
whispered:

"He's touched! He's a good sort, but touched. He's gone clean
out of his head, that's all you can say. He sits up too much at
night, poor lad. The English languages have finished him off,
damn them!"

After that Makar, valiantly working in the solitude of his room,
listened undistrubed to the cocks' nocturnal chorus. Day after
day he worked in the fields with the women and boys weeding the
grain; but each evening, after his supper of cabbage soup and
milk, he sat down before his *English Self-taught* primer and
patiently waited till midnight. A few evenings later he was
joined by old Shchukar, who knocked quietly at the door and
asked:

"May I come in?"

"Yes, come in. What have you turned up for?" Makar greeted
him with the not very friendly question.

"Well, it's like this . . ." Shchukar stammered. "Maybe I sort
of long for your company, my dear Makar. I just thought I'd
come along and sit with you."

"Why, are you a woman, that you've started longing for me?"

"Sometimes an old man feels a longing more than any woman.
And my job's a rather dreary one: all the time with stallions and
stallions. Those dumb animals have got me down. Go and speak
kindly to them and all they do is chew oats and wave their tails.
And what can I get out of that? And then there's that goat, blast
his hide! When does that insect sleep, Makar? I've only got to
close my eyes at night for the devil to start walking over me. The

times he's gone for me with his hoofs when I've been half asleep!
He frightens me to death, and then, no matter how tired my eyes
are, I can't get off to sleep, and that's the end of it. He's such a
damned dangerous insect that he gives me no peace at all. He
spends all night marching round the stable and the hayloft. Let's
kill him, shall we, Makar, my boy?"

"You get such ideas out of your head. The collective-farm goats
aren't in my charge; Davidov's their commander. Go and talk to
him."

"God forbid! I didn't come along to talk about the goat, but
simply to be company for you. Give me an interesting book and
I'll sit beside you as quiet as a mouse in its hole. It'll be more
cheerful for you, and me too. I shan't get in your way at all."

After thinking it over, Makar agreed. Handing the old fellow
a hefty Russian dictionary, he said: "All right, sit with me and
read; only read to yourself. Don't make any noise with your lips,
and don't sneeze. In short, I don't want to hear a sound from
you. We'll smoke when I give the order. Is that clear?"

"I agree to everything, except about sneezing. Supposing I
suddenly get an attack of sneezing, what am I to do? With my
job my nose is always full of hay dust. Sometimes I sneeze even
in my sleep; so what can I do about it?"

"Fly out and fire your gun in the passage."

"Ah, Makar, my boy, my gun's old and rusty. Before I can get
out to the passage I shall have sneezed a dozen times and blown
my nose half a dozen."

"Then you'll have to move faster, old man."

"A maid moved fast to get a husband, but the groom failed to
turn up. But some kind fellow came along to help her in her
trouble. And d'you know what that girl became even without the
wedding crown? A fine woman! And that's what may happen to
me. I'll hurry; but if I get into trouble while I'm running, you'll
put me outside. I see that as clear as water."

Makar laughed and said: "Just get a move on: you mustn't
risk upsetting your authority. So keep quiet and don't put me off
my work. You just read and become a cultured old man."

"May I ask one more little question? Don't frown, Makar: it'll
be my very last."

"Well? Spit it out."

Shchukar fidgeted nervously on the bench, and mumbled: "You see, it's like this . . . it's not much . . . but all the same, my old woman quickly gets annoyed with me over it. She says I won't let her sleep. But how can I help it: that's what I want to know."

"Get down to brass tacks!"

"That's just what I am doing. You see, I'm ruptured, and because of that, and maybe other troubles as well, I get a terrible rumbling in my belly. I thunder away just like a thundercloud. And when that starts, what are you and I to do? Will that take your mind off your books too?"

"Get out into the passage, and don't let's have any thunders and lightnings here. Is that clear?"

Shchukar nodded, sighed deeply, and opened the dictionary. At midnight, with Makar to guide him and explain, he heard the cocks crowing properly for the first time in his life. Three nights running they sprawled across the window sill side by side, shoulder to shoulder, and Daddy Shchukar whispered enthusiastically:

"My God, my God! All my life I've been treading on the cock's tails—I was brought up among chickens—but I never found their singing so beautiful before. But now I've come to like it. Makar, my boy, that Maidannikov demon—how he crows, doesn't he? Just like General Brusilov, that's it exactly."

Makar frowned, but he answered in a subdued whisper: "A fine idea that! You should hear our Soviet generals, Daddy: that's where you'll hear our real voices. What was your Brusilov? To begin with, a former Tsarist general, and so a suspect; secondly, he was an intelligentsia in spectacles. I expect he had a voice like Arkashka's dead cockerel, which we ate. Even voices have to be judged from the political angle. To give you an example: in our division we had a bass, the best bass in the whole of the army. He turned out to be a rat—he went over to the enemy. And d'you think I regard him as a bass now? The bald-headed devil! He's not a bass now, he's a mercenary fistula!"

"But Makar, my boy, surely the cocks aren't affected by politics?" Shchukar asked timidly.

"Oh yes they are. Well, we've talked quite enough. You sit down at your book and I at mine, and don't bother me any more

with your stupid questions. Otherwise I'll turn you out without thinking twice."

Old Shchukar became an enthusiastic devotee of the cock crows. It was he who persuaded Makar to go and look at Maidannikov's cock. They turned into the yard as if they were calling on business. Kondrat was out in the fields, ploughing, so Makar talked to his wife. He asked casually why she wasn't out weeding, with his eyes fixed on the cock strutting importantly about the yard. It was a very solid and dignified bird to look at, with fine rusty-red plumage. Makar was satisfied with his scrutiny. As he went out of the gate he nudged the taciturn Shchukar and asked:

"Well?"

"His looks match his voice. He's not a cock, he's a bishop."

The comparison didn't please Makar, but he made no comment. They had almost arrived at the collective-farm office when Shchukar's eyes started to roll with fright, and he seized Makar's shirt sleeve.

"Makar, my boy, supposing they kill . . . No, not me, God forbid, but the cock! For God's sake! They'll slit his throat: I'm sure they will."

"But why should they? What are you getting at?"

"Why, can't you see? He's an old bird, he's my age, and maybe older. I can remember that cock even when I was a boy."

"Cut out the lies, Daddy. Cocks don't live till they're seventy, it's against the laws of nature."

"All the same, he's old; he's gone all grey round the cheek; didn't you notice?" Shchukar objected.

Makar turned on his heel. He walked back with such a long, swift stride that Schhukar had to take little runs to keep up with him. They quickly arrived at Maidannikov's yard. Makar wiped the sweat from his forehead with the lace handkerchief he had kept in memory of Lushka, while Shchukar panted with gaping mouth, like a hound that has been chasing a fox for half a day. The glittering saliva ran off his violet tongue over his straggly beard.

Kondrat's wife came up and welcomed them with: "Have you forgotten something?"

"I forgot to tell you that you're not to kill your cock."

Shchukar twisted his body into the shape of a question mark, stretched his hands out, wagged his dirty fore-finger, and, breathing heavily, hissed the words: "God save you . . ."

Makar gave him a dirty look and went on. "We want him as a breeder for the collective farm, so we'll buy him from you or make an exchange. Judging by the look of him he comes of pure thoroughbred blood; his parents may have come from England or Holland in order to start new breeds in Russia. You don't know, do you? I don't know either, but, in any case, whatever happens he's not to be killed."

"But he's no good for breeding, he's too old. We intended to kill him for Trinity Sunday and get a young one in his place."

Shchukar nudged Makar with his elbow and said: "What did I tell you?" But Makar took no notice of him, continuing his persuasive argument with Mrs. Maidannikov.

"Old age is no reproach: we'll use him for breeding; we'll feed him properly with wheat soaked in vodka, and he'll start making up to the little hens like a flame to a post. So you're not to destroy that valuable bird on any account, understand? Well, that's fine! And Shchukar will bring you round a young cock this very day."

The same day Makar bought a cock from Diemka Ushakov at a reasonable price, and sent Shchukar with it to Mrs. Maidannikov. But a rumour sped merrily through the village that for some unknown reason Makar Nagulnov was buying up all the cocks, wholesale and retail, and was paying through the eyes and nose for them. Razmiotnov was fond of a joke, and he could hardly fail to react to such activities. When he heard of his friend's extraordinary behaviour he decided to check the truth of the story himself. Late one night he turned up at Nagulnov's room.

Makar and Shchukar were sitting at the table with their noses deep in stout volumes. The lamp-wick was turned up too high, and the lamp was smoking. Black smuts were sailing about the room, the charred paper shade resting on the glass was stinking, and the silence was like that in the first class of a primary school during a writing lesson. Razmiotnov entered without knocking, and stood coughing at the door. But neither of the two diligent readers took any notice of him. Smothering a smile, he asked in a loud voice:

"Does Comrade Nagulnov live here?"

Makar raised his head and stared fixedly at Andrei. No, his nocturnal visitor was not drunk, though his lips were quivering with an almost irresistible desire to laugh aloud. Makar's eyes flashed a little, but he said calmly: "Go along and sit with the girls, Andrei: you can see I've no time to waste on you."

As Makar showed no sign of sharing his own cheerful mood, Razmiotnov sat down on the bench and lit a cigarette, asking in a more serious tone: "But really, what have you bought them for?"

"For noodles and cabbage soup. Did you think I was going to make them into ices for our young ladies?"

"Of course I hadn't thought of ices; but I couldn't help wondering what you wanted all those cocks for, and why they had to be cocks."

Makar smiled. "I like cockscombs made into noodles, that's all. You couldn't help wondering about my purchases, but I can't help wondering why you haven't bothered to go out and give a hand in the weeding, Andrei."

"And what do you order me to do out there? Keep an eye on the women? That's the brigadier's job."

"Not to keep an eye on them, but to do some weeding yourself."

Razmiotnov laughed merrily and dismissed the idea with a wave of the hand. "Are you suggesting I should go out and help them pull up rape? Excuse me, brother. That's not a man's job; and, besides, I'm not just an ordinary collective farmer. I'm the chairman of the village Soviet."

"That's not a very big bug. I tell you straight out you're about as good as nobody. Why can I go and pull up rape and other weeds like the rest, while you can't?"

Razmiotnov shrugged his shoulders. "It isn't that I can't, but I just don't feel inclined to lower myself in the eyes of the Cossacks."

"Davidov doesn't mind what work he does, nor do I. So why do you push your cap to the back of your head and sit for days in your Soviet, or tuck your filthy document case under your arm and go dragging about the village all high and mighty? Can't your secretary even manage to issue a certificate saying

how many a man has in his family? Drop that idea, Andrei! Go
along to the first brigade tomorrow and show the women how a
hero of the civil war can work."

"Are you mad, or is this your idea of a joke? You can kill me
on the spot, but I'm not going." Razmiotnov angrily flung away
his cigarette butt and jumped up. "I don't want to be everybody's laughing-stock. Weeding's not a man's job. I suppose
you'll be telling me next to go and hoe the potato plants?"

Calmly tapping his pencil stump on the table, Makar said:
"Wherever the Party sends a man, that's a man's job. Supposing,
for instance, they say to me: 'Nagulnov, go and chop off some
counter-revolutionary's head,' then I'll go with pleasure. Supposing they say: 'Go and hoe the potato plants,' I shan't like it, but
I'll go. If they tell me to go and help the milkmaids milk the cows
I shall grind my teeth, but all the same I'll go. The unfortunate
animal may try to get away from me, but I'll milk her to the best
of my ability. Damn her!"

"If you were to milk a cow with those paws of yours she'd be
on the ground in no time at all."

"She'd be on the ground, and I'd pick her up again, but I'd
milk her to the victorious end—till I'd squeezed the last drop out
of her. Get that?" Without waiting for an answer he continued
in a meditative tone: "You think it over, Andrei old boy, and
don't be too proud of your manhood and your Cossack-hood. As
I understand it, our Party honour doesn't consist in that sort of
thing. The other day I went to the district to present myself to
the new secretary; on the way I fell in with the Party secretary
of Tubyanskoe village, and he asked me: 'Where are you off
to? Not to the district committee, by any chance?' 'Yes,' I said.
'To see the new secretary?' 'That's right,' I said. 'Good, then you
see those people mowing over there? You'll find him among
them.'

"And he pointed with his whip across the steppe to the left.
I look and see haymaking in full swing, six mowing machines at
work. 'Are you mad?' I asked, 'haymaking so early?' And d'you
know what he said? 'We're not mowing grass but scrub and
thistles; we've decided to make silage of it.' I asked him: 'Did
you decide on that off your own bat?' 'No,' he answered, 'the
secretary arrived yesterday and asked us what we intended to

do with the scrub. We said we turned it in to lie fallow, but he laughed and said: "Ploughing it up's a crack-brained idea; there'd be more sense in mowing it for silage." ' "

Makar was silent for a moment, staring at Razmiotnov searchingly.

"Did you see him?" Razmiotnov asked impatiently.

"Of course. I turned off the road, drove a couple of kilometres across the steppe, and came to two britzkas: some old johnny was making gruel over a fire, and an ugly mug of a youngster as healthy as a bull was lying under one of the britzkas, drumming his heels and whisking off the flies with a twig. He didn't look like a secretary: he lay barefoot, and his mug was as pitted as a sieve. When I asked after the secretary the lad grinned and answered: 'He took my place on the mower this morning; that's him over there, forking off the hay.' I dismounted, tied my horse up to the britzka, and went across to the mowers. I let the first mowing machine go by; an old gaffer was sitting on it in a straw hat, a ragged shirt rotten with sweat, and canvas trousers smeared with cart grease. I felt he wasn't the secretary. The second was driven by a young fellow with cropped hair, no shirt on, all his body gleaming like butter with sweat; he shone in the sun just like a sabre blade. Well, I thought, he obviously can't be the secretary. A secretary wouldn't ride on a mowing machine with no shirt on. Then I look along the line, and all the others had their shirts off too. Think that out: how are you to tell which is the secretary? I thought I'd know him by his intelligent face, so I let them all go by. But damn it all, I couldn't tell that way either. They were all stripped to the waist, they were all as alike as two pennies, and not one had got the word 'secretary' written on his forehead. So much for judging by the intelligent face! Every one of them looked intelligent! Cut all the hair off the hairiest of priests and put him in a bath-house together with soldiers, and you'd never know he was a priest. It was just the same here."

"Don't talk like that about holy men, Makar my boy: it's a sin," Shchukar, who so far had not opened his mouth, said timidly.

Makar gave him an angry look and went on. "I returned to the britzkas and asked the lad which of the mowers was the

secretary. But the ugly mug said the secretary was the one without a shirt. And I said to him: 'You clean out your eyes, you've got flies in them; except for some old fellow not one of the men on the mowers is wearing a shirt.' He crawled out from under the britzka, rubbed his eyes, and how he laughed! I looked and had to laugh with him: while I'd been walking back to the britzka the old gaffer had taken off his hat and shirt, and now he was driving at the head of the line only in his trousers. His bald head shone and the wind drove his grey beard over his shoulder. He sailed along over the scrub like a swan. Well, I thought, and that's that! A district secretary with town ideas has brought them the latest fashion: to go chasing over the steppe naked; and he's even got that feeble old gaffer to be indecent like the rest. Ugly mug pointed out the secretary to me. I go across to him, and walk along beside the mowing machine, introducing myself and saying I was on the way to the district committee to make his acquaintance. But he just laughed, halted the horses, and said: 'Jump up and drive this pair: I'll get acquainted with you, Comrade Nagulnov, while we're mowing.' I turned the lad who was driving the horses off his seat, sat in his place, and touched them up. And by the time we'd done four stretches of mowing the secretary and I had got to know each other. He's a fine fellow: we've never had any secretary like him before. 'I'll show you how we work in the Stavropol district,' he said. 'You Cossacks wear neat stripes down your trousers, but we make a cleaner job of mowing.' And he laughed. 'We'll see who drives better,' I told him. 'The boaster can brag as much as he likes, and the burner only burns itself.' He asked me all about our village and everything, and then said: 'You ride home, Comrade Nagulnov; I'll be coming along to see you all before long.'"

"What else did he say?" Razmiotnov asked, now thoroughly interested.

"Nothing of any importance. Oh yes, he asked about Khoprov: he wanted to know whether he was an active worker. 'A fine active worker he was,' I said; 'he made me weep.'"

"And what did he say to that?"

" 'Then why did they kill him, and his wife too?' he asked. 'The kulaks will kill a man for anything,' I said. 'They didn't like him, so they just killed him.'"

"He pulled a face as though he was chewing a sour apple, and grunted: 'Hm, hm!' But he didn't say anything I could understand."

"But where did he hear about the Khoprovs?"

"How the hell should I know? I expect the district G.P.U. informed him."

Razmiotnov silently smoked yet another cigarette. He sat thinking with such concentration that he completely forgot what he had come to see Nagulnov about. As he said good-bye he smiled and looked right into Makar's eyes. "Now I've got it all sorted out. At first light tomorrow I'll go off to the first brigade. Don't worry over me, Makar. I shan't spare my back in the weeding. But you're to let me have a litre of Vodka on Sunday, and no dodging."

"You'll have it, and we'll drink it together if you weed well. But go out early, and set the women a good example. Well, all the best." And Makar returned to his book.

Round about midnight, when a profound silence had settled over the village, he and Shchukar listened enthusiastically to the cocks. Each had his own way of enjoying the melodious crowing.

"It's just like in a cathedral," Shchukar whispered beatifically, lisping in the fullness of his feelings.

"Just like in a cavalry regiment," Makar said, gazing dreamily at the sooted lamp-glass.

Chapter 5

Razmiotnov was the only one to see Davidov off to join the second brigade. He went with a britzka which was taking rations out from the warehouse, and a little clothing from the families of the ploughers.

Davidov sat with his legs dangling over the side, huddled like an old man and looking about him indifferently. Through the

jacket flung round his shoulders his shoulder-blades showed angularly. He had not had a shave for many days. Tight curls of black hair slipped from under the cap thrust on his head, and hung over his greasy jacket collar. He looked the picture of misery and dejection.

Razmiotnov thought as he watched him with knitted brows: "Ah, that Lushka's thoroughly got him down. That bloody female! She's made her mark on him all right, and how! Look what love does to the likes of us: he was a man once, but now he's worse than a cabbage stump."

Others could express their own opinions, but Razmiotnov did really know what "love does to the likes of us." He recalled various incidents in his own life and sighed bitterly. But he put on a cheerful smile as he went off to the village Soviet. On the way he fell in with the Party secretary, Makar Nagulnov. Makar looked as dry and spruce as ever, even a little foppish with his irreproachable military bearing. He held out his hand to Razmiotnov without speaking, and nodded after the britzka rattling off along the street.

"Have you noticed what's happening to Comrade Davidov?"

"He's gone rather thin," Razmiotnov replied evasively.

"When I was in his position I got thinner and thinner every day. But there's only one thing to be said about him: he's a weakling. You might as well sprinkle him with holy water and put him in his coffin. He stayed in my house; he saw what sort of creature she was. Before his eyes I fought my family counter-revolutionary, and now look: he's got hooked. When I saw him today, believe me my heart thumped like mad. He's gone quite thin and sheepish: he wouldn't look at me. And, by God, what keeps his trousers up round him, poor devil? He's going rotten right before our eyes. My former spouse should have been treated as a kulak away back in the winter and sent to the cold country together with her ragged Timoshka. She might lose some of her heat there!"

"But I didn't think you knew . . ."

"Bah! as if I didn't know! Everybody else knows, so why shouldn't I? Do I go around with my eyes shut? The devil can have her so far as I'm concerned. I don't care who she gets mixed

up with, so long as the bitch doesn't touch my Davidov, doesn't ruin my dear comrade. That's how things stand at the moment."

"You should have warned him. Why didn't you?"

"That would have been awkward. He might have thought I was trying to turn him against her out of jealousy or something. But you weren't involved: why didn't you speak? Why didn't you give him a stern warning?"

"With a Party reprimand!" Razmiotnov smiled.

"He'll earn himself a reprimand from elsewhere if he goes around doing nothing. But you and I are his comrades, and we should warn him; we mustn't leave it any longer. Lushka's such a snake that if he gets tied up with her he won't only die before the coming of the world revolution, he may go completely lame in the hoof. He'll get galloping consumption or syphilis or something, you mark my words! When I got shut of her I felt just as if I'd been born again. But now I'm no longer afraid of catching V.D., I'm learning English fast, I've achieved quite a lot off my own bat, without any teachers, I'm attending properly to Party affairs, and I don't avoid doing other work if it comes my way. In a word: in my bachelor state my hands and legs are free and my head's clear. But although I never drank vodka when I was living with her I was sort of drunk every day. My boy, so far as we revolutionaries are concerned women are pure opium for the people. I'd have that written into the Party constitution in capital letters, and I'd have every Party member, every true Communist and sympathizer read that great saying every night before going to bed and every morning three times on an empty stomach. And then you'd never have any devils getting into the mess our Comrade Davidov is in now. Why, when you stop to think, Andrei, just imagine how many good men have suffered from the woman's accursed seed! You couldn't count them all. How much waste they've been the cause of, how much drunkenness; how many Party reprimands have been given to good lads because of them; how many men are sitting in prison on their account! It gives you the shudders to think of it."

Razmiotnov was lost in thought. For a time they walked along without speaking, sunk in memories of the distant and recent past, and of the women they had known. Makar Nagulnov

dilated his nostrils, pressed his thin lips together, and walked as though on parade, throwing back his shoulders, setting his feet down firmly. All his bearing indicated that he was impervious to female charms. But Razmiotnov smiled, then despairingly waved his hand, or twisted his fair, curly whisker and narrowed his eyes to two slits, like a well-fed cat. From time to time, evidently when he had some particularly vivid memory of a woman he had known, he grunted, as though he had drunk a large glass of vodka. Between the lengthy silences he exclaimed somewhat incoherently: "Well, well! What a woman she was! Now, that's the truth. Pah, blasted female!"

Gremyachy Log was left behind, hidden round a bend, and the spacious steppe, too expansive to be taken in with one glance, held Davidov in its embrace. Drawing in deep breaths of the intoxicating scent of the grass and the moist black earth, he gazed out towards the distant ridge of burial tumuli. Somehow those mounds, dove-blue in the distance, reminded him of the storm-tossed waters of the Baltic. Unable to resist the quiet melancholy which took possession of him, he sighed deeply and turned away his suddenly moistening eyes. Then his abstracted gaze picked out a hardly perceptible speck in the sky. A black steppe eagle, a dweller among the burial mounds, majestic in its loneliness, floated in the chilly zenith, slowly, almost imperceptibly losing height as it circled. Its broad, square-cut wings, widespread but unmoving, carried it lightly along below the clouds, and the oncoming wind greedily licked and pressed its dull black plumage against its powerfully boned chest. When, careening a little at the turn, it again sped eastward, the sun lit it up in front and below, and then Davidov imagined he saw white sparks, momentarily glowing and fading, flying along the greyish-white edging of its wings.

Steppe without rim or bound. Ancient mounds half hidden in a dove-blue haze. A black eagle in the sky. The quiet rustle of the grasses before the wind. Davidov felt small and lost in these vast expanses as he ran his yearning gaze over the steppe, which exhausted by its very endlessness. And during these moments his love for Lushka, the bitterness of the parting, and his un-

quenched desire to see her again seemed petty and insignificant. A feeling of loneliness, of being cut off from all the living world held him firmly in its grasp. It was a feeling similar to that he had known during his life as a sailor, years before, when he had had to take the look-out on his ship at night. How strangely long ago that was! It could almost be a long-forgotten dream.

The sun scorched more and more fiercely. The gentle southern wind began to blow harder. Unthinking, he began to nod; and he dozed off, his body gently swaying over the pot-holes and bumps of the neglected earthen steppe road.

The horses were skinny little beasts; his driver, the elderly collective farmer Ivan Arzhanov, was taciturn and, according to general opinion, not quite right in the head. He took great care of the horses, which had recently been put in his charge, and so almost all the way to the field camp they dragged along at such a boring and lazy pace that at last Davidov, waking up from his doze, could stand it no longer. He asked sternly:

"What's the matter, Daddy Ivan? D'you think you're carrying earthenware to market?"

At first Arzhanov ignored the question, and turned his back on Davidov. But at last he said in a grating tone: "I know what earthenware 'pot' I'm carrying, but even if you are the collective-farm chairman you can't make me slog unnecessarily, brother."

"But who's asked you to slog unnecessarily? You might at least put them into a trot downhill. You've got no weight on at all, you could say we're travelling empty, and that's a fact."

After a long silence Arzhanov reluctantly said: "The animals themselves know when they ought to go at a walk, and when at a trot."

Davidov began to get really angry. Not making any bones about it, he exclaimed indignantly: "But that's too much! What d'you think the reins have been put in your hands for? What are you sitting in the driver's seat for? Here, give me the reins!"

Arzhanov replied rather more readily: "The reins have been put in my hands to drive the horses, so as they go where we want them to, and not where we don't. If you don't like my sitting beside you I can get down and walk; only I'm not going to hand the reins over to you, shout as much as you like, brother."

"But why not?" Davidov asked, vainly attempting to look into

Arzhanov's face; but the old man obstinately refused to turn his
way.

"Well, would you hand your reins over to me?"

"What reins?" Davidov did not see at first what the old man
was driving at.

"Why you've got the reins of all the collective-farm in your
hands; the people have handed over all their husbandry to you
to manage. Would you hand those reins over to me? I doubt it!
You'd say: 'You're mad, brother!' And that goes for me: I don't
ask you for your reins. So don't you ask for mine!"

Davidov snorted merrily. All his recent anger had evaporated.
"Well, but supposing there's a fire in the village, would you drive
with a barrel of water at this same disgusting pace?" he asked,
and waited with some interest for the old man's reply.

"They don't send such as me with barrels to a fire."

Looking sidelong at Arzhanov, Davidov noticed the tiny furrows of a suppressed smile below his weather-beaten, prominent
cheekbones. "Then what sort do they send, in your view?"

"People like you or Makar Nagulnov."

"But why?"

"You're the only people in the village who like driving fast, and
you yourselves live at a gallop. . . ."

Davidov laughed outright, smacking his knees and throwing
his head back. Panting with laughter, he asked: "So if a fire was
to break out, Makar and me would be the only people who could
put it out?"

"No, of course not. All you and Makar would do would be to
bring up the water. You'd go galloping around with the horses
for all they were worth, and they'd scatter lather all over the
place; but it would be us collective farmers who'd put the fire
out, some with buckets, some with billhooks, some with axes.
And the man to issue orders at the fire would be Razmiotnov,
no one else. . . ."

"And people think he's not quite right in the head!" Davidov
thought, genuinely astonished. After a minute he asked: "And
what makes you appoint Razmiotnov and no one else as fire-
brigade commander?"

"You're an intelligent lad, but you're not very quick in the up-
take!" Arzhanov said with a laugh. "Anyone who lives like him

should be given the job, because of his morals. You and Makar live at a gallop, you give yourselves no peace day or night, and you give nobody else any peace either; and so, because you're energetic and spendthrift you carry water around without stopping; you can't put out a fire without water, can you? Now, Andrei Razmiotnov, he lives at a trot, little by little; he doesn't drive himself unnecessarily, and never oversteps the mark so long as you don't show him the knout. So what is he to do, seeing he's the ataman? Just stand around, and give orders, shout, organize confusion, get between people's legs. But we, the people I mean, just go on quietly, we live step by step, we have to do our job without unnecessary fuss and haste, the job of putting out the fire. . . ."

Davidov slapped Arzhanov on the back, turned him round so that they were face to face, and looked closely into his slyly smiling eyes and the kindly, thick-bearded features. Smiling faintly, Davidov said: "But as for you, old Ivan, you're only a goose."

"Well, and so are you, Davidov, and not the least of the geese, either."

They drove on at a walking pace as before, but now Davidov no longer urged Arzhanov to hurry, for he realized that he would not shift the old man. As they talked about collective-farm and other matters he grew more and more convinced that his driver was very far from being weak-minded: he expressed his opinions pointedly and intelligently, but he had his own personal and distinctive measure for everything. When the field camp appeared in the distance, with the smoke curling thinly upward from the field kitchen close by it, Davidov asked:

"But seriously, Daddy Ivan, have you driven your horses at a walking pace all your life?"

"Yes, I have."

"Why didn't you tell me of your strange habit before? I wouldn't have come with you, and that's a fact."

"But why should I praise myself? Now you've seen for yourself how I drive. When you've driven with me once you won't want to a second time."

"Why do you hope that?" Davidov smiled.

Arzhanov did not answer the question directly, but said eva-

sively: "In the old days I had a neighbour who was a carpenter, and a heavy drinker. He had wonderful hands, but he drank terribly. He'd keep off it for a time, but the moment he smelt the glass he went on the rampage for a month. He drank everything off himself down to the last stitch, the dear fellow!"

"Well?"

"Well, you see his son never touches a drop. . . ."

"Come on, out with it; don't wrap it up."

"I haven't time to put it more clearly, my dear man. My father was a great hunter, and an even better horseman. When he was in the army doing his service he always took the regimental first prize for horse-jumping, sabre-play, and trick-riding. When he returned from service he took a prize every year in the district horse shows. Although he was my own father he was a bad influence, may he inherit the heavenly kingdom! He thought a lot of himself, and used to go swaggering about. He had a trick of heating a nail in the kitchen stove every morning and curling his whiskers with it. He liked to show off in front of people, but especially the women. But my, he could ride! May the Lord not hold it against him! If he had to go off to the district centre on business he'd lead his service horse out of the stable, saddle it, and start off at a gallop. He'd spur his horse through the yard, set him to jump over the fence, and his forelock would go streaming behind him. He never rode at a trot, still less a walking pace. He'd gallop all the twelve miles to the centre, and all the twelve miles back. He had a risky trick of chasing hares. Note, I said hares, not wolves. He'd start a hare out of the scrub, head it off from the ravine, overtake it and either cut it down with his whip or gallop his horse over it. Time and time again he was thrown when galloping flat out, and hurt himself, but he just wouldn't give it up. And the horses he destroyed for us! Within my own knowledge he finished off six horses, either by riding them to death or breaking their legs. He ruined Mother and the rest of us completely. One winter he rode two horses to death under him. They would stumble when galloping flat out, would hit the frozen ground, and that'd be the end. We'd see Father coming back on foot, carrying the saddle over his shoulder. Mother would howl as though lamenting for the dead, but Father—did he worry? He'd lie up for three days and groan a bit,

but before the bruises had had time to fade on his body he'd be getting ready for the hunt again. . . ."

"If he rode the horses to death, how did he manage to escape?"

"A horse is a heavy animal. When it falls going all out it flies over and over more than once before it comes to rest on the ground. But my father just kicked his feet free of the stirrups and flew off the horse like a swallow. And he strikes the ground and gets knocked unconscious, lies as long as it takes to come round again, then he gets up and marches home on foot. He was brave all right, the devil. And he had bones like forged iron."

"You're right, he must have been strong," Davidov said in an admiring voice.

"Strong or not, there was a strength which did him in in the end."

"Why, what happened?"

"He was killed by Cossacks of his own village."

"What for?" Davidov asked inquisitively, lighting a cigarette.

"Let me have a cigarette too, my dear man."

"But surely you don't smoke, Daddy Ivan?"

"I don't smoke seriously, but I play with a cigarette sometimes. And as I recalled that old story my throat went all dry and salty. What did they kill him for, you may well ask. He deserved it, of course. . . ."

"But all the same?"

"He was killed over a woman; because he had a lover. She was married. And her husband got to hear of it. He was afraid to meet Father in a fight face to face. Father wasn't very big, but he was very strong, and so the woman's husband got his two brothers to help him. It happened one Shrovetide. The three of them lay in wait for Father down by the river one night. God be merciful, how they beat him up! They beat him with stakes and with iron or something. . . . When Father was brought home next morning he was still unconscious, and as black as iron all over. He had lain senseless on the ice all night, and it couldn't have been easy for him out there, could it? It was a week before he began to talk and understand a bit what was said to him. In the end he got to be his old self, but he didn't get out of bed for two months; he coughed up blood and talked very slowly, very, very slowly. All his inside was mashed. His friends came to see

him, and they asked him: 'Tell us who beat you up, Fiodor? Let us know, and we'll . . .' But he kept his mouth shut and only smiled a little, looked everywhere but at them, and, when Mother went out, he whispered: 'I don't remember, brothers. I'm in debt to so many husbands.'

"Mother went down on her knees to him again and again, asking him: 'My darling Fiodor, do tell me at least who beat you up. Tell me for the love of Christ, so that I may know whose destruction I'm to pray for.' But Father put his hand on her head as if she was a child, stroked her hair, and said: 'I don't know who it was. It was dark, I didn't recognize them. They came up behind me and hit me on the head, they knocked me down, and I didn't have time to see who dandled me on the ice.' Or he'd smile a little smile and tell her: 'D'you want to recall old things, my little darling? Mine was the sin, and mine is the responsibility.' They sent for the priest to shrive him; and to the priest, too, he said nothing. He was a terribly determined man."

"How d'you know he didn't tell the priest?"

"I lay under the bed and listened. Mother made me. 'Ivan,' she said, 'crawl under the bed and listen; maybe he'll tell the Father who beat him up.' But Father didn't say a word about them. Five times he replied to the priest's question: 'I'm a sinner, Father'; then he asked: 'Tell me, Father Mitry, are there any horses in the next world?' The priest evidently got worried and said again and again: 'What are you saying, Fiodor, slave of God? How can there be any horses there? You should be thinking about the salvation of your soul.' He spent a long time with Father, shriving him and trying to persuade him, but Father wouldn't say a word; he only said at last: 'So you say there aren't any horses there? Pity! In that case there's nothing for me to do in the next world. I shan't die, and that's the end of it.' The priest hurriedly gave him the sacrament and went out very annoyed; in fact he was quite angry. I told Mother all I'd heard; she started to cry and said: 'Our bread-winner lived a sinner, and he'll die a sinner.'

"In the spring—the snow had already melted—Father got up, walked about the house for two days, and on the third day I saw him putting on his quilted coat and fur cap. And he said to me: 'Go, Vania, my boy, and saddle the little mare for me.' At

that time we had just one three-year-old mare left on the farm.
Mother heard what he said and cried all in tears: 'What good
are you for riding now, Fiodor? You can hardly stand on your two
feet. If you haven't any pity for yourself at least have pity on me
and our little children.' But he just laughs and says: 'Mother, in
all my life I've never ridden at a walking pace. Let me sit once
more in the saddle before I die, and ride round the yard at a slow
walk just once. I'll only ride round twice and then I'll go back
into the house.'

"I went and saddled the mare, and led her to the veranda
steps. Mother brought Father out by the arm. He hadn't shaved
for two months, and in our dark little hut it wasn't possible to
see how much he'd changed. . . . But now I looked at him in the
sunlight, and I began to boil inside with tears. Two months before, Father had been as black as a raven; but now his beard
had gone half grey, and his whiskers too; and the hair on his
upper cheeks was quite white, like snow. . . . If only he hadn't
smiled with a sort of tortured smile I mightn't have started to cry;
but then I simply couldn't hold back my tears. He took the
reins from me and gripped the mare's mane; but his left hand
had been smashed to pulp, and it had only just healed up. I
wanted to help him up, but he wouldn't let me. He was terribly
proud, was Father. And he was ashamed of his weakness. Of
course he tried to fly into the saddle like a bird, just like he'd
used to; but it didn't work that way. He rose in the stirrup, but
his left hand let him down, the fingers opened and he fell headlong on his back. Mother and I carried him into the house. Before he'd only coughed up blood; but now it came up from his
throat like up a pipe. Mother couldn't put down the kneading
trough till evening; and she had no time to wash out the blood-
stained towels. She sent for the priest. He came during the night
and gave him the Extreme Unction; but Father was a terribly
strong man. It wasn't till the third day after the Extreme Unction, late in the afternoon, that the mortal agony came upon
him. He tossed about the bed; then he jumped up, looked at
mother with absent but cheerful eyes, and said: 'After Extreme
Unction you mustn't step on the ground with bare feet, so they
say; but I'll stand up for just a bit. . . . I've walked and ridden
a lot about this earth, and I'm really sorry to leave it. Mother,

give me your little hand; it has had to work hard in this life.'

"Mother went over to him and took him by the hand. He lay down on his back, was silent a while, and then said almost in a whisper: 'And she's had quite a lot of tears to wipe away because of me. . . .' He turned his face to the wall and died; he went to the next world to look after St. Vassily's droves of horses."

Obviously overcome by his memories, Arzhanov was silent for a long time. Davidov gave a little cough, and asked:

"Listen, Daddy Ivan; but how d'you know your father was beaten up by the husband of that . . . well, of his woman, and her husband's brothers? Or did you only guess?"

"Why d'you think I guessed it? Father himself told me the day before he died."

In his surprise Davidov rose slightly in his seat. "He told you?"

"Yes, and quite simply, too. In the morning Mother went to milk the cow. I was sitting at the table doing my lessons before going to school, and I hear Father whisper: 'Vania, my boy, come over here.' I go over. He whispers: 'Bend down closer.' I bend down. He says very quietly: 'Now listen, little son; you're thirteen now, and when I'm gone you'll be the master of this house, so remember: Averian Arkipov and his two brothers Afanasya and crooked Sergei beat me up. If they'd killed me outright I shouldn't have borne them any malice. I even asked them to kill me there on the river, while I was still conscious. But Averian said to me: "You won't have an easy death, you snake. You go on living a cripple, swallow your bellyful of blood, get the taste of it and then die." That's why I still bear anger against Averian. Death is standing at my head, but all the same I feel bitter against him. You're little now, but you'll grow up to be a big man: remember my sufferings and kill Averian. Don't tell anyone what I've just said to you, not to Mother, nor anyone in the world. Swear you won't tell!' I swore. My eyes were dry, and I kissed the cross which my father wore at his chest."

"Pah, you devil! This is just like it was among the Caucasian Circassians in the old days," Davidov exclaimed, deeply moved by the story.

"The Circassians have hearts, but have the Russians stones instead of hearts? My dear man, people are alike the world over."

"And is there any more to tell?" Davidov asked impatiently.

"We buried Father. I came back from the cemetery, stood in the best room with my back against the doorpost, and made a little mark above my head with a pencil. Every month I measured my height and made a mark: I wanted to grow up quickly, so that I could do for Averian. And I became the master of the house. At that time I was just gone twelve, and besides me Mother had seven more children, all smaller than me. After Father's death Mother often fell ill, and, my God, the need and misery we had to suffer! No matter how good-for-nothing Father had been, even if he did like his bit of fun, he knew how to work too. Some folk thought he was a wicked man; but to us children and Mother he was our own father: he'd fed us, clothed us, and shod us; for our sakes he'd bent his back from spring to autumn in the fields. I had bony shoulders then, and a feeble sort of backbone, but I had to carry all the farm on that back and work like any grown-up Cossack. When Father was alive four of us had been going to school; but when he died we all had to give it up. I taught Nurka, my little ten-year-old sister, to do the household chores and milk the cow; my smaller younger brothers helped me on the farm. But I never forgot to measure myself against the doorpost every month. That first year I didn't grow much: sorrow and need didn't allow me to grow properly. But I watched Averian like a little wolf in the reeds watching a bird. I knew every step he took, where he went, where he drove or rode to: I knew everything.

"Sometimes the other boys of my age would organize all sorts of games of a Sunday; but I never had time to join in, I was the head of the house. They'd go off to school on week-days, but I collected the cattle in the yard. I felt ashamed even to bitter tears because of my bitter life. And little by little I began to keep away from my boy-friends, I grew unsociable, as silent as a stone, and didn't like being among people. And then people began to say that Vania Arzhanov was not far off being weak in the head, that I was touched. 'Damn them, the whole lot of them!' I thought. 'Would they grow wiser if they had a life like mine?' And then I came to hate my fellow villagers altogether: I couldn't stand any of them. Give me just one more cigarette, my dear man."

He took the cigarette awkwardly. His fingers were perceptibly

trembling. It took him a long time to light up from Davidov's cigarette, with his eyes closed, absurdly pouting his lips and sucking
noisily.

"But what about Averian?"

"Well, and what about Averian? He lived as he wished. He
could never forgive his wife her love for my father, he beat her
to death, he drove her into her grave before twelve months
were out. In the autumn he married again, a rather young girl
from our village. 'Well, Averian,' I thought, 'you won't have a
long life with your young wife. . . .'

"Unbeknown to Mother I began to save money, and in the
autumn, instead of driving to the nearest granary-collection
centre, I drove all the way to Kalach and sold a cartload of wheat,
and bought a single-barrelled gun and ten cartridges to fit it in
the market there. I tried the gun on the way back, and wasted
three shots. It was a filthy little gun; the hammer didn't always
break the percussion cap; out of three cartridges two misfired;
only the third bullet worked. I hid the gun under the eaves of the
shed when I got home, and didn't tell anyone what I'd bought.
And now I began to watch Averian all the time. Nothing happened for a long while. Either there were people around, or
something or other indicated that I was not to shoot him. All the
same I waited for my day. The main thing was that I didn't want
to kill him in the village: that was the trouble. On the first day of
the Blessed Virgin he drove off to the district market; and he
went alone, without his wife. I found out that he'd gone by himself, and I crossed myself, for if he hadn't I'd have had to kill
them both. For a day and a half I didn't eat, or drink, or sleep. I
lay in wait for him in a ravine at the roadside. I prayed fervently
in that ravine: I asked God that Averian might return from the
centre alone, not in the company of other Cossacks from our village. And the merciful God heard my boyish prayer. Late in
the afternnon of the second day I saw Averian coming along. I'd
let so many carts go by, my heart had beaten violently so many
times, when I saw his horses coming along the road in the distance. He was alone. He drew level with me, and I jumped out
of the ravine and said: 'Get out, Daddy Averian, and pray to
God.' He turned as white as a wall, and reined in the horses. He
was a full-grown man and a sturdy, tough Cossack, but what

could he do to me? I had a gun in my hands. He shouted: 'What d'you think you're up to, you little snake?' I said to him: 'Get out and go down on your knees. You'll soon learn what I'm up to.' But he was brave, the enemy! He jumped out of the britzka and rushed at me with bare hands. . . . I let him come quite close, as near as that clump of scrub there, and fired point blank. . . ."

"But supposing it had missed fire?"

"Well, then he'd have sent me to join my father and to help look after the droves in the next world."

"And what did happen?"

"At the shot the horses galloped off, but I didn't move. My legs gave way beneath me, I was trembling all over like a leaf in the wind. Averian lay close by me, but I couldn't take a single step towards him; I raised my foot and put it down again; I was afraid of falling over. That's how much it shook me. But I pulled myself together somehow or other, walked over to him, spat into his face, and turned out the pockets of his trousers and jacket. I took out his wallet. In it was twenty-eight paper roubles, one gold five-rouble piece, and two or three roubles in small change. I counted it all later, when I got home. Evidently he'd spent the rest of his gains on a present for his young wife. I flung away the empty wallet and jumped back into the ravine. It's a long time ago now, but I remember it all so clearly: as if it had happened only yesterday. I dug a hole in the ravine and hid the firearm and bullets. As soon as the first snows fell I dug up my property at night, brought it into the village and buried the gun in someone else's pasturage, in an old hollow willow."

"Why did you take the money?" Davidov asked sternly, angrily.

"What?"

"Why did you touch it? I ask."

"I needed it," Arzhanov answered simply. "At that time we were even more eaten up by need than lice."

Davidov jumped down from the britzka and walked for a long time without saying a word. The old man was silent too. Then Davidov asked:

"And was that the end of it?"

"No, it wasn't, dear man. The investigating authorities arrived

and rummaged about and dug. . . . But they went away again empty-handed. Who was going to think of me? Soon after, while he was wood-cutting, crooked Sergei, Averian's brother, caught a chill, fell ill, and died: he got inflammation of the lungs. And then I began to be worried; I thought: 'Supposing Afanasya dies a natural death, and my hand, the hand Father blessed to punish the enemies, should be left hanging in the air?' So I got busy—"

"Wait!" Davidov interrupted him. "Your father only mentioned Averian, but you intended to get all three, did you?"

"What does it matter what Father said? Father had his own will, and I had mine. And so I got busy. . . . I shot Afanasya through the window as he was having supper. That night I measured myself against the doorpost for the last time, and then I washed all the marks off with a rag. And I sank the gun and the other bullets in the river: I hadn't any use for them any more. I'd fulfilled my father's and my own will. Soon after, Mother took to her bed. One night she called me to her, and asked: 'Did you kill them, Vania, my dear?' I answered: 'Yes, Mummy.' She said not another word, only took my right hand and laid it on her heart."

Arzhanov shook out the reins, and the horses moved more briskly. Looking at Davidov in a childlike fashion with his clear grey eyes, he asked: "And now you won't ask me any more why I don't drive horses fast?"

"I understand perfectly," Davidov replied. "You ought to be a water-cart driver and drive bullocks, Daddy Ivan. Fact!"

"I've asked Yakov Lukich several times to let me, but he won't agree. He wants to have the laugh on me to the end. . . ."

"Why does he?"

"When I was a lad I lived with him for eighteen months as a farm-hand."

"You don't say!"

"I do say, my dear man. I take it you don't know that all his life Ostrovnov had labourers working on his farm?" Arzhanov screwed up his eyes craftily. "He did, my dear man, he did. Some four years back, when they began to put on the taxes, he drew in his horns, he wound himself into a coil, like a snake before it strikes. And if it hadn't been for the collective farms and

the lower taxes, Yakov Lukich would have given himself away, you can be sure of that. He was one of the most vicious of all our kulaks; but you've warmed the snake in your bosom."

After a long silence Davidov said: "We'll put that right; we'll deal with Ostrovnov if he deserves it. But all the same, Daddy Ivan, you're a man with a queer twist."

Arzhanov smiled and gazed thoughtfully into the distance. "Well, yes, I've a queer twist, I agree. Take a cherry tree: it has lots of different twigs. I went and cut off one twig to make a little knout: knouts made of cherry wood are more reliable. And the tree grew, the darling, also with a queer twist in it, in its branches, its leaves, its beauty. But I whittled the twig, and here it is. . . ." Arshanov took a knout from under the seat and showed it to Davidov: a handle of brown cherry wood with dry, shrivelled bark. "And here it is. It's not much to look at. And man's just like that: without a queer twist he's just naked and wretched, like this knout. There's Nagulnov learning some foreign language: he's got a twist. For twenty years Daddy Kramskov's been collecting all sorts of match-boxes: another twist. A drunken man goes along the street, stumbles, and goes and rubs his back against the fence. He's queer too. My dear Mr. Chairman, if you deprive a man of any twist he'll be as bare and boring as this knout."

Arzhanov held out the knout and added, still smiling thoughtfully: "Take it in your hands and think it over; maybe you'll get some light into your head."

Davidov angrily pushed his hand away. "Go to the devil! I can think and get to the bottom of things without that."

And all the rest of the journey to the camp they said not another word.

Chapter 6

The brigade was in the middle of its mid-day break. With a bit of a squeeze, the roughly made table accommodated all the ploughmen and drivers. As they ate they occasionally exchanged

salty masculine jokes, or businesslike comments on the quality
of the gruel the cook had prepared.

"She never does salt it sufficiently. She's not a cook, she's an
affliction."

"When there's little salt in it you won't dribble; and you can
put more salt in if you wish."

"But me and Vashka are eating out of the same dish; he likes
it without salt, and I like it salted. How can we share the same
dish? Answer me that if you're so clever."

"Tomorrow we'll plait a braid and divide your dish in half
with it, and then you'll be happy. Oh, you numskull! Couldn't
you think of such a simple idea for yourself?"

"Well, brother, all your mind is in your beard, and you haven't
any more."

The cross-talk and joking would never have ended, but someone noticed the britzka coming along in the distance, and the
keenest-eyed among them, Pryanishnikov, put his hand over his
mouth and whistled softly:

"Here's Vania Arzhanov coming, he's got mind enough; and
he's bringing Davidov with him."

They put down their spoons with a clatter, and all eyes
stared impatiently at the spot where the britzka had disappeared
into a ravine.

"To think we've lived to see it! He's coming out to take us in
hand again," Agafon Dubtsiev, the brigadier, said with suppressed indignation. "I've just about had enough. You can strain
your peepers as much as you like, I'm tired of blinking; I've no
desire to see him, I'm too ashamed."

Davidov felt a glow of pleasure as they all rose as one man to
greet him. He went up to them with great strides, and they
stretched out their hands to him. Their faces—the men's tanned
almost black, but the women's faces only a deep brown—lit up
with smiles. The girls and women never really tanned: they
wrapped themselves up so closely in their white kerchiefs when
at work that only narrow slits were left for their eyes. Davidov
smiled as he scanned those familiar faces. Now he had become
part of their lives; they were genuinely glad to see him, and
greeted him as one of themselves. Such were the thoughts that

flashed through his head, and his heart beat with joy. As he spoke his voice rose higher and sounded rather strained.

"Hello, you backward toilers! Would you give your visitors some food?"

"Anyone who's come to stay we'll feed, but we shan't feed anyone who's only come on a short visit as a guest: we'll just speed his going with low bows. That's right, isn't it, Brigadier?" Pryanishnikov said, raising a laugh from the others.

"I expect to be with you for some time." Davidov smiled.

Dubtsiev roared in his deafening bass voice: "Book-keeper! Put him down for full rations from today on; and, cook, pour him out some gruel, as much as his belly will hold."

Davidov went round the table, giving each one a handshake. The men exchanged their customary strong grip with him, but as the women looked into his eyes they were embarrassed and held out hands like icicles: their own Cossacks were not in the habit of coddling them with so much attention, and hardly ever condescended to hold their hands out to a woman.

Dubtsiev seated Davidov beside himself, and laid a hot and heavy hand on his knee. "We're glad to see our dear friend Davidov again."

"So I see. Thank you."

"Only, don't start nagging at us at once. . . ."

"But I haven't any intention of nagging."

"Oh yes you have; you can't do without it. And a good talk will do us good too. But keep quiet for the present. Don't go and spoil our appetites while we're eating."

"I can wait," Davidov laughed. "We've got to have a good talk, but I shan't start at the table. We'll keep off it somehow, shan't we?"

"Of course we must keep off it," Dubtsiev said firmly to a roar of laughter, and was the first to pick up his spoon again.

Davidov sat silent, concentrating on his food, keeping his head well down over the dish. He paid little attention to the quiet conversation of the ploughmen, but all the time he felt someone's gaze fixed steadily on him. When he had finished the gruel he sighed with relief: he was really satisfied for the first time for many days. Licking the wooden spoon like any child, he raised

his head. Across the table a girl's eyes stared at him fixedly, un-
brokenly, and in those eyes was such an expression of burning,
untold love, hope, and humility that for a moment he was embarrassed. He had already fallen in with this large-handed, full-
grown, and good-looking seventeen-year-old girl at meetings in
the village and in the street, and whenever they met she had
smiled at him bashfully and graciously, and her suddenly flaming
face had conveyed her confusion. But now there was something
different—something grown-up and serious in her look.

"What wind blows you to me and what need have I of you, my
dear child! And what need have you of me? You must have lots
of lads hanging around you, and yet you fix your eyes on me. Oh,
you short-sighted creature! Why, I'm twice your age, I've been
wounded, I'm ugly, pockmarked, and you don't see it. . . . I
don't need you, my unhappy child! You manage without me," he
thought, as he gazed abstractedly into her flushed face.

She cast down her eyes and turned away a little when she met
his glance. Her eyelashes fluttered, and her large, work-rough-
ened hands trembled visibly as she fingered the folds of her old,
dirty blouse. So naïve and open in her childlike simplicity was
she in her feelings that she did not know how to conceal them.
And only a blind man could fail to have noticed them before this.

Kondrat Maidannikov turned to Davidov with a laugh. "Don't
stare at our Varvara like that; you've already sent the blood rushing to her face. Go and wash, Varvara; then perhaps you'll cool
down a little. But how can she? She's lost all the strength in her
legs. She's been working with me as my driver, and she hasn't
given me a moment's peace: she kept on asking when you'd be
coming out. 'How do I know when he's coming; do shut up,' I
told her. But she pecked away at me with her questions from
morn till night like a woodpecker at a dry tree."

As though to prove that her legs had not failed her the girl
turned sideways and, lightly bending her knees, leaped across the
bench on which she had been sitting and went off to the shed,
muttering something angrily with blanched lips. She waited till
she reached the shed, then turned round and shouted in a quivering voice: "Daddy Kondrat . . . Daddy . . . you're not . . .
telling the truth."

The only answer was a roar of laughter from the men around the table.

"She gets well away before she answers back," Dubtsiev said with a smile. "She's safer at a distance."

"But what did you make the girl blush for? You shouldn't have done it," Davidov said in a discontented tone.

"You don't know her yet," Maidannikov said condescendingly. "She's quiet enough when you're around, but if you weren't here she'd be at the throat of any one of us without thinking twice about it. She's got teeth, that girl has! She's not a girl, she's a thunderstorm. Did you see how she jumped up where she was sitting? Just like a wild goat. . . ."

Varvara's decidedly naïve, girlish love for him hardly flattered Davidov's masculine self-esteem; all the brigade had known of it for a long time, but this was the first he had heard or noticed it. How different it would be if other eyes than Varvara's were to gaze at him with such perfect devotion and love! In an attempt to dispel the awkward atmosphere he said jokingly: "Well, thank you, cook and wooden spoon. You've given me a full belly."

"Your thanks, Chairman, should be in recognition of the great efforts your right hand and broad mouth have put out, and not to the cook and the spoon. Would you like some more?" the stout, majestic-looking cook inquired, rising from the table.

Davidov looked at her enormous girth, her broad back and unembraceable waist with open amazement. "Where did you get her from?" he asked Dubtsiev in an undertone.

"They made her at Taganrog metallurgical works to our special order," the book-keeper, a pert young fellow, answered.

"But how is it I've never seen you before?" Davidov asked the cook, and his tone conveyed his astonishment. "It'd take enormous calipers to measure you, and yet I don't remember seeing you before, Mother."

"Oh, so now I've got a little son, have I?" the cook snorted. "How can I be your mother when I'm only forty-seven? You haven't seen me before because I never leave my house in the winter-time. With my fat and short legs I'm no good for walking in the snow, I get stuck in it even on the level. So all the winter

I sit at home without stirring, spinning wool, knitting shawls, earning my keep one way and another. I'm no good for walking in the mud either: I'm like a camel, I'm afraid of my feet going both ways when I tread on slippery spots. But when the dry weather set in I got this job as cook. But don't call me mother, Comrade Chairman. If you want to live at peace with me, call me Daria Kuprianovna, and then you'll never go hungry so long as you're with the brigade."

"I'm perfectly willing to live at peace with you, Daria Kuprianovna," Davidov said with a smile. He stood up and bowed to her with the utmost gravity.

"That'll be better both for you and me. But now hand me your dish, I'll give you some sour milk for sweet," she said, highly pleased with Davidov's civil manners. She poured out the sour milk with generous hand, putting a good kilo into his dish, and bobbed low as she handed it to him.

"But why did you become a cook rather than going into production?" he asked. "With all your weight one push on the plough handle would send the blade half a yard into the ground, and that's a fact."

"I've got a weak heart. The doctor says it's fatty degeneration. I find it hard enough even as a cook. As soon as I start on the pots and pans my heart begins to thump right up in my throat. No, Comrade Davidov, I'd not be any good as a ploughman. Those dances are not to my music."

"She's always complaining of her heart; but she's seen three husbands into the grave," Dubtsiev remarked. "She's outlived three Cossacks, and now she's looking for a fourth. But no one seems anxious to volunteer: they're afraid to marry her; she'd ride them to death."

"You pockmarked liar!" the cook exclaimed angrily. "Is it my fault that not one of my three Cossacks had any guts? They were all weak and sickly. The Lord didn't give them a long life, but am I to blame for that?"

"But you helped them to their death," Dubtsiev held to his point.

"How did I?"

"You know how. . . ."

"Don't twist: out with it!"

"It's all quite clear already. . . ."

"Come on, say it straight out, or else keep your tongue still."

"You know how you helped, with all your loving," Dubtsiev said cautiously.

"You're a pockmarked fool!" she shouted in a rage, raising her voice high above the Cossacks' laughter. With one sweep of her arms she gathered up half the dishes on the table.

But the imperturbable Dubtsiev was not to be disposed of so easily. He took his time finishing his sour milk, wiped his whiskers with his hand, and then said: "Of course I may be a fool, and I may be pockmarked. But when we come to such questions, my girl, I can get to the bottom of it easily enough."

This made the cook swear at him so juicily that the laughter rose even louder; and Davidov, crimson with laughter and embarrassment, could hardly get out the words: "Well, what d'you think of that, my lads! I never heard such language, not even in the navy."

But Dubtsiev kept a perfectly straight face and shouted with exaggerated ardour: "I'll swear any oath. I'll kiss the cross, but I stand by my words, Daria: your love despatched three husbands to the next world. Three, mark you! You've only got to think it over for a minute. . . . And what did Volodya Grachev die of last year? He used to visit you too. . . ."

He was not allowed to finish his sentence. He ducked energetically as a heavy wooden dish went whistling past his head like a shell fragment. He nimbly threw one leg over the bench and fled. Ten yards from the table he suddenly leaped to one side and dodged as a pewter utensil flew past him with a swish, scattering sour milk in all directions and falling far out in the steppe. Standing with straddled legs, Dubtsiev threatened the cook with his fist and shouted: "Now, Daria, take it easy! Chuck what you like, but not earthenware basins. I shall deduct labour days from your tally for every dish that's broken, by God I will. Follow Varvara's example and get behind the shed; you'll find it easier to argue your case from there. Do what you like, I stand by what I said; you've buried three husbands, and now you're working your temper off on me. . . ."

Davidov had difficulty in restoring order. The men sat down to

smoke not far from the shed, and Kondrat Maidannikov, still panting with laughter, remarked:

"This sort of thing goes on every day either at dinner or supper. Agafon went around with one cheek bruised for a week after Daria went for him with her fists. But he won't stop making fun of her. You'll never get back home in one piece, Agafon: she'll either knock out your eyes or twist your leg off for you. You'll pay for your jokes. . . ."

"She's not a woman, she's a Fordson tractor," Dubtsiev said in an admiring tone, stealthily watching the cook as she went past. Pretending he hadn't noticed her, he raised his voice: "No, brothers, it'd be a sin not to admit it. I'd marry Daria myself if I hadn't got one wife already; but I'd only be married to her for a week, after that I'd be done for. Strong as I am I couldn't stand more than a week of it. And I don't want to die just yet. What pleasure would I get out of condemning myself to death? I fought all through the civil war, and survived, so am I to die through having a bit of fun with a woman? I may be a pockmarked fool, but I've got my head screwed on the right way. I'd manage to stick it with Daria for a week, but then one night I'd quietly slip out of bed and dance across on tiptoe to the door, out into the yard and full speed back home. Believe me, Davidov, I'm not lying, I swear it by the true God, and in any case Pryanishnikov, him over there, he wouldn't let me. One day he and I arranged to give Daria a hug because she's such a good cook. He took her from the front, and I from the back, and we tried to join hands. But we couldn't do it, it was too far round. So we called over the book-keeper—he's a youngster and no coward—but he was afraid to come too close, so she'll go for ever and ever without being hugged. . . ."

"Don't you believe the old devil, Comrade Davidov," said the cook, now smiling without a trace of her recent temper. "Why, if he weren't to tell some lie today he'd die of regret tomorrow. At every step he takes he lies, and he was born lying."

After a smoke Davidov asked: "How much land have you got left to plough?"

"A hell of a lot," Dubtsiev answered reluctantly. "More than one hundred and fifty hectares. We still had one hundred and fifty-eight to do yesterday."

"Fine work, and that's a fact!" Davidov said coldly. "What have you been getting up to out here? Putting on acts with the cook?"

"There's no need to talk like that."

"But how is it the first and third brigades have finished ploughing days ago, and you're not finished yet?"

"Davidov, let's all get together this evening and talk it over frankly, but now let's go and get on with the ploughing," Dubtsiev suggested. It was a reasonable proposal, and after thinking it over for a minute the chairman agreed.

"What oxen can you let me have to plough with?" he asked.

"Take mine," Kondrat Maidannikov advised. "They're used to work and they work well, and we've two yoke of young bullocks at the health resort at the moment."

"What health resort?" Davidov asked in surprise.

The smiling Dubtsiev explained: "They're rather weak, they lie down on the job, and so we unyoked them and turned them out to graze down by the pond. There's good, nourishing grass there; let them get up their strength. As they are now they're no good to anybody. They came through the winter very thin, and we were working them day after day, so they went off colour, and they can't draw the plough, that's all. We tried harnessing them singly with old bullocks, but nothing but trouble came of that. You take over Kondrat's bullocks: his advice is good."

"But what will he do?"

"I'm sending him home for a day or two. His wife's not very well, she didn't even send him out a change of underwear, and she asked Vania Arzhanov to tell him to come home."

"That's different. If you hadn't said that, I might have thought you were sending him to a health resort too. I can see you've all got the health-resort atmosphere. . . ."

Dubtsiev winked at the others surreptitiously, so that Davidov wouldn't notice, and they went off to harness up the oxen.

Chapter 7

At sunset, when he reached the end of the furrow Davidov unharnessed the oxen and untied the reins from their horns. He
sat down on the grass edging the furrows, wiped the sweat from
his brow with his jacket sleeve, rolled a cigarette with trembling
hands, and only then realized how terribly tired he was. His
back was aching, he had a queer, twitching sensation behind his
knees, and his hands shook as if he were an old man.

"Shall we find the oxen again at dawn?" he asked Varvara.

She stood facing him on the upturned soil. Her small feet in
worn, over-large shoes were sunk up to the ankle in the crumbling
earth. Pushing the dusty grey kerchief back from her face, she
answered: "Oh, we'll find them: they won't go far at night."

Davidov closed his eyes and smoked greedily. He wanted to
avoid looking at the girl. But she stood beaming with a happy
and weary smile, and said quietly:

"You've worn me out and the oxen too. You don't rest enough."

"I've worn myself right out," he said grumpily.

"You should take more rests. Daddy Kondrat seems to rest
quite a lot, he gives the oxen a chance to breathe, yet he always
ploughs more land than anyone else. You've worn yourself out
because you're not used to it . . ." She wanted to add "my
dear," but took alarm at the thought and pressed her lips firmly
together.

"That's true: I haven't got used to it yet," he agreed.

He struggled up from the ground, and trudged along the furrow towards the camp, lifting his aching feet with difficulty. For
a time the girl followed him; then she drew level and walked
at his side. In his left hand he carried his faded, ragged sailor
blouse. During the day he had bent down to see to the plough
and had caught his collar in the handle. Straightening up suddenly, he had ripped the blouse right down. The day was hot,
and he could have managed very well without it, but with this
girl around it was impossible for him to work bare to the waist.
In his embarrassment he drew the edges of the blouse together,

and asked if she had a pin. She said unfortunately she hadn't. He looked glumly in the direction of the camp. It was at least a mile and a half away. "All the same I'll have to do it," he thought, and, swearing under his breath in his chagrin, he said:

"Listen, my droopy Varia, wait for me here: I'm going back to the camp."

"What for?"

"I'll take off these bits of rag and put on a jacket."

"You'll find it hot working in a jacket."

"But I'm going all the same," he said obstinately.

Damn it all, he really couldn't parade around without a stitch to his back. Whatever happened he couldn't let this innocent child see what was tattooed on his chest and belly. True, the tattooing on his two broad breasts was modest and even rather sentimental: the naval artist had skilfully devised two doves. If Davidov wriggled a little the blue doves came to life, and when he wriggled his shoulders they touched each other with their beaks as though kissing. That was all. But on his belly . . . The picture there had given him a good deal of anxiety. Once during the civil war the twenty-year-old sailor had got dead drunk. He lay flat out on a lower bunk dressed only in his trunks, and two drunken friends from a minesweeper, who were first-class tattooers, had worked on him, giving full rein to their unbridled imaginations. Davidov had stopped going to the baths after that, and on medical inspections he had always insisted that only male doctors should examine him.

When he was demobilized and went to work in the factory he ventured to go to the baths again. Covering his belly with both hands, he found a free tub, and was soaping his head thoroughly when he heard a quiet chuckle coming from the lower bench. He splashed his face free of soap and saw an elderly, bald-headed citizen openly examining the picture on his belly and giggling quietly, thoroughly enjoying himself. Davidov deliberately poured the water out of the heavy oak tub and brought it down on the nosy gentleman's head. The man closed his eyes without finishing his examination, and lay down quietly on the floor. Davidov washed himself just as deliberately, poured a full tub of ice-cold water over the bald head and, when the man's

eyelids began to flutter, made for the cooling room. Since then he had completely given up the pleasure of steaming himself thoroughly in a Russian steam bath, preferring to wash at home.

At the very thought that Varvara might get so much as a glance at his decorated belly he went hot and cold, and drew the creeping edges of his blouse closer round him.

"You unyoke the oxen and let them graze. I'm off," he said with a sigh. He was not at all pleased at the prospect of going right round the ploughed land, or stumbling for nearly two miles over the furrows, all because of a stupid accident.

But Varvara explained his behavior in her own way. "My darling doesn't like working with me without a shirt on," she decided. Grateful for this evidence of his consideration for her, she resolutely kicked off her shoes. "I'll run there quicker than you," she told him.

Before he could make any objection she was flying like a bird towards the camp. The swarthy calves of her nimble legs twinkled over the black furrows, and, caught by a head wind, the ends of her white kerchief fluttered over her back. She ran bent a little forward, pressing her fists against her swelling breasts, thinking of one thing only: "I'll run and bring him his jacket . . . I'll run quick and please him, and then he'll give me just one kindly glance today and may even say 'Thanks, Varia.'"

Davidov stood watching her progress for some time; then he unharnessed the oxen and stepped out of the furrows. Not far off he found some bindweed twined round a bush, and stripped a long trailer of its leaves. With this tendril he laced the edges of his blouse together. Then he lay down on his back and at once fell asleep, feeling as if he had fallen into something black and soft which smelt of the earth.

He woke up because something was crawling over his forehead: a little spider or some other insect probably. Frowning, he rubbed his hand over his face and dozed off again. But something slipped over his cheek, crawled along his upper lip, tickled his nostrils. He sneezed and opened his eyes. Varia was squatting on her heels beside him and quivering with restrained laughter as she tickled his face with a dry blade of grass. He seized her slender wrist, but she made no attempt to release her hand. She

only dropped down on one knee, and her laughing face suddenly turned anxiously expectant and humble.

"I've brought you your jacket: get up," she whispered almost inaudibly, and feebly tried to release her wrist.

He opened his hand. Her hand, large and sunburnt, dropped on his knee. She closed her eyes and heard the ringing, rapid beating of her heart. She was still waiting for something, hoping for something. . . . But he said nothing. His chest rose and fell calmly and evenly; not a muscle quivered in his face. Then he sat up, tucking his right foot under him. With an indolent movement he put his hands in his pocket and felt for his tobacco pouch. Now their two heads were almost touching. He dilated his nostrils and caught the subtle, faintly spicy perfume of her hair. All her body was scented with the noonday sun, with sundrenched grass and that inimitable, fresh, and enchanting scent of youth which no one has ever yet been able to convey in words.

"She's a dear, sweet little girl," he thought, and sighed. They rose to their feet almost simultaneously and stood for a few seconds looking into each other's eyes without speaking; then he took the jacket from her hands and smiled kindly with only his eyes.

"Thank you, Varia."

That was just what he said: "Varia," not "droopy Varia." So at last he had said the words she had hoped for when she ran for the jacket. Then why did tears start to her grey eyes and why did her thick eyelashes quiver? What was the girl crying for? She wept soundlessly, with a quiet, almost childlike helplessness, drooping her head. But he saw nothing: all his attention was given to rolling a cigarette, trying to avoid wasting any of the tobacco. He had finished his stock of cigarettes; his tobacco was almost all gone too, and so he was economizing, rolling small, neat cigarettes sufficient for only five or six good draws.

She stood for a moment or two vainly trying to calm herself. Then, turning sharply on her heels, she went off to the oxen, calling back over her shoulder: "I'll go and bring up the oxen."

Even then he did not catch the tremor in her voice. He nodded, lit his cigarette, and stood thinking, working out how many days it would take for the brigade to plough all the land allocated to it if it relied entirely on its own resources, and wondering

whether it wouldn't be better to transfer several teams from the stronger third brigade.

She was not inhibited from crying when he could see her tears. She cried with delight, and the tears rolled down her swarthy cheeks, and she wiped them away with the ends of her kerchief.

Her first, maidenly love had come up against his indifference. But he was blind in love matters, he had no understanding of a woman's feelings, nor did he ever realize what was happening until a long time after, when it was too late. As he harnessed the oxen he noticed grey streaks on her cheeks, the marks left by the tears which she had shed but which he hadn't noticed. He said reproachfully:

"Ah, you droopy Varia! Why, you haven't washed yourself today. I can see that."

"How can you?"

"Your face is all streaked with dirt. You should wash every day," he said in an admonitory tone.

Now the sun had set, but they were still trudging wearily towards the camp. The shadows fell across the steppe. The thorn-covered ravine was engulfed in mist. The deep blue, almost black clouds in the west slowly changed colour: first their lower fringes were touched with dull purple, then the bloodily red sun-glow shone right through them, rapidly crept upward and embraced the sky in a broad arc. "He doesn't love me," the girl thought sorrowfully, bitterly compressing her full lips. "There'll be a strong wind tomorrow, the ground will dry up during the day, and then it'll be hard work for the oxen," he thought discontentedly, looking up at the blazing afterglow.

All the way back to the camp Varia was bursting to say something, but something restrained her. When they had only a little farther to go she called up all her resolution. "Give me your blouse," she asked quietly. Afraid he would refuse, she put a note of entreaty into her voice: "Give it to me, please."

"What for?" he asked in amazement.

"I'll sew it up, and so perfectly you won't even notice the seam. And I'll wash it."

He laughed aloud. "Why, it's rotten with sweat. There's noth-

ing to patch it to, as they say. No, my dear droopy one, that blouse has done its service: Kuprianovna can have it for rags to wash the shed floor."

"Let me have a try, and you'll see," she asked insistently.

"All right, then, but it'll be a sheer waste of your labour."

It was unseemly for her to arrive in the camp carrying his striped blouse in her hands; it would cause too much talk and joking at her expense. She took a sidelong, surreptitious look at him and, turning her shoulder to hide what she was doing, thrust the warm little bundle into her bodice. She felt a strange, disturbing feeling as the dusty blouse touched her bare breast; it was as though all the burning warmth of his strong, masculine body had entered into her. Her lips went dry, little drops of sweat stood out on her narrow white forehead, and even her step grew suddenly cautious and unsure. But he did not notice anything, did not see anything of all this. The next minute he had forgotten that she had his filthy blouse in her keeping, and, turning to her, he exclaimed cheerfully:

"Look, Varia, they're welcoming the conquerors. The bookkeeper's waving his cap to us. That means you and I have done a good day's work. Fact!"

After supper the men lit a camp fire not far from the shed, and sat down around it to smoke.

"Well, now we'll have our heart-to-heart talk. Why have you been working so badly? Why have you taken so long over the ploughing?" Davidov asked.

"The other brigades have more oxen," the younger Beskhlebnov answered.

"Yes, but how many more?"

"Why, don't you know? The third have got eight yoke of oxen more, and say what you like, that means four ploughs. The first has two ploughs more, so they're stronger than us too."

"And yet the plan we've been set is bigger," Pryanishnikov interjected.

Davidov smiled wryly. "And by how much is it bigger?"

"By thirty hectares, or even more. You can't turn that lot over with your nose."

"But you confirmed the plan in March, didn't you? What's the point of crying over it now? We based everything on the quantity of land allotted to each brigade, didn't we?"

Dubtsiev said quietly: "Nobody's crying, Davidov: that's not the point. The oxen in our brigade had a bad time during the winter. And when we socialized the cattle and fodder we found we had less hay and straw. You know that as well as we do, and you've got no cause to pick holes in us. I agree, the ploughing has gone on too long, the majority of our oxen have proved a poor lot of beasts; but we ought to have distributed the fodder properly, and not like you and Ostrovnov thought: what was handed in from the better farms should have gone to feed the thin cattle. But now what's happening? The others have finished ploughing, and they're getting their oxen ready for the haymow; but we're still struggling along with our oxen."

"Then let's give you a hand; Liubishkin will help," Davidov proposed.

"Well, we won't say no. We're not proud," Dubtsiev declared, with the silent assent of the other Cossacks.

"Now, it's all clear," Davidov said thoughtfully. "It's clear that we in the office and all the rest of us went wrong. We distributed the fodder last winter according to the territorial arrangements, so to speak. That was a mistake! But how the hell are we to blame? We made the mistake, we'll put it right. Going by output, I mean the daily output, you haven't achieved bad figures, and yet the result as a whole is rotten. Let's work out how many ploughs to transfer to you, to get you out of the mess. Let's put it all down in black and white, and then we'll take our mistakes into account for the haymow and distribute our forces differently. How many more mistakes can we make?"

For a couple of hours they sat round the fire, arguing, calculating, swearing at one another. The most active speaker among the Cossacks was Atamanchukov. He spoke ardently and made some sensible suggestions; but, happening to glance at him casually while Beskhlebnov was making some venomous remarks about Dubtsiev, Davidov saw such an icy hatred in his eyes that he raised his eyebrows in astonishment. Atamanchukov swiftly lowered his eyes and touched the chestnut growth of hair round his Adam's apple; and when a moment or two later he looked

across at Davidov again and their eyes met, his gaze had an
affected friendliness, and every furrow in his face was expressive
of good-natured unconcern. "He's an artist!" Davidov thought.
"But why did he give me such a devilish look? Is he still upset
because I put him out of the collective farm in the spring?"

Davidov could not know all that had happened in the spring.
When Polovtsiev heard that Atamanchukov had been expelled
he had sent for him at night. Grinding his massive jaws together,
he had said through his teeth: "What are you playing at, idiot? I
want you to be an exemplary collective farmer, not an enthusiastic fool who goes and gets himself into trouble over nothing, and
will get everybody else and the cause as a whole into trouble if
he's questioned by the G.P.U. You go down on your knees if necessary in the collective-farm general meeting, you son of a bitch,
but see to it that the meeting doesn't confirm the brigade's decision. Not a shadow of suspicion should fall on any of our people
until we've started."

Atamanchukov didn't have to go down on his knees: acting on
Polovtsiev's order, Yakov Lukich and all who thought like him
went as one man to his defence, and the meeting did not confirm
the brigade's decision. Atamanchukov was let off with a social
reprimand. After that he had lain low, had worked well, and had
set the sluggish workers an example of responsible attitude to
labour. But he could not entirely conceal his hatred for Davidov
and the collective-farm system, and at times it showed itself in
an indiscreet remark, or a sceptical smile; or furious sparks flashed
in his dark-blue eyes like burnished steel, and at once died away
again.

It was midnight before they were able to determine the extent
of the aid the second brigade required and the date by which the
ploughing should be finished. Davidov went on sitting by the fire
to write a note to Razmiotnov there and then, and Dubtsiev decided to go back to the village at once, without waiting for the
dawn, to get oxen and ploughs from the third brigade out to the
fields by noon, and together with Liubishkin to choose the best
ploughmen. They had a last silent smoke round the dying fire,
then went off to lie down and sleep.

Meanwhile a different sort of conversation was taking place
by the hut. Varia was carefully washing Davidov's sailor blouse

in a plain iron basin, and the cook stood beside her, talking in a deep, almost masculine voice.

"What are you crying for, you little fool?"

"It smells of salt. . . ."

"Well, what of it? Everybody who works makes his under-clothes smell of salt and sweat, not perfume and scented soap. What are you bellowing about? He hasn't said anything unkind to you, has he?"

"No, of course not, Auntie."

"Then what are you opening the flood-gates for, you fool?"

"I'm not washing a stranger's blouse: it's my own dear one's," the girl said, bending low over the basin and choking back her sobs.

After a long silence the cook put her arms akimbo and ex-claimed angrily: "I've had just about enough of this. Varia, girl, lift your head at once."

The wretched seventeen-year-old girl raised her head, and two tear-stained but happy eyes gazed at the cook. "Even the salt in his blouse is dear to me. . . ."

Daria Kuprianovna's mighty breasts tossed violently with her laughter. "Oh well, I can see you're a real young woman now, Varia."

"Why, what was I before: unreal?"

"Before? Before you were only wind; but now you're a young woman. So long as a lad isn't ready to fight another lad over the girl that's in love with him he's not a lad but a kid. And so long as a girl only bares her teeth and flashes her eyes she's not a young woman but wind in a skirt. But when her eyes turn wet with love, when her pillow won't dry because of her tears at night, then she's a real young woman. Get that, little idiot?"

Davidov lay inside the hut, his arms behind his head, but sleep wouldn't come. "I don't really know these people in our collective farm; I don't know what they live by . . ." he thought remorse-fully. "First it was getting rid of the kulaks, then organizing the collective farm, then these economic questions. So I haven't had time to take a good look at them, to get to know them better. But, damn it, what sort of chairman am I if I haven't got to know

the people yet? Yet it isn't so simple as all that. Look at how Arzhanov turned out. Everybody thinks he's a bit simple-minded, but he's no nitwit, far from it. The devil got into that bearded satyr from the very beginning. He crawled into his shell when he was a child and slammed the door, and now try to get into his soul! Does he let you in? I should say not! And take Yakov Lukich: he's another lock with a secret key. I must keep him under my nose and watch him properly. He was a kulak, that's obvious, but he's working conscientiously now; probably he's afraid because of his past. . . . But I shall have to turn him out of his job as manager: he'll have to work as a rank-and-file collective farmer. And I don't get Atamanchukov either: he looks at me like an executioner at a condemned man. But why? He's a typical middle-peasant, and he was with the Whites—but which of them wasn't? That's not the answer. I've got to think hard about all this: I've done enough trying to run the farm blindly, not knowing who I could really rely on, who I could genuinely trust. Ah, sailor, sailor! If the lads in the shop found out how you're running this business they'd tear you limb from limb."

The women drivers lay down to sleep in the open outside the hut. Through his doze Davidov heard Varia's thin voice and Kuprianovna's baritone.

"What are you pressing up against me for like a calf to a cow?" the cook said, laughing and half choking. "D'you hear, Varia? I've had enough of your cuddling me. Shift away, for Christ's sake! You're as hot as a stove. D'you hear what I said? I shouldn't have lain down beside you. How hot you are! You aren't ill, are you?"

Varia's quiet laugh was like the cooing of a dove. Smiling sleepily, Davidov imagined them lying side by side and thought as he dropped off: "What a dear little girl she is! She's big now, all ready for a husband, but she's a child in her outlook."

He did not wake up till dawn was fully come. No one was left in the shed, nor could he hear any men's voices outside; the ploughmen were already out on the land; he was the only one still lying on the broad bunk. He jumped up briskly, put on his leg-rags and boots, and at once noticed that his blouse had been washed clean and neatly sewn up with small stiches, and was now placed with a clean shirt at the head of the bunk. "How did she get hold of the shirt? I came out here without a stitch, I know

that, so how did the shirt get here? What a little devil!" he thought in surprise. To convince himself that it was not a dream he touched the cool linen with his hand.

Only when he had put on his blouse and went outside did he learn the truth. Varia, now dressed in a fine blue blouse and carefully ironed black skirt, was washing her feet by the water barrel. She was as rosy and fresh as the early morning. She smiled at him with her crimson lips, and her widely set grey eyes shone with joy, just as they had yesterday.

"Had a good rest, Chairman? Slept well?" she asked in a smiling tone.

"Where were you last night?"

"I went off to the village."

"But when did you come back?"

"I've only just arrived."

"Did you bring me this shirt?"

She nodded, and a look of anxiety appeared in her eyes. "Why, shouldn't I have done it? Shouldn't I have gone to your room? I just thought that striped shirt of yours was hopeless. . . ."

"You're a great girl, Varia. Thank you for everything. But what are you all togged up like that for? My goodness! She's even got a ring on her finger!"

She turned the simple silver ring round and round on her finger in her embarrassment, and stammered: "Everything I had on was as filthy as mud. So I went and saw Mother and changed my clothes. . . ." Suddenly, mastering her bashfulness, she saucily flashed her eyes. "I wanted to put on shoes, too, so that you'd take one look at me during the day; but you can't walk far in shoes over the furrows."

Davidov laughed outright. "Now I shan't take my eyes off you at all, my swift-footed little deer. Well, go and harness up the oxen; I'll have a wash and come along at once."

But before he had had time to wash, Kondrat Maidannikov turned up.

"Why've you come back so soon?" Davidov asked with a smile. "You asked for two days off."

Kondrat waved the question away. "It's boring at home. My wife's got up. She was shaking with fever, but what can I do? I turned round and came back. But where's Varia?"

"She's gone to harness up the oxen."

"Well, I'll go and plough, and you wait here for the guests. Liubishkin's bringing out eight ploughs. I caught them up half-way, and Agafon was riding at the head of them all on a white mare like Kutuzov. And here's more news for you: yesterday evening, after dark, someone shot at Nagulnov."

"Shot at him? What d'you mean?"

"What I say. Just a shot from a rifle. Some swine tried to pick him off. He was sitting in the lamp-light by the open window. The bullet passed close to his temple and scorched the flesh, but that's all. He's got a tic, though, as the result, either through the burn or because he's mad about it. Otherwise he's whole and well. The militia have arrived from the district and are sniffing around. But the business is dead meat already. . . ."

"I'll have to leave you tomorrow: I must go back to the village," Davidov said. "So the enemy's raising his head again, Kondrat?"

"So much the better. Let him raise his head. It's easier to chop it off then," Maidannikov said calmly, and began to change boots.

Chapter 8

After midnight solidly massed, heavy, and sombre clouds swept over the sky, a dreary autumnal drizzle began to fall, and soon the steppe grew very dark, cool, and still, like a deep, raw cellar. An hour before dawn a wind blew up, the clouds crowded on one another and scurried across the sky, the rain, which had been dropping straight down, now drove in an eastward slant from the bottom of the clouds to the very ground. Then it stopped as unexpectedly as it had started.

Just before sunrise a horseman rode up to the brigade hut. He unhurriedly dismounted, and tied the reins to a nearby haw-thorn bush. He walked as unhurriedly up to the cook, who was bustling round a small stove half buried in the earth, and greeted her. She did not reply. She was down on her knees with her

elbows and her mighty breasts resting on the ground, her head cocked on one side, blowing with all her lungs at the charred chips, vainly trying to get a fire going. The chips were wet with the rain and dew, and would not catch; the smoke billowed into her puffy crimson face, and the ash flew up in grey clouds.

"Pah, may you be damned three times over, cooking in such conditions!" the infuriated cook exclaimed, panting and coughing with the smoke. She flung herself back and raised her head, put up her hands to adjust the hair breaking from below her kerchief, and noticed the new arrival standing in front of her.

"You should put the chips in the hut for the night, Mother. You haven't enough wind in your nostrils to set wet wood alight. But let me give you a hand." He gently pushed her aside.

"There are plenty of instructors like you wandering about the steppe! You see whether you can set it alight, and I'll see how much wind you've got in your nostrils," the cook snorted. She readily made room for him, and gave him a good looking-over.

He was short and not particularly impressive-looking. The shabby beaver jacket fitted him closely, and was drawn tight round him with a military belt. The khaki trousers, neatly patched and darned, and the rather ancient leg-boots, covered to the tops with a grey crust of mud, had also obviously done supplementary service for their owner. The smart Kuban hat of silver karakul, gloomily drawn down over his eyebrows, was in quite unexpected contrast to the rest of his poverty-stricken attire. His swarthy face was good-natured, his simple snub nose wrinkled absurdly when he smiled, and his black eyes gazed out on the wide world with condescending and intelligent derision.

He squatted down on his heels, then took out a cigarette lighter and a large flat flask with a ground-glass stopper from his jacket inner pocket. In a minute the small chips of wood, sprinkled with gasoline, were burning merrily.

"That's the way to do it, Mother!" he said, jokingly smacking the cook on her fleshy shoulder. "I'll give you this flask as a keepsake. If your kindling ever gets damp, splash some of this over the chips and everything will go like one o'clock. Take this gift from me, and the next time you've got some hot food ready you can expect me as your guest. A full plate, piled up!"

Putting the flask into her bosom, she thanked him with un-

usual graciousness. "Well, thank you very much, my good man, for your little present. I'll try to do you proud! But what do you carry that bottle around with you for? You're not a veterinary surgeon, are you? Not an expert on cows?"

"No, I'm not a cattle doctor," the man replied evasively. "But where are the ploughmen? Surely they're not still asleep?"

"Some of them have gone off to the pond to get the oxen, others are already out ploughing."

"Is Davidov here?"

"He's in the hut. He's overslept, poor man! He wore himself out yesterday, he's a hard worker. And he went to bed late."

"What was he doing up so late?"

"The devil only knows. He came back late from the ploughing, and then he felt he'd got to go and look at the winter wheat—it was sown before the collectivization. He walked right to the head of the valley."

"But whoever goes and looks at growing wheat in the dark?" The stranger smiled, wrinkling his nose and looking interrogatively into the cook's round, shining face.

"It was still light when he went, but he was late getting back. The devil knows why he was so late; maybe he was listening to the nightingales. And what our nightingales sing in the Thorny Ravine is beyond belief. They sing in so many different voices you can't ever get to sleep. They pour out their souls, damn them! Sometimes as I lie and listen to them bitter tears come to my eyes. . . ."

"But why?"

"What d'you mean, 'why'?" You lie and think of when you were young, and all sorts of things that happened to you then. My dear man, it doesn't take much to make the tears come pouring out of a woman's eyes."

"But did Davidov go all by himself to look at the wheat?"

"He's still going around without a guide, thank God; he's not blind. But who are you, by the way? What have you come for?" The cook suddenly turned wary and pursed her lips severely.

"I've got a little business with Comrade Davidov," the stranger said, again evasively. "But I'm in no hurry, I can wait till he wakes up. Let the toiler sleep his fill. And while the wood's burning up, you and I can sit and have a chat about things."

"But when shall I get the potatoes done for all my men if I waste time chattering with you?" she asked.

The bright young man was not put off by the question: without saying a word he took a penknife out of a pocket and tried its blade on his thumbnail. "Bring the taters here, I'll help you do them. I'm ready to spend all my life working as assistant to such an attractive cook as you, provided you smile on me at night. . . . Just as you are now."

She went even more crimson with pleasure, but she shook her head with hypocritical compassion. "You're rather thin, my poor lad. Your body's rather thin for me. I might quite possibly smile on you one night, but you'd never notice, you'd never see it. . . ."

The visitor settled himself comfortably on an oak block, and screwed up his eyes as he gazed at the smiling cook. "I can see like an owl at night."

"Maybe, but it wouldn't be because you couldn't see, but because your keen little eyes would be filled with tears. . . ."

"So that's what you're like!" The stranger laughed quietly. "Take care, fatty, or you'll be the first to wash your face with tears. I'm only kind in the daytime; at night I give such fat bodies as you no mercy. Though you plead and cry."

Kuprianovna snorted, but she glanced at the saucy stranger with measured approval. "Be careful, my dear! The boaster can boast too much, and the lamenter can lament more than enough. . . ."

"We'll decide when the morning's come who's going to lament and who's going to sleep and stretch himself comfortably. Give me the potatoes, magpie, we don't want to sit here all day doing nothing."

She went to the hut and brought back a full bucket of potatoes, swaying from the hips as she walked. Still smiling, she sat down on a low stool opposite the visitor. She watched as he peeled the thin potato skins off in spirals with the knife in his nimble, swarthy fingers, and said with satisfaction: "You're sharp with your hands as well as with your tongue. You'll make me a good assistant."

The visitor worked swiftly, but made no comment. Some minutes later he asked: "Well, and how's Davidov getting on? Have the Cossacks taken him to their hearts, or haven't they?"

"Oh, he's all right. He's a brave lad and straight, like you. Our people like such as don't make or ask for a lot of show."

"He's straight, you said?"

"Quite simple."

"So he's a bit stupid, eh?" The visitor gave her a crafty look from under his Kuban cap.

"Do you regard yourself as a bit stupid, then?" she asked sarcastically.

"I wouldn't have said so. . . ."

"Then why turn Davidov into a fool? You're very like him, you know. . . ."

The visitor was again silent, smiling to himself, and taking rare looks at the talkative cook.

In the east the lurid band of the sunrise had been hidden by clouds. The wind, rested during the night, rose on its wings and brought the trilling sounds of nightingale song from the Thorny Ravine. The visitor wiped his knife blade on his trousers, and said:

"Go and wake Davidov up, or he'll sleep till winter."

Davidov came barefoot out of the hut, sleepy and frowning. Glancing casually at the stranger, he asked gruffly: "Brought mail from the district committee? Hand it over."

"No mail, but I'm from the district committee. Put your boots on, Comrade Davidov; we've got to have a talk, you and I."

Scratching his tattooed chest, Davidov looked at his visitor condescendingly. "I kind of feel that you're a plenipotentiary from the district committee. . . . I'll be back in a moment, Comrade."

He dressed swiftly, put his boots on his bare feet, hurriedly splashed his face with water that smelt sourly of the oak barrel, and bowed with a touch of ceremony. "I'm Siemion Davidov, Chairman of the Gremyachy collective farm."

The visitor went up to him and put his arm round his broad back. "Well, that's an official way of introducing yourself, I must say. And I'm Ivan Nesterenko, the district-committee secretary. And now we know each other let's take a walk and have a heart-to-heart talk, Comrade Chairman. Have you got much ploughing left to do?"

"Quite a bit. . . ."

"So the master hasn't got the hang of it all yet?" He took Davidov by the arm and gently led him in the direction of the ploughlands.

Taking a sidelong glance at him, Davidov said reservedly: "We've made a mistake." But suddenly he took fire, surprising even himself. "But you must realize, my dear secretary, that I'm only a kid in agriculture. I'm not trying to excuse myself, but I wasn't the only one who made the mistake. . . . It's new work to me. . . ."

"I see and I understand. Don't get so worked up."

"I wasn't the only one who made the mistake; all the lads I rely on went wrong with me. We didn't distribute our forces properly. Get me?"

"I get you. And there isn't anything very terrible in that. It's not such a serious failure: you can put it right as you go along. You've already received reinforcements in men and cattle? Good! As for the distribution of forces, and the proper allocation of those forces to each brigade, learn the lesson for future reference, for the haymow, for instance, but especially for the harvesting. You've got to think it all out thoroughly in advance."

"That's a fact!"

"Well, now come and show me where you've been ploughing, where your strip is. I'd like to see how the Leningrad working class manages on the Don soil. . . . I shan't have to write to the Party committee secretary at the Putilov works and complain of your lack of enthusiasm, shall I?"

"You can judge of that for yourself."

Nesterenko's small but strong hand gripped Davidov's elbow still more firmly. Glancing at the secretary's simple, open features, Davidov suddenly felt so free and at ease that an involuntary smile touched his lips. It was a long time since any of the Party authorities had talked with him so humanly, with such friendly simplicity.

"D'you want to check up on the quality, Comrade Nesterenko? Quite seriously?"

"Of course not, of course not! I simply want to have a look; I'm curious to see what the working class is capable of when it's not at the bench or the lathe but on the land. If you wish to know, I come of an old family of Stavropol peasants, and I'm curious to

see what the Cossacks have taught you. But perhaps you've been
taught by some Cossack girl, and she's taught you to plough shallow? Watch your step: don't come under the baneful influence of
the Gremyachy girls. Among them are hussies who'll teach you
the devil knows what, experienced sailor though you are. They'll
have you off the right road before you know where you are.
Maybe one of them's already done it?"

The secretary talked with a cheerful freedom, apparently not
particularly careful in what he said. But Davidov sensed that
there was something behind this jesting tone of his, and he grew
wary. "Does he know anything about Lushka, or is he casting
his hook at random?" he wondered a little anxiously. But he fell
in with the secretary's bantering tone.

"When a woman goes off the road or goes wrong she cries:
'Ai! Ai! Ai!' But a man, if he's a real man, doesn't say a word: he
just seeks the right road. That's a fact!"

"So I take it we are to regard you as a real man?"

"Well, what do you think, Comrade Secretary?"

"What I think is this: real men are more to my mind than
those who talk and shout; and if you should happen to get off the
right road, Davidov, then don't shout, but just whisper into my
ear. And I'll help you to get back onto the firm path somehow
or other. Agreed?"

"Thank you for that," Davidov said seriously. But he was thinking: "There's a son of Beezlebub for you! He's sniffed it all
out. . . ." To take off the effect of his serious tone he added: "I
must say we've got an extremely kind district secretary, something unique."

Nesterenko stopped dead, turned to Davidov, and, pushing
his luxurious Kuban cap to the back of his head and wrinkling
his nose with a smile, he retorted: "I'm kind because when I was
young I myself didn't always walk along the straight path. There
are times when a man strides along as though on parade, but then
he gets his feet entangled and he finishes up the devil knows
where. Anyway, he gets off the track, and he struggles through
the brambles until decent people lead the young fool back onto
the road. So now you see, sailor lad, where my goodness was
born! But I'm not always kind irrespective . . ."

"The proverb says that a horse has four legs but it can stumble," Davidov warily interjected.

"If a good horse stumbles a time or two he can be trained to do better; but there are horses which stumble at every step. Teach them what you like, struggle with them as much as you like, they'll try to count every little hummock they come to with their nose. And why keep such a nag in the stable? Turn him out!"

Davidov was silent, smiling to himself. The allusion was so obvious that it needed no explanation.

They walked slowly along to the ploughed land, and just as slowly, hiding behind an enormous lilac cloud, the sun rose behind them.

"This is my section." Davidov pointed with assumed unconcern to the level line of furrows stretching away into the distance.

With an imperceptible nod bringing his cap right down over his eyebrows, Nesterenko went striding across the damp furrows. Davidov, following a little behind him, noticed that the secretary from time to time pretended to remove a burr from inside the leg of his boot but really was measuring the depth of the furrow. At last he had to burst out:

"Why don't you measure openly? Why are you being so diplomatic about it?"

"You might pretend you hadn't noticed," the secretary barked back. When they came to the farther edge of the ploughed land he halted and remarked with insulting condescension: "In general not bad, but the furrows are uneven, as if a lad had ploughed them. In some places they're deeper, in some they're shallower, and at times they're very deep. Probably that's because you don't know the job properly; but it might also be because you weren't in a good humour when you set your hands to the plough handles. Bear in mind, Davidov, that bad temper is good only in war-time; then a touch of spleen helps you to fight. But when you're ploughing you've got to be a cordial sort of man, because the earth likes to be treated equably and kindly. That's what my dead father always told me. Well, and what are you thinking about, you dry-land sailor?" he suddenly exclaimed, and gave Davidov a powerful nudge with his shoulder.

Davidov went staggering, and didn't realize at first that he was

being challenged to a fight. But when the secretary laughed and gave him another powerful charge, he planted his feet wide apart and crouched a little forward. They took hold of each other, trying to get a grip on each other's belt.

"By the belt or how?" Nesterenko asked.

"As you like, only no tricks: no tripping."

"And no overhead throws," Nesterenko grunted, puffing a little with the effort of trying to put his opponent down.

Davidov took a good grip of the secretary's taut, muscular body and at once realized that he had to deal with an experienced wrestler. Davidov might have been the stronger, but Nesterenko excelled him in mobility and dexterity. More than once, when their two faces were almost touching, Davidov saw cheeks flooded with a swarthy flush, insolently glittering eyes, and heard the stifled whisper: "Come on then, come on, working class! What are you treading around in one spot for?"

For a good eight minutes they struggled over the ploughed land until quite exhausted. Davidov hoarsely said:

"Let's get onto the grass, or we'll give up our souls to God. . . ."

"Where we began, there we shall finish," the secretary murmured between his gasps of breath.

Exerting his last strength, Davidov somehow managed to bring his opponent down on the ground, and that ended the contest: they fell locked together, but, in falling, the chairman turned the secretary over and came down on top. Throwing out his legs, pressing on Nesterenko with all the weight of his body, Davidov could hardly get the words out for panting:

"Well, what d'you say now, Secretary?"

"What is there to say? . . . I pass! You're strong, working class! It isn't all that easy to get me down: I've gone in for wrestling ever since I was a child."

Davidov got up and magnanimously held out his hand to his defeated adversary. But the secretary leaped to his feet like an uncoiling spring and turned his back.

"Brush me down!"

With a gentle yet masculine warmth Davidov carefully brushed the clumps of dirt and blades of old grass from Neste-

renko's back with his great paw. Then their eyes met again, and they both roared with laughter.

"You should have let me win, if only out of respect for my Party position. What would it have cost you? Ah, you Leningrad bear! You've got no sense of decency, no respect for authority. Look at that smile! Right up to your ears and all your mug beaming with satisfaction, like a young wife."

"I'll bear it in mind next time, and that's a fact," Davidov said, still smiling. "But you musn't put up such resistance: why, you buried yourself right up to your knees in the soil and just wouldn't give way. Ah, Nesterenko, Nesterenko! You're just an unfortunate Stavropol medium peasant and petty proprietor, as our Makar Nagulnov would put it. As a Party secretary you should know very well that the working class ought to be on top every time; it's historically justified. Fact!"

Nesterenko whistled humorously and shook his head. His Kuban cap slipped down over the back of his neck, and clung there as though by a miracle. He said with a laugh: "Next time I'll put you down without fail. And then we'll see what Marxist justification you'll try to find. The worst of it is that the cook saw us struggling like a couple of boys, and what will she think of us? She's sure to say we've gone clean crazy. . . ."

Davidov dismissed the possibility unconcernedly. "We'll appeal to our youth; she'll understand and forgive. But now let's talk, Comrade Nesterenko, for time's passing, that's a fact."

"Let's find a drier spot where we can sit down."

They settled down on a clayey mound, an abandoned marmot hillock, and the secretary began to talk quietly and slowly.

"Before I came out here I spent some time in Gremyachy. I made the acquaintance of Razmiotnov and all the active members left in the village. I know Nagulnov already: he came out to see us in the district committee. I've already said this to him and Razmiotnov and I repeat it to you: you're not getting on well with the job of drawing good collective farmers into the Party, not getting hold of men who're devoted to our cause. And there are some good lads in the collective farm, don't you agree?"

"That's a fact."

"Then, what's wrong?"

"Even the good men are waiting. . . ."

"What for?"

"To see how things turn out with the collective farm . . . And meanwhile they're digging their own gardens."

"You've got to stir them up a bit; they'll be getting sluggish in their thinking."

"We are stirring them up little by little, but we haven't much result to show so far. But I think there'll be an increase in our group by autumn, that's a fact."

"And until then you'll just sit around with folded arms?"

"No, why? We shall work; but we shan't press them."

"I'm not suggesting any pressure. I simply think you musn't miss any opportunity to bring in one outstanding worker after another, explaining the Party policy to him in language he understands."

"That's what we are doing, Comrade Nesterenko," Davidov assured him.

"You say you're doing it, but all the same the group isn't growing. And that looks more like inaction than action. All right, we'll wait a little longer and see how things go. Now to turn to another matter: I want to point out defects of a different kind. I came here to get to know you, to sniff around, so to speak, and then to have a heart-to-heart talk. You've had a Party education and you won't seriously claim that you're young. Your youth has gone, and at such a pace that you'll never overtake it or bring it back. And don't expect any allowance because of your proletarian origin, your inexperience, and so on; on the other hand you needn't expect any special, inflexible severity such as certain Party leaders are fond of." He was speaking more energetically now. "In my view some rather unintelligent behaviour has crept into our Party life, and with it we've got certain phrases like: 'clear up the shavings,' 'clean things up with sand,' 'rub them down with emery cloth,' and the like. You'd think we weren't dealing with human beings but with pieces of rusty old iron. But what does it all amount to in reality? And note that these phrases are spouted mainly by men who never shaved a shaving off metal or wood in their lives, and never held an emery block in their hands, if I know anything. Man's a fine piece of work, and you have to handle him with the greatest of care.

"I'll tell you a story. In 1918 the order and discipline in our detachment was so bad it couldn't have been worse. It wasn't a Red Guard detachment, it was a Makhno bandit group, honest! And then, at the beginning of 1919 we were sent a Communist commissar from the Don miners. He was getting on in years, an old daddy with a bit of a stoop, and black whiskers drooping like those of Taras Shevchenko. But with his arrival there was a complete change. The men were the same, and yet they weren't: it was just as though they'd all been reborn. There wasn't one case calling for disciplinary measures, not to mention bringing a man before a revolutionary tribunal: and that not a month after the commissar arrived. How did he get hold of them? By his spirit: that's how he did it, the cunning devil. He talked to every man, he had a decent word for each of them. If a man showed signs of fear before going into battle, he encouraged him with a heart-to-heart talk; and he pulled up those who were too venturesome, but he did it so that it never entered their head to get wild with him. He'd just whisper into their ear: 'Don't strain against the reins, you idiot! They'll only kill you, and then what would we do? Why, if you were to go, the whole squad, not to mention the company, would be done for.' Of course the hero was flattered to think the commissar had such a good opinion of him, and after that he'd fight just as well, but without any dare-devilry.

"Our commissar had only one weakness: whenever we occupied some large village or a Cossack district centre he went all limp. . . ."

The word was so unexpected that Davidov turned sharply round to face the secretary, and nearly fell backward off the marmot mound. Slipping and clinging to the damp soil of the steep, wind-carved side with his fingers, he exclaimed: "What d'you mean, 'limp'?"

Nesterenko laughed quietly. "I used the wrong word. I don't mean he went limp, but he started to rummage through the libraries owned by the wealthy merchants, the landowners, and anyone else who bought books in those days. He'd take all the books he wanted and confiscate them without further argument. You won't believe it, but he carted four cartloads of books around with him, a whole library on wheels, and he fussed as

much over them as he did over the ammunition: every britzka was covered with a tarpaulin, the books were packed back to back, and he had straw laid under them. And whenever we, bivouacked, or made a halt, or had a breathing space between fights, he'd hand out books to us and order us to read them; and then he'd check up on whether we had or not.

"I was young then, and more interested in girls; and I must admit I dodged reading. But I was almost illiterate, and as stupid as a cork. One day he handed me a packet because I hadn't read the book he'd given me. He spent two days questioning me about the book, but I couldn't tell him a single thing. And he said to me—he always took you aside to talk about such things, he wouldn't speak in front of everybody, he wouldn't shame you like that—and he said to me: 'What do you think? Are you going to live like Ivan the Fool? I saw you making up to some girl yesterday evening; but you might as well cut your nose off: no literate girl wants an illiterate dolt like you, she'd be bored with you in five minutes; you're just a lout and a clot; your mind isn't getting any bigger, because you haven't got one and never did have; you haven't acquired one yet. Men who're literate have all the masculine qualities of the illiterates, so taking it by and large they've got the advantage. Get that into your head, you young ninny!'

"Well, what answer could I make to that?

"For a good fortnight he nagged me and ragged me; he all but reduced me to tears, but all the same he got me into the habit of reading, and then I got such a passion for books that you couldn't drag me away from them. I remember his kind words to this very day. To tell the truth, I don't know who I owe more to for my knowledge and education: my dead father or that commissar."

He was silent for a few moments, meditating. Evidently his memories had saddened him. But soon, hardly concealing his guileful smile, he was overwhelming Davidov with questions again.

"Do you do any reading in your spare time? I suppose you just glance through the papers? And of course you haven't much spare time, have you? But, by the way, are there any interesting books in your reading room? You don't know? Then shame on

you, brother! Have you ever been to your reading room? Only twice? My dear boy, that won't get you anywhere. I thought better of you, representative of the Leningrad working class. Now I have got something to write to your works about. But don't worry, I shall write in my own name: 'Davidov, who used to work in your factory, and is now one of the twenty-five thousand mobilized for collectivization and is chairman of the Stalin collective farm, both he and the farmers he's in charge of, have a great need of books. They urgently require popular political and economic literature, books on agriculture, cattle-breeding, and farming generally. It would be fine if you could send them a selection of literature, too, both classics and modern. As patron of the collective farm, please send them a small library without charge, some three hundred books, say, to the following address.' Well, is that all right? You don't want me to write? Of course not. Then do it yourself, out of your collective-farm resources: get hold of a library of at least two or three hundred books. Of course you'll say you haven't any money. Bosh! You can find it. Sell a couple of your old oxen, don't beggar yourself, the devil won't get you! And then you'll have your library, and what a library! I reckoned it all out yesterday in your office, and I decided you've got more draught animals than you need for the amount of land in the farm. What are you wasting fodder on them for? Get rid of them. Do you know how many of your oxen are over ten years old? You don't? Pity! But I can help you out in your ignorance: you've got ten yoke of oxen over ten years old. A good farmer doesn't keep such old rubbish in his yard: he feeds them up and sells them. Get that?"

"I get it, all right; but we've already decided to sell the surplus livestock in the autumn, including the old oxen. Our experienced farmers have advised me on that already."

"And now the cattle are being fattened up?"

"No. But the old oxen are working, that I do know."

"Who were the experienced farmers who advised you to sell them in the autumn?"

"Our manager, Ostrovnov, and someone else; I don't remember now. . . ."

"Hm, interesting! Your manager was a kulak right down to five minutes before the collectivization, so he knew his job. Then

how could he give you such nonsensical advice? Sell the oxen
in the autumn, and keep them under the yoke till then? If you do
you'll be selling skin and bones. I'd give you different advice:
turn all the cattle you intend to sell out to graze, and fatten
them up; put them on concentrates and sell them during the
summer, when there isn't much livestock on the market and
meat's high. In the autumn, meat will be plentiful enough without your cattle and you'll get a lower price. You've got a surplus
of grain. So what's the idea? You please yourselves, I don't intend to interfere in your affairs. All the same, think it over. . . .
In any case you can fatten up a couple of old bullocks and sell
them at once. After all, the money won't be going into drink, but
into books. To cut the cackle: see to it that you've got a library
within two months: first point. Transfer the reading room at
once from its present ramshackle hut to one of the good kulak
houses, the very best, and make no mistake: second point. I'll
send you out a good lad to run the reading room and I'll tell him
he's got to have public readings every day: third point."

"Hold up with your points," Davidov pleaded, crimson with
mortification. "In good Russian I tell you there'll be a library;
that disposes of point one. I'll transfer the reading room to a
good house tomorrow; that's disposed of point two. But wait a
bit with point three. I've already got someone in mind to run
the reading room, an outstanding youngster and a first-rate
agitator. But he's working in production at present, that's the real
trouble. I think the Young Communist League will meet us half-
way, and I'll put the lad on the job."

Nesterenko listened to him attentively, nodding his head, an
impenetrable expression on his face, only his eyes smiling.
"There's nothing I like better than a commander who's
energetic and takes the right decisions quickly. But listen to
something more I have to say about your reading room. I visited
it yesterday. I tell you the accommodation isn't what I'd call
pleasant. It's horribly bare and desperately neglected. Dust on
the window sills. The floors not washed since God knows when.
It stinks of mildew and I don't know what else. It smells just
like a funeral vault, by God! But worst of all, the books! You can
count them on your two hands, and they're old, to make matters

worse. On one shelf I found a poster rolled up; it was yellow with age. I unrolled it, looked at the picture, and read:

> 'The girls all love to see our troops;
> The toothless women mumble away;
> The fathers too are deeply moved;
> These boys, great lads, are ours, they say.
> Beat the enemy back and front.
> Ploughman, as you turn over the soil,
> Know that the workmen are pleased as punch
> To be defending your precious toil.'

"Ah, I thought, this is an old acquaintance! I read that poster, and promptly forgot it again—away back in 1920, on the Wrangel front. Demian Biedny's words are good for today too. But don't you agree that in 1930 it would be better to have something more up to date, something with more relation to the present time, to collectivization, for instance? . . ."

"You use your eyes all right and you're quick on detail," Davidov mumbled more approvingly than discontentedly, though he was still smarting under the ticking off.

"It's my job to use my eyes and to help put right any defects in the work, and I do so with full understanding of your position, Siemion. But all this is by way of introduction, and the main story has yet to come. You came out here to the brigade, you abandoned the collective farm, you handed over all its administration to Razmiotnov. But you know very well that it's difficult for him to carry the whole burden at such a time; he just can't manage it. You know that, don't you? And yet you came out here."

"But you yourself went driving a mowing machine over the Tubyanskoe fields the other day. Or do you deny the force of example?"

Nesterenko irritably waved the question aside. "I worked in the Tubyanskoe fields for a few hours to get to know the people. This is a different matter; you came out to the brigade because of difficulties in your personal affairs. Any difference? I've got a feeling you ran away from Lukeria Nagulnova. Or am I mistaken?"

The blood ebbed from Davidov's face. He turned away,

plucked aimlessly at the grass, and said thickly: "I heard . . ."

But Nesterenko cautiously, gently laid his hand on Davidov's shoulder, drew him closer, and said: "Don't take offence. Did you think I was just measuring the depths of your furrows for no reason? In certain places you ploughed deeper than any tractor. You poured out your spite on the earth, and you transferred your feeling of injury to the oxen. From all I hear from those who know you it looks as if your affair with Lukeria's coming to an end. Is that right?"

"It looks like it."

"Well, I can only say I'm sincerely glad. Only don't go on putting things off too long, my dear Siemion. The people like you, but it isn't well that they're feeling sorry for you. Get that? They really are feeling sorry for you. Just because of that worthless liaison. When people, as is their Russian habit, feel sorry for poor or ill folk that's as it should be. But when they begin to feel pity for an intelligent young fellow like you, and their leader into the bargain, nothing can be more shameful and horrible for him. And the main thing is that this stupid fascination of yours for a worthless female, and she only recently your comrade's wife, is getting in the way of everything, in my view. How else can we explain the unforgivable letdowns in your work, in Nagulnov's work? You've got yourselves tied into a devilish knot, and if you don't untie yourselves the district committee will have to cut it. Understand that!"

"Maybe it would be better for me to leave Gremyachy?" Davidov asked irresolutely.

"Don't talk rot!" Nesterenko broke in harshly. "If you've made a mess of yourself the first thing to do is to clean yourself up; then you can talk about going away. I'd rather you told me one thing: d'you know Yegorova, the teacher? She's a Party member too."

"Yes, I've met her." Davidov smiled rather ineptly as he recalled his first meeting with the quite young and extremely shy teacher in the winter, when the kulak farms were being broken up. When she was introduced to him she held out her clammy hand awkwardly, and blushed fierily; she was hardly able to stammer out the words: "I'm the teacher, Liuda Yegorova."

Davidov had suggested to Nagulnov at the time: "Take the young Communist teacher into your brigade. Let the girl see what the class war is really like." But Nagulnov had stared glumly at his long, swarthy hands and had replied: "You take her in your brigade. I've got no use for her. She teaches the lowest classes, and my boy gets two marks from her instead of one, for she cries her eyes out together with him. Who was responsible for accepting such a girl into the Young Communist League? D'you call her a Young Communist? She's nothing but spittle in a skirt."

Nesterenko knitted his brows and looked at Davidov censoriously. "What are you smiling at, I'd like to know? What's so funny about my question?"

Davidov tried awkwardly to explain the reason for his amusement. "It's nothing. I simply remembered some little point concerning that teacher. She's a very modest sort. . . ."

"Remembered little points! You've chosen a right moment to be amused!" Nesterenko exclaimed, evidently really annoyed. "You'd do better to remember that that modest little teacher's the only Young Communist in your village. A large village like yours, and you haven't got a Young Communist group going. That's not a little point! Who's responsible for that? Nagulnov first and foremost, and you, and I as well. And yet you're still smiling. . . . That's not a pleasant smile, Siemion Davidov. And don't plead that you've had other more important matters to attend to. Every task which the Party puts into your hands is important. It's quite another matter how we manage to deal with them."

Davidov was beginning to get rather annoyed too, but, controlling his feelings, he said: "Comrade Nesterenko, you've only spent one day in Gremyachy Log and yet you've managed to discover all these shortcomings and defects in our work, and you've noticed my behaviour. What on earth would have happened if you'd been living here ever since last January? I'd have had to listen to your comments for a whole week, and that's a fact."

The last sentence rather amused Nesterenko. He narrowed his eyes impudently, and jogged his companion in the ribs with his

elbow. "I suppose you wouldn't admit that if I hadn't merely visited Gremyachy but had worked side by side with you possibly there wouldn't have been so many shortcomings?"

"I grant there wouldn't have been so many, but there would have been some, all the same. You're not Stalin any more than I am, and you'd go wrong like anyone else, and that's a fact. I can see many of my mistakes, but I don't put them all right, and certainly not all at once: that's my trouble, brother. One day last spring the schoolmaster took all his boys out into the fields to hunt marmots. I happened to go by but I didn't stop and speak to them; I didn't know then and I still don't know how and what that old teacher lives on. I tell you I've done worse things than that. In the winter he sent me a note asking for a cart to bring him some firewood. D'you think I let him have a cart? I forgot all about it. Other things occupied my time and my thoughts. I'm ashamed when I recall it even now. You're right, too, in regard to the Young Communists. We've let that important matter slide, and of course I'm very much to blame for that, and that's a fact."

But Nesterenko wasn't to be appeased simply with penitent confessions. "It's all to the good that you admit your mistakes, and it's clear you haven't quite lost all sense of shame. But the net result is that the Young Communists haven't grown in numbers, and the teacher hasn't had his wood. It's action that's wanted, my dear Siemion, and not just remorse," he urged insistently.

"Everything will be put right, everything will be done, I give you my word. But you, I mean the district committee, must help us to organize a Young Communist group. Send us one or two Young Communist boys and girls, even if only for temporary work. I tell you quite seriously, Yegorova's no good whatever as an organizer. She's too shy to walk this earth, so how can you expect her to handle the youngsters, especially ours?"

Now at last Nesterenko was satisfied. "That's talking! We'll help with the Young Communists, I promise you; but let me add a little more to your self-criticism. Your co-operative asked you to let them have two carts to collect goods from the district in time for the first of May celebrations, didn't they?"

"They did."

"And you didn't let them have them?"

"It couldn't be done. We were ploughing and sowing, both at once. There wasn't time for trading."

"And so it wasn't possible to let them have two carts? Rubbish! Bosh! You could have, and without serious harm to the field work. But you didn't manage it, you didn't want to, you didn't think the question out enough, didn't ask: 'How will this affect the spirit of the collective farmers?' And so the women of Gremyachy trudged all the way to the district for the things they needed most: soap, salt, matches, and paraffin, and that on the very eve of the holiday. And then what did they say to one another about our Soviet regime? Or don't you care what they say? But did you and I fight the Whites for our women to curse our Soviet government? Or doesn't that matter to you? You and I didn't fight for them to curse our own government. Not on your life!" he shouted, his voice unexpectedly rising to a shrill tone, then falling to a whisper: "Do you really mean to say you don't see such a simple truth as that, Siemion? Wake up, Comrade! Come to your senses!"

Davidov kneaded the dead cigarette end with his fingers and sat with pursed lips, staring at the ground. He had always been slow to give vent to his feelings; no one could ever accuse him of sentimentality, whatever else they might charge him with. But now some force took command of him, and he gave Nesterenko a powerful hug and even brushed his lips against the secretary's unshaven cheek. His voice quivered with emotion as he said:

"Thank you, Comrade. My warm thanks. You're a fine fellow, and it'll be easy to work with you, not like with the previous secretary, Korchinsky. You've said some hard things, but they're true through and through, and that's a fact. Only for God's sake don't think I'm past hoping for. I'll do all that's necessary; we'll all try to do what's wanted. I shall reconsider a lot of things, I've got plenty to think about now. . . . Believe me, Comrade Nesterenko."

The secretary was just as moved, but he gave no sign of it; he coughed and screwed up his black, serious eyes. Davidov noticed that he was shivering all over. After a moment he said quietly: "I believe in you and the other lads, and I put my hopes in you as much as I do in myself. Keep that firmly in mind, Siemion Davidov. Don't try to pull the wool over the eyes of the

district committee or me, don't dare to let us down. We Communists are soldiers in one regiment, and under no circumstances should we ever lose the feeling that we stand shoulder to shoulder. You know that very well. And now see to it that we have no more unpleasant conversations like this one, damn them! I don't like them, though I have to have a lot of them. I have a talk like today's and get wild with a good friend like you, and afterwards I can't sleep all night, I get a feeling round my heart . . ."

Davidov took a firm grip of Nesterenko's hand and looked into his face. He was astonished. The man he now saw sitting beside him was not the previous cheerful talker, not the sociable fellow who was ready to have his bit of fun and even a wrestling bout, but elderly and very tired. His eyes seemed suddenly to have aged: there were deep furrows round the corners of his mouth, and even the swarthy flush on his bony cheeks had faded and turned yellow. In a few minutes he had completely changed in his personality.

"Time I was off; I've spent too long as your guest," he said, rising heavily from the marmot mound.

"You're not feeling ill, are you?" Davidov asked anxiously. "You seem to have gone all queer."

"You've guessed right," the secretary said dispiritedly. "I've got a bout of malaria coming on. I picked it up years ago in Central Asia, and I can't get rid of the blasted germ nohow."

"But what were you doing in Central Asia? What necessity drove you there?"

"You don't think I went there to pick apricots, do you? I was liquidating the counter-revolutionary bandits; but I can't liquidate my own personal malaria. The doctors drove it into my spleen, and now I have to put up with it. But that's all by the way. What I want to say as my last word is: the counter-revolutionaries have begun to get busy in our district, and in the neighbouring district too, in the Stalingrad area. They think they can pull off something yet, the devils! But what is it the song says? 'They wanted to beat us, to beat us; They gathered to defeat us.' "

" 'But neither were we scared, we too were all prepared,' " Davidov said, finishing the verse.

"Exactly. All the same we need to keep our ears washed out." Nesterenko thoughtfully scratched one eyebrow and croaked angrily: "It can't be helped; I've got to deprive myself of something that's rather precious. . . . As you and I have sworn friendship, accept this toy as a present from me. It may come in useful. Nagulnov has had his warning: you look out too, or you may be in for something worse. . . ."

He took out a dully gleaming Browning from his jacket pocket and put it in Davidov's hand. "That's not much of a defence. I dare say a locksmith's tool is more reliable," he added.

Davidov gripped his hand tightly and muttered thickly, half choking with his feelings: "Thank you for your comradely . . . What can I say? . . . Well, it's a fact, your friendly thoughtfulness. My warm thanks."

"May it do you good!" Nesterenko jested. "Only, keep your eyes peeled: don't let yourself down. You know old fighters tend to grow more thoughtless with the years. . . ."

"So long as I live I shan't let myself down; or if I do I'll lose my head in doing it," Davidov assured him. He put the pistol in his trouser hip pocket; but he took it out again and looked anxiously first at the weapon then at Nesterenko. "It's rather awkward. . . . You can't be left without a weapon. Take it back; I don't need it."

But the secretary gently pushed his hand away. "Don't worry, I've got a spare one. That one I've given you was expendable, but the other I guard as the apple of my eye. It was a present, a nameday present. I suppose you imagine I served in the army and fought five years for nothing?" He winked and even attempted to smile; but the smile was painful, tortured. He shivered feverishly, wriggled his shoulders in an attempt to control his trembling, and said in spasms: "Yesterday Shaly was boasting about his present. I went and saw him, and sat drinking tea with honey, talking about life; and he took your locksmith's tool out of his chest and said: 'In all my life I've been given two presents: a tobacco pouch from my old woman when she was still going around with the girls and casting looks at me, the young smith; and this tool personally from Comrade Davidov for my shock work in the forge. Two presents in all my long life. And you could never reckon up the amount of iron I've dan-

gled in my hands during all that smoke-stained life of mine. And
so I don't keep these presents in the chest, but right by my heart.'
He's a good old man. He's spent a fine, hard-working life, and,
as we say, God grant that every man may bring the people as
much benefit as that old smith has with his two strong hands.
And so you see your present is far more precious than mine."

They walked swiftly back to the hut. Now Nesterenko was
shivering violently.

Rain came on again from the west. Low, ragged clumps of
cloud, the first harbingers of dirty weather, floated over. The
young grass and the damp black soil gave off an intoxicating
scent. The sun, which had shone for a brief while, hid behind the
clouds, and, beating the fresh wind with their broad wings, two
steppe eagles flew up into the invisible heights. The stillness that
presages rain covered the steppe like soft felt; only the marmots
whistled piercingly and anxiously, sure sign that a prolonged
downpour was on its way.

"Lie up a bit in our hut before you go. The rain will catch you
on the road: you'll get soaked and then you'll have to take to
your bed," Davidov urged him. But Nesterenko flatly refused.

"I can't. I've a meeting at three. And the rain won't catch up
with me. I've a good horse."

As he untied the reins and tightened the saddle girths his
hands shook like those of a decrepit old man. He swiftly embraced Davidov, sprang with unexpected lightness onto his horse's
back, and shouted as he set off at a smart trot: "I'll get warm as
I ride."

Hearing the quiet clop of horse hoofs, Kuprianovna peered
out of the hut like dough out of a trough, and clapped her hands
bitterly. "Gone already? How could he go without his breakfast?"

"He's feeling ill," Davidov said as he stood gazing after the
secretary.

"Oh, my unhappy head!" Kuprianovna exclaimed regretfully.
"Such a good fellow, and we haven't fed him. Although he's an
official, as anyone can see with half an eye, he wasn't ashamed to
peel my potatoes for me while you were snoring, Chairman. He's
not like our dear little Cossacks; there's no comparison! Expect
them to help you? Not on your life! All they can do is guzzle

with three throats and brag till the new moon. But help the cook? Don't dare even to ask! But that visitor spoke to me very kindly. So kindly and sincere he was, you'd never think of a better in a hundred years." Finically pursing up her lips, she lauded the secretary to the skies, taking sidelong glances at Davidov the while to see what impression she was making.

He was not listening to her; he was going over his conversation with Nesterenko. But once the cook started to chatter she found it difficult to stop.

"And you're a fine one too, Davidov, damn your eyes! You might have whispered to me that he was intending to go. And I, old fool that I am, I didn't guess, that's the worst of it. I expect he'll be thinking the cook deliberately kept out of his way in the hut, though I was ready to serve him with all my soul. . . ."

Davidov still said nothing, and the cook went on unhindered.

"Look how he rides his horse! You'd say he was born under a horse and grew up on a horse. He doesn't stir or sway, the eagle. He's a born Cossack, with all the old-time bearing, too," she declared rapturously, not removing her enchanted gaze from the departing horseman.

"He's not a Cossack, he's a Ukrainian," Davidov said abstractedly, and sighed. Now Nesterenko had gone he felt sad.

At his remark Kuprianovna flashed up like dry tinder. "You tell those yarns to your grandmother! I tell you straight he's a true Cossack! Are your eyes gummed up, or what? You can tell by his seat even at this distance, and when he's around you can see he's of Cossack leaven by his figure, the way he carries himself, and the way he behaves with women; he's not like those timid . . ." she added pointedly.

"All right, let him be a Cossack if you wish, but it doesn't make me get hot under the collar either way," he said in a conciliatory tone. "But d'you think he's a good sort? I expect you talked a lot to him before you woke me up?"

Now it was the cook's turn to sigh, and she sighed with all the power of her mighty chest, with such fervour that her old blouse split right down the seam under her arm. "You could search a long time . . ." she answered slowly, with deep feeling. Suddenly, for no apparent reason she began to bang the dishes

about, aimlessly setting them out on the table, yet not so much setting them out as flinging them around as they came to her hand and wherever they happened to fall.

Chapter 9

Davidov walked along with an unhurried but steady stride. As he reached the top of a rise he halted and looked back towards the brigade camp, now completely deserted, at the ploughed fields sweeping up the opposite slope almost to the horizon. Say what they like, he had worked at full stretch during the past few days, and they musn't be upset if he worked his driver, Varvara, and Kondrat's oxen so hard. It would be interesting to see this section of the farm again in October: if all went well it would be covered with the bushy green of winter wheat, the morning frosts would silver it, and at midday, when the sun warmed the earth, floating low in the pale, almost white sky, the winter wheat would sparkle with all the colours of the rainbow as though after a heavy downpour, and every little drop would reflect the chilly autumnal sky and the feathery white clouds, and the fading sun.

From this distance the ploughed land extended like an enormous expanse of black velvet opened to its full width and edged by the green of the grassland. Only on the very verge, on the northern slope where the clay rose close to the surface, was there an uneven fringe which showed ruddy brown patches. The rolls of black turned-over earth, whitened by the ploughshares, showed dully along the furrows, and suddenly he caught sight of a bluish-grey patch standing out against the black soil: Varia Kharlamova had abandoned her work, since it was no longer of any interest to her, and was slowly trudging back to the camp, her head bowed low. Kondrat Maidannikov was sitting smoking at the edge of the furrow. What could he do without his assistant? His oxen, useless without the driver and surrounded with swarms of clegs, could give him no satisfaction now.

Noticing Davidov standing on the ridge, Varia also halted, briskly took off her kerchief, and gently waved it. That silent, diffident challenge brought a smile to Davidov's lips. He waved his cap in reply and set off without looking back again.

"She's a very wilful girl! Very pleasant, but really quite wilful and spoilt! But are any girls not spoilt? Aren't they always full of flirtatiousness? In all my days, dreaming or waking, I've never seen one that isn't. As soon as a beauty reaches the age of sixteen or seventeen she begins to tog herself up, does all she can to make herself look even more attractive, and then begins to try her power and will on the likes of us. Fact!" he reflected. "Here's this child taking it on herself to tame me, and unconsciously revealing all her character. All right, nothing will come of it; we Baltic men are old birds. But what's she going back to the hut for? She's in no hurry, she's taking her time, so evidently Kondrat hasn't sent her back for something; she's going to please herself, out of her own stupid girlish whim. Surely it can't be because I've left the brigade? That really would be disgusting, an utter violation of labour discipline. If she's going for some good reason, then by all means let her; but if it's just a whim, she'll get it hot at the next brigade meeting, for all her youth and her beautiful personality. Ploughing isn't a Sunday game, so please work properly." He began to grow irritable.

He had a strange feeling that he was being torn in two: on the one hand he was indignant with Varvara for her wilful conduct, but on the other, as a man he felt flattered by the possibility that she had abandoned her work because of him.

He remembered an old friend of his in Leningrad, a former sailor like himself. When he started chasing any girl he used to take Davidov aside and whisper like any conspirator, in a serious tone: "Siemion, I'm working for a *rapprochement* with the enemy. If I show signs of wavering, support me on the flanks; but if I go under, please cover my shameful retreat." As he recalled those distant days he smiled and thought: "No, it isn't wise to work for a *'rapprochement'* with this 'enemy.' Varia's not my age, and not my kind. And, besides, if I don't steer clear of her, and I get sunk, the collective farmers will think I'm nothing but a skirt-chaser. But I'm a fine devilish sort of skirt-chaser, when I don't even know how to get free of Lukeria. No, in all conscience

I couldn't play about with Varia. She's as pure as the dawn of a
fine day. . . . And as I haven't yet learnt what serious love is,
there's no point in my being a plague to the girl. Cast off, sailor
Davidov, and at once! I must keep away from her. First I must
have a talk with her, only I must do it very carefully, so that she
doesn't take offence, and then I'll keep off." So he decided, with
an involuntary sigh.

Thus meditating on the not very cheerful turn his life in
Gremyachy Log had taken, and on the tasks the new district
secretary had set him, his mind turned back to Lukeria. "How
am I to untie that knot painlessly? Makar's right: if you can't
get a knot undone with your fingers or teeth you've got to cut it.
What a she-devil she is! It's going to be devilish hard for me to
give her up for good. Yet why should it be? How is it Makar found
it so easy, while I find it difficult? Haven't I any character? That's
a point that never occurred to me before. But perhaps it wasn't
really easy for Makar, only he didn't show it? I expect that's the
truth of the matter; he was able to conceal what he went
through, and I can't."

Without realizing it he had now covered a considerable distance. Close to a wayside hawthorn bush he lay down in the
shade to rest and smoke, and began to turn over in his mind
who had tried to shoot Nagulnov. But then he angrily cut his
thoughts short. "We knew already there were swine left in the
village even after we broke up the kulaks. I'll have a talk with
Makar and find out the details, then possibly I shall get a clue.
There's no point in my worrying my brains uselessly."

To shorten his journey he turned off the road and struck a
course straight across the virgin soil. But he had not gone more
than a few hundred yards when he crossed some invisible boundary and found himself in a different world: his leg-boots were no
longer rustling through the heavy-grained cats'-tail grass, the
ground was no longer spangled with flowers, the heady scent
of luxuriantly flowering grasses had faded, and before him
stretched a wide expanse of grey and gloomy steppe.

So joyless was this barren earth, which looked as though it had
recently been devastated by fire, that he seethed with fury. Looking around him, he realized that he had come to the head of the

Biriuk valley, to the area of virgin soil which Yakov Lukich had once referred to in a meeting of the farm administration. "In the Caucasus for some reason the Lord God piled up all the land into mountains. He raised all the earth into stupid bumps, so that you can't drive or even walk through them. But what I don't understand is why He was annoyed with us Gremyachy Cossacks. Almost two thousand hectares of good land He's salted down so that for ages it hasn't been possible to plough or sow it. It's all right for grazing in the spring, but that doesn't last long, and then you can spit on that God-accursed earth and never set foot on it again till the following spring. And all the good we get from it is some six weeks when the village sheep crop semi-starvation rations off it, after which it's only mentioned in our reports and it harbours nothing but lizards and snakes."

Davidov walked more slowly, making his way round the extensive saline ruts, striding across the deep round holes trodden out by the hoofs of cows and sheep, and licked smooth by their rough tongues. The spongy, salty soil looked like grey-grained marble.

As far as the Wet Ravine, some three miles farther on, this dismal area extended. In places it was white with the smoky plumes of feather-grass, with dried-up patches of salt marsh cracking in the heat; a flowing, shifting mirage floated over it as it panted fierily in the mid-day sun. But even this dreary soil had its own undying, flourishing life: from time to time red-legged crickets started up with a crack from under Davidov's feet; grey lizards, the colour of the soil, crawled about noiselessly; marmots whistled to one another anxiously; a harrier floated low over the steppe, rocking as it turned and blending with the feather-grass; and trustful skylarks fearlessly allowed Davidov to walk almost right up to them; they flew up reluctantly and, gathering height till they were lost in the milky grey haze of the cloudless sky, trilled away there more faintly but more pleasantly.

For some reason the skylarks greatly favoured this dreary scrap of earth; they flew here very early in the spring, as soon as the first patches of soil appeared in the thawing snow, weaved nests from last year's withered grass, reared their young, and delighted the steppe till late in the autumn with their simple

song, familiar to the human ear from childhood. Davidov all but trod on one such nest cunningly fashioned in a hollow left by a horse hoof. He drew his foot back in alarm and bent down. But the nest was old and deserted. Tiny feathers, clinging together after the rain, and shards of eggshell were scattered around it.

"The mother's taken her young away. It would have been interesting to see the young skylarks. I don't remember ever seeing one when I was a child," he thought. He smiled wryly: "Every little bird makes its nest and brings up its young; but I've been hobbling around an old bachelor for nearly forty years, and I still don't know whether I shall ever see children of my own. . . . Get married in my old age, is that the programme?"

He laughed aloud as for one moment he imagined himself a solid, married man with a corpulent wife like Kuprianovna and a numerous progeny. He had seen such family portraits in the windows of provincial-town photographers. And this sudden thought of marriage seemed so inept and absurd that he shrugged it off, and strode back to the village in a more cheerful mood.

He did not go to his quarters, but straight to the collective-farm office. He was impatient to get Nagulnov's report on all that had happened while he was away.

The spacious grass-grown office yard was deserted; only the neighbour's chickens were lazily pecking at the dung outside the stable, and under the shed the goat stood sunk in a profound, aged contemplation. Seeing him, the animal, which rejoiced in the name of Trofim, came to life, shook his beard enthusiastically, trod the ground for a moment, then rushed to cut him off. Suddenly he lowered his head, militantly raised his docked tail, and broke into a gallop. His intentions were so obvious that Davidov smiled and halted, making ready to meet the bearded brawler's attack.

"Is that the way you welcome the collective-farm chairman? I'll play football with you, you old demon," he said. Neatly dodging, he seized the animal's arching horns. "And now we'll go along to the office to get justice done. You bully and drone!"

Trofim at once lost all his truculence. He humbly minced along at Davidov's side, occasionally shaking his head in an attempt to free his horn. But when they reached the bottom step to the veranda he put up a resolute resistance, braking with all four

feet. When Davidov stopped, he trustfully stretched out his head and sniffed at his pocket, absurdly wriggling his grey lips.

Davidov shook his head reproachfully and said as expressively as he could: "Ah, Trofim, Trofim! An old fellow like you, a collective-farm pensioner, we might say. But you don't stop your idiotic pranks, rushing to fight everybody and then, if nothing comes of it, beginning to beg for bread. That's not good enough; it's downright disgraceful. Well, and now what can you smell?"

Beneath his tobacco pouch and matches he found a dry crust of bread. He carefully cleaned it of tobacco and took a good sniff at it, then held it out on his palm. The goat drooped his head in a pleading, wheedling manner, looked at Davidov with the dreaming eyes of an old satyr, barely sniffed at the crust, and then, snorting contemptuously, walked away with a dignified air.

"Not very hungry!" Davidov said, a little peeved. "You lousy devil, you've never been in the army or you'd have eaten it up with pleasure. It smells a bit of tobacco, but what of it? You must have a lot of blue blood in you, you old rogue; you're very fastidious, and that's a fact."

He threw away the crust, went onto the cool porch, picked up a mug and dipped it into the water pitcher, and drank thirstily. Now at last he realized how tired he was with the heat and the walk.

Only Razmiotnov and the book-keeper were in the office. When he saw Davidov enter, Razmiotnov smiled.

"So you're back, serviceman? Well, that's a load off my shoulders. I've had trouble enough with this collective-farm work; God forbid that I should have any more. First there's no coal in the smithy, then the water-wheel in the plantation breaks down, someone else comes along with some urgent requirement, and someone else doesn't turn up in time. . . . Such a nerve-racking job is quite out of keeping with my character. If I had to sit here for another week I'd be in such a state of nerves that the very sight of me would be painful."

"How's Makar?"

"He's alive."

"I know he's alive, but what about his contusion?"

Razmiotnov knitted his brows. "Well, what sort of contusion can you get from a bullet? They didn't shoot at him from a three-

inch gun. He shook his head a little, moistened the scratch with vodka, and drank what remained of the bottle; and that's the end of the story."

"Where is he now?"

"He's gone off to the brigade."

"But how did it all happen?"

"Very simple: Makar was sitting by the open window the night before last, and the new student, old Shchukar, was sitting at the other side of the table. And someone took aim at Makar with a rifle. Who it was, only the dark night knows. But one thing is clear: the fellow who fired was a bungler."

"Why is it clear?"

Razmiotnov raised astonished eyebrows. "Would you miss your aim with a rifle at thirty paces? Next morning we found the spot he'd fired from; we found the empty cartridge case. I measured the distance myself: exactly thirty paces from the fence to the window."

"You can miss your aim at night even at thirty paces."

"No, that's impossible," Ramiotnov objected hotly. "I wouldn't. If you like, we'll put it to the test: you sit tonight where Makar was sitting, and let me have a rifle. With my first bullet I'll drill a hole clean between your eyebrows. So it's obvious that the man who fired must have been an amateur and not a real soldier."

"I'd like more details."

"I'll report everything as it happened. About midnight I heard shots fired in the village: a single rifle shot, then two rather fainter, like from a pistol, and then another rifle shot: you could tell it by the sound. I snatched my pistol from under my pillow, pulled on my trousers as I ran, and rushed into the street. I ran to Makar's place: the shooting had come from that direction. For some idiotic reason I thought Makar must be playing about. . . .

"I was there like greased lightning. I knocked at the door; it was bolted, and I could hear someone groaning inside. I charged at the door with my shoulder, broke away the bolt, ran into the house, and struck a match. In the kitchen I saw a couple of feet sticking out from under the bed. I seized them and pulled. By all the saints, under the bed someone squealed just like a pig. I tell you straight it scared me, but I went on hauling. I dragged the legs into the middle of the room, and saw it wasn't a man

at all, but Makar's old housewife. I asked her where Makar was, but she couldn't get a word out for terror.

"I ran into Makar's little room and stumbled over something soft. I fell over, jumped up again, and went all hot: so they've killed Makar, I thought; it's him lying here. Somehow I managed to strike a match and took a look: there was Daddy Shchukar lying on the floor and staring up at me with one eye, while he kept the other shut. He'd got blood on his forehead and cheek. I ask him: 'Are you alive? And where's Makar?' But he only asks me: 'Andrei, tell me for God's sake, am I alive or not?' His voice was as gentle and thin as if he was really giving up the ghost. I reassured him: 'If you can talk you must be still alive; but you're already stinking of death.' He burst into bitter tears and said: 'It must be my soul leaving my body, that's why there's such a stink. But even if I'm alive now I shall die without fail shortly, I've got a bullet in my head.'

"What damned rot!" Davidov interrupted impatiently. "But why was there blood on his face? I don't get it. Was he wounded too?"

Laughing aloud, Razmiotnov went on. "No one was wounded; the shot missed. So I went in, closed the shutters just in case, and lit the lamp. Shchukar went on lying very quietly on his back, only he closed the other eye too, and folded his hands over his chest. He lay there as if he was in his grave, not stirring, as good as a corpse and good for nothing more. In a very feeble, very polite tone he asked me: 'For Christ's sake go and fetch my old woman. I'd like to say good-bye to her before I die.'

"I bent down and shone the lamp on him." Razmiotnov snorted, hardly able to control his laughter. "By the light I could see he'd got a splinter of wood sticking in his forehead. Apparently the bullet sent a splinter flying from the window sill, and it hit Shchukar on the head, pierced the skin, and he, like the fool he is, thought it was a bullet and fell down. Without being killed, the old man was dying before my eyes, but I couldn't straighten up for laughing. Of course I pulled the splinter out and told him: 'I've removed your bullet; now get up. There's no point in your lying there. But tell me, where's Makar got to?'

"I saw the old fellow was cheering up a bit, but he seemed unwilling to stand on his feet while I was around; he shuffled about

over the floor, but didn't get up. All the same, even as he lay there the old driveller nagged away. 'When the enemy shot me,' he said, 'and struck me with a bullet right in my forehead, I dropped as though I'd been scythed down, and I went right off. But Makar put out the lamp, jumped through the window, and vanished. That's the sort of friend he is to me,' he said. 'Here am I lying wounded almost to death, but he goes and abandons me to the mercy of the enemy and hides himself in his fright. Show me the bullet that all but did for me, Andrei. If God grants me my life I'll keep it under the holy pictures as a lasting memory.'

" 'No,' I tell him, 'I can't show you the bullet, it's smothered in blood, and you might go right off again if you saw it.' At that the old man grew even more cheerful, turned nimbly onto one side and asked: 'What d'you think, Andrei? Seeing as I've been hero-ically wounded and suffered such an attack from the enemy, may I get a medal from the higher authorities?' But that really got up my nose: I pushed the splinter into his hand and said: 'Here's your bullet. Put it behind the icon and keep it; and now hop off to the well, wash away your heroism, and put yourself into decent state, for you stink like a cattle cemetery.'

"He went out into the yard, and Makar turned up soon after, panting like a hard-driven horse. He sat down at the table and said nothing. But when he'd got his breath he remarked: 'I didn't get the scum. I shot twice. It was dark. I couldn't get him in the sights: I took aim along the barrel and missed him. But he stopped and fired at me again. It felt just as if someone had tugged at my tunic.' He drew aside the edge of his tunic, and there just above the belt was a bullet hole. I asked him: 'Have you any idea who it was?' But he smiled wryly: 'I haven't the eyes of an owl. I only know it was a young man, judging by the way he moved. An older man couldn't run like that. I couldn't have caught him even if I'd been on horseback.' 'But why did you behave so rashly?' I asked him. 'You went after him without knowing how many there were. Supposing there'd been a couple more hiding behind the fence: where would you have been? They could have let you come right up to them and fired at you point-blank.' But you can't talk to Makar. 'What else was I to do?' he said. 'Put the lamp out and crawl under the bed?'

"And that's the whole of the story. All Makar's got as the result of the shot is an attack of catarrh."

"But how did he get that?"

"How should I know? That's what he says, but I'm surprised myself. Well, what are you laughing at? He really has got catarrh terribly bad since that shot. His nose is streaming all the time, and he sneezes in bursts like a machine gun."

"It's all pure ignorance," the book-keeper, an elderly Cossack who had been a regimental secretary at one time, said discontentedly. He pushed his spectacles in their tarnished silver frame up on his brow, and said dryly: "Comrade Nagulnov's simply revealing his ignorance, that's all."

"We have to be more and more responsible for ignorance these days," Razmiotnov said sarcastically. "You've had a good education, you click away on your abacus and you write every letter with flourishes and tails, but it wasn't you they shot at, it was Nagulnov." Turning back to Davidov, he continued. "Early next morning I went to see how he was, and he was having such an argument with the quack that the devil himself couldn't have made sense of it. The quack said he'd got catarrh because he'd caught cold sitting by the open window at night; but Makar would have it that he'd got catarrh because the bullet had affected a nerve in his nose. The quack asked: 'But how could the bullet affect the nerve when it passed above the ear and scorched your temple?' But Makar tells him: 'It's nothing to do with you how it touched the nerve; the fact is it did affect it, and it's your job to cure my nervous catarrh, and not express your opinion on something you know nothing about.'

"Makar's as stubborn as the devil, but the old quack's even worse. 'Don't try to get me all muddled with your stupid ideas,' he says. 'When a nerve is affected one eyelid twitches, but not both; or one cheek twitches, and not both. So how is it you've got catarrh not in one nostril but in both? It's obvious you've caught cold.'

"Makar was silent for a bit; then he asks: 'Tell me, company doctor, has anyone ever boxed your ears?'

"I sat down close to Makar just to be on the safe side, to seize his hand if necessary. But the quack did just the reverse: he

shifted farther away, looked towards the door, and said rather uncertainly: 'No, God has been kind and nobody has. But why do you ask?'

"Makar asks him again: 'Well, supposing someone hits you on your left ear, do you think you'll hear the sound of the blow only in the one ear? Take it from me, you'll hear a ringing in both ears like all the church bells at Easter.'

"The quack rose from the table and edged towards the door, and Makar went on: 'But don't get fussed up, sit down on your chair; I've no intention of boxing your ears. I'm simply putting the case, d'you see?'

"The quack was all ready to fly to the door, but when Makar said that, he sat down again on the very edge of his chair. But he kept glancing at the door all the same. Makar clenched his fist, examined it as if he'd never seen it before, and asked again: 'But if I was going to give you that little treat a second time, what would happen then?' The quack got up and started edging towards the door again. He took hold of the handle, and then he said: 'You do talk rubbish! Your fists have got nothing whatever to do with medicine and nerves.' 'On the contrary, they've a great deal to do with them,' Makar contradicted him, and once more he asked him to sit down and remain seated politely on his chair. But the quack started to sweat and declared he was terribly anxious to go off and see his patients. But Makar flatly said the patients could wait a few minutes, and he hoped that in the future he would be able to give the quack five out of five on this subject."

Davidov smiled wearily; the book-keeper laughed with a quiet, aged laugh, covering his mouth with his hand; but Razmoitnov went on with a perfectly straight face.

"'Well, now,' said Makar, 'if I hit you a second time in the same place, don't imagine that tears will flow only from your left eye. They'll flow from both eyes, like the juice from a ripe tomato, I guarantee that. And it's just the same with nervous catarrh: if it streams from your left nostril it must stream from your right as well. Get that?' But the quack plucked up courage and said: 'Don't try to be so clever; you know nothing about medicine. You just take the drops I shall prescribe for you.' You should have seen Makar jump! He sprang almost up to the ceil-

ing and bawled in an unnatural voice: 'I know nothing about
medicine? You old enema! In the German war I was wounded
four times, I had contusions twice and gas poisoning once; in the
civil war I was wounded three times; I've attended thirty field
and other hospitals, and you say I know nothing about medicine!
Why, do you know, you feeble old Seidlitz powder, how the doctors and professors treated me? Not even in your dreams have
you ever met such learned men, you old fool.' But at that the
quack really let himself go. Goodness knows where he got the
pluck from, but he stormed at Makar: 'I don't care if learned
men did treat you; all the same, so far as medicine's concerned
you're simply a cork.' To which Makar replied: 'And so far as
medicine's concerned you're simply the hole in a doughnut. All
you're good for is cutting the umbilical cord of new-born babes
and setting old men's ruptures. You know about as much about
nerves as a sheep does about the Bible. You've never learnt a
thing about the science of nerves.'

"And so they went for each other hammer and tongs, and the
quack flew out of Makar's room like a ball of thread. Then Makar
cooled down a little and said to me: 'Go along to the office, and
I'll treat myself with some remedies of my own; I'll rub some fat
on my nose, and follow you in a moment or two.' He turned up
an hour later, and you should have seen what he looked like.
His nose had swollen and turned blue so that it looked like an
aubergine, and it was all twisted to one side. He must have dislocated it in rubbing it. And the stink of sheep fat that came from
him, from his nose I mean, filled the whole office. That was the
ointment he'd made up for himself. I looked at him and, believe
me, I couldn't stop laughing. He grew frightfully angry and
asked me: 'What are you laughing at, you stupid fool? Have you
found a shining button on the road, or what? What are you so
pleased about, you son of Tofim? You've got as much sense as
our goat, but there you are laughing at decent people.'

"He went off to the stable, and I followed him. He took a
saddle, saddled a little sorrel pony, and led it out of the stable, all
without saying a word. I could see he was mad because I'd
laughed. I ask him: 'Where are you off to?' And he answers
glumly: 'I'm going out to the fields to cut some brushwood and
give myself a whipping.' 'But what for?' He didn't answer. I

went with him. We walked right to his place without saying a word. At the wicket gate he threw the reins to me and went into the house. When he came out again he was carrying his gun in its holster and the holster on a strap, as it should be, and in his hands he had a towel. . . ."

"A towel?" David exclaimed. "But why a towel?"

"I've already told you he's got catarrh terribly and no handkerchief is big enough, and even out in the steppe he didn't like the idea of knocking the juice from his nose on to the ground as we do." Razmiotnov smiled faintly. "Don't condemn him too much: after all, he's learning English, and he can't let anyone think he's not educated. That's why he took a towel instead of a handkerchief. I said to him: 'Makar, you should bandage your head and cover the wound.' But he flared up, and roared back: 'D'you call this a wound, damn you? I don't need any of your ladylike handling. I'll ride out to the brigade, the wind will blow on the wound, the dust will be sprinkled over it, and it will heal up like a scratch on an old bitch. You keep your nose out of other people's business and clear off with your idiotic suggestions.'

"I could see he was horribly put out over his quarrel with the quack and my laughing, and I advised him very warily to keep his gun out of sight. 'So any scum can shoot at me now, and I've got to ride around blowing a tin trumpet, have I?' he shouted. 'I've carried my gun in my pocket these last eight years, it's made a hopeless hole, and I've had enough of it. From now on I shall wear it openly. I didn't steal it, I earned it with my blood. D'you think it was presented to me in the name of Comrade Frunze for nothing, and with a silver plate bearing my name on the butt into the bargain? You're mad, my boy, and you're sticking your nose into other people's business again.' So he mounted the pony and rode off. As he rode through the village I could hear him blowing his nose into the towel as though he was blowing a trumpet. But you speak to him about the gun, Siemion. After all, it isn't wise to display it in front of everybody. He'll listen to you."

Razmiotnov's words had long since ceased to make any impression in Davidov's mind. Propping his head on his hands, he stared at the dented, ink-stained table, recalled Arzhanov's story, and thought: "All right, let's agree that Yakov Lukich is a kulak; but why should I suspect just him? He'd never lift a rifle; he's too

old and cunning. And, besides, Makar said it was a young man,
quick on his feet. But supposing Lukich's son thinks the same way
as his father? Even so, we can't sack Yakov Lukich from his job
as manager without definite proof; if he's got mixed up in some
plot it would only put him on his guard, and it would warn the
others too. Besides, Lukich wouldn't go in for such activities on
his own. He's a cunning old devil, and wouldn't risk his skin in
such a business for anything. So we've just got to carry on with
him as before and not give him any hint that we suspect him;
otherwise the whole affair will fold up. I must ride to the district
at the first opportunity to have a talk with Nesterenko and the
head of the G.P.U. Our G.P.U. flaps its ears, but now the enemy's
beginning to flap from rifles by night. Yesterday at Makar, tomorrow at me or Razmiotnov. If we do nothing, one single
bloody scum may pick us all off in three days. All the same,
Yakov Lukich isn't likely to get himself mixed up in counter-revolutionary activities. He's too calculating, that's a fact. And what
would be the sense of it? He's got his job as manager, he's a
member of the administration, he lives well, he's in clover. No,
I just can't believe he'd want to go back to the old times. There's
no return to those days, he must see that. It would be different
if we'd got a war on with one of our neighbours: then he might
get active. But I don't believe he's up to anything just now."

Razmiotnov broke in on Davidov's thoughts. He stared silently
for some time at his friend's clouded face, then asked in a businesslike tone: "Have you had breakfast?"

"Breakfast? What makes you ask?" Davidov answered ab-
sently.

"You're so thin, you look bloody awful. Your cheekbones are
sticking through your flesh, and your cheeks are baked dry with
the sun."

"Back on the old subject again?"

"No; I'm quite serious, believe me."

"I haven't had any breakfast. I didn't have time to, and in any
case I don't want any; it's been too hot to eat ever since early
morning."

"Well, I'm feeling peckish. Come along with me, Siemion, and
we'll have a bite," he suggested.

Davidov agreed, though reluctantly. They went out into the

yard, and a dry, hot wind from the steppe, scented with wormwood, blew at them fierily.

At the wicket gate Davidov halted and asked: "Do you suspect anyone, Andrei?"

Razmiotnov shrugged his shoulders and slowly opened his
arms wide. "The devil only knows! I've turned it all over in my
mind again and again; I've gone over all the Cossacks in the
village; but I haven't been able to think of anything. Some devil
has set us a problem, and now we can rack our brains. A comrade
from the district G.P.U. rode into the village and looked all over
Makar's house; he questioned him and Shchukar, Makar's housekeeper, and myself. He looked at the cartridge case we found,
but there's not a mark on it. And then he rode away again.
'There's only one deduction to be made,' he said before he went.
'You've got an enemy somewhere among you.' Makar said: 'Aren't
you clever! Do you think friends shoot at one another sometimes?
Clear off to the end of the world. We'll sort it out without your
help.' The G.P.U. man only sniffed, got on his horse, and rode
away."

"D'you think Ostrovnov would be up to such a trick?" Davidov
asked cautiously.

Razmiotnov had raised his hand to lift the gate latch, but in
his astonishment he let his hand drop. He laughed. "What's the
matter with you, are you crazy? You mean Yakov Lukich? What
in heaven's name would he do such a thing for? Why, he's afraid
of the creak of a cart, and yet you can think up such bosh. Cut off
my head if you like, but he'd never do it. Anyone but him."

"But how about his son?"

"You're right off the target again. If you're going to poke
blindly with your finger, you might as well point at me. No, this
problem's more difficult. . . . This is a lock with a secret cipher."

For breakfast Razmiotnov's old mother dished up the usual
thin wheat gruel, only parsimoniously larded with fat. But when
she brought in a plateful of fresh ridge cucumbers from the garden, Davidov cheered up. He ate two of them with great relish,
enjoying their scent of earth and sun, drank a mug of home brew,
and got up from the table.

"Thank you, Mother; you've fed me well. And thanks especially for the cucumbers. They were good, there's no denying it."

The kindly old woman set her palm against her cheek mournfully. "But where could you expect to get cucumbers from, my dear? You haven't a wife, have you?"

"I haven't got hold of one yet, I haven't had the time." Davidov smiled.

"If you've never had the time to get hold of a wife, you can't expect to be provided with early cucumbers. Why don't you get a garden and plant things for yourself? Here's my Andrei been left on the shelf too. And if he hadn't got a mother he'd be stretching out his legs with starvation. But his mother does manage to feed him somehow or other. I feel sorry for you whenever I see you. Here's my Andrei jogging along on his own, and Makar, and you too. Don't you all feel ashamed of yourselves? Strong bulls like you going about the village, and every one of you a hopeless failure with the women! I can't believe you'll all be left on the shelf. It's absolutely shameful, there's no other word for it."

Razmiotnov laughingly bantered her. "Nobody will have us, Mother."

"Of course they won't, and no one ever will if you go around as bachelors for another five years. By that time you won't be fit for anything to any woman; you'll be too old. And I'm not just thinking of the girls, either. You're too old for any girl now."

"You're right. The girl's won't come after us; and we don't want widows. Feed another man's children? I'd be hanged first," Razmiotnov retorted.

Obviously this was an old bone of contention, and Davidov felt rather awkward and kept his mouth shut.

Thanking his hospitable friends, he went off to the forge. Before the village commission took over the farming implements from the smith, he wanted to examine the repaired mowers and horse-drawn rakes, expecially since he had had a hand in the work.

Chapter 10

The old smithy, which stood on the very edge of the village, welcomed Davidov with its familiar smells and sounds: the hammer clanged away as usual in the hands of the smith, obedient to his every movement; the asthmatic wheezing of the ancient bellows could be heard over quite a distance; and, as always, the pungent fumes of burning coals and the unforgettable exhalation of hot iron billowed through the wide-open doors.

The forge stood in an isolated and lonely spot. The scent of dust and goosefoot came from the nearby cart track. Wild hemp and scrub were growing on the sinking roof with its thatch of reeds held firmly in place by turves. Innumerable sparrows were fussing about in the thatch. They had their homes permanently under the eaves, even in the winter, and their incessant twittering provided a kind of accompaniment to the living clangour of the hammer and the ring of the anvil.

Shaly greeted Davidov as an old friend. The smith was bored with his life, spending all day and every day in the company of the adolescent youth who was his assistant, and he was obviously very glad to see the chairman. As he stretched out his rough, iron-hard hand he said cheerfully in his booming voice:

"It's a long time since you were last here, Chairman. You forget the proletariat, you never drop in to see us. You've grown stuck-up, young man, that's very clear. You say you've come to see me? Tell me another! You've come to look at the mowers; I know you, young man! Well, come on then, let's go and look at them. I've set them out as though they were on parade, like Cossacks at a review. Come on now. But look them over without picking holes. You yourself gave me a hand with them, so you've got no right to complain now."

Davidov examined every machine closely and thoroughly. He found no fault in the repairs, with the exception of two or three petty defects. But he thoroughly upset the old smith. Shaly followed him around from machine to machine, wiping the

sweat from his livid face with his leather apron, and at last muttered dicontentedly:

"You're a very finicky master, I must say! All your fault-finding doesn't mean a thing. Now what are you sniffing at? What are you looking for now, I want to know? D'you think I'm a gypsy, or what? He taps around with his hammer, bustles about like a priest's old wife, then gets back into his britzka, touches up his horses, and have we ever seen him here since? No, my lad; everything has been done thoroughly, like I'd do it for myself, and there's no point in your sniffing around and picking holes like you are."

"I'm not picking holes in you, Sidorovich. What are you getting all worked up for?"

"If you'd been examining everything without trying to find fault you'd have been finished ages ago. But you're still dancing around every machine, still sniffing and feeling. . . ."

"My work has taught me to believe with my eyes, but to feel with my hands." Davidov made a joke of it.

But when he subjected one rickety, dilapidated harvester which had belonged to Antip Grach to a particularly critical examination, Shaly was highly amused. His discontent completely evaporated. Seizing his beard in his fist, winking at nobody in particular, and smirking cunningly, he said sarcastically:

"Get down! Get right down on the ground, Davidov. What are you strutting around it like a cock for? Crawl on your belly and try the driving chain with your teeth. Why feel it as if it was a girl? Try it in your teeth. Ah, you lousy smith! Don't you recognize your own work? You repaired that mower entirely on your own. I tell you straight, young man, every bit of it's your work. But you don't see it and don't recognize it. Why, you'd marry a girl in the evening and wouldn't recognize your young wife next morning. . . ."

He enjoyed his joke, thundering with laughter, coughing and waving his hands. But Davidov was not at all put out, and replied:

"You needn't laugh, Sidorovich! I recognized that low-powered, medium-peasant machine at first glance, and my work on

it too. But I'm checking up on it so that I shan't regret it when it goes into action. If some disaster occurred with that machine, you'd be the first to say in front of everybody: 'There you are! I trusted Davidov with a hammer and pincers, and look at the mess he's made of it.' Now, wouldn't you?"

"Of course I would. And why not? The man who does the job is responsible for it."

"But you say I didn't recognize it. I did, my old friend, but I check my own work strictest of all."

"So you don't trust yourself?"

"Sometimes. . . ."

"That's all to the good, young man," the smith agreed, and he suddenly turned serious. "Working with iron is a responsible sort of job, and you don't learn to be a master at it in five minutes. Oh no. . . . You know, we smiths have a true saying: 'Trust the anvil, the hand, and the hammer, but don't trust your own mind.' It doesn't matter whether it's a large works or a small forge, it's responsible work, and I tell you so once and for all. But I remember last year the district head of the raw hides and skins collection department was billeted on me: he came out to do some work in our village. Me and my wife made him welcome, we treated him as if he was our own child, but would he talk? Not on your life, neither with me nor my old woman. He thought us too low. He sits down at the table and says nothing; he gets up from the table and still says nothing. He comes back from the village Soviet and says nothing; he goes out and says nothing. Ask him what we like about politics or agriculture, he barks back: 'That's nothing to do with you, old man.' And that's all the talk we had from him. He lived with us three days very quiet and peaceful, saying nothing, and on the fourth he began to talk. In the morning he said to me all high and mighty: 'Tell your old woman not to bring me my potatoes in the frying pan, but on a plate; and she's to lay a towel on the table, and a serviette of some sort. I'm a cultured man,' he says, 'and I'm a responsible district worker too; and I don't like your country manners.'

"I grew real mad with him and I says: 'You're not a cultured man, you're a stinking nit. If you're so cultured, eat from what the food's handed to you on, and wipe your mouth with whatever's given you. We've never had any serviettes in this house,

and my old woman has smashed all the plates. I won't take a penny from you; my old woman doesn't know what to do to please you, where to seat you, or how to make you more comfortable for the night. But you carry your nose higher than the roof with your: "I'm a responsible worker." How are you responsible?' I ask him. 'When you're on duty you collect hare and marmot skins. That's all your responsibility amounts to. You're not responsible at all. But take me, now: I'm a responsible worker. After the chairman and the Party secretary I'm the most important man in the village, because without me they wouldn't be able to plough or mow. I've got work with iron in my hands,' I tell him, 'but yours is only skins. So who's the most important really, you or me? You call yourself a responsible worker, and I think I am. If you and I are both responsible, how can we live together comfortably in the one kitchen? We just can't. Take your document case, my dear man, and let the four winds blow you where they will. As for me, I've got no use at all for such a stuck-up fellow.'"

Davidov's eyes narrowed till the pupils were hardly visible. Shaking with laughter, he asked quietly: "So you turned him out?"

"Once and for all. That very instant. He cleared out, and the responsible son of a bitch didn't even say thank you for the bread and salt."

"Oh, you're a great lad, Sidorovich."

"Great lad's got nothing to do with it; I'd be ashamed to put up with such a guest."

After a smoke Davidov started again on his inspection of the implements; he did not finish till after midday. As he said goodbye to Shaly he thanked him sincerely for his conscientious work, and asked: "How many labour days were credited to you for the repairs?"

The old smith's face clouded, and he turned away with the comment: "When Yakov Lukich does the reckoning, keep a close hand on your pocket."

"What has Yakov Lukich got to do with it?"

"Because he sets the book-keeper his own rules. The book-keeper puts down whatever he tells him to."

"All the same, how many did they reckon to you?"

"Almost nothing, my lad; a fly's leg."

"How was that?"

Such an unpleasant look came over the normally good-natured smith's face that he might have been seeing not Davidov but Yakov Lukich standing in front of him. "Why, because he doesn't want to reckon anything at all for my work. I spend a day in the forge, and he sets down one labour day. Whether I've done any work there or only made myself cigarettes, it's all the same to him. Maybe I've earned five labour days doing the repairs, but he puts down one just the same. I could break myself in half over the anvil, but I still wouldn't earn more than one labour day. So I don't get very fat on what you pay me, my lad. It keeps a man alive, but he wouldn't want to get married on it."

"That's not payment from me," Davidov said sharply. "That's not the collective-farm payment. Why didn't you tell me about this before? It's disgusting!"

Shaly was embarrassed, and he was obviously reluctant to reply. "What could I say, my lad? I just didn't like to. I sort of felt bad about it. I thought of complaining to you once and for all, but then I thought you'd say: 'There's a pig for you: he's never satisfied. . . .' So I held my tongue. But now I'll speak out, and I'll say even more. They're good enough to take into account such work as they can see—the repair of a plough, say, or a cultivator, or any implement that can be seen. But if it's some small job, like shoeing a horse, or making horse-shoes, or pincers, parts for a granary, and all that sort of small job, they don't allow anything for it at all and don't even want to hear about it. But I don't think that's fair, because you can spend a lot of time over such small things."

"You keep on saying 'they.' Who are these 'they'? The book-keeper's the only man who keeps the accounts and he answers for it to the administration," Davidov said angrily.

"The book-keeper keeps the accounts, but Lukich adjusts them. You tell me how it ought to be, but I tell you how it is in reality."

"It's pretty bad if that's how it is in reality."

"Well, that's not my fault, my lad, it's yours."

"I know that without needing you to tell me. It must be put right, and quickly. I'll call a committee meeting tomorrow and

we'll question Yakov Lukich. . . . We'll talk to him good and proper!" Davidov said resolutely.

But Shaly only smiled into his beard. "He's not the one you ought to talk to. . . ."

"Well, who is, then, in your view? The book-keeper?"

"No, to yourself."

"To me? Hm. . . . Well, let's have it!"

Searchingly, as though weighing up Davidov's strength, Shaly ran his eyes over him from head to foot, then began slowly. "Stand by, my lad. I'm going to say some rude things to you. I'd rather not, but they've got to be said. I'm afraid others won't dare to say them."

"Come on, then, let's have it!" Davidov encouraged him. He already had a feeling that the talk would not be pleasant, and he was afraid above all that the smith would start on his relations with Lukeria. But the old fellow began on quite a different tack.

"Looking at you now, you look like a real chairman; but dig deeper into you and you're not chairman of the collective farm, you're just an old patch, as they say."

"Now, that's very nice to hear!" Davidov exclaimed with rather forced amusement.

"Not so very nice," Shaly went on harshly. "There's nothing nice about it, I tell you once and for all. Here you go wriggling under the mowers, you check up on things as a good master should, and you spend time in the fields, and you take a hand in the ploughing. But what goes on in your office you don't see and don't know anything about. You should spend less time roaming about the fields and more time here in the village; then things would go better. But you're a ploughman, and a smith: it's just like in the song: 'A reaper in the field, and a player on the bagpipe.' And Ostrovnov manages everything in your place. You've let the power fall from your hands, but Ostrovnov has picked it up. . . ."

"Carry on," Davidov said curtly. "Carry on, don't mince your words."

"Nor will I," Shaly readily agreed. He seated himself comfortably on the platform of a mower, beckoned to Davidov to sit down beside him, and, noticing that his lad was standing at the smithy door, listening to their conversation, he stamped his foot

and roared: "Clear out, you little devil! Can't you find yourself
something to do? So you'd like to hear everything we say, would
you, you son of a sow? I'll take off my strap and flay you alive.
And then you'll know! What a stupid brat, for the Lord's sake!"

The lad, his little eyes glittering with laughter in his smutty
face, dived like a mouse into the dark interior of the forge, and at
once the bellows began to wheeze hoarsely and lividly glowing
flames started up from the furnace. But Shaly smiled benevolently and said:

"He's an orphan and I'm teaching him to be a smith. You can't
get any of the grown-up lads to work in the forge. The Soviet
regime's spoilt them once and for all. Every one of them wants to
be a doctor, or an agronomist, or an engineer; but when we old
'uns die out, who's going to mend the people's boots, patch their
trousers, or shoe their horses? It's just the same with me: I can't
get any young man to come and work in the smithy: they all fly
from the smoke like a devil from incense. So I had to take on this
little Ivan. He's a smart little devil, but the way he tyrannizes
over me, you just wouldn't believe. He goes off to work in some
one else's orchard in the summer, but I'm still held responsible
for him; or he leaves the forge altogether and slips away to catch
gudgeon, or he thinks up some other idea; he's absolutely good for
nothing. He lives with his aunt, but she can't manage him, so I
have to put up with his tryranny. But I can only swear at him; I
can't raise my hand to strike an orphan. That's the way it is, my
lad. In my lifetime I've turned out ten good smiths, and today
my pupils are setting up anvils in forges in several villages, and
one is even working in a factory at Rostov. That's not to be
laughed at, my lad, you've worked in a factory yourself and you
know they don't take on just anybody. I'm proud to think that
when I die there'll be more than a dozen followers of my trade
left in the world."

"Let's talk about business. What other defects do you find in
my work?"

"There's one defect you have got: you're only the chairman at
meetings; in the day-to-day work it's all Ostrovnov. That's where
all the trouble begins. I realize that in the spring you had to get
to know the ploughing teams, and to learn how to plough yourself; that's not bad for a chairman. But why you're letting your-

self go to rot in the fields now, I just can't understand. Surely the director of the factory where you worked didn't spend days on end at the bench? I just don't believe it!"

He went on talking for a long time of the weaknesses in the collective farm, things Davidov had failed to notice, things which Yakov Lukich, the book-keeper, and the warehouseman had diligently kept from him. But every word of his talk led up to the charge that behind all the obscure happenings since the very start of the collective farm was one man: the seemingly quiet and peaceable Yakov Lukich.

"But why haven't you ever said all this straight out at a meeting? Aren't you so keen on the collective farm after all? And yet you say: 'I'm a proletarian.' What sort of damned proletarian are you if you only mutter into your fist, yet when we hold a meeting you have to be hunted for with a lantern?"

Shaly hung his head and sat for a long time without opening his mouth; he turned over and over a blade of grass, and the grass blade looked so odd, so fragile and weightless in his great blackened, almost iron-hard fingers that Davidov could not help smiling. But the old smith fixedly studied something at his feet, as though his reply depended on his examination. After a long silence he asked:

"In the spring you were in favour of kicking Atamanchukov out of the collective farm, weren't you?"

"I did raise the matter at the general meeting. But what of it?"

"And did you chuck him out?"

"No, unfortunately not. But we should have."

"Unfortunate or not, that's beside the point. . . ."

"Then, what is the point?"

"Can you recall who spoke against the proposal? You can't? Then I'll remind you: Ostrovnov, and Afonka the storeman, and Liushna, and twelve others. It was they who got your good advice rejected, and turned the people against you. So you see Ostrovnov is not the only one in it."

"Go on."

"Oh, I can go on. You ask why I don't speak out at the meetings? I might speak once, or twice, but the third time I wouldn't have a voice to speak with. I'd be struck down in this very smithy and with the very piece of iron I'd just heated in the fur-

nace and nursed in my hand, and that would be the end of my speaking at meetings. No, my lad, I've grown too old to speak; you do it yourselves, I want to go on enjoying the smell of hot iron in my forge."

"I think you're exaggerating the risk a bit, and that's a fact," Davidov said. But the smith's words had made a deep impression on him, and his voice sounded uncertain.

Shaly stared at him hard, and screwed up his black, bulging eyes humorously: "Maybe I do exaggerate, as an old man will. But you, my lad, you don't see the danger at all. Your young way of rushing about has completely blinded you. I tell you that once and for all."

Davidov did not comment. Now it was his turn to be sunk in thought, and now it was he who turned over something in his hands: not a blade of grass but a rusty old screw.

The sun had long since passed its zenith. The shadows were shifting, and the hot, slanting rays burned the smithy roof, the mowing machines standing a little way off, and the dusty wayside grass. A profound afternoon silence hung over Gremyachy Log. All the house shutters were closed, the streets were deserted, even the calves which had been wandering idly about the alleys all the morning had hurried down to the river and were sheltering in the dense shade of the osiers and willows. But Davidov and Shaly were still sitting in the broiling sun.

"Let's go inside, where it's cool; I'm not used to this heat," Shaly said, wiping the sweat from his face and bald head. "An old smith's like an old lady: they don't like the sun, they like their bodies to be in the cool; each has his own way of cooling himself."

They moved into the shade and sat down on the warm earth on the northern side of the forge. Drawing very close to Davidov, Shaly hummed away like a bee entangled in bindweed.

"Did they kill Khoprov and his wife? They did. But what did they kill them for? Because they were drunk? No, my lad, that's just it. . . . That was dirty work. They don't kill a man for no reason at all. And I with my stupid old man's mind argue this way: if he hadn't pleased the Soviet government he'd have been arrested and killed after being sentenced. He wouldn't have been done in quietly. But as he was done in quietly, by night,

and his wife too, it's obvious he didn't please the enemies of the Soviet regime. It can't be otherwise. And why did they kill his wife, I ask you? Why, so that she shouldn't give the murderers away to the authorities. She recognized their faces. But the dead tell no tales, things are more peaceful with them, my lad. It can't be otherwise, I tell you flat."

"We know all this without you telling us, we can guess so much. But who killed him, no one knows." Davidov was silent for a moment or two, and then resorted to cunning. "And no one ever will know."

But Shaly didn't seem to hear that last remark. He gripped his grizzled beard in his fist and smiled broadly. "It's very pleasant here. In the old days I remember a certain incident, my lad. Just before the harvest I tired four wheels for a wealthy Tauride farmer. He came to collect the wheels, as I remember, on a week-day; it must have been a Wednesday or a Friday, as it was a fast-day. He paid me, praised my work, and gave his men, who had driven the horses here to be shoed, a good tip for beer. They drank his health. Then I paid for a round and they drank that too. He was quite a rich Ukrainian, but a good-hearted man, such as you rarely find among the rich. And he took it into his head to have a good time. But I had work to do: it was the busiest season of the year, with I don't know how many orders to tackle. And I says to him: 'You drink with your work-men, Trofim Denisovich. You carry on, but I can't: I've got too much work to do.' And he agreed. They went on filling them-selves up with vodka, and I went off to the smithy. There was a roaring in my head, but I kept my feet all right, and my hands were firm. And yet, my lad, I was downright drunk. To make things worse, a troika with tinkling bells drives up to the smithy. I go out, and see the landowner Selivanov sitting in a light basket tarantass under an umbrella. He was known all over our district as a terribly proud man and one of the world's worst bastards. His coachman unfastens the traces from the offside trace-horse, and I saw the man's hands were trembling and as white as a wall. He hadn't been keeping his eyes on his job, and the horse had lost a shoe. And the gentleman let him have it: 'You so and so, I'll sack you, and I'll fling you in prison; through you I may be late for my appointment.' And so on. But you

know, my lad, under the Tsarist regime we Don Cossacks didn't bend our backs over-much to the landowners. And so it was with Selivanov: I'd have been perfectly ready to spit and grind it out with my foot just to show what I thought of him, though he was one of the richest of our landowners. So I go out all gay with vodka, and stand by the door, and I hear him letting fly at the coachman. And the sight made my blood boil, my lad. Selivanov sees me and shouts: 'Hey, smith, come here!' I felt like telling him: 'If you want something come and fetch it.' But I had a better idea: I went up to him, smiling as though he was one of the family, went right up to the tarantass, held out my hand, and said: 'Hallo, brother! How are you getting on?' In his surprise his gold spectacles fell off his nose; if they hadn't been held with a black ribbon they'd have been smashed. He puts his spectacles back on his nose, but I keep my hand held out, and it was as black as soot, filthier than mud. But he pretended he didn't see my hand; he frowned as though he'd bitten something bitter, and said through his teeth: 'Are you drunk? Who d'you think you're holding your hand out too, you filthy mug?' 'Oh, I know,' I says; 'I know only too well who you are. You and I are like blood brothers; you shield yourself from the sun under an umbrella, and I in the forge under my earthen roof. You're quite right, I've drunk too much for a working day; but you don't drink only on Sundays like the working people either, your nose is all red. So you and I are both of noble line. And if you don't like to give me your hand because yours is white and mine's black, that's a matter for your conscience. When we die you and I will both go white just the same.'

"Selivanov said nothing, he only chewed his lips, and his face changed. 'What do you want?' I ask him. 'Your horse shod? We'll soon get that done. But you're wasting your breath swearing at your coachman. He's obviously tongue-tied when you're around. You'd do better to swear at me. Come with me into the smithy, brother, and close the door tight; then you try swearing at me! I like people who're ready to take a risk.'

"Selivanov says nothing, but his face changes more and more. It goes white, and then red, but he still says nothing. I shod his horse, and then went back to the tarantass. He pretended he didn't see me; he holds out a silver rouble to the coachman and

says: 'Give this to that boor.' I take the rouble from the coachman and fling it into the tarantass at Selivanov's feet; and I
smile as though a bit surprised and say: 'What are you thinking
of, brother? Does a man take money from his relative for such a
small thing? I sacrifice it to your poverty; drive off to the pub
and drink my health with it.' At that my landowner didn't go
white or red, but sort of blue, and he screams at me in a shrill
voice: 'I drink to your health? May you drop down dead, you
scum, you cur, you Socialist, you so and so! I'll complain to the
district ataman. I'll have you flung in prison.' "

Davidov laughed so heartily that the sparrows took off from
the smithy roof in alarm. Shaly rolled himself a cigarette.

"So you didn't get on well with your 'brother'?" Davidov
asked.

"No, I didn't."

"But what happened to the money? Did he throw it out of the
tarantass again?"

"If he had I'd have flung it straight at him. . . . He drove off
with his rouble. I wasn't concerned about the money. . . ."

"Then what were you concerned about?" Davidov laughed so
youthfully and infectiously that Shaly, too, had to laugh. He dismissed the question with a wave of the hand:

"I've made a bit of a fool of myself. . . ."

"But tell me, Sidorovich, what are you telling me all this for?"
He stared hard at the old smith, but Shaly only waved his hand
again and laughed thunderously, hollowly.

"Oh, do tell me, don't keep me in suspense," Davidov implored, momentarily forgetting their previous serious talk.

"What is there to say? You see, my lad, he called me a cur,
and a scoundrel, and I don't know what else; and in the end he
all but choked, he stamped his feet in the tarantass and roared:
'You Socialist, you so and so.' In those days I had no idea what a
Socialist was; I knew what revolution meant, but I didn't know
the word 'Socialist.' And I just thought it must be an extra strong
terrible curse. So I lets him have it back: 'You're a Socialist yourself, you son of a bitch; and clear off out of here before I knock
some of the fat off you.' But next day I was hauled up before
the district ataman. He asked me all about it, laughed just like
you have now, and let me go without putting me in prison. He

was an officer, but he came of a poor family, and he felt flattered that a simple smith could put it over on a rich landowner. Before letting me go he said: 'You be more careful, Cossack; don't let your tongue wag so much, for the times are such that you can be shoeing horses today, and tomorrow you may be shod on all four hoofs, so that you can go by stages to Siberia without slipping. Understand?' 'I understand,' I says, 'your excellency.' 'Well, off with you and don't leave a smell of you behind. I'll tell Selivanov I've flayed you alive.' That's how things were in those days, my lad. . . ."

Davidov rose to return to the village; but the talkative old smith dragged him down by his shirt sleeve, seated him beside himself again, and unexpectedly asked:

"So you say nobody will ever know who killed the Khoprovs? That's where you're wrong, my lad. People will know. Of course they'll know: only give them time."

It was evident that the old man knew something, and Davidov decided to tackle him directly.

"Who are you hinting at, Sidorovich?" he asked straight out, staring into Shaly's eyes, as bloodshot as a bull's.

The smith glanced at him and answered evasively: "In such a matter it's only too easy to make a mistake, my lad. . . ."

"Yes, but all the same?"

Hesitating no longer, Shaly laid his hand on Davidov's knee, and said: "Well, then, my assistant, an agreement's more valuable than money: if anything happens, don't bring me into it. Agreed?"

"Agreed."

"Well, that dirty business didn't happen without Lukich having a hand in it. I tell you that once and for all."

"Well, brother . . ." Davidov drawled in a disillusioned tone.

"I was 'brother' to Selivanov, but I'm old enough to be your father," Shaly retorted angrily. "I'm not saying Yakov Lukich killed the Khoprovs himself, but I do say it wasn't done without his having a hand in it. You've got to realize that, my lad, if God hasn't done you a wrong in giving you too little sense."

"But proof?"

"Why, are you setting yourself up as the investigator now?" Shaly jested.

"Now we've gone so far you can't try to joke it off, Shaly. Speak straight out what's in your mind. There's no point in you and I playing hide and seek."

"You're a poor sort of investigator, my lad," Shaly declared with conviction. "Don't be in such a hurry, rein yourself in, and I'll speak straight out once and for all, and you'll have time only to rub your eyes. . . . But you've gone and got yourself tied up with Lushka. And what the devil do you need her for? Couldn't you find any better woman than that hussy?"

"That's not your business," Davidov snapped.

"You're wrong, my lad. It's not only my business, but all the collective farm's business."

"How d'you make that out?"

"Because now you've got tied up to that camp-following bitch you've started to work much worse. You've got an attack of chicken blindness. But you say it's not my business. My lad, this isn't just your misfortune, but our collective-farm misfortune. I suppose you think your goings on with Lushka aren't known; but the village knows all about you down to the last stitch. Some days we old men get together and argue how we can separate you from Lushka, may she be stricken with the palsy. And why do we? Just because females like her don't drive men to work but drag them away from it. And that's why we're worried about you. You're a good, quiet lad, and you don't drink. In a word, you're not too bad; but that filthy whore has exploited your goodness, she's riding astride you and driving you. And you know yourself how she drives you: she drives you, and then she goes boasting about it to everybody: 'You see the sort of men I ride?' Ah, Davidov, Davidov, you haven't found the right woman. One Sunday we old men were sitting on the ledge around Beskhlebnov's hut, and you went past. Old Beskhlebnov gazed after you and said: 'We ought to have weighed our Davidov on the scales to see what he weighed before he started chasing after Lukeria and what he weighs now. I reckon she's reduced his weight by half. There's something wrong here: she's got the fine flour and we the siftings.' Believe me, my lad, when he said that, I felt ashamed for you. If you'd been just my apprentice in the smithy, nobody'd have said a word; but you're the head of our farm. And to be the head's a big thing, my boy. It wasn't for

nothing that in the old days, when they used to whip the Cossacks for the least thing at the Cossack assemblies, we had the
saying: 'Let so and so be red so long as his head's clear.' But the
head of our collective farm isn't so very clear; it's a little fud-
dled. Our head's got messed up hanging around Lushka and it's
been smeared with pitch. You find some decent girl, or a
widow, say, and nobody would have said a word. But you . . .
Ah, Davidov, Davidov, you've got your eyes bunged up. And I
think you've lost weight not because of your love for Lushka but
through your conscience. Your conscience is making you go thin,
I tell you flat."

Davidov stared at the road running past the smithy, at the
sparrows having a dust-bath. His face had turned perceptibly
pale; bluish patches showed on his cheeks. "Well, close the
shop!" he said thickly, and turned to the old smith. "I'm getting
sick of this."

"But when a man's drunk he feels better after being sick,"
Shaly said in a casual tone.

Recovering a little from his awkwardness and embarrassment,
Davidov said curtly: "You give me proof that Ostrovnov was in
it. Without proof and facts what you say sounds like slander.
Ostrovnov's upset you, and so you're trying to get back at him,
that's a fact. What proof have you got? Tell me."

"You're talking nonsense, my lad," Shaly answered harshly.
"Why should I be upset by Lukich? Because of my labour days?
In any case I shan't give up my rights, I'll get them credited to
me. But I haven't any proof: I wasn't lying under Khoprov's
bed when they killed him and murdered his wife, my cousin."
The old man sat listening to a rustle beyond the wall and raised
his powerful, thick-set body from the ground with unexpected
ease. He stood for a moment listening intently, then with a lazy
movement drew his soiled leather apron over his head, and remarked:

"I tell you what, my boy; come along to my place. We'll drink
a mug of cold milk where it's cool, and we'll finish our conversation there. I tell you in secret . . ." He leaned across to Davidov,
but his hollow whisper could probably be heard in all the nearest houses of the village. "That little devil of mine is listening to
us, I'll bet. He's a nail to fit any hole, and he won't let me talk to

anyone without his pricking up his ears. My God, the tyranny
I have to put up with from him. He's disobedient and lazy, and
completely spoilt. But he's good at our job, I must say. Whatever
he takes on himself to do he does well. And besides, he's an orphan. That's why I put up with all his tyrannies. I want to make
a man of him, so that he can take over all I know."

Shaly went into the forge, flung his apron down on a bench
filthy with smuts, curtly said: "Come on!" and strode off home.
Davidov would have liked to end the talk so as to go and quietly
think over all the smith had told him. But the question of the
Khoprovs' murder was still unsettled, and he followed the smith
waddling in front of him like a bear. He felt it would be awkward to walk all the way back to the house without saying a
word, so he asked:

"How many have you got in your family, Sidorovich?"

"Just myself and my deaf old woman, that's all. . . ."

"Didn't you have any children?"

"We had a couple when we were young, but they died before
they could get used to the world. And my wife had a third still-
born, and after that she didn't have any more. She was young
and healthy, but something put a spell on her. No matter what
we did, how we tried, it was no use. She went on foot all the
way to the monastery at Kiev to pray for a child, but that didn't
help either. Before she went I told her: 'Bring me back something in your skirt, even if it's a little Ukrainian, but do bring
back something.'" He sniffed quietly and ended: "She called
me a stupid old fool, prayed to the icon, and went off. From
spring to autumn she walked on pilgrimage, but it was all for
nothing. Since then I've brought up several orphans and taught
them the smith's trade. I'm terribly fond of kids, but the Lord
saw fit not to allow me to rejoice over my own. That's life, my
lad. . . ."

It was dim, quiet, and cool in Shaly's neat and clean best
room. A yellow light seeped through the shutters, closed to
keep out the sun. The floor had been washed recently, and smelt
of thyme and more faintly of wormwood. The smith brought up
a sweating jug of milk from the cold cellar, set two mugs on the
table, and sighed.

"My wife's been ordered off to the orchards; she doesn't suffer

from the heat, the old cholera! And so you ask what proof I've got? I tell you once and for all: the morning after the Khoprovs were murdered I went to see their bodies; you see, Khoprov's wife had been godmother to one of my children. But they wouldn't let anyone into the hut; a militia-man stood at the door waiting for the official investigator to arrive. So I hung about the steps. And on the steps I noticed a footprint that seemed familiar. . . . There were several footprints, but one was over to the side, by the balustrade."

"What made you think it looked familiar?" Davidov asked, now thoroughly interested.

"It had an iron on the heel. It was quite a fresh trace, made during the night; it was as plain as print, and that shoe was familiar. I'd swear there's only one man in all the village wears such iron on his boots. And I couldn't make any mistake, for I gave them to him myself."

Davidov impatiently set down his mug with the milk unfinished. "I don't follow this. Speak more plainly."

"There's nothing to follow, my lad. In the days when we were still individual farmers, a couple of years ago, one early spring Yakov Lukich came to the smithy and asked me to rim the wheels of his britzka. 'Do it now, while you haven't a lot of work on hand,' he said. He brought the britzka along, and sat with me in the smithy chatting for half an hour or so. He got up to go, but stopped by the furnace, looking at some iron scrap, picking it over. As you know, I've always got a lot of scrap iron lying about. He found two old steel heels from English boots—they'd been lying about ever since the civil war—and he said: 'I'll have these, Sidorovich; I'll nail them on my boots. I'm getting old, I put more and more weight on my heels, and I never have time to mend the heels of my boots and shoes!' 'You take them, Lukich,' I told him. 'I don't mind giving them away to a decent sort like you. They're steel, and they'll last you your lifetime, unless you go and lose them.' He put them in his pocket and went. Of course he's forgotten the incident, but I remember it. So I couldn't help feeling suspicious. I asked myself: 'Why was that footprint there?' "

"Well, go on," Davidov encouraged the deliberate old man.

"So I thought I'd try and see Lukich and notice what marks

he made with his heels. I made a point of going and seeing him, and said I'd come about iron for the ploughshares. I glanced at his feet, but he was wearing felt boots. It was rather frosty at the time. I asked him casual like: 'Have you seen the murdered couple?' 'No,' he said. 'I can't stand the sight of dead people, especially when they've been murdered. I've got weak nerves for that sort of thing. But all the same I'll have to go along there in a few minutes.' Then I ask him: 'When did you see Khoprov last?' 'Oh, some time ago,' he answered. 'Last week. Now we know the sort of scum we've got living among us,' he added. 'He was a peaceable sort, never upset anyone. May their arms wither, curse them!'

"I went hot all over. There he sat talking like a Judas, but my knees knocked together as I thought: 'You dog, you were there last night, and if you didn't use the ax yourself you brought someone who had a light hand with you.' But I didn't let him see I suspected anything. All the same, the idea of checking up on his footprints stuck in my head like a nail in a horseshoe. Had he lost that present of mine from his boots or hadn't he? I had to wait a couple of weeks before he stopped wearing his felt boots and put his leather ones on again. The weather turned warmer, the thin snow melted, and I left my work in the smithy and deliberately went across to the farm office. He was there, and he had his boots on. Some time after I'd arrived he went out into the yard. I followed him. He turned off the path to go to the granary. I looked down at his tracks, and there were my steel heels printed as clear as clear. In all the two years since I gave him them they hadn't come off."

"Why the hell didn't you say anything at the time, damn you? Why didn't you report it to the proper quarters?" The blood rushed to Davidov's face. In his chagrin and anger he brought his fist down hard on the table.

But Shaly looked him up and down with a far from friendly look and asked: "What, my lad? Looking for an even bigger fool than yourself? I thought of that before you did. But I'd have been reporting it to the investigator three weeks after the murder, and would there have been any footmark on the steps then? I'd have looked a mighty big fool."

"You should have spoken up the very same day. You're a lousy

coward; you were afraid of Ostrovnov, and that's a fact."

"There's something in that too," Shaly readily assented. "It's dangerous to cross Ostrovnov, my lad. Ten years back, when he was younger, he and Antip Grach quarrelled one harvest, and Antip gave him a good hiding. But before a month was out Antip's summer kitchen caught fire. It was built close to his house, and the wind that night was in the right direction, blowing straight from the kitchen to the house. And so the house caught alight. The whole place went up in flames, and they couldn't save the sheds either. Antip had a fine house then, but now he's living in a hut thatched with straw. That's what it means to cross Lukich. He doesn't forgive things that are long past, not to mention things that happened yesterday. But that's not the point, my lad. I couldn't make up my mind to tell the militia-man of my suspicions. Something held me back. Nor could I be absolutely sure that Yakov Lukich was the only one wearing steel heels. I had to check up on it: during the civil war half the village wore English boots. And within an hour the Khoprovs' steps had been trodden by so many people that it would have been impossible to tell a camel's from a horse's hoof. So you see it isn't all that simple, my lad, if you think it over properly. All the same, I did invite you today not just to come out and look at the mowing machines but to have a heart-to-heart talk."

"You thought of it rather late; your mind works slowly," Davidov said reproachfully.

"It isn't too late yet, but if you don't open your eyes it soon will be, I tell you that once and for all."

Davidov hesitated before answering, carefully choosing his words. "So far as I and my work are concerned, you've said the truth, Sidorovich, and I thank you for it. I've got to reorganize my work, and that's a fact. But that old devil will see through it at once."

"That's true," Shaly agreed.

"But so far as your labour days are concerned we'll have the matter reviewed and put right. We'll have to go carefully with Ostrovnov, seeing as we haven't caught him out in anything. We need time. Not a word to anyone about our talk. D'you hear?"

"I'll be like the grave," Shaly assured him.

"Have you got anything more to say? Otherwise I must be getting off. I've some business to settle with the school headmaster."

"Yes, I have. Give Lukeria the gate once and for all. She'll be the end of you. . . ."

"Oh, to hell with you," Davidov exclaimed furiously. "You've already spoken about her, and that's enough. I thought you might have something worth while to say before I went, but you go back to that old—"

"Now, don't fly off the handle, listen carefully to an old man. I'm not talking to no purpose, and you ought to know that you're not the only man in her life just at present. And you'd better drop the bitch once and for all, if you don't want a bullet in your brain."

"And where would the bullet come from?" Davidov's firm lips quivered in a disbelieving smile. Shaly noticed that smile and exploded:

"What are you grinning at? You thank God you're still walking about alive, you blind man. I can't for the life of me think why he shot at Makar, and not you."

"And who's 'he'?"

"Ragged Timoshka, that's who. I just don't understand why he thought of shooting Makar. That's another reason why I asked you to come along; I wanted to warn you. But you grin away like my lad Ivan."

Davidov involuntarily thrust his hand into his pocket, and leaned forward with his chest against the table. "Timoshka? Where's he come from?"

"He's a runaway. Can't you guess?"

"Have you seen him?" Davidov asked quietly almost in a whisper.

"Today's Wednesday, isn't it?"

"Yes."

"Well, then, it was on Saturday night I saw him with your Lushka. That evening our cow didn't come home with the village herd, and I went out to look for her. I was driving the damned creature home somewhere about midnight, and came upon them both not far from the village."

"You're sure you're not mistaken?"

"D'you think I took you for Timoshka?" Shaly smiled sarcastically. "No, my lad; I've got sharp eyes, though I am old. They must have thought the cow was wandering about by herself in the dark. But I was following her; they didn't see me at first. Lushka said: 'Bah, a blasted old cow! It's a cow, Timoshka, and I thought it was a man.' And then she saw me. She was the first to jump up from the ground, and Timoshka scrambled up after her. I heard the click of a revolver cock, but he didn't say a word. I just said very calmly: 'Sit down, sit down, good folk. I shan't get in your way; I'm driving my cow home: she got away from the herd.'"

"Well, now I understand it all," Davidov said more to himself than to Shaly. He rose heavily from the bench, put his left arm round the smith's shoulders, and gripped his elbow firmly with his right hand. "Thank you for everything, Ippolit Sidorovich," he said.

That same evening he told Nagulnov and Razmiotnov of his talk with Shaly, and proposed that they should inform the district G.P.U. at once that Timofei the Ragged was somewhere in the village. But Nagulnov listened to the news without turning a hair, and objected:

"We don't want to inform anyone. They'll only go and make a mess of things. Timoshka's no fool, he won't be living in the village. And as soon as one of those district G.P.U. men turn up, he'll hear of it and clear out."

"But how can he get to know of it if the G.P.U. men come secretly, at night?" Razmiotnov asked.

Nagulnov gave him a benevolently sarcastic smile. "You've got the mind of a child, Andrei. The wolf always sees the hunter first, and the hunter sees the wolf after."

"Then what do you suggest?" Davidov asked.

"Give me five or six days and I'll bring in Timoshka dead or alive. But you and Andrei look after yourselves at night; don't go out late and don't strike a light. That's all you're asked to do. The rest is my business." He flatly refused to say any more.

"All right, then, it's up to you," Davidov said. "Only bear in mind: if you let Timoshka go he'll go into hiding and we'll never find him."

"Don't worry; he won't get away." Nagulnov smiled quietly and let his dark lashes droop over his eyes, momentarily eclipsing their glint.

Chapter 11

Lukeria was living with her aunt. The little hut, with its thatch of rushes, lopsided shutters, its walls sagging with age and settling into the ground, clung to the very edge of the river bank. The yard was overgrown with grass and scrub. Lukeria's aunt, Alexeevna, had only one cow and a small garden. A low wattle fence enclosed the yard on the river side, and in the fence was a gap which Alexeevna used to pass through to bring water from the stream for her cabbages, cucumbers, and tomatoes.

By the gap, thistles proudly raised their crimson and violet caps; wild flax grew thickly; the tendrils of pumpkins intertwined with the wattle, between the stakes, patterning the fence with little bells of yellow flowers. Of a morning the fence glimmered with the stars of bindweed, and from a distance it looked like a carpet of extraordinary weave. The spot was lonely and quiet. And Nagulnov took pleasure in the sight of it as early next morning he walked along the river bank past Alexeevna's yard.

For two days he took no action; he was waiting for his catarrh to go. On the third, as soon as it was dark he put on his padded quilted jacket and stealthily went out into the street to make his way down to the river.

All night—it was moonless and dark—he lay among the flax under the wattle fence. But nobody came to the gap. At sunrise he went home, had several hours' sleep, then rode out to the first brigade, which had begun to mow the hay. But with the oncoming of darkness he was lying once more close to the gap.

About midnight he heard the house door creak gently. Through the wattle he saw a woman's form, wrapped in a dark shawl, come out to the steps. He recognized Lukeria.

She walked slowly down the steps, stood for a moment or two, then went through the yard and turned into the alley. Makar noiselessly followed some ten paces behind her. Quite unsuspecting, not looking back, she made her way to the common. She was well outside the village when Makar's catarrh gave him away: he sneezed violently. He dropped flat to the ground. Lushka turned round impetuously. She stood motionless for a moment or two, rooted to the spot, pressing her hands to her chest, breathing spasmodically, heavily. Her bodice suddenly grew too tight for her, and the blood thudded in her temples. Mastering her alarm, she walked slowly, fearfully, towards Makar, taking very short steps. He lay with his elbows resting on the ground, watching her from under his brows. She came to a halt some three paces from him and asked in a choking voice:

"Who is it?"

He scrambled to all fours, and pulled his jacket over his head. He did not speak. He had no desire for his wife to recognize him.

"Oh Lord!" she whispered in terror and fled back to the village.

Makar went and woke up Razmiotnov before dawn the next morning. As he sat down on the bench he said morosely: "I only sneezed once, but that spoilt everything, damn it. You must help me, Andrei, otherwise we shan't catch Timoshka now."

Less than half an hour later they drove up to Alexeevna's yard in a two-horsed britzka. Razmiotnov tied the horses to the fence and led the way up the steps. He knocked on the crooked door.

"Who's there?" Alexeevna called in a sleepy voice. "What do you want?"

"Get up, Alexeevna, or you'll oversleep the cow," Razmiotnov said boldly.

"Who is it?"

"It's me, Razmiotnov—the Soviet chairman."

"What devil brings you here at this unearthly hour of the morning?" she asked peevishly.

"I've something I want to see you about."

The door bolt rattled, and she opened to them. Razmiotnov

and Nagulnov entered the kitchen. The aunt hurriedly dressed
and lit the lamp without saying a word.

"Is your lodger at home?" Razmiotnov glanced towards the
bedroom door.

"Yes. But what do you want with her at this time of the morning?"

Without answering, he knocked on the door and called: "Hey
you, Lukeria! Get up and dress. I give you five minutes, military
fashion."

Lukeria came out barefoot, with a shawl flung round her bare
shoulders. The swarthy flesh of her calves set off the spotless
white of the lace on her underskirt.

"Dress yourself!" Razmiotnov ordered, reproachfully shaking
his head. "You might at least have put on your skirt. Ah, you're a
shameless hussy!"

Lukeria looked her two visitors up and down, and put on a
dazzling smile. "Why, we're all friends here. What have I got to
be shy about?"

Though she was still half asleep she looked maidenly fresh
and beautiful. Smiling and gazing at her with unconcealed admiration, Razmiotnov enjoyed the sight of her. Makar looked
with a heavy, unwinking stare at Alexeevna, who was leaning
against the stove.

"What have you called for, my dear guests?" Lukeria asked,
adjusting her slipping shawl with a coquettish wriggle of her
shoulders. "You're not looking for Davidov, are you?"

She smiled triumphantly, insolently narrowed her flashing eyes,
and tried to catch her husband's gaze. He turned his face towards her, looked at her calmly and heavily, and, letting the
words come just as heavily and calmly, he answered:

"No, it's not Davidov we're looking for; it's Timofei the
Ragged."

"Well, you won't find him here," she said easily though she
wriggled her shoulders as though she felt cold. "You want to
look for him in the cold parts where you exiled him to, my
eagle. . . ."

"Cut that out," Makar said, calmly still, though he was beginning to lose control of himself.

His chilly calm, which evidently was not what she expected, infuriated her, and she went into the offensive. "It didn't happen to be you who followed on my heels when I went for a walk on the steppe, was it, my dear husband?"

"So you did guess!" Makar's lips quivered in a hardly perceptible smile.

"No, I didn't guess in the darkness, and you frightened me out of my wits, my dear. But after I got back to the village I guessed it was you."

"What was such a bold hussy as you afraid of?" Razmiotnov asked coarsely, speaking with deliberate roughness in order to break the spell her beauty was casting over him.

She set her arms akimbo and withered him with a furious look. "Don't call me a hussy. You go and say that sort of thing to your own Marynka; maybe Diemid the Silent will bash your face in as you deserve. But it's easy to insult me, I've got no one to defend me. . . ."

"You've got more than you need," Razmiotnov sneered.

But she paid no further attention to him. Turning to Makar, she asked: "And what were you following me for? What do you want of me? I'm a free bird, I fly wherever I wish. If my little friend Davidov had been with me he wouldn't have thanked you for following us."

Makar suddenly turned pale, the muscles worked in his cheeks, but with a great effort he held back his retort. The others heard his fingers cracking as he clenched his fists. Razmiotnov tried to put an end to the conversation, which was taking a dangerous turn.

"Well, we've had a chat, and that's enough. Dress yourself, Lukeria, and you too, Alexeevna. You're under arrest, we're taking you to the district centre at once."

"What's this for?" Lukeria asked.

"You'll find out when you get there."

"But supposing I won't go?"

"We'll tie you up like a sheep and carry you. And we shan't give you any chance to kick. Now, get a move on!"

For several seconds she stood irresolute; then she stepped backward and, with a swift movement, slipped through the bedroom door, slammed it behind her, and tried to fasten it by the

inside hook. But without any great effort Makar charged the door open, went in, and shouted:

"We're not playing with you! Get dressed, and don't try to get away. I shan't chase after you, you little fool. A bullet will do that for me."

Breathing heavily, she sat down on the bed. "You go out, and then I'll dress."

"You dress at once. You've got nothing to be shy about. I've seen you in all sorts of states!"

"Oh well, damn you!" she said wearily but without a hint of spite.

She threw off her skirt and nightshirt and stood naked, alluring in her youthful beauty, then went brazenly to the chest and opened it. Makar did not look at her: his indifferent, almost frozen gaze was fixed on the window.

Five minutes later, dressed in a modest chintz dress, she said: "I'm ready, dear old Makar." And she raised her unexpectedly meek and rather sorrowful eyes to his face.

In the kitchen Alexeevna was already dressed. She asked: "Who am I to leave the house in charge of? Who's going to milk the cow? Who's going to look after the garden?"

"We'll see to all that, Auntie, and when you come back you'll find everything just the same as it is now," Razmiotnov assured her.

They went into the yard and climbed into the britzka. Razmiotnov united the reins, waved the knout vigorously, and sent the horses off at a spanking trot. He halted them outside the village Soviet and jumped down.

"Well, women, get out!" He led the way onto the porch, struck a match, and opened the door of the dark storeroom. "Come in and make yourselves comfortable."

"And when are we going to the district?" Lukeria asked.

"We'll drive there when it's daylight."

"Then why did you bring us here in the britzka, and not on foot?" she persisted.

"To do you proud." Razmiotnov smiled in the darkness. He could hardly tell the inquisitive woman that she and her aunt had been brought in the britzka because Makar and he didn't want anyone to see them on their way to the Soviet.

"We could have got here quite easily walking," Alexeevna said. Crossing herself, she went into the storeroom. Suppressing a sigh, Lukeria followed her without speaking. Razmiotnov locked the door, and then called loud enough for them to hear:

"Now, listen to me, Lukeria! We shall give you food and drink. In the corner to the left of the door you'll find a pot for your convenience. Please sit quiet, don't make any noise, and don't bang on the door, or I swear we'll tie you up and gag you. This isn't a joke. Well, so long! I'll come and see you during the morning."

He fastened a second padlock to the main door of the village Soviet, then went to Nagulnov, who was waiting for him by the steps. There was a pleading note in his voice as he said: "I'll keep them in there three days, but I can't make it any longer. It's as you wish, Makar, but if Davidov gets to hear of it there'll be trouble for you and me."

"He won't hear. Stable the horses and then take the prisoners something to eat. Thank you. I'm going home. . . ."

It was not the once dashing and straight-backed Makar who walked through the greying darkness of the early morning, along the deserted by-ways of Gremyachy Log. He stooped a little; he trudged along with his head hanging dejectedly; from time to time he pressed his big, broad palm to his left breast.

To avoid Davidov, he spent all day out mowing in the steppe, and did not return to the village till nightfall. On the evening of the second day, before going off to his ambush he dropped in to see Razmiotnov, and asked: "Davidov hasn't been looking for me, has he?"

"No. To tell the truth I've hardly seen him myself. We've been building the bridge over the river these past two days, and I've spent all my time there and running back here to see to the prisoners."

"How are they?"

"Yesterday Lushka was so mad it was terrible. I go to the door, and she can't find names fit to call me. She swore, the blasted hussy, worse than a drunken Cossack. Where on earth did she ever learn such wisdom? I forced her to shut up. Today she's been quieter. She's crying."

"Let her cry. She'll be lamenting over the dead before long."

"Timoshka won't let you get a sight of him," Razmiotnov said dubiously.

"He'll come." Makar banged his fist on his knee; his eyes, swollen with sleepless nights, glittered. "Where can he go without Lushka's help? He'll come."

And Timofei did come. Abandoning all caution, on the third night, about two in the morning, he turned up at the gap. Was it jealousy that drove him to the village? Or hunger? Possibly both. In any case he could not keep away any longer.

As silently as an animal he stole along the path from the river. Makar did not hear any rustle of soil under his feet, not a snap of dry twig or scrub. When the outline of a man bent a little forward suddenly appeared only five paces away, Makar started with surprise.

Timofei stood listening tensely, not stirring, a rifle in his right hand. Makar lay still among the flax and held his breath. For a second his heart beat twice as fast, then it returned to its normal flow; but his throat went dry and rough.

A corn-crake sounded its grating cry down by the river. At the far end of the village a cow lowed. Somewhere in the meadowland on the other side of the river a quail sent a noisy rattle through the night.

Makar could have shot Timofei easily on the spot: his enemy stood with his body turned slightly to the right, his left side swung forward in an easy attitude. He was still listening intently.

Makar quietly put the barrel of his pistol in the crook of his left arm. The sleeves of his jerkin were wet with dew. He hesitated a moment. He was not some kulak dog to shoot his enemy out of hand. Without shifting his position he called: "Turn round to face your death, you scum!"

Timofei leaped forward and sideways as though on a spring. He threw up his rifle. But Makar was even quicker. In the misty silence the pistol shot was muffled.

Dropping his rifle, sagging at the knees, Timofei sank to the ground slowly, very slowly, it seemed to Makar. He heard the sound of Timofei's head striking dully, heavily on the hard, firmly trodden path.

Makar lay perfectly still for a good fifteen minutes. "They don't

come in a flock just to visit one woman, but it's just possible he's
got friends hiding and waiting down by the river," he thought,
straining his hearing. But an unbroken silence hung all around.
The crake, which had stopped calling when the shot sounded,
began to grate away again, timorously and disconnectedly. Dawn
came on fast. The livid streak in the eastern edge of the indigo
sky lengthened and widened. Makar rose and went to Timofei.
The dead man was lying on his back, his right arm flung straight
out. His eyes were wide open, fixed but with a vital gleam still.
Those dead eyes seemed to be delighting with exultant, speech-
less amazement in the faint, fading stars, the little opal clouds
with silver fringes melting in the zenith, and all the boundless
expanse of the sky, veiled with a translucent haze lighter than
the finest smoke.

Makar nudged the body with the toe of his boot, and quietly
asked: "Well, so you've done roaming, you enemy?"

Even in death he was handsome, this spoilt darling of the
women. A dark strand of hair fell over his brow, white and un-
touched by sunburn; his full face had not yet lost its fine rosy
freshness of complexion. His curling upper lip, fringed with a
fluffy black whisker, was turned up slightly, revealing his gleaming teeth: and the faint shadow of an astonished smile lurked in
the full mouth, which only a few days before had been exchanging passionate kisses with Lushka. "But you've been living well
all the same, my lad," Makar thought.

At that moment he had no feeling of bitterness, or of satisfaction, only an oppressive weariness as he calmly scrutinized the
dead man. All the emotions which had disturbed his being
through the long days and years, all that had sent the hot blood
rushing to his heart and had made it constrict with injury and
jealousy, had gone completely.

He picked up the rifle and, fastidiously knitting his brows,
searched Timofei's pockets. In the left-hand jacket pocket he felt
the shape of a hand grenade; in the right were only four cartridge clips. He had no documents.

Before leaving him, Makar took another glance at Timofei.
Only then did he notice that the dead man's embroidered shirt
must have been washed quite recently, and his khaki trousers
were neatly patched at the knees, obviously by a woman's hands.

"So she fed and looked after you not at all badly," Makar thought bitterly, as very heavily he set his foot on the step of the gap.

Despite the early hour Razmiotnov met Makar at the wicket gate, and took the rifle, cartridges, and hand grenade from him. In a satisfied tone he said: "So you got him? He was a brave fellow, he didn't know what fear was. . . . I heard your shot, so I got up and dressed. I was on my way here to find you when I saw you coming. I felt easier then."

"Give me the keys to the village Soviet," Makar asked.

Razmiotnov guessed what he had in mind, but he asked in turn: "Are you going to let Lushka out?"

"Yes."

"That's a mistake."

"Shut up!" Makar said thickly. "I still love her, the good-for-nothing. . . ."

He took the keys, turned round without a word, and, shuffling his feet along, went off to the village Soviet.

The passage was dark, and he fumbled for a moment or two before he found the keyhole. Throwing the door wide open, he called quietly: "Lukeria! Come out for a second."

The straw in the corner rustled. She came to the door without saying a word, adjusting her white kerchief over her head with a weary gesture.

"Come out on to the steps." He stood aside to let her pass.

On the steps she clasped her hands behind her back and leaned against the handrail, still saying nothing. Was she needing support? She waited, silently. Like Andrei Razmiotnov, she had not slept all night, and she had heard the quiet shot just before dawn. Doubtless she guessed what Makar was about to tell her. Her face was pale, but in their dark sockets her dry eyes had an expression he had never seen in them before.

"I've killed Timofei," he said, looking straight into her black, tormented eyes. He involuntarily shifted his gaze to the painful furrows which had settled so swiftly in the corners of her capricious, sensual mouth. "Go home at once, collect your things into a bundle, and clear out of the village for good; otherwise things will be bad for you. You'll be brought to trial."

She still said not a word. He fidgeted awkwardly, searching in

his pockets for something. At last he held out a lace handkerchief, crumpled and grey with dirt.

"This belongs to you. You left it behind when you went . . .
Take it. I don't need it any longer. . . ."

With cold fingers she thrust the handkerchief into the sleeve
of her crumpled coat.

He took a deep breath, and said: "If you want to say good-bye
to him, he's lying by the gap leading from your yard."

They parted in silence, never to meet again. As he went down
the steps he carelessly nodded good-bye to her, while she gazed
long at him and bent her proud head in a deep bow. Had she
perhaps expected this last meeting with her stern and solitary
husband to take a different turn?

Chapter 12

The fine, hot days hastened the ripening of the grass in the dry
hollows, and at last the third brigade of Gremyachy Collective
Farm joined in the steppe haymaking. The mowers of the brigade
drove out to the steppe on Friday morning, and on Saturday
evening Nagulnov dropped in to see Davidov. He sat a long
time silent, huddled up, unshaven, looking as though he had
aged during the past few days. For the first time Davidov noticed in the dark scrub of his firm chin the frosty gleam of grey
hairs.

For some minutes the two sat smoking silently, for neither
wished to be the first to begin. But, before going, Nagulnov
asked:

"It looks as if all Liubishkin's people have gone out to the
mowing, but have you checked up on them?"

"All those who were assigned have gone, but what of it?"

"You might ride out tomorrow morning and see how things are
going with them."

"They've hardly got out there yet, and you want me to check
already? Isn't it rather soon?"

"Tomorrow's Sunday."

"Well, what of it?"

Nagulnov's dry lips were touched with a hardly noticeable smile. "Most of the people in the third brigade are a bit pious; they're devotees of opium, especially the ones who wear skirts. It's true they've gone out to mow, but they won't mow a single swathe on Sunday. If you're not careful, some of the women will be going all the way to the church at Tubyanskoe. But the work won't wait; the weather may change; and then instead of ricks we shall only get enough hay for a dog's litter."

"Good! I'll ride out early and check up. Of course I shan't let any of them be away from work. Thanks for warning me. But why is it that only Liubishkin's brigade is so pious, as you put it?"

"Well, there are plenty in the other brigades too, but they're thicker on the ground in the third."

"I follow. But what are you thinking of doing tomorrow? What about your visiting the first brigade?"

Nagulnov answered reluctantly: "I'm not going anywhere. I'm spending a few days at home. I've sort of gone flabby. . . . Just as though I'd been given a good thrashing."

It had become a rule in the Gremyachy Party nucleus that while field work was going on, every Communist was bound to be out on the job. Nagulnov's presence in one of the brigades was absolutely necessary at the moment, but Davidov fully understood how his comrade felt, and he replied:

"All right, Makar, you stay at home. Maybe that will be better. One of the executives ought to be in the village in any case."

As though he had said all he had come to say, Nagulnov went out without saying good-bye. But a minute or two later he came back, smiling guiltily. "My memory's gone just like a sieve. I even forgot to say 'so long.' When you get back from the brigade, drop in and tell us how the pious ones are getting on, whether they've got their eyes fixed on the ground under the horses' hoofs or the cross on Tubyanskoe church? Tell those christened freaks it was only in ancient times that Christ sent manna down from heaven in years of famine; the Cossacks can't expect Him to get the hay ready for the winter, so they needn't put their hopes in Him. In a word, give them a good dose of anti-religious propaganda. You know well enough what arguments to use. I'm sorry I'm not go-

ing with you, I might be of great help in the anti-religious field.
I'm not very good at talking, I know that, but my fist is always
ready for any discussion. Once I leave its mark on him my opponent can't protest; it's easy enough to make objections standing up, but what objection can anyone make lying down? Lying-
down objections aren't taken into account!"

He brightened up abruptly and added, his eyes flashing more
cheerfully:

"I'll come out with you after all, Siemion. Before an hour's up
you and the women will be going at it hammer and tongs over
this question of religious misunderstanding, and then I can be of
great help. You know our women: they didn't peck you to death
in the spring, so they'll do it without fail this time. But you won't
go under if I'm with you! I know how to handle that devil's
seed!"

Controlling his desire to laugh aloud, Davidov dismissed the
suggestion in some alarm. "No, no! Of course not! I don't need
your help at all. I can manage. After all, perhaps you're exaggerating. The people understand what needs to be done much better
than they did in the early days of collectivization, that's a fact.
You're still measuring them by the old yardstick, and that's another fact."

"I can go, or I needn't, it's as you wish. I thought I might be of
some assistance to you. But seeing you're such a proud hero,
you get on with it."

"Don't take offence, Makar. But you'd make a poor fighter
against religious prejudices, and you might spoil things completely. Really you might."

"I don't want to argue with you about it," Nagulnov said curtly.
"Only take care you don't come a cropper. You're used to looking these former individual farmers in the face, but I make propaganda among them as my partisan conscience tells me. Well,
I'm off. So long!"

They shook hands vigorously, as though they would not be
meeting again for a long time. Nagulnov's hands were hard and
cold as iron, and that unexpressed, lurking pain again appeared
in his eyes, which had lost their vivid gleam. "He's finding
things hard just now," Davidov thought, firmly repressing his
feeling of compassion.

Nagulnov put his hand to the door latch but turned back and, looking away to one side, said in a rather hoarse voice: "My former spouse, your beauty, has cleared out of the village. Had you heard?"

Davidov still did not know that Lukeria had said good-bye to Gremyachy Log for ever several days before, and he answered with conviction: "That can't be! Where could she go without documents? I expect she's living quietly with her aunt, waiting till the talk about Timofei dies down. Of course it would be awkward for her to mix with people just now. Her affair with Timofei took a bad turn. . . ."

Makar smiled sarcastically and felt like saying: "You and I didn't find things any easier with her, did we?" But what he did say was: "She's got a document, and she cleared out on Wednesday. You can take that as certain. I myself saw her on the high road at dawn; she had a small bundle in her hand, with clothes in it, I expect. She stood for a moment at the top of the hill, looked back at the village, and then I saw no more of her, the evil spirit! I asked her aunt where she'd gone off to. But the aunt knows absolutely nothing. That's all there is to tell. She's done her dancing, the flighty bitch!"

Davidov made no comment. His former feeling of shame and embarrassment in Makar's presence attacked him with new strength. Trying to appear unconcerned, and gazing past Makar, he said quietly: "Well, and good riddance to her. There's no one left to pity her."

"She never did need anyone's pity; but as far as love was concerned, Timoshka had us both corked up, brother. And that's a fact, as you'd say. Well, why sniff? You don't like the truth? Nor do I, brother, but you can't get away from it. It was very easy for Lukeria to give both you and me the knock, my boy. And why? Because she's not a woman but an absolute devil. D'you think she ever grieved over the world revolution? Not on your life. She hadn't any use at all for collective farms, or Soviet farms, or the Soviet regime itself. All she wanted was to go and have fun, to do as little work as possible, to wag her tail as much as possible. And that was her entire non-Party programme. To keep a woman like her at your side you need to smear tar on your hands, to seize her by the skirt, to close your eyes and forget

everything else in the world. But if you doze off for a second, she'll slip out of her skin, out of her skirt, like a reptile, and go off in the clothes she was born in to have fun with the boys. That's what she's like. That's why she clung to Timofei. He used to wander through the village with his accordion on Sunday, and he'd go strolling past my place, and Lushka would shake with the ague and just couldn't wait for me to go out. How could you or I hope to keep such a wagtail at our side? Throw up the revolution and all our Soviet work for her sake? Buy a three-bank accordion to play? Sheer loss! Loss and bourgois degeneracy. Let her go off to the nearest bough to hang herself, but you and I mustn't turn our backs on our Party ideals for the sake of such worthless filth as she is, Siemion."

He was speaking energetically again; he straightened up, his cheeks flushed. Then he leaned against the doorpost, rolled a cigarette, lit it, and, after two or three deep draws, said more calmly and quietly, almost in a whisper:

"I must admit, Siemion, I was afraid my late spouse would give tongue when she saw Timofei dead. Not she! Her aunt told me she went up to him without a tear, without a cry, dropped down on her knees beside him, and said very quietly: 'You flew to me, my fine eagle, but you flew straight to your death. . . . Forgive me for not being able to warn you against your danger.' Then she took off her kerchief, took a comb out of her hair, combed back his forelock, and kissed him on the lips. Then she left him. She walked away and didn't look back once."

He said no more for a moment or two; then he raised his voice again, and Davidov caught a badly concealed note of pride in his hoarse tone.

"And that was all the good-bye she said to him. Good, wasn't it? The damned hussy showed she'd got a strong heart inside her. Well, I'm off. So long."

Evidently that was what Makar had come for! Davidov saw him to the wicket gate, then returned to his darkened room and flung himself fully dressed on his bed. He had no desire to think; he wished only to forget everything in sleep. But sleep would not come.

Again and again he cursed himself for his imprudence, his in-

discreet liaison with Lushka. She hadn't had the least feeling of true love for him. Timofei had come back, and she had broken with Davidov without thinking twice, had turned to Timofei again, had gone headlong after the man she really loved. Evidently the old saying that first love is never forgotten was true. She had left the village without a word to Davidov; she hadn't even said good-bye. But, after all, what need had she of him? She had said good-bye to the one who even in death was dear to her, so where did Davidov come in? All things are governed by their own laws. His not very respectable affair with Lushka had come to an end in the middle of a sentence, like a feeble, unfinished letter. And that was all!

He tossed and turned on his narrow pallet, cleared his throat, twice got up to smoke, dozed off just before dawn, and woke up again when it was broad daylight. His brief sleep had not refreshed him. He felt as though he had a hangover: he was tormented with thirst; his head ached unbearably; his throat was dry; and at times he felt a little sick. Going down painfully on his knees, he spent some time looking for his boots, feeling under the bed and the table, looking in perplexity at the empty corners. But when he rose to his feet he saw that he had his boots on. He swore furiously and muttered: "You're in a bad way, sailor! I congratulate you. You couldn't be worse, and that's a fact. Blast that Lushka. Gone four days, but she still haunts me. . . ."

He went out to the well, stripped to his waist, and splashed the icy water over his burning, sweaty back, groaning and coughing, soaking his head. Then, feeling rather better, he went off to the collective-farm stable.

Chapter 13

Within the hour he was in sight of the third brigade camp. Even when some distance away he could see that there was something wrong: a good half of the mowers were not working, hobbled

horses were wandering about the steppe, nobody was raking up the dried swathes of hay, and as far as the eye could reach he could not see a single stook.

Six Cossacks were playing cards on a blanket spread out close to the brigade covered wagon; a seventh was stitching a sole on an old boot; an eighth was comfortably asleep in the shade by one of the wagon's back wheels, his nose buried in a crumpled, filthy canvas coat. When they saw Davidov coming, the players sluggishly clambered up, all but one who was reclining on his elbow, slowly and thoughtfully shuffling the pack of cards and evidently meditating on his losses.

Davidov turned pale with rage; he ran up to the Cossacks and cried in a voice quivering with anger: "Is this what you call work? Why aren't you mowing? Where's Liubishkin?"

"But today's Sunday," one of the players answered uncertainly.

"D'you think the weather will wait for you? Supposing it rains?"

He turned his horse so sharply that the animal stepped on the blanket; taking fright at the strange feel beneath its hoofs, it reared and took a great leap sideways. He swayed violently and almost lost his stirrups, but he kept his seat. Flinging himself back, he drew the reins tight, and when he had the dancing horse under control again he shouted even louder: "Where's Liubishkin, I asked you?"

"He's over there mowing, the second mower to the left of the rise. But what are you shouting your head off for, Chairman? Mind you don't lose your voice," Ustin Rikalin retorted. He was a stocky little Cossack with bleached eyebrows that grew right across the bridge of his nose, and a face pockmarked all over.

"What are you idling around here for? I'm asking the whole lot of you!" Davidov all but choked with his anger.

They were silent for a moment; then the ailing and peace-loving Alexander Nechayev, who lived next door to Davidov, spoke up.

"You see, there's nobody to take charge of the horses, that's the trouble. All the women and many of the girls have gone off to church, so we've got to keep holiday whether we like it or not. We asked them not to go, damn them, but they wouldn't hear of

staying. We couldn't keep them here anyhow. We asked them, we pleaded with them, but they just wouldn't listen, believe me, Comrade Davidov."

"Granted that I believe you, but why aren't you men at work?" he asked with rather more restraint, but still unnecessarily loud of voice.

The horse under him would not quiet down; it flinched and set its ears back, all its flesh quivering beneath its fine skin. Controlling it firmly with a tight rein, stroking its warm, silky neck, he waited patiently for their reply. But for some reason there was a long silence.

"I tell you the women have gone off. We've got nobody to work with," Nechayev answered reluctantly, looking round at the others to have their support.

"What d'you mean, you've got no one? There are eight of you idling around here: you could get four mowers into action, couldn't you? Of course you could! But you're amusing yourself playing cards. I didn't expect you to take such an attitude to our collective farm, and that's a fact."

"Well, what did you think? Did you think we're cattle, not human beings?" Ustin asked in a challenging tone.

"And what d'you mean by that?"

"Do workers in the factories have days off?"

"They do, but the works don't stop on Sundays, and the workmen in the shops don't sit down to play cards like you. Get that?"

"I expect they have other shifts working on Sundays, but we have to do it all ourselves, we're like the damned! We're in the horse-collar from Monday to Saturday, and we can't get out of it even on Sunday. What sort of order d'you call that? Does the Soviet government stand for that sort of thing? It says there shouldn't be any differences among the toiling people; but you twist the law, you try to turn it to your own advantage."

"What was that? What the hell did you say?" Davidov exclaimed. "I want to make sure there's hay in the winter and for all your own cows too, get that? And is that to my advantage? My personal advantage? What are you talking such rot for, you windbag?"

Ustin waved his hand in a gesture of supreme contempt. "All

you worry about is getting the plan done on time, whether the grass grows or not. You gave us a lot of pipe-dreams about our cattle, and I believed you. But in the spring the cattle had to carry the seed grain from the district to Voiskovoi village, and how many bullocks left their bones by the wayside then? So many you couldn't count them. But now you're throwing dust in our eyes!"

"The Voiskovoi collective-farm bullocks died on the road because creatures like you had buried their grain in the ground. You joined the collective farm, but you hid your grain. We had to sow something, didn't we? And so we had to drive the bullocks along a frightful road to get the seed grain, and that's why they died. Fact! Surely you know that?"

"You're only concerned about carrying out the plan, that's why you're making all this fuss over the hay," Ustin obstinately grumbled.

"Why, am I going to eat the hay myself? I'm working for the general good. What's the plan got to do with it?" Davidov stormed, losing all patience.

"Don't shout, Chairman; you won't frighten me with your shouting and thundering. I've served in the artillery. Well, supposing we agree you're working for the general good. But in that case why strain the people's sinews by making them work day and night? That's where the plan comes in. You're trying to earn the praise of the district authorities, and the district are doing the same with the region; but we have to pay for it all. D'you think the people don't see through it? They see, all right, but how can they get away from you officials? Take you, for instance, and others like you. We can't remove you from your positions can we? No! And so you do just anything that comes into your head. But Moscow's a long way off; Moscow doesn't know what games you get up to here. . . ."

Despite Nagulnov's presentiments, Davidov was destined that day to come into conflict not with the women, but the Cossacks. But that didn't make his task any the easier. By their tense silence he realized that shouting wouldn't help; rather, it would ruin everything. He had to be patient, and to try the most reliable method: that of persuasion. As he stared into Ustin's angry fea-

tures he thought with relief: "It's lucky I didn't bring Makar with me. There'd have been a fight by now."

To gain time to think of how to deal with Ustin and any others who thought of supporting him, he asked: "Ustin Mikhailovich, when I was elected Chairman did you vote for me?"

"No, I didn't. Why should I have voted for you? You were brought to us like a cat in a sack. . . ."

"I came of my own choice. . . ."

"That makes no difference, you came like a cat in a sack. So why should I have voted for you, when I hadn't any idea what you were like?"

"But are you against me now?"

"What else could I be? Of course I am."

"Then raise the question of removing me at the next collective-farm meeting. As the meeting decides, so let it be. Only, you must give sound arguments for your proposal, otherwise you'll regret it."

"I shan't speak. You needn't be afraid, there's plenty of time for that. But while you are our chairman, tell us what you've done with our rest-days."

That was easy enough to answer, but Ustin didn't give Davidov the chance even to open his mouth.

"Why is it that in the district centre the young ladies in the offices paint their faces, powder themselves, and stroll about the streets all day, and go to dances in the evening, or go and watch the pictures, while our women and girls have to wash themselves with sweat even on Sundays?"

"In the working season, in the summer—"

"It's always a working season with us, both winter and summer. All the year round is one long working season."

"I mean to say—"

"There's no point in your wearing out your tongue to no purpose. And there's nothing you can say."

"Wait a bit, Ustin!" He raised his hand in an endeavour to check the Cossack's flow.

But Ustin interrupted him with a rapid machine-gun burst of words. "As it is, here am I standing before you like a workman, and you're sitting in the saddle like a master."

"Wait a bit I ask you, as man to man."

"There's nothing I need wait for. Wait or not, we'll never hear a true word from you."

"Will you let me speak?" Davidov shouted, turning livid.

"Don't bawl at me! I'm not Lushka Nagulnova." Ustin drew in deep breaths through his dilated nostrils and talked loud and fast in a strained, high-pitched voice. "Whatever you think, we're not going to let you brag to the wind. You can wag your tongue as much as you like at the meetings, but out here it's us that's going to do the talking. And don't throw up the cards against us, Chairman. In our collective farm we're the masters: we'll work if we want to, but if we don't want to, then we'll take a rest. And you can't force us to work on holidays, you thin-guts!"

"Have you finished?" Davidov demanded, hardly able to control himself.

"No, I haven't. And I'll tell you something else: if you don't like our way of doing things you can clear off to the devil's dam where you came from. Nobody asked you to come to our village, and we'll manage to get by without you, God grant! You're not the light of our eyes."

This was open provocation. Davidov realized quite well what Ustin was after, but he could control his feelings no longer. Spots danced before his eyes, and for a full minute he stared almost unseeing at the Cossack's closely knit eyebrows, his round face, dissolving and revolving before him. He had a vague feeling that his right hand, gripping the whip handle, was flooding with blood, growing heavy; a sharp, burning pain attacked his knuckles.

Ustin stood with straddled legs confronting him, his hands casually thrust into his trouser pockets. He seemed suddenly to have achieved a poise, and, confident that he had the silent support of the Cossacks behind him, sure of his own superiority, he smiled calmly and insolently, narrowing his blue, deep-sunk eyes. But Davidov turned whiter and whiter; his blanched lips moved silently; he was unable to get out a single word. He wrestled obstinately with himself; he strained all his will to bridle his blind, unreasoning fury, to hold himself back. Ustin's voice seemed to be coming from a long way off, but he distinctly un-

derstood what the Cossack was saying, and caught the derisive note in that voice.

"What are you gaping like a fish for, and not saying a word, Chairman? Have you swallowed your tongue, or is it that you've nothing to say? I thought you wanted to have a talk; but anyone would think you'd filled your mouth with water. It's clear you can't fight the truth. No, Chairman, you'd better not come up against us, and don't get all het up over trifles. You'd better slip peacefully off your horse and come and have a game of nap with us. That calls for intelligence, brother; that's not like running a collective farm."

One of the Cossacks standing behind him laughed quietly, then coughed the laugh back. For a brief second there was an ominous silence. The only sounds to be heard were Davidov's violent breathing, the mowing machines clattering away in the distance, and the carefree skylarks singing their hearts out in the azure, invisible to the eye. They were not in the least concerned with the excited men gathered round the wagon.

Davidov slowly raised the whip above his head and touched up his horse with his heels. Ustin reacted at once: starting forward, he seized the horse's bit with his left hand and pressed close up against Davidov's leg.

"You're not thinking of using your whip, are you? Go on, try it!" he said quietly, menacingly. His cheekbones stood out prominently; his eyes glittered with challenging merriment, with impatient expectation.

But Davidov brought his whip down vigorously against the leg of his dust-red boot and, looking down at Ustin, vainly trying to smile, answered: "No, I'm not going to strike you, Ustin. You needn't hope for that, you White! But if you'd come my way ten years back things would have been different. Then I'd have sent you sick for ever, you counter-revolutionary!"

Pushing the Cossack away gently with his foot, he dismounted.

"All right, Ustin, you've taken hold of the bit, so now take the horse and tie it up. You invite me to play cards with you? Right-ho, with pleasure! Hand them over, and that's a fact!"

The argument had taken a very unexpected turn. The Cossacks exchanged glances, then silently began to squat down round the horse-cloth. Ustin tied up the horse to a cart wheel and

sat down opposite Davidov, tucking his legs under him Kalmik
fashion, from time to time giving him swift glances. He was confident he had come out on top in his clash with the chairman,
and so he decided to continue the conversation:

"But you still haven't said anything about rest-days, Chairman. You've tucked the question under the pillow."

"You and I have still got to have a good talk," Davidov promised significantly.

"And how am I to take that? You're not threatening me, are
you?"

"No. Why should I? We've sat down to play cards, so let's
put everything else aside. There'll be plenty of time for talk
later."

But the more Davidov calmed down, the more agitated Ustin
became. Before the first round of cards was finished he flung his
hand down angrily on the blanket and embraced his knees with
his arms.

"What the devil are we playing for? We'd do much better to
talk about our rest days. D'you think, Chairman, that we Cossacks are the only ones worried about them? Not on your life!
Early yesterday morning I went out to harness the horses, and
the bay mare sighed with grief and told me in so many words:
'Ah, Ustin, Ustin, what sort of life is this collective-farm life? I'm
worked on the week-days, the collar isn't taken off my neck day
or night, and I'm not even unharnessed on holidays. It wasn't like
this in the old days. In the old days they didn't work me on Sundays, but only drove to pay visits, or for weddings. In the old
days my life was far and away better.' "

The Cossacks laughed under their breath. Their sympathies
appeared to be all with Ustin. But they were expectantly silent
when Davidov put his hand to his Adam's apple for a moment,
then said quietly:

"But whom did she belong to before the collective farm, that
interesting mare you're talking about?"

Ustin screwed up his eyes craftily and even gave a little wink.
"You don't think she belonged to me, do you? D'you think she
was using my words? No, Chairman, you're wrong there. That
mare belonged to Titkov; she's been dekulakized. On his own
farm she was fed differently from how she is in the collective

farm; she never even smelt chaff in the winter, Chairman; she almost wore out all her teeth chewing nothing but oats. She didn't just exist; she lived in luxury, as you might say."

"So she's an old mare, is she, seeing she's worn out her teeth?" Davidov asked in a casual way.

"Oh, she's old, all right; she's going downhill," Ustin readily agreed, not suspecting any trick.

"Then you're wasting your time listening to that talkative old mare," Davidov said with conviction.

"Why am I?"

"Why, because from a kulak mare you can only expect kulak talk."

"But she's the collective farm's now. . . ."

"Outwardly you're a collective farmer, but in reality, judging by the tunes you sing, you're a kulak."

"Well, that's going too far, Chairman. . . ."

"I'm not going too far: a fact remains a fact. And besides, if the mare's so old, did you enjoy listening to her? In her old age she's worn out all her mental powers. She wouldn't have talked with you like that if she'd been younger and more intelligent."

"Then how would she have talked?" Ustin asked, now rather more on his guard.

"She should have told you: 'Ah, Ustin, Ustin, you're just a kulak ass-licker. During the winter, you son of a bitch, you didn't do a stroke of work; and you didn't do any in the spring either, you pretended you were ill. And even now you don't want to do a decent day's work. What will you feed me on during the winter, and what will you yourself eat next winter? If we go on working like this you and I will both die of starvation.' That's how she should have talked to you."

His last words were almost lost in a roar of laughter. Nechayev laughed like a girl, giggling and squealing. Gerasim Zyablov laughed heartily in his bass tones, jumping to his feet and then squatting down ridiculously, slapping the legs of his boots as though he were doing the Cossack dance. Old Tikhon Osietrov seized his grey beard in his fist and yelled in a high-pitched voice:

"Lie down flat, Ustin, and don't lift your head! Davidov's trampled over you good and proper."

But Davidov was surprised to see that Ustin also laughed, not in the least put out, nor was his laughter forced or artificial.

When the merriment died away to some extent, Ustin was the first to say: "Well, Chairman, you've got the better of me. I didn't think you'd get out of my grip so neatly. But as for my being a kulak ass-licker, you've got no cause to say that. And in regard to my not being ill in the spring but only pretending, you've got no cause to say that either. Excuse me for putting it this way, but you're lying."

"Prove it."

"How can I prove it?"

"With facts."

"What facts can I give you in this joking talk?" he asked. He was more serious now, and he smiled uncertainly.

"Stop playing the fool!" Davidov said angrily. "Our talk is far from being a joke, and what you had in mind wasn't a joke in the least. As for the facts, here they are: you hardly do any work in the collective farm, you try to get the less intelligent element to follow you, you talk to others in a way that's dangerous for you, and today, for instance, you managed to stop the men from going to work. Through your activities half the brigade isn't working. So where the devil is the joke?"

Ustin's humorously raised eyebrows dropped and met again in a single straight, firm line across the bridge of his nose. "So because I mention the rest-days I at once become a kulak ass-licker and counter-revolutionary, do I? So you're the only one allowed to talk, and our job is just to hold our tongues and wipe our lips with our sleeves. Is that it?"

"That's not the only reason," Davidov retorted hotly. "All your behaviour's crooked, and that's a fact. What are you going on about rest-days for, when during the winter you had as many as twenty such days in a single month? And not only you, but all the others who're sitting around here. What did you do in the winter apart from housing the cattle and sorting the seed corn? You lay around on the warm stoves! So what right have you got to organize rest-days for yourselves at the very height of the working season, when every hour's precious, when the mowing is in danger? Now, out with it straight!"

Ustin sat silent, staring fixedly, without blinking, at Davidov. Tikhon Osietrov spoke up in his place:

"There's no point in our muttering behind our palms, Cossacks. Davidov's right. Our mistake's come out, now it's for us to put it right. Our work is like that; we can't take a holiday just when we like, and in fact most of our holidays come in the winter season. It was just the same in the old days, when we had our own farms. Which of us ever got his field work finished before the Blessed Virgin's Day? You'd hardly got the grain in when it was time to be ploughing again. Davidov's right, and we were wrong to let the women go off to church this morning. As for our sitting down here to pass the summer, I won't even mention it. Let's face it, we're in the wrong. We've condemned ourselves, and that's all there is to be said. But it was you, Ustin, who sent us wrong, you trouble-making devil!"

Ustin exploded like gunpowder. His blue eyes darkened and glittered angrily. "Haven't you got a mind of your own then, you bearded fool? Or did you leave it at home?"

"That's just it: it looks like I did forget it at home."

"Well, run off to the village and fetch it."

Nechayev covered his mouth with his narrow hand to hide his smile, and asked the disconcerted Osietrov in a thin, quavering voice: "I hope you hid it properly—your mind, I mean, Tikhon Gordeich."

"Why, what are you worried about?"

"Well, today's Sunday . . ."

"And what of it?"

"More than likely your daughter-in-law did some cleaning up first thing this morning. I expect she swept the floor, and if you happened to leave your mind lying about under a bench or the stove she will have swept it right out into the yard, you can be sure of that. And there the chickens will peck it to bits in no time. Supposing you had to live out the rest of your life with no mind at all, Gordeich! That's what has me worried."

They all laughed, but the Cossacks' laughter was not particularly cheerful. None the less, the tension had been eased. As often in such circumstances, joking had averted the quarrel which was on the point of breaking out. Osietrov, too, cooled down a little, and only retorted:

"You've got nothing you could forget at home, Alexander; you just haven't any mind at all. Have you shown yourself any wiser than me? Your wife's on her way to Tubyanskoe this very moment, and you didn't refuse a game of cards either."

"My fault, my fault," Nechayev joked back.

But Davidov was not satisfied with the way the conversation was going. He wanted to pin Ustin down.

"All right, so let's finish the question of the rest-days once and for all," he said, looking straight at Ustin. "Did you work very hard last winter, Ustin Mikhailovich?"

"I worked as many days as was necessary."

"But just how many?"

"I didn't count."

"Then how many labour days have been credited to you?"

"I don't remember. And what are you on to me all the time for? Go and reckon them up if you've got nothing better to do. It's boring to be doing nothing."

"I don't need to reckon them up. Even if you've forgotten, it's not for me, the collective-farm chairman, to forget." With fingers still trembling a little he took out and turned over the pages of the notebook which he always carried about with him. "I've found your name, you hard worker! And here are your results: During January, February, March, April, and May you worked . . . I'll tell you in a minute . . . you earned only twenty-nine labour days. Well, what's your opinion? Worked hard, didn't you?"

"That's not a lot of labour days to have to your credit," one of the Cossacks said to Ustin reproachfully. But he was not prepared to give way.

"I've still got half the year before me, and we count our chickens in the autumn."

"We'll count our chickens in the autumn, all right, but we count our earnings every day," Davidov retorted sharply. "You can put this in your pipe and smoke it, Ustin: we shan't stand any idlers in the collective farm. We'll drive out all the saboteurs double quick. We don't need any drones. You stop and think where you're going. Osietrov's got almost two hundred labour days to his credit; the rest of your brigade have all earned over a hundred; even men like Nechayev, who isn't all that fit, have

about a hundred. But you've earned exactly twenty-nine! You ought to be ashamed!"

"My wife's sick; she suffers from women's ailments, and she's on her back for weeks on end. And in addition I've got six children," Ustin said moodily.

"But how about yourself?"

"What about myself?"

"Why don't you work at top pressure?"

Once more Ustin's cheeks flamed crimson, and unpleasant glints appeared in his blue, angrily narrowed eyes.

"What are you staring at me for? Why only gaze at my mug?" He agitatedly shook his left fist; the blue veins swelled in his short, thick neck. "What am I to you? Lushka Nagulnova, or Varia Kharlamova, who's pining for you? Take a look at my hands, and then ask about my work!"

He flung his hands out vehemently; on his right hand he had only the index finger; where the others should have been was only brown, wrinkled skin.

In his embarrassment, Davidov scratched his nose. "Well, how was I to know? . . . Where did you lose your fingers?"

"In the Crimea, on the Wrangel front. You called me a White just now, but I'm as rosy as a ripe watermelon! I was with the Whites, then I chummed up with the Greens for a fortnight, and I was with the Reds. I served with the Whites, but I didn't fight more than I could help: I did all I could to keep in the rear. But when I fought the Whites you'll be pleased to know that's when I lost my fingers. My drinking hand, the one that holds the glass, is sound enough." He wriggled the stumpy fingers of his left hand. "But as you see, my eating hand has nothing to get a grip with. . . ."

"Cut off by a shell fragment?"

"A hand grenade."

"Then how did your forefinger escape?"

"It was lying on the release. I killed two Wrangel men myself that day. I had to pay for them somehow, didn't I? The Lord God was angry with me for shedding blood, so I had to make a sacrifice of four fingers to Him. I reckon I got off cheap. In His stupidity He might have demanded half my head."

Gradually Davidov's calm was communicated to Ustin. Now

they were talking amicably, and the devil-may-care Cossack cooled down; his usual ironic little smile reappeared on his lips.

"You should have sacrificed your last finger too: what's the good of it to you now?"

"Well, you're quick to dispose of other people's goods, Chairman! I need that one in my work more than ever."

"But what do you need it for?" Davidov asked, suppressing a smile.

"D'you think I can't make use of it? At night I threaten my old woman with it if she doesn't do what I want her to; in the daytime I peck at my teeth with it, and mystify good people. Because I'm badly off we have meat in our cabbage soup about once in a twelve-month; but each day after dinner I walk along the street pecking at my teeth with this finger and spitting out. And everybody thinks: 'Just look how well that damned Ustin lives! He has meat to eat every day, he's never without it.' And then you ask what I need one finger for? It does its job. Let the people think I'm well off. Right or wrong, it's flattering."

"You're clever with your tongue," Davidov commented, unable to avoid smiling. "But will you go out and mow today?"

"After such a pleasant talk of course I will."

Davidov turned to Osietrov, who was the oldest Cossack in the group. "How long is it that your women set out for Tubyanskoe?"

"Why, it might be an hour, but not more."

"And how many went?"

"A dozen. They're a lot of sheep, those women: where one goes all the rest follow like a flock. Sometimes one bad sheep leads all the rest astray. Just like we gave way to Ustin: he planned to take a day off from mowing, may the old hag seize him!"

Ustin laughed good-naturedly. "So I'm to blame again? Don't pile other people's sins on to me, longbeard! The women went off to the service, and what had I to do with that? It was Mrs. Atamanchukova and another of our old women who turned them off the right path. They came out from the village at first light and began to make propaganda among our women: 'Today's the festival of the holy martyr Glikeria, but you women are thinking of going out to mow! Aren't you afraid of such a sin?' And so they got them away. I asked the two old women: 'What Lukeria are

you referring to? Not Mrs. Nagulnova, surely? She's a great martyr, certainly. She's always ready to suffer with any man who happens to come along.' And you should have seen how those old women flared up and went for me! Old Atamanchukova even swung her crutch to hit me, but luckily I turned away just in time, or I'd have had an egg on my forehead like a Dutch goose. And then our own women went for me; they clung to me like burrs in a dog's tail, and I only got away by sheer force. Why am I so unfortunate? This is one of my off-days. You reckon it up, friends: in one day I've managed to quarrel with the old women, and with our own women, with the chairman, and with old greybeard Gordeich. And to do all that takes intelligence!"

"You can do it, all right. You don't need to get your intelligence from your neighbours for that. Ever since you were a kid you've quarrelled with everybody, like a fighting cock. But you mark my words, a quarrelsome cock always has a bloody comb," Osietrov warned him.

But Ustin didn't appear to hear him. Looking at Davidov with insolent, fearless eyes, he went on: "On the other hand we're in luck's way with propagandists today. They've come out to us on foot and on horseback. If the railway was nearer they'd be riding out to us on the engines. But you want to take a lesson from our old women on how to do real propaganda, Chairman. They're older than you, and more cunning, and they've got more experience. They talk quietly, they persuade people gently, and are always polite about it, and that's how they gain their ends. Their powder always flashes. But how do you go about things? You'd hardly reached our camp before you were bawling all over the steppe: 'Why aren't you at work?' Who talks to the people like that these days? Under the Soviet regime the people have taken out their pride from their store-chests, and they've got no respect for anyone who comes shouting at them. To put it bluntly, they don't like being tickled, and it's to the point to mention that even in Tsarist times the atamans didn't shout too much at the Cossacks: they were afraid of upsetting the village elders. And so it's high time you and Nagulnov understood that those days are gone, and the old habits have got to be dropped. D'you think I'd ever have agreed to go out mowing today if you hadn't piped down? Not on your life. But you pulled yourself up a bit,

you changed from anger to friendliness, you agreed to have a game of cards with us, you talked to the point, and I agreed to everything: both to play cards and to build stooks."

Davidov felt really annoyed with himself as he listened to Ustin's reproaches. For, after all, this more than usually quick-witted Cossack was right, up to a point. He was right, if only in saying that Davidov shouldn't have begun by shouting and swearing. That was precisely why he had lost the exchange at first. How had he come to lose his temper? He had to admit that he had; little by little he was imitating Nagulnov's rough way of handling people; he had let himself go, as Razmiotnov would have put it, and now he was faced with the result: he was sar-castically advised to take a leaf out of the book of two old crones who worked cautiously, stealthily, and who gained their ends without putting a foot wrong. It was all as clear as daylight. He should have ridden up to the camp quietly, should have talked quietly, should have argued with the people and convinced them that a holiday mood was impermissible at this stage. But he had shouted at them, and at one point he had all but resorted to his whip. One hasty action might have destroyed all the work he had put into building up the collective farm, and then most likely he would have had to hand in his Party card to the dis-trict committee. That would have been a personal disaster, and at the very thought he felt a chill down his back.

Absorbed in these unpleasant reflections, he stared fixedly at the cards scattered over the blanket and thought: "I've paid heavily for buying that ten of spades!" It wasn't easy for him to admit his lack of self-control, but he found the strength to say, almost despite himself: "You're quite right, Ustin, I did strain my throat unnecessarily. But it was rather shameful to find you weren't out at work, don't you think? And you hardly talked in a whisper to me, did you? But of course we could have come to some agreement without swearing at each other. Well, we won't talk about it any more. Go and harness a pair of your best horses into a cart, and you, Nechayev, harness another good pair into this drozhki."

"You're not going to drive after the women, are you?" Ustin asked in open amazement.

"You've hit it exactly. I shall try to persuade them to come back to work today."

"But d'you think they'll do as you ask?"

"We shall see. Persuasions are not orders."

"Well, then, may the Lord God, and the Madonna of Czesto-chowa help you! Listen, Chairman, take me with you, will you?"

"Come on, then," Davidov agreed at once. "But will you help me talk them into it?"

Ustin twisted his cracked lips into a smile. "My assistant will help you; I'll take him along with me for sure."

Davidov stared at him in perplexity. "What assistant?"

Without a word, the Cossack deliberately sauntered over to the covered wagon and from under a pile of coats took out a long, newish-looking knout with a smart leather fringe to its handle. "This is my assistant. Fine, isn't he? You wouldn't believe how convincing he is. Let him start whistling and he'll persuade them, all right, he'll win them over. Don't worry because I'm left-handed."

"Drop that." Davidov knitted his brows. "I won't let you lay your little finger on the women, though I'd be delighted to try out your assistant on your own back."

But Ustin only crinkled up his eyes humorously. "Some old boy wanted to try the curd dumplings, but the dog ate the curds first. I'm privileged, I was wounded in the civil war. A good whipping only makes women fatter and quieter—I know that from experience with my own wife. Who ought to be whipped, if not women? Why be so shy about it: let me put the whip properly across two or three of them, and the others will come running like the wind and leap on the cart before you know where you are."

Evidently considering the conversation at an end, he picked up bridles lying under the wagon and went off to bring in the horses. Nechayev and the other Cossacks, with the exception of Osietrov, hurried after him.

"Aren't you going off to mow too, Tikhon Gordeich?" Davidov asked.

"I just wanted to have a word with you about Ustin. May I?"

"Out with it."

"Don't be angry with the fool, for God's sake. He goes quite wild when he feels the rein under his tail," Osietrov pleaded. But Davidov interrupted.

"He's not a fool, he's an open enemy of our collective farm. We've had to fight men like him and we'll go on fighting them without mercy."

"But how can you call him an enemy?" Osietrov exclaimed in surprise. "I tell you he only gets a bit beside himself when he's mad, that's all. I've known him ever since he was a kid, and he's always been as prickly as a hedgehog as long as I can remember. Before the revolution, our elders whipped him I don't know how many times for his obstinacy in the village assemblies, the rascal. They used to whip him so hard he couldn't sit or lie down, but it rolled off him like water off a duck's back. He'd cool his ass for a week and then be up to his old tricks again, never letting anybody have any peace, picking holes in everybody, like a dog searching for fleas! And so keen on it too! Why should he be an enemy of the collective farm? He's been against the rich all his life, and you should see the sort of life he lives himself. His hut's lopsided, all but falling down; he's only got one wretched little cow and a few mangy sheep. All his life he's never had a penny to bless himself with. In one pocket he's got fleas on a noose, and in the other lice on a chain, and that's all he possesses in the world. And his wife's sickly, he's overrun with kids, they're terribly badly off. Maybe that's why he's always so quick to snap. And you call him an enemy! He's no enemy, he's just a bellyful of wind."

"He doesn't happen to be a relation of yours, does he? Why are you speaking up for him?"

"That's just the point, he is a relation of mine."

"So that's why you're so anxious to help him?"

"Well, and why not, Comrade Davidov? He's got six kids round his neck, and all of them little ones, but he has a tongue like a besom. I've told him I don't know how many times: 'Put a stop to your tongue, Ustin. You'll talk yourself into some misfortune. In the heat of the moment you'll say something that'll get you packed off to Siberia, and then you'll start to bite your tongue.' But he always comes back with: 'Do people go around on all fours in Siberia, then? I don't suppose the wind will blow

me away there any more than it does here; I'm too used to it.'
And a fool like that's not worth twenty roubles. But what would
happen to his children then? In times like these they can be
made orphans before you know where you are."

Davidov closed his eyes, and stood a long time thinking. Maybe
it was his own colourless, dreary childhood he was recalling.

"Don't let his foolish remarks upset you," Osietrov repeated.

Davidov passed his hand over his face and started, as though
the words had brought him back to himself. "Listen, Tikhon
Gordeich," he said slowly. "I shan't touch Ustin for the moment.
Let him work in the collective farm as well as he can, we shan't
put him on heavy work; let him do whatever he can manage. If
at the end of the year he's short of labour days we'll help him;
we'll let him have grain from the collective-farm general fund for
his kids, understand? But you tell him from me on the quiet:
if he tries to stir up mud against me again in the brigade or
thinks he can get people to take the wrong road, it won't be good
for him. Let him think over what he's doing before it's too late. I
don't intend to joke any more with him, and you can tell him so.
It's not him I'm sorry for; it's his children."

"Thank you for those kind words, Comrade Davidov. Thank
you, too, for not bearing anger in your heart against him." The
old man bowed, and the gesture made Davidov fume again.

"What are you bowing to me for? I'm not an icon. I'll do what
I've said I'll do without your bows."

"It's a custom from the old days. We always bow when we're
thanking anyone," Osietrov answered with dignity.

"Well, all right, old man! But tell me, now: how are Ustin's kids
off for clothes? And how many of them are going to school?"

"In the winter they all sit on the stove just as they are; they've
got nothing they can go out in. In the summer they run about in
their old rags. They were given a few things out of the property
taken from the kulaks, but it wasn't enough to cover their
nakedness. And last winter Ustin kept his oldest boy away from
school because he had nothing to wear; neither clothes nor
boots. He's big for his age, he's twelve, and he's ashamed to go
about in gypsy rags."

Davidov furiously scratched his head and abruptly turned his
back on the old man. "Go and get on with the mowing."

His voice sounded thick and unpleasant. . . . Osietrov stared at his gloomily bent back, bowed once more, and slowly went off to join the others.

Recovering a little from his agitation, Davidov turned and gazed after Osietrov, thinking: "Strange lot, these Cossacks! Just try to find out what sort of fruit this Ustin is! An open enemy or simply a blustering brawler who says the first thing that comes into his head? Never a day passes without their giving me new clues to crosswords. How to get to the bottom of each of them, the devil take the lot of them! Well, I will get to the bottom of them! If necessary I'll eat not a pound but a whole sack of salt with them, but one way or another I'll get to the bottom of them. Fact!"

Ustin broke into his meditations; he came riding up at a gallop, leading a second horse by the bridle. "Why harness up the drozhki, Chairman?" he asked. "We'll take the bigger wagon. I don't suppose the women will be shaken to pieces in it, if they do agree to come back."

But Davidov had already thought out his plan of campaign, and knew what he would need the drozhki for, if he managed to win the women over.

After some forty minutes of hard driving they saw a colourful crowd of women dressed in their Sunday best slowly toiling along a summer field road up a further slope. Ustin drew his drozhki level with the wagon.

"Well, Chairman, get your feet well planted on the ground! The women will be organizing a second performance for you in a minute or two."

"The blind man said: 'We'll see,'" Davidov answered briskly, slapping the reins down over the horses' backs.

"You're not afraid?"

"Why should I be? There are only twelve or so of them."

"But supposing I take their side?" Ustin asked, smiling mysteriously.

Davidov stared into his face, but could not make up his mind whether the Cossack was joking or serious.

"How will things go then?" Ustin asked again, and now his face was without a smile.

Davidov reined in his horses sharply, climbed out of the wagon, and went across to the drozhki. He put his hand into his right-hand coat pocket and took out the pistol which Nesterenko had given him. Laying it on Ustin's knees, he said: "Take this toy and keep it well away from temptation. If you happened to take their side I'm afraid I mightn't be able to resist the desire to put a bullet through your head."

He gently took the knout from Ustin's sweating hand and with a great swing of his arm flung it far into the steppe. "Now get a move on. Speed up your horses, Ustin Mikhailovich. But take a good look to see where your knout has fallen. We'll pick it up on the way back, that's a fact. And when we get back to the camp you'll hand over my pistol. Get cracking!"

When he reached the knot of women he dashingly drove round them and drew up the wagon across the road. Ustin halted his horses alongside.

"Well, my handsome beauties, and how are you today?" Davidov greeted the women with forced gaiety.

The boldest of them spoke up for the crowd. "We're all right, if you're not joking."

He jumped down from the wagon, took off his cap, and bowed. "In the name of the collective-farm committee I ask you to return to work. Your husbands have sent me after you. They've already started mowing."

"We're not going to a fair, we're going to mass," an elderly woman with a crimson, sweating face replied indignantly.

He pressed his crumpled cap to his chest with both hands. "After the haymow you can pray as much as you like, but there isn't time for it now. Look: clouds are coming up, and there isn't a single rick standing in your sector yet. The hay will be lost. It'll all rot. And if the hay's lost next winter we shall lose the cattle. After all, you know that better than I do."

"Where did you see the clouds?" a young girl asked sarcastically. "The sky's as clean as fresh washing."

He wriggled out of the argument. "The barometer points to rain, and clouds have nothing to do with it. There's bound to be

rain before long. Come on, my dear women; you can go and do
your praying next Sunday. What difference does it make to you?
Get in, and we'll drive you back like the wind. Get in, my dears,
the work won't wait."

He put all he knew into persuading his collective-farm
women, and didn't spare flattery. They began to fidget irresolutely, to whisper to one another. Unexpectedly Ustin came to
his aid: quietly stealing up behind Nechayev's tall and burly
wife, he seized her by the arms and, taking no notice of the
blows which the laughing woman showered on him, half carried her at a trot to the wagon and gently lifted her into the
back. The other women scattered in all directions, laughing and
squealing.

"Get into the wagon of your own free will or I'll bring the
knout to you," he bawled at the top of his voice, rolling his eyes
savagely. But then, roaring with laughter, he added:

"Get in, get in, I shan't touch you. Only do get a move on,
you long-tailed devils!"

Drawing herself up to her full height, adjusting the shawl
slipping off her head, Nechayev's wife shouted: "Come on, jump
in, women. Have I got to wait for you? Look at the honour
we've been done: the chairman himself has come out to fetch us."

The women swarmed around, laughing and jostling one another, giving Davidov sly glances as they unceremoniously
climbed into the wagon. Only two old women were left on the
road.

"Have we got to walk to Tubyanskoe all on our own, you
damned devil?" one of them, old Mrs. Atamanchukova, said,
and gave Davidov a hateful look.

But Davidov summoned up all his sailor gallantry, bowing low
and clicking his heels together. "You don't have to walk, old
ladies. Here's a drozhki specially for you: get in and ride there,
and pray to your heart's content. Ustin Mikhailovich will drive
you. He'll wait till you've finished your mass, and then bring you
back to the village."

Every minute was precious and he could not wait for the old
women's agreement. He took them by the arm and led them to
the drozhki. Mrs. Atamanchukova tried to resist, but Ustin
pushed her on from behind, gently and respectfully. They got

them somehow into the drozhki. As he shook out the reins, Ustin said very quietly to Davidov:

"You're as cunning as a devil, Davidov!"

It was the first time he had addressed his chairman by his sur-name. Davidov made a mental note of the fact, and smiled half-heartedly: his sleepless night and the emotional strain were be-ginning to tell on him, and his longing for sleep was almost irresistible.

Chapter 14

"It's a fine sight of grass we've got this year. If the rain doesn't mess things up and we get all the mowing done in good weather we'll be loaded down with hay," Agafon Dubtsiev said as he came into Davidov's modest office and sat down wearily on the bench, grunting like an old man.

Not until he had made himself thoroughly comfortable did he put his faded peaked cap down beside him, wipe the sweat from his sunburnt, freckled face with the sleeve of his cotton shirt, and turn with a smile to Davidov, the book-keeper, and Yakov Lukich, who were sitting at the table.

"Greetings, Chairman; and your good health, you office clods!"

"Farmer Dubtsiev has arrived," the book-keeper snorted. "Take a good look at the old boy, Davidov. Well, d'you call your-self a farmer, Agafon?"

"Why, what do you think I am?" Dubtsiev turned on the book-keeper in a challenging tone.

"Anything you like—except a farmer."

"Then give it a name!"

"Well, it's rather awkward to say exactly what you are . . ."

Dubtsiev frowned, his face clouded, and his swarthy features seemed to turn even darker. He retorted impatiently: "Now, don't you try anything on me, you tell me straight out what you think I am. And if your words choke you I'll give you a thump on the back and you'll start talking at once."

"You're a perfect gypsy, that's what you are!" the book-keeper said in a tone of conviction.

"How d'you make that out? Why a gypsy?"

"Oh, that's quite simple."

"Even a flea doesn't bite simply, but with intent. So now explain your insulting remark."

The book-keeper removed his spectacles, and scratched behind his ear with his pencil. "Don't get annoyed, Agafon, but just listen to me. Farmers work in the fields, don't they? And gypsies ride from village to village getting the people to tell them where things are being left about unguarded, and then stealing them. And that applies to you. What have you come back to the village for? Not to steal, I hope. But if not, then it can only be to cadge something. Is that correct?"

"Well, as for cadging . . ." Dubtsiev began irresolutely. "Why, can't I drop in to see you sometimes? Aren't we allowed to come into the village at all, not even on business? Do you forbid that, you clod in spectacles?"

"Do tell us frankly what you have come for," Davidov asked with a smile.

However, Dubsiev pretended he hadn't heard the question. He looked around the shady room, and sighed enviously. "Some people live well; may they sit on a hedgehog! Shutters half closed, the floor washed with cold water; it's quiet, and dark, and cool. Not a single fly, not a single mosquito buzzing around. But out in the steppe, damn it all, the sun soaks into you from morn till eve; during the day insects suck your blood as if you were cattle; all sorts of filthy flies cling to you as tightly as a pestiferous wife; and all night the mosquitoes won't give you any peace. And they're not just ordinary mosquitoes either, they're lifeguard size. You wouldn't believe it, brothers, but every one is almost as big as a sparrow, and when they suck your blood they grow even bigger than a sparrow, that's the honest truth. To look at, this kind of mosquito is yellowish and frightening, and it's got a sting at least a couple of inches long. Let such a little devil pierce through your coat and with a single sting he gets right down to the living flesh, by God! The tortures we suffer from all kinds of flying vermin, the blood we shed, it's like the civil war all over again."

"You can tell a good yarn, Agafon," Yakov Lukich laughed, and added admiringly: "If you go on like that you'll beat old Shchukar before long."

"What yarn am I telling? You're sitting here where it's cool; but you ride out into the steppe and you'll find out for yourself," Dubtsiev snapped. But the smile took a long time to fade from his rascally, half-closed eyes. He would have been prepared to continue his hypocritically lachrymose story of the brigade's miseries and trials if Davidov had not interrupted him.

"We've heard enough. Don't put on an act, don't come whining and pulling a long face to us. Tell me straight out: what have you come in for? To ask for help?"

"That wouldn't hurt. . . ."

"But what are you orphans short of? Daddies or mummies?"

"You like your joke, Davidov, but we too saw the funny side of it at first."

"I'm not asking in joke. What are you short of: people?"

"And people too. On the slopes of the Thorny Ravine—you've seen it for yourself—the grass is almost too good. But you can't run mowers over those steep slopes, and we've so few men to mow with scythes, it's enough to make a cat weep. It'll be a terrible pity if such good grass should go to waste."

"We might be able to let you have two or three more mowing machines, from the first brigade perhaps?" Davidov said, insinuatingly.

Dubtsiev sighed mournfully and gazed at Davidov with sad and questioning eyes. He hesitated over his reply, sighed again, and said: "I won't say no. An old maid wouldn't refuse even a hunchback. This is how I see it: our work in the collective farm is for everybody's benefit, and I don't regard it as any disgrace to accept help from another brigade. That's right, isn't it?"

"That's right enough. But don't you think it rather a disgrace to mow with other people's horses for a couple of days?"

"What other people's horses?" Dubtsiev's tone expressed such genuine astonishment that Davidov found it difficult to suppress a smile.

"D'you mean to say you don't know? Who drove off two pairs of Liubishkin's horses when they were out to graze? It looks as if the book-keeper's right: there's a bit of the gypsy about you.

You like to cadge for things, and you're not altogether indifferent to other people's horses."

Dubtsiev turned away and spat contemptuously. "D'you call them horses? Those nags came wandering into our brigade of their own accord; nobody drove them there. And, besides, how can they be other people's when they belong to our collective farm?"

"But why didn't you return those nags to the third brigade at once, instead of waiting till their masters came and unharnessed them from your mowers?"

Dubtsiev laughed aloud. "Fine masters they are! Couldn't find their horses for two days in their own parts! D'you call them masters? They're not masters, they're sleepwalkers. Anyway, this is all a matter of the past: Liubishkin and I have made it up, so there's no point in bringing it all up again. I've not come here for help, but on important business. I couldn't leave the haymow unless I had a special reason, could I? If the worst comes to the worst we'll manage without any outside help and with our own strength. But that old clod Mikheich the book-keeper has to call me a gypsy! I think that's damned unfair. If we're really in desperate need we'll ask for help, and even then we'll only do it gritting our teeth in our pride. But what does poor dear Mikheich understand about farming? He was born on the beads of an abacus, and he'll die on them. Let me have him in my brigade for a week or so, Davidov. I'll set him to work forking hay off the mower, and I'll drive the horses myself. I'll teach him how to work! He ought to feel the sweat in his eyes for once in his life."

The banter was in danger of turning into a wrangle, and Davidov averted it with the hurried question: "Then what's the important business you've come about, Agafon?"

"Well, how am I to put it? . . . Of course it's important to us, but how you'll take it we don't know. To cut it short, I've brought in three applications, written in pencil, of course. We asked our book-keeper for a piece of indelible pencil, dissolved the lead in hot water, and made ink for our applications that way."

Davidov was all ready to give Dubtsiev a good dressing-down for his "independent attitude," but he asked interestedly: "What are the applications for?"

Disregarding the question, Dubtsiev said: "As I understand it

we ought to take them to Nagulnov. But he wasn't at home, he's out with the first brigade, so we decided to hand these papers over to you. Am I to take them back again?"

"But what are the applications for?" Davidov asked impatiently.

Dubtsiev's face suddenly turned serious; not even a shadow of his previous bantering expression was left. He unhurriedly took a scrap of bone comb out of his breast pocket, combed back his sweaty hair, and assumed an air of dignity. Then, controlling his agitation and carefully choosing his words, he began: "All of us, that's all three of us, are volunteers in this matter. We wish to join the Party. And so we ask our Gremyachy Party group to accept us in our Bolshevik Party. We've been turning it over this way and that for many nights; we've had lots of talks about it, but we've decided to join with one accord. Before we settled down for the night we'd go off into the steppe and begin to criticize each other; but all the same we all had to admit that the other two were worthy to join the Party. But as you decide, so it will be. One of us made much of the fact that he'd served with the Whites, but I told him: 'You served with the Whites under compulsion as a rank-and-file Cossack for five months, but you went over to the Red Army voluntarily and served as a section commander for two years. So your later service wipes out the earlier, and you're fit for the Party.' The other said that you— Davidov, that is—had asked him to join long ago, but he refused because he was fond of his own bullocks. But now he says to me: 'How can I be fond of them any longer, when the kulaks' sons are reaching for their guns and want to bring back the old regime? I mentally give up all regret for the bullocks which were mine, and for all my other livestock, and I subscribe to the Party, so as to stand behind the Soviet government just as I did ten years ago in the same ranks as the Communists.' I think just the same, and so we've written out our applications. To tell the truth, none of them is written very clearly, but . . ." Here Dubtsiev squinted at Mikheich and ended: "But, you see, we weren't taught to be book-keepers and secretaries. On the other hand, every word we've written is the solemn truth."

He wiped the copious sweat from his brow with his hand once more and, bending his body over a little to the left, care-

fully took the applications, wrapped in newspaper, out of his right-hand trouser pocket.

The request was so unexpected that there was silence in the room for a good minute. Nobody said a word, but each had his characteristic reaction to Dubtsiev's remarks: the book-keeper stopped in the middle of a column, pushed his spectacles back on his brow in astonishment, and stared idiotically, unblinking, at Dubtsiev with his short-sighted eyes; Yakov Lukich, unable to conceal a gloomy and contemptuous smile, turned to the window. As for Davidov, his face beamed, and he flung himself back in his chair so violently that it slipped away with him on it, and creaked miserably.

"Accept our papers, Comrade Davidov." Dubtsiev unfolded the newspaper and handed over several sheets torn from a school exercise book, covered with large, uneven writing.

"Who wrote out the applications?" Davidov asked, and his voice rang through the room.

"The younger Beskhlebnov, myself, and Kondrat Maidanni-kov."

Taking the papers from him, Davidov said with restrained emotion: "This is a very moving fact, and it's a great event for you, Comrade Dubtsiev, and for Comrades Maidannikov and Beskhlebnov, as well as for us members of the Gremyachy Party group. I shall hand your applications to Nagulnov today. But now ride back at once to the brigade and warn the comrades that we shall consider their applications at an open Party meeting on Sunday evening. We shall hold it in the school, at eight o'clock. There must be no late arrivals; turn up punctually. But I'm sure you'll see to that. After dinner on Sunday harness up your best horses and drive into the village. Oh, and one other thing. Have you any other kind of vehicle in your camp, apart from wagons?"

"We've got a britzka."

"Well, then, be so good as to come to the village in that." He smiled again with a child's glowing smile, but he winked as he added: "And turn up dressed like bridegrooms. This only happens once in your lifetime, brother. It's an event. . . . It's like youth, my boy: it comes once in a lifetime. . . ."

Evidently he had difficulty in thinking of appropriate words:

he paused, deeply moved, then suddenly asked rather anxiously: "But is the britzka a decent one?"

"It's quite good: it's got four wheels. It's all right for carrying dung, but it's all scratched and broken. People couldn't ride in it in the daytime, only at night, in the dark. It must be at least my age, and Kondrat says our Cossacks fought Napoleon at Moscow in it."

"That's no good!" Davidov said decisively. "I'll send old Shchukar out for you with a springed drozhki. I tell you such an event occurs only once in a lifetime."

He wanted to ensure that the step now being taken by these three men, whom he liked greatly and trusted, should be made a solemn act, and he stood thinking: what else could be done to make the great day even more memorable?

"We must get the school cleaned and whitewashed before Sunday so that it looks like new," he said at last, gazing at Ostrovnov with a far-away look. "Get the area all round it swept up and scatter sand in the front and in the school yard. D'you hear, Lukich? And get the floors and the desks scrubbed, and the ceilings washed. Give the rooms a good airing: in short, have the place put in perfect order."

"But supposing so many turn up that the school won't hold them all?" Yakov Lukich asked.

"We ought to organize a club; that's what we need," Davidov said in a quiet, dreamy voice instead of answering. But he came back at once to reality. "Don't let children and juveniles into the meeting; then there'll be room for everybody. But whatever happens, the school must be given a . . . well, a holiday look."

"But how about seconders? Who'll sign for our lives?" Dubtsiev asked before he finally left.

Davidov answered, as he firmly gripped Dubtsiev's hand: "You're worried about seconders? They'll be found. This very evening I'll write out recommendations for all three of you, and that's a fact. Well, a good ride back. Give my greetings to all our mowers and tell them not to let the grass stand too long and not to let the hay dry too long in the swathes. Can we rely on the second brigade?"

"You can always rely on us, Comrade Davidov," Dubtsiev replied with unwonted seriousness, and he bowed and went out.

Very early next morning Davidov was disturbed by the master
of the house in which he lived.

"Get up, slugabed, a mounted messenger has galloped in from
the field of battle to see you. Ustin's come in bareback from the
third brigade: he's not properly dressed and he looks as though
someone's beaten him up."

The Cossack was grinning from ear to ear, but Davidov, still
half asleep, did not get the drift of the man's remarks at once,
and asked unconcernedly:

"What is it?"

"I tell you a courier has galloped in all beaten up; he's come
for help, I should think. . . ."

At last Davidov caught the import of the Cossack's words,
and he dressed himself hurriedly. In the porch he hastily
splashed his face with warm water, unpleasantly so because it
had been standing all night, and went out to the veranda.

Ustin Rikalin was standing on the bottom step, holding his
horse's reins in one hand and with the other soothing the young
mare, which was treading excitedly after the fast gallop. His
faded, blue cotton blouse was torn in several places right down
to the lower hem and hung around his shoulders only by a miracle; a large black bruise extended from the cheekbone to his
chin, and his left eye was half closed by a livid swelling. But his
right eye glittered angrily.

"Who's handled you like that?" Davidov asked in concern, forgetting even to say good morning as he came down the steps.

"It's robbery, Comrade Davidov. Robbery, banditry, there's no
other word for it," Ustin cried hoarsely. "Aren't they a lot of sons
of bitches to do such a thing? Oh, stand still, you God-damned
mare!" He swung his hand furiously at the horse, which had almost trodden on his foot.

"Can't you talk sense?" Davidov asked him.

"I couldn't think of more sensible words! Call them neighbours? May they be burnt in the fire, may they be shaken with
relapsing fever, the parasites! How d'you like this? Our Tubyanskoe neighbours—may they be choked with a wagon shaft—
drove up under cover of the night to Kalinov fields and carried
off not less than thirty ricks of our hay. At dawn this morning I
saw two wagons still being loaded with our own natural-born

hay, but everything else was cleaned up, not a single rick to be seen anywhere. I jumped on a horse and galloped up to them. 'What the hell are you doing, you so-and-sos? What right have you got to cart off our hay?' One of them laughed, the reptile: 'It was yours, but now it's ours. Don't mow other people's grass.' 'What d'you mean by "other people's"? You've come too far, can't you see where the boundary post is standing?' But he says: 'You open your eyes and look: the post's behind you. This land has belonged to Tubyanskoe ever since the beginning of time. God repay you for your labour in mowing our hay for us.' So they were playing tricks with the boundary posts, were they? I pulled him down off the wagon by his leg and gave him a couple of blows between the eyes with my damaged hand so that he could see more clearly and wouldn't get other people's land mixed up with his own.

"I gave him a good hard punch, and he went flying: he wasn't very firm on his feet. Then three more of them came running up. I managed to make one kiss the ground, but after that there wasn't much I could do in the way of beating them, for there were four of them. And one man can hardly tackle four, can he? Meanwhile our people were running up to join in the fight, but the four of them decorated me properly like an Easter egg, and ruined my shirt completely. Aren't they a lot of swine? How can I go and show myself to my old woman? Beat me up if you like, but why seize me by my shirt and rip it off my back? Now what am I to do with it? Use it for a scarecrow in the garden? Why, even a scarecrow would feel shy about standing in such a rag, and if I tear it up to make ribbons for the girls, they won't wear them, it's not the right sort of material. One of those Tubyanskoe fellows had better not meet me alone in the steppe! He'll return to his wife as black and blue as I am now."

Davidov laughed as he put his arm round Ustin. "Don't grieve; you can get a new shirt, and the bruises will fade before the wedding."

"Before your wedding?" Ustin sneered.

"Before the first that takes place in the village. So far I haven't got engaged to anyone. But d'you remember what the old gaffer said to you last Sunday? 'A quarrelsome cock always has a bloody comb.' "

Davidov smiled, but he was thinking: "It's simply wonderful that you've started to fight over our collective-farm hay and not your own individual property. It's a very moving fact."

But Ustin drew back, affronted. "It's all right for you to grin, Davidov, but all my ribs are cracking. You can't joke your way out of it; you put your leg across a horse and ride off to Tubyanskoe to get our hay back. We managed to save those two wagon-loads, but think how much they carried off during the night. In return for their stealing our hay, they can cart it right home to our village: that'll be only fair." He painfully stretched his swollen, blood-caked lips into a smile. "You wait and see: the hay will be brought back by their women; their Cossacks will be afraid to visit us. But it was the Cossacks who came and stole it, and they'd chosen such a fine lot of lads that when all four of them started to caress me with their fists I felt quite sick. They wouldn't let me down to the ground, they wouldn't let me fall, though I asked them to with tears in my eyes. They passed me round from hand to hand until our own Cossacks ran up. I didn't spare my fists, either. But, as they say, force will break a straw."

He tried to smile again, but only knitted his brows and waved off the idea. "You should have seen our Liubishkin: you'd have laughed till you cried. He ran round and round us, squatting down like a bitch about to leap a hedge, and bawled like mad: 'Smash them into smithereens, boys! Beat them up: they can stand a lot of bruising, I know them!' But he didn't join in himself, he kept well away. Daddy Osietrov flared up and shouted at him: 'Go and help them, you castrated ram! Or have you got carbuncles on your back?' But Liubishkin was almost in tears as he roared back: 'I can't. I'm a Party man and a brigadier into the bargain. Smash them into smithereens and I'll hold myself back somehow.' So he ran round and round us, squatting down and grinding his teeth together to hold himself in. . . . But there's no point in wasting more time: go and have your breakfast quick, and meantime I'll find a horse and saddle it for you, and we'll ride out to the brigade together. Our folk said I wasn't to show myself among them again without you. We don't intend to let those blockheads have our hay for nothing."

Regarding the question of Davidov's riding to Tubyanskoe as

settled, Ustin tied his mare to the balustrade and went off to the office yard. "I must go and see Polyanitsa, the Tubyanskoe chairman," Davidov thought. "If they took the hay with his knowledge there'll be no avoiding a quarrel with him. He's as stubborn as a mule. But all the same I'll have to go."

He hurriedly gulped down a mug of fresh milk, ate a dry crust of bread, and was ready just as the unusually sprightly Ustin, attired in a new shirt, galloped up to the wicket gate on Nagulnov's little dun horse.

Chapter 15

Although he and Davidov had only met a few times in the district committee and they knew each other chiefly by repute, Nikifor Polyanitsa, a former locksmith in a Dnepropetrovsk metallurgical works, one of the 25,000 workers commandeered for the collectivization and now chairman of Tubyanskoe collective farm, welcomed Davidov as if he were an old friend entering the farm office.

"Why, if it isn't our dear Comrade Davidov! The Baltic sailor! What wind has brought you to our altogether backward collective farm? Come and sit down, you're a very welcome guest."

Polyanitsa's broad, freckled face beamed with an artificial, crafty smile; his little black eyes gleamed with apparent affability. But this excessively friendly welcome put Davidov on his guard, and, replying curtly to the greeting, he sat down and looked about him leisurely.

To his eyes this collective-farm office had a strange appearance: the spacious room was lavishly decorated with dusty flowers in ochre-coloured censers and clay pots; the furniture consisted of ancient Viennese chairs with dirty wooden stools nestling among them like orphans; beside the door was a shapeless, ragged divan with its rusty springs sticking through the upholstery; pictures cut out of Soviet popular magazines were pasted on the walls, while cheap lithographs showed the christening of

Rus in Kiev, the siege of Sevastopol, the battle of Shipka, and the Japanese infantry going into the attack during the Russo-Japanese War. Above the chairman's table hung a yellowing portrait of Stalin, and on the opposite wall a highly coloured, flyblown advertisement of the Morozov cotton mill gladdened the eye. In this picture a dashing toreador in raspberry-hued jerkin had wrapped a loop of thread round an enraged bull's horns, and now one hand was restraining the rearing animal, while the other negligently rested on a sword. At his feet lay an enormous, half-unwound reel of white thread: its label clearly read: "No. 40."

The furniture was completed by an enormous chest banded with strips of white tinplate. Probably it served Polyanitsa instead of a fireproof safe: documents of high importance were evidently kept in it, for it was fastened with a granary padlock almost as big as itself.

As he ran his eyes round this office Davidov could not help smiling; but the chairman put his own construction on the smile.

"As you can see, we've made ourselves comfortable," he said contentedly. "It was all saved from the former kulak owner; everything in the room's just the same; I only had the bedstead and featherbed and pillows put into the cleaner's room; otherwise all the comfort has been kept, as you see. No ceremony, no officialism! I must admit I'm fond of home comfort, and I like people who come and see me to feel at their ease, just as if they were at home. Don't you agree?"

Davidov shrugged his shoulders, and made no comment. He went straight to his business. "I've got something unpleasant to discuss with you, neighbour."

Polyanitsa's cunning little eyes almost vanished in the fleshy folds of skin, and gleamed slatily like tiny pieces of anthracite. He raised his thick black eyebrows. "What unpleasantness can there be between good neighbours? You alarm me, Davidov. You and I have always been like two fish in water; and now quite suddenly you fling this at me: 'something unpleasant to discuss.' I just can't believe it. Say what you like: I don't believe it."

Davidov stared hard into Polyanitsa's eyes, but he was unable

to deduce anything from their expression. That face was as good-natured and inscrutable as before, and the friendly, imperturbable smile was frozen fast on his lips. The chairman of the "Red Ray" collective farm was evidently a natural artist: he had perfect self-control and played his hand intelligently.

"Our hay . . . was it by your orders that it was carried off last night?" Davidov asked without beating about the bush.

Polyanitsa's eyebrows rose still higher. "What hay, friend?"

"Just ordinary steppe hay."

"This is the first I've heard of it. Carried off, did you say? By our Tubyanskoe people? It can't be ture. I don't believe it. Shoot me, execute me, but I shall never believe it. Bear in mind, Siemion my friend, that our collective farmers are exceptionally honest toilers in our socialistic fields, and your suspicions are insulting not only to them but to me too as their collective-farm chairman. I ask you, friend, to keep that seriously in mind."

Suppressing his rising anger, Davidov calmly answered: "Now listen, my would-be friend: I'm not Litvinov, and you're not Chamberlain, and there's no point in our being diplomatic with each other. Was the hay carted off by your orders?"

"Again I ask, friend, what hay are you talking about?"

"Oh, this is like a fairy tale: this is where we came in," Davidov exclaimed angrily.

"Bear in mind, friend, that I'm asking you a serious question. What hay are you referring to?"

"The hay on the Kalinov fields. Our hayfields lie side by side around there, and you've simply stolen our hay, that's a fact."

As though delighted that the misunderstanding had been cleared up so satisfactorily, Polyanitsa smacked his hand down on his shanks and roared with laughter. "You should have started there, my friend. But you kept harping on one note: hay, hay, hay! The question is: what hay? Either by mistake or deliberately, your people went and mowed our land in the Kalinov fields. And we carted off that hay with every legal right and justification. Is that clear, friend?"

"No, my would-be friend, it's not clear. If it was your hay, why did you carry it off by stealth, at night?"

"That's the brigadier's affair. Night work's better for the ani-

mals, and for human beings too. Don't your people ever work at night? If not, they should. It's much better to work at night, especially a light night, than in the heat of the day."

Davidov laughed sarcastically. "As it happens, just now the nights are dark, that's a fact."

"Well, you know, even on a dark night you can't miss your mouth with the spoon."

"Especially if other people's porridge is in the spoon!"

"Now, drop that, friend. Bear in mind that your insinuations are a serious insult to the honest and fully politically conscious farmers of 'Red Ray,' as well as to me, their chairman. Say what you like, we're toilers, not swindlers. Bear that in mind."

Davidov's eyes flashed, but he kept his control and retorted: "You can drop your fine words, my would-be friend, and let's get down to business. Do you know that last spring three boundary posts were shifted on both sides of the Kalinov valley? Your honest collective farmers shifted those posts, straightened out the boundary line, and so took from us at least four or five hectares of land. Do you know that?"

"Friend! Where did you get that from? Bear in mind that your suspicions are a serious insult to people who're not the least bit guilty—"

"Stop dodging and think it out," Davidov broke in, beginning to boil. "D'you think I'm a child, or what? I'm talking to you seriously, but you keep putting on these turns and acting injured innocence. On the way here I myself rode out to the Kalinov fields and checked up on what our collective farmers had told me: the hay's been carted off and the posts have been shifted, that's a fact. And you can't get away from that fact."

"I've no intention of getting away from anything. I'm all here, you can take me with your bare hands, but . . . before you take me, you'd better tar them. Tar your hands well, friend, otherwise I may slip out of your clutches like an eel, bear in mind . . ."

"What your Tubyanskoe people have done is called arbitrary seizure, and for that you'll answer, Polyanitsa."

"That, my friend, has to be proved first, so far as shifting the boundary posts is concerned. We've only got your bare word for that. Your hay doesn't carry any marks."

"The wolf doesn't care whether the sheep is marked or not."

Polyanitsa smiled faintly, but he shook his head reproachfully. "Ai, ai, ai! So now you're comparing us with wolves. Say what you like, I don't believe anyone would pull up the posts and shift them."

"Then ride out there and see for yourself. Are the marks where they stood still visible? They are. Where they've been pulled up the soil's looser and the grass lower, and you can see the marks of the round holes as plain as the palm of your hand. That's a fact. Well, what do you say to that? If you like we'll ride out there together. Agreed? No, Comrade Polyanitsa, you can't wriggle away from me. Well, shall we go, or what?"

He puffed at his cigarette, waiting for an answer; Polyanitsa was silent too, smiling imperturbably. In that flower-bedecked room the air was stifling. Flies beat against the dirty window-pane and buzzed monotonously. Through the gaps between the heavy, brilliantly green leaves of a fig tree Davidov saw a young, very stout, but still beautiful woman come out on to the veranda; she was dressed in a nightshirt with short sleeves, tucked into an old skirt. Shielding her eyes from the sun with her hand, she gazed down the street and, suddenly coming to life, shouted in an unpleasantly raucous voice:

"Fenka, you damned girl, drive the calf home. Can't you see the cow's come back from the herd?"

Polyanitsa also gazed through the window at the woman's full, milk-white arm bare to the shoulder, at the abundance of red hair broken loose from under her kerchief and stirring in the breeze. For some reason he sighed and chewed his lips. "She's our cleaner; she lives here and keeps the place clean. Not a bad woman, but she's got a bad habit of shouting. I simply can't break her of it. . . . There's no point in my riding out to the fields, Davidov. You've been there and seen, and that's good enough. But I'm not going to return the hay, that's definite, and so that's the end of it. The matter's under dispute, the land distribution was made some five years ago, and it's not for you and me to settle such an issue between Tubyanskoe and Gremyachy."

"Then who should?"

"The district organizations."

"Good, I agree. But the dispute over the land's a separate is-

sue; meanwhile, you return the hay. We mowed it: it belongs
to us."

Evidently Polyanitsa had resolved to put an end to this pointless conversation. He no longer smiled. His right hand was lying inert on the table, but now the fingers gently spread apart
and made a V sign. Drawing Davidov's attention to it with a
glance, he briskly said, for some reason slipping into his native
Ukrainian: "D'you see that? There's my answer. And now, so
long; I've got work to do. Keep well."

Davidov smiled sarcastically. "I think you've got a queer way
of arguing. D'you really mean to say you're so short of words
that you stick your fingers up like a fruit vender? D'you want me
to complain to the public prosecutor about you over this wretched
hay?"

"Complain to whom you like, by all means. To the prosecutor
if you like, or to the district committee. But I shan't return the
hay and I shan't give back the land, bear that in mind," he answered, again resorting to Russian.

There was no point in wasting further words; Davidov stood
up and gazed at the chairman thoughtfully. "Looking at you,
Comrade Polyanitsa, I'm amazed: how could you, a worker, a
Bolshevik, get so quickly involved in petty property ownership
right up to your ears? You start off by boasting of your kulak
comfort, you say the room's been preserved exactly as it was. But
if you ask me, you've preserved not only the kulak furniture
but its spirit too. And that's a fact. In six months you've got
completely soaked in it. If you'd been born twenty years
earlier you'd have made a perfect kulak, I tell you that as a
fact."

Polyanitsa shrugged his shoulders, and his glittering eyes
again almost vanished under the folds of skin. "I don't know
whether I'd have made a kulak or not. But you, Davidov, would
certainly have been a priest, or at least a church official."

"And how d'you make that out?" Davidov was genuinely astonished.

"Why, because you, a former sailor, have got sunk right up to
your ears in religious prejudices. Bear in mind that if I was secretary to the district committee I'd have you hand in your Party
ticket for your goings-on."

"What goings-on? What are you talking about?" Davidov raised his shoulders to his ears in astonishment.

"Stop pretending. You know very well what I'm talking about. All our Party group here are fighting religion; we've discussed the question of closing the church twice at our general collective-farm and village meetings. And then what do you do? You're sticking a spoke in our wheel, bear that in mind, that's what you're doing."

"Go on talking; I'll be interested to hear what spokes I'm sticking in your wheels."

"But what are you doing?" Polyanitsa went on, now obviously working himself up. "You're driving old women to church on Sundays in the collective-farm drozhki so that they can attend the service, that's what you're doing. And bear in mind that that sort of thing upsets our women. You this and that, they say to me, you want to close the church and turn it into a club; but the Gremyachy chairman shows his respect for believing women and even gives them horses so that they can ride to church on Sundays."

Davidov could not help laughing aloud. "So that's what you're driving at? So that's the religious prejudices I'm guilty of having? Not a very terrible crime."

"Maybe it isn't to you, but it couldn't be worse for us, bear in mind," Polyanitsa continued heatedly. "You make up to the collective farmers, you want everybody to think well of you, but you're undermining our anti-religious work. I must say you're a fine Communist! You accuse others of having petty bourgeois tendencies, but you yourself get up to the devil knows what. Where's your political consciousness? Where's your Bolshevik idealism and no compromise with religion?"

"Wait a bit, you idealistic gasbag. Take the bends more carefully. What d'you mean by 'making up'? D'you know why I sent the old women here in the drozhki? D'you know what I reckoned on doing when I arranged that?"

"I spit on your reckonings from a lofty belfry. You can reckon as much as you like, but don't mess up our reckoning in the struggle with the priests. You please yourself, but I shall raise the question of your behaviour with the district committee, bear that in mind."

"I must confess I thought you had more sense, Polyanitsa,"
Davidov said commiserately, and walked out without saying
good-bye.

Chapter 16

By the time he reached Gremyachy Log, Davidov had decided
not to raise the issue of the Tubyanskoe seizure of land and hay
with the district prosecutor. Nor did he want to put it in the
hands of the district Party committee. Before taking any action
he felt that he must definitely establish to whom the disputed
land had belonged in the old days.

As he went over his conversation with Polyanitsa he thought
bitterly: "Well, that lover of flowers and home comfort's an old
brand! You can't say he's clever, not at all, but he's cunning:
like most fools he's got a simple sort of cunning. But don't put
your finger into his mouth! Of course he agreed to their carting
off the hay, but that's not the main point: it's the posts. They
couldn't have shifted them on his instructions. He wouldn't dare
to go so far as that; it'd be too risky. But supposing he knew
they'd shifted the posts, and simply winked at it? That would
mean he's a damned rotten skunk. His collective farm's only ex-
isted six months, and to begin by seizing your neighbours' land
and stealing is to demoralize the collective farmers completely.
That's driving them back to their old ways as individual farmers.
Use any means, don't despise any trick, in order to grab more
for yourself. No, that won't pass. As soon as I've established that
the land really belongs to us I'll ride over and see the district committee; let the brainy ones tick us off: me over the old women,
and Polyanitsa for badly educating the collective farmers."

The measured trot of the horse lulled him into a doze, and
suddenly in the grey haze of his drowsiness he clearly saw the
stout woman standing on the veranda in Tubyanskoe. He
twisted his lips scornfully, and sleepily thought: "She's got a lot

of surplus meat and fat on her carcass. In this heat she must go about in an absolute lather, that's a fact." His all too ready memory immediately recalled Lushka's maidenly, shapely figure, her springy gait, and the charming gesture with which her slender hands adjusted her hair, while she looked up from under her brows with kindly, twinkling, all-knowing eyes. He started as though someone had unexpectedly jostled him, straightened up in the saddle, and, frowning as though with pain, angrily brought his whip down on his mount and put it into a gallop.

These days his unkind memory was always playing tricks on him: at quite inept moments, in the middle of a business conversation, in times of meditation, or in his dreams it continually revived Lukeria's image, which he so desperately wished, but was unable, to forget.

He arrived in Gremyachy at noon. Ostrovnov and the book-keeper were having an animated conversation about something, but the moment he opened the door a dead silence fell in the room. Tired with the heat and the ride, he sat down at the table and asked: "What were you two arguing about? Has Nagulnov been in the office at all?"

"No, he hasn't," Ostrovnov answered after a moment, giving the book-keeper a swift glance. "We weren't arguing, we were talking over various questions, chiefly connected with the farm. Well, are the Tubyanskoe people going to bring back our hay?"

"They're asking us to get some more ready for them. Whom does that land belong to really in your view, Lukich?"

"Who's to say, Comrade Davidov? It's not at all clear. At first it was allotted to Tubyanskoe—that was before the revolution; but under the Soviet government the upper part of the Kalinov fields came to us. During the last redistribution in 1926 the Tubyanskoe people got our share cut down a bit, but where the boundary ran I don't know, for my land lay in the opposite direction. Some two years ago Titok, the kulak we expelled, was mowing there. Either he mowed without permission or else he bought the land on the quiet from one of the poor Cossacks. I can't say which it was, for I don't know. But what could be simpler than to ask the district land surveyor, Comrade Shportnoi?

He could sort it out at once by the old maps, and show where the boundary ran. It was he who made the land allotment in 1926, and if he doesn't know, who should?"

Davidov rubbed his hands with pleasure, and brightened up. "That's an excellent suggestion. Of course Shportnoi should know who the land belongs to. I thought the land allocation must have been made by land surveyors from the regional land office. Go and find Shchukar at once, and tell him to harness the stallions into the drozhki and drive to the district to see Shportnoi. I'll write him a note."

Ostrovnov went out. But some five minutes later he came back with a grin stretching from ear to ear. He beckoned Davidov with his finger. "Come to the hayloft and look at this remarkable sight."

The dead mid-day silence, which occurred only during the most oppressively hot days of summer, hung everywhere in the village, including the office yard. The air was heavy with the scent of grass wilting in the sun; from the stables came the smell of dry horse dung, and when Davidov went into the hayloft his nostrils drew in such a strong, spicy scent of freshly mown, hardly dry hay that for one moment he thought he must be out in the steppe, right beside a newly tossed stook.

Opening one wing of the door, Yakov Lukich stepped aside and let Davidov go in first, saying in an undertone: "You'll enjoy the sight of those two turtledoves. You'd never believe that an hour ago they were fighting for life and death. Apparently they arrange an armistice when they're asleep."

Until his eyes got used to the darkness Davidov could see nothing except a shaft of sunlight falling straight through an opening in the roof and piercing into the top of the hay carelessly piled in the middle of the shed. But then he distinguished old Shchukar sleeping on the hay, and Trofim, rolled into a ball, at his side.

"The old man was chasing the goat with a knout all morning, but, as you see, now they're sleeping together," Lukich said aloud, waking Shchukar up. He had hardly raised himself up on one elbow when Trofim sprang out of the hay with all four feet, leaped to the ground, put his head down, and shook his beard militantly.

"Good folk, did you ever see such a horned devil?" Shchukar asked in a feeble, weary voice, pointing to the goat. "All night long he's been pawing around in the hay, scraping, snorting, grinding his teeth, and the damned animal hasn't let me have a moment's sleep. I've had several fights already with him this morning, but then he tucked himself up to sleep beside me; the unclean spirit put him right down at my side. But now he's all ready for another fight. I can't go on being persecuted like this. It looks like it'll be war to the death: sooner or later either I shall put an end to his life or he'll drive his horns into my chest below my bellows, and it'll be God have mercy on old Shchukar. I tell you one of us will have a sticky end with this horned devil around."

Unexpectedly the knout found Shchukar's hand; but before he could even wave it, Trofim took two great leaps into a dark corner and there, clattering his hoofs challengingly, watched with phosphorescently gleaming eyes. The old fellow laid the knout down and mournfully shook his head.

"Did you see the nimble insect? The knout's my only protection from him, and even that doesn't always work, because the anathema lies in wait for me in the most unexpected places. For days and nights on end I never put the knout down. I simply can't get away from that goat. He turns up at the most awkward moments. Take yesterday, for instance: I had to go into a quiet corner behind the shed for a very important and urgent job. I took a good look all around, and there wasn't a sign of him. 'Ah well,' I think, 'praise be, he's taking a rest somewhere where it's cool or wandering round the houses nibbling the grass.' With my mind at ease I went behind the shed, and I'd just made myself all nice and comfortable when that damned animal comes charging at me, doing his best to gore me in the side. Like it or not, I had to get up. . . .

"I drove him off with the knout and had just settled down again when he came back. He tried this trick on me so many times that I didn't want to go any more. D'you call that living? I've got rheumatism in my legs, and I'm not a youngster, to squat down and get up again as if doing P.T. I get a trembling in the legs and colic in my loins. I might very easily die in some quiet spot while I'm squatting. At one time I could squat for

half a day, but now I almost have to ask someone to support me under the arms. That's what that accursed goat has reduced me to. Pfooh!"

He spat violently, and rummaged in the hay, muttering and cursing.

"You should learn to live like a civilized being, and make use of the closet, not go wandering behind sheds," Davidov advised him with a laugh.

Shchukar looked at him sorrowfully, and waved his hand in a gesture of despair. "I can't. My soul won't let me. I'm not one of your town dwellers. All my life I've been used to doing what I need to do in the open air, with the wind blowing all around me. Even in winter, in the deepest frost, you can't drive me into a shed, and when I go into one of your conveniences my head swims with the strong smell and I'd drop if I didn't get out quick."

"Well, in that case I can't help you. You'll just have to make the best of it. But now harness the stallions into the drozhki and drive to the district for the land surveyor. We need him urgently. Do you know where Shportnoi lives, Lukich?"

Getting no answer, he looked around; but, knowing from experience how long it took Shchukar to get ready, Lukich had gone off to the stable to harness the horses himself.

"I can drive to the district in a minute, that's nothing for me," Shchukar assured Davidov. "But tell me one thing, Comrade Davidov: why is it that any animal which used to belong to a kulak is exactly like its old master in its character: terribly dangerous and cunning beyond words? Take that monster Trofim, for instance: why hasn't he ever gone for Yakov Lukich, say, instead of always picking on me? It's because he recognized him by his smell as a kulak relation, and so he doesn't touch him, but pours out all his spite on me.

"Or you take any kulak cow: you can be quite sure she never gives the collective-farm milkmaid as much milk as her former kulak mistress. Well, perhaps that's only as it should be: she fed her with beet, and swills, and other fruit; but the milkmaid throws her a handful of dry last-year hay and sits and dozes under the udder, waiting for the milk to come out on its own.

"I asked Makar about this once, but all he said was: 'It's the

class war.' He didn't explain what the class war was, he just laughed and went about his business. But what the devil do I need this class war for, if it means that whenever I go about the village I have to watch every bitch with fear and trembling because she once belonged to a kulak? It doesn't say on her forehead whether she's an honest bitch or comes of former kulaks. And if she's a kulak bitch, my class enemy, as Makar says, what ought I to do? Dekulakize her? But how can you dekulakize her? Can you strip her of her fur coat? It just isn't possible. She's much more likely to let the soul out of your own skin. So it's clear you've got to tie her up first, and then strip the fur off her. I put this idea to Makar the other day, but all he said was: 'In that case, you stupid old man, you'd kill off half the dogs in the village.' Only I don't know which of us is stupid, him or me. It's still an open question, but in my view it's Makar who's a little stupid, not me. Will the department for raw-hide collection accept dogs' skins? It will. And how many dekulakized bitches are roaming about all over the country without masters and out of control? Millions! So if we strip them all of their skins and make hides of them and knit stockings from their fur, what will be the result? The result will be that half Russia will be going about in chrome-leather boots, and they'll be cured of their rheumatism for ever and ever. My grandmother told me of that way of curing rheumatism: there's not a surer remedy in all the world, if you wish to know. But I don't need to explain to you. I suffer from rheumatism myself and the only remedy for it is stockings made from dogs' fur. Without them I'd have been crawling about like a crab long since."

"Daddy, are you thinking of driving to the district today?" Davidov found an opportunity to ask.

"I'm quite thinking of doing so, but don't you interrupt: you just listen. And when I got that great idea of working up dog skins I didn't sleep for two days on end. I thought and thought of the financial gain it would bring to the state and, even more important, to me. And so I decided to tell Makar about it. I went and put it all to him and said: 'Makar, my dear, I'm an old man. I've got no need of any capital or reward, and I'd like to make you happy for all the rest of your life. You write to the central government about my idea, and you'll get an order just like the

one you were given in the war. And if you get some money for it in addition, you and I'll share it fifty-fifty.'

"Anybody else would have bowed down to my feet and thanked me. Well, he thanked me, all right! You should have seen the way he jumped up from the chair! And heard how he let fly with his swearwords. 'The older you get, the stupider you get!' he roared at me. 'You haven't got a head on your shoulders: it's an empty pot,' and he called me an old so and so, and this and that, and such and such: the air was so thick a fly couldn't have flown in it. And all because of my mind! A wise man he proved to be, all right! Wouldn't eat it himself, but wouldn't let anybody else eat it either. I sat and waited till he got a dry throat, thinking to myself: 'He can jump around as much as he likes: all the same he'll sit down in the same place on the chair as before.'

"Of course Makar got tired of swearing at last. So he sat down and asked: 'Have you had enough?' That made me mad with him, though he and I are good friends. 'You've lost your breath,' I say to him, 'take a rest and then start all over again. I'll wait; I'm in no hurry. But what on earth are you swearing like that for, Makar? For an idea like this you'll be printed in the papers all over Russia.' But at that he slammed the door and tore out of the house as if I'd poured boiling water into his trousers.

"That same evening I went to see the teacher and ask his advice: after all, he's an educated man. But in my view all these scientists have got a bug, and a big bug too. D'you know what he said? He just smirked and said: 'All great people have suffered persecution for their ideas, so you must suffer too, Daddy.' There's comfort for you. He's not a teacher, he's a pain in the neck. What's the point of telling me about suffering? I had the cow almost in my hands, but I didn't see so much as her tail. And all through Makar's pigheadedness. And he calls me his friend! All through him it's nothing but trouble at home. I bragged to my wife that maybe the Lord God would send us a cow in reward for my mental activity. And of course He's sent it, hold your pocket open wide! But now my old woman keeps nagging away at me like a saw: 'Where's that cow you promised me? Lying again, were you?' And so I have to suffer all manner of persecutions from her. Seeing that great men have always suffered persecution, God's arranged for me to do the same. . . ."

Leaning against the doorpost, Davidov laughed inwardly. Growing a little calmer, Shchukar began deliberately to put on his boots and, taking no more notice of his chairman, went on with his story:

"But dogs'-hair stockings are a golden remedy for rheumatism. I went about in them myself all winter; I didn't take them off once, and although by the spring my feet were all festered, and my old woman drove me out of the house because I stank of dog, all the same I cured myself of my rheumatism and went about dancing a whole month, like a young cock around a hen. But what good came of it all? None whatever. For in the spring I was stupid enough to get my feet wet again and I had another bad attack. But it won't last long; I'm not over-worried about that ailment. Once let me put on my healing stockings and I'll be dancing about like a youngster once more. The only trouble is my old woman refuses to spin the dogs' hair and knit me stockings any longer. The smell of dog makes her head swim, and as she twists the spindle she starts to hiccup, and then she chokes and chokes, and at last she gets so bad she brings up all her insides. Well, God be with her; I don't need her help. I washed the hair myself, dried it in the sun, and spun it myself too, and knitted my stockings. Necessity, my boy, forces you to learn all sorts of unpleasant jobs.

"But that's not the whole of the trouble: it's only the half. The worst is that my old woman's nothing but an asp and basilisk. Two summers ago I was knocked over with rheumatics in the legs. And then of course I remembered the dogs'-hair stockings. So one morning I enticed our neighbour's bitch onto the porch with rusks and stripped her clean like a real born barber. I only left tufts of hair around her ears for decoration, and on the end of the tail so she could keep the flies off. You wouldn't believe it, but I got nearly twenty pounds of hair off her."

Davidov hid his face in his hands and groaned in the effort to suppress his laughter. "Isn't that rather a lot?" he asked.

But such captious questions never caught Shchukar at a loss. He unconcernedly shrugged his shoulders and magnanimously conceded a point. "Well, it might have been a little less, say ten or twelve pounds. After all, I didn't weigh it. And that bitch was as hairy as a merino sheep. I thought I'd have enough hair to last

me to the end of my days. But no, I only managed to get one
pair knitted before my old woman got hold of the rest and burnt
the lot in the yard. It's not a wife I've got, she's a savage tigress.
In evil-doing she's as wicked as that thrice-damned goat; she
and Trofim are a pair of boots, by God I'm not lying. To get that
bitch to stand quietly while I sheared her I had to feed her with
enormous quantities of rusk, and look what came of it!

"Only the poor bitch didn't come out of it well either. When
I'd finished she broke away and seemed to be pleased because
I'd relieved her of unnecessary hair; she even waved her tufted
tail in her delight. But then she tore down to the river, and as
soon as she saw her reflection in the water she howled for shame.
Afterwards I was told she waded into the river and tried to
drown herself. But the water in our river wouldn't come up to a
sparrow's knee, and she didn't think of jumping down a well,
she hadn't got all that sense. And of course you wouldn't expect
her to have. After all, she's an animal or an insect, so to speak.

"For three days on end she lay howling under our neighbour's
granary and never crawled out: evidently she didn't like showing herself to people in such a state. She cleared right out of the
village, and wasn't seen any more till the spring. But as soon as
she'd grown her hair again she turned up at her master's house.
She was a bashful little bitch, shyer than any woman, by God I'm
not lying.

"After that I decided that if ever I had to shear a dog again
I wouldn't touch a bitch, I wouldn't rob her of her clothing and
put her to womanly shame, but choose some dog. They're not so
shy: you could scrape them with a razor and they wouldn't turn
a hair."

"Will you be finished with your fairy tale soon?" Davidov interrupted. "It's time you were off. Get a move on!"

"One moment! I'll just put my boots on and then I'm ready.
Only don't interrupt me for Jesus' sake, or my thoughts will get
turned aside and I shall forget what we were talking about.
And so, as I was saying: Makar seems to have an idea I'm stupid,
but he's greatly mistaken. He's young to oppose me: he's swim-
ming in shallow water, and all his berries are on the surface;
but as for me, the old cock sparrow, you can't get me into barren

chaff, no, that you can't! It's no sin for him to borrow my ideas. That's just the point."

The old man had obviously got one of his attacks of garrulity. He had grown expansive, as Razmiotnov put it, and now it was almost impossible to stop him. Davidov, who always treated the old fellow with kindly courtesy and almost felt pity for him, none the less decided to stop his story-telling at all costs.

"Wait a bit, Daddy, hold your horses. You've got to drive quickly to the district to bring back Shportnoi the land surveyor. D'you know him?"

"I don't only know your Shportnoi but all the other dogs in the district."

"You're a specialist on dogs, that's a fact! But I want Shportnoi, understand?"

"I'll bring him back, I've said I will, haven't I? I'll bring him back like a bride to the altar, and that'll be that. Only don't interrupt me. What an unpleasant habit you've got of interrupting a man! You're getting worse than Makar, that's God's truth. He at least shot Timoshka, he's a Cossack hero, and he can interrupt me if he likes, I'll still respect him. But what have you done to be called a hero? Why should I have any respect for you? Now, if you'll shoot that goat with your revolver, seeing as he's spoilt all my life, I'll pray to God for you till I'm dead, and I'll respect you just as much as Makar. Makar's a hero. He's learnt all there is to learn and he's studying English: he understands everything as well as I do; he's a leading expert even on cock-crows. He turned Lushka out himself, but you, like a fool, nursed her in your bosom. And he settled that enemy Timoshka with a single bullet. . . ."

"Get your boots on quick! What are you fidgeting around like that for?" Davidov lost his patience.

Grunting and shuffling about on the hay, old Shchukar snarled: "I'm tying the thongs round my boots, can't you see? It's the devil's own job to tie them in the dark."

"Then go out into the light."

"I'll manage it here somehow. Ye-e-es, that's the sort he is, my Makar. He's not only studying himself, but he's trying to teach me. . . ."

"What's he teaching you?" Davidov asked with a smile.

"All sorts of things," the old man answered. "I've started to learn foreign words: how d'you like that?"

"You need foreign words as much as a dead man needs poultices. Get yourself dressed smarter," Davidov said, still smiling.

The old man snorted like an angry cat. "Smarter! Fine thing to say! You've got to be smart when you're catching a flea or when you're running away from another man's wife at night and her husband's chasing you, right on your heels. I can't find my knout nohow, may it catch a disease! I had it in my hands only a moment ago, and now it's fallen through the ground. And without a knout I won't budge an inch: I'm afraid of that goat. Glory be, I've found it. But where's my cap? You haven't seen it by any chance, have you, Comrade Davidov? It was lying right by my head. Well, praise be, I've found my cap too, now I've only got to find my coat and I'll be ready. Ah, that unclean spirit Trofim! He must have tossed and worried it into the hay, and it'll take me all day to find it. Aha! I remember now, I left it at home. Why should I need it in this heat? I'd no cause to bring it here at all."

Davidov glanced through the doorway and saw Ostrovnov soothing the stallions, gently stroking and whispering to them. "Yakov Lukich has harnessed the horses, and you're still getting ready. When will you stop fidgeting around, you old docked cock?"

Shchukar cursed loud and long. "This is my unlucky day, damn it! Really, if the truth must be told, it wouldn't be wise to drive to the district. All the signs are against it. I've found my cap but now I've lost my tobacco pouch. Is that a good sign? Of course it isn't. There's bound to be some misfortune on the road, there'll be no avoiding it. Now I can't find my pouch. I wonder if Trofim's swallowed it? Perhaps we could put off the drive till to-morrow? All the signs are unfavourable. . . . In the holy book . . . in Matthew, I've forgotten which chapter . . . but, damn it, it doesn't matter . . . it doesn't say for nothing: 'If you, traveller, have made ready for a journey and you notice bad omens, stay at home and don't stir out of the house.' So you decide seriously, Comrade Davidov: am I to go today or not?"

"You'll go at once, old man," Davidov sternly ordered.

Sighing, but no longer swearing, Shchukar slipped down on his back off the hay and went to the door, shuffling his feet, dragging the knout behind him and casting fearful glances back at the goat lurking in the darkness.

Chapter 17

Having managed to get Shchukar away, Davidov decided to go along to the school to decide what else could be done to give the place a festive air on Sunday. He also wanted to have a chat with the headmaster and estimate with his help what kinds and quantities of building materials would be needed for the school repairs and when the work could be started, so as to have it in thorough repair by the beginning of the new school year.

Only during the last few days had he abruptly realized that they were about to enter the most intensive period of field activity since his arrival in Gremyachy Log: they had still not finished haymaking, but the grain was almost ready for harvest; the winter rye was beginning to darken in the ear; the barley was ripening almost simultaneously; the weeds were growing luxuriantly; and the areas of collective-farm land under sunflower and Indian corn, vast in extent by comparison with the days of individual farming, were silently calling for weeding; and the wheat harvest would be upon them quite soon.

There was so much to be done before the grain was harvested: as much hay as possible had to be carted into the village; the threshing floors had to be prepared for threshing; the task of shifting all the former kulak granaries into one central spot had to be completed; the one steam thresher on the farm had to be overhauled. Innumerable other little and big tasks were awaiting his attention, and each required his close and incessant care.

He climbed the old, creaking steps to the spacious school veranda. At the door a sturdy barefoot girl about ten years old stepped aside to let him enter.

"Are you a pupil, my dear?" he asked kindly.

"Yes," the girl quietly replied, looking up at him boldly.

"Where does your headmaster live?"

"He's not at home; he's gone with his wife across the river to water the cabbages in his garden."

"That's a pity. Is anyone else in the school?"

"Our teacher, Liudmila Sergeevna."

"But what's she doing here?"

"She's busy with the backward children." The girl smiled. "She teaches them every day after dinner."

"So she's pulling them up?"

The girl nodded.

"Excellent!" Davidov said approvingly, and went into the twilit passage.

From the depths of the long corridor came children's voices. As he walked round unhurriedly and examined the empty classrooms with an expert eye, through a half-open door in the end classroom he saw about a dozen small children sitting in the front row of desks, with the young school teacher in front of them. Short, thin, and narrow-shouldered, with cropped curly flaxen hair, she looked more like a girl in her teens than a teacher.

Davidov had not set foot inside a school for a long time, and he felt strange as he stood at the classroom door, crushing his faded cap in his left hand. He felt all his old feeling of respect for school, and a pleasant tremor born of memories of his distant childhood. He hesitantly pushed the door wide open and, coughing, but not because he had any tickling in his throat, asked the teacher quietly: "May I come in?"

"Come in," she answered in her thin, girlish voice. She turned to look at the intruder, and raised her eyebrows in astonishment. But then, recognizing him, she said in some embarrassment: "Please come in."

He bowed awkwardly. "Good morning. Excuse my butting in, but I shan't be a minute. . . . I just wanted to look round this last classroom. I've come in regard to repairs. I can wait."

The children stood up and replied in a ragged chorus to his greeting. As he glanced again at the teacher he could not help thinking: "I'm just like a former patron of the school, one of the strict moneybags. Now I've frightened the girl, and she's blushing. I would go and turn up at such a moment!"

She came over to meet him. "Come in, please, Comrade Davidov. I shall be finished with the lesson in a few minutes. Please
sit down. Shall I send for Ivan Nikolaevich?"

"And who is he?"

"The headmaster. Don't you know him, then?"

"Oh yes, I know him. No, don't trouble; I'll wait. May I stay
here while you finish the lesson?"

"Why, of course. Sit down, Comrade Davidov."

She looked at him and talked to him, but she still felt some
embarrassment: she was blushing furiously, down to her collar-
bone, and her ears were crimson. That was more than Davidov
could stand, if only because whenever he saw a woman blushing he began to blush too, and so he always felt even more embarrassment and discomfort.

He sat down on the chair she set for him beside the small
table. Then, going across to the window, she began to dictate,
syllabizing each word:

"Mo-ther is cook-ing. Have you written that down, children?
She is cook-ing din-ner for us. Put a full stop after 'us.' I repeat . . ."

After writing the sentence a second time, the children stared
at Davidov inquisitively. He put on a serious look and ran his
fingers over his upper lip, pretending to stroke his moustache.
But he gave them a humorous wink. They began to smile, and
good relations seemed on the point of being established. But
the teacher started to dictate another sentence, and they bent
over their exercise books again.

The classroom smelt of sunlight and dust and the stuffiness
of a building rarely aired. The bushes of lilac and acacia which
pressed close up to the window did not provide any real shade;
the wind rustled the leaves, and patches of sunlight twinkled
over the well-scrubbed floor.

Knitting his brows in his concentration, Davidov occupied
himself with estimates: "We shall need not less than two cubic
metres of pine boards; some of the floorboards need replacing.
The window frames are good, but I'll have to find out what state
the double frames are in. Must buy a crate of window glass. I
doubt whether we've got a single sheet in stock, and I can't imagine the boys not breaking the window sometimes, that's a fact.

It would be a good idea to get hold of some white lead, but we'd need an awful lot to paint the ceilings, the door frames, the window frames, and everything else. I must get the exact figures from the carpenters. The veranda must be repaired. We could do that from our own resources: we'll saw up two willows, and that's that. The repairs are going to cost a bit. The shed in the yard must be thatched with straw. There's a hell of a lot to be done, that's a fact. We'll get the granaries finished, and then we'll turn all the carpenter brigade on to the school. It would be a good idea to repaint the roof, but where's the money coming from? I'll get it somehow, even if I die in the attempt. But there's no need to go as far as that; we'll sell a couple of our surplus bullocks, and there's the money. We'll have to fight the district executive committee over those bullocks, otherwise nothing will come of it. But I'll get myself in a jam if I sell them without permission. All the same I'll risk it. Surely Nesterenko will support me?"

He took out his notebook and wrote: "School: boards, nails, glass—a crate. Green paint for the roof. White lead . . . Linseed oil . . ."

As he wrote down the last word a small, damp ball of chewed paper blown through a tube struck his forehead and remained clinging to the skin. He started at the unexpected sting, and one of the boys sniggered into his hand. A quiet ripple of laughter ran through the desks.

"What's the matter?" the teacher asked sternly.

Removing the ball from his forehead, Davidov swiftly ran his smiling eyes over the children. Their dark and fair little heads were all bent low over the desks, but not one hand was writing.

"Have you finished, children? Now write the following sentence. . . ."

He waited patiently, keeping his eyes fixed on the bent heads. One of the boys slowly, stealthily raised his head, and Davidov at once recognized an old acquaintance: none other than Fiodot Ushakov, whom he had met in the fields the previous spring, was staring at him through the narrow slits of his eyes, and the boy's crimson lips were extended in a broad, uncontrollable grin. Davidov looked at that impudent face, and almost laughed aloud. He hurriedly tore a sheet out of his notebook, put it into

his mouth, and began to chew, taking swift glances at the teacher and winking saucily at Fiodot. The boy stared at him with goggling eyes, and covered his mouth with his hand to hide his smile.

Relishing Fiodot's impatience, Davidov deliberately and thoroughly rolled the mashed paper into a ball, put it on the thumb nail of his left hand, and screwed up his left eye as though taking aim. Fiodot puffed out his cheeks and drew his head down fearfully between his shoulders, for that ball of paper was by no means small. When, choosing a suitable moment, Davidov gently flicked the ball to Fiodot, the boy ducked so violently that he cracked his forehead against the desk. He straightened up and looked hard at the teacher, goggling anxiously, then began to rub his reddening brow with his hand. But Davidov, shaking with soundless laughter, turned away and hid his face in his hands.

Of course he was behaving in an outrageously childish fashion, and he should have remembered where he was. Recovering his control, he gave the teacher a sidelong, guiltily smiling look, but saw that she had turned to the window and was trying to suppress her laughter too. Her thin shoulders were quivering, and she raised a crumpled handkerchief to her eyes to wipe away the tears.

"Now, there's a strict patron for you," Davidov thought. "I've ruined the lesson completely. I must slip out of here."

Putting on a serious look, he glanced at Fiodot again. The boy was already fidgeting once more at his desk, as lively as quicksilver. He pointed to his mouth, and then parted his lips: where once there had been a gap, two broad bluish-white teeth were visible. They were not yet fully grown, and they had such amusing little teeth on each side that Davidov had to smile.

A quiet feeling of happiness came over him as he studied the children's heads bent over the desks, and remembered that many years ago he too, like Fiodot's neighbour, had had the trick, when writing or drawing, of putting his head right down on the desk and sticking out his tongue, as if it helped him in his difficult task. And once more, as in the spring when he had first met Fiodot, he thought with a sigh: "It'll be an easier life for you, my boys, and you're already finding life easier. Otherwise what

did I fight for? Surely not for you to sup sorrow with a soup spoon, like I had to?"

He was aroused from his reverie by Fiodot, who was bobbing up and down as though on hinges. When he succeeded in attracting Davidov's attention he made urgent signs asking him to show his teeth. Davidov waited for the teacher to turn her back, and then, throwing out his hands to convey his affliction, he revealed his teeth. Seeing the familiar gap in the chairman's mouth, Fiodot quietly clapped his hands and smiled with the utmost satisfaction. All his exultant attitude said more eloquently than words: "So I've gone one better than you. My teeth have grown again, but yours haven't."

But a moment or two later there was an incident that gave Davidov the shivers every time he thought of it for a long time after. Fiodot, growing over-bold, quietly tapped on the desk to attract Davidov's attention, and when he looked vaguely in the boy's direction Fiodot drew himself up importantly, put his right hand into his trouser pocket, took out and then swiftly put back—a hand grenade. It all happened so quickly that for a moment Davidov only blinked furiously. But then he turned pale.

"Where's he got that from? Is the firing pin in position? Supposing he knocked it against the seat, then . . . Oh, hell, what should I do?" he thought with a burning feeling of horror, closing his eyes and not even conscious of the cold sweat that larded his forehead, chin, and neck.

He must do something about it at once. But what? Get up and try to take the grenade away by force? But supposing the kid got frightened and struggled out of his hands, or, worse still, threw the grenade away, not knowing that it might kill him and the others. No, that wouldn't do. Still sitting with his eyes closed, he painfully tried to think of a way out, while his imagination pictured the yellow flash of the explosion, a sudden, wild shriek, children's mutilated bodies.

Only then did he feel the drops of sweat slowly rolling down his forehead, over his nose, tickling his eyes. He felt in his pocket for a handkerchief, and his fingers touched the penknife an old friend had given him many years before. An idea occurred to him like a flash: he wiped the sweat away with his sleeve, took out the knife, and began to examine it so closely that

one would have thought he had never seen it before. In between
he took sidelong glances at Fiodot.

It was rather old, that pen-knife, and blunt, but its mother-of-
pearl sides shone dully in the sunlight, and in addition to two
blades, a screwdriver, and corkscrew, it had a pair of small but
excellent scissors. He showed off all these valuable accessories
with extreme deliberation, occasionally shooting glances at the
boy. Fiodot was enthralled: he could not remove his gaze from
the pen-knife. It was no ordinary knife, it was a perfect treasure. Davidov tore a clean page out of his notebook and swiftly
cut out a horse's head with the scissors. At that, Fiodot's rapture
knew no bounds.

As soon as the lesson ended, Davidov went to Fiodot and
whispered: "Did you see the knife?"

The boy swallowed hard and nodded without speaking.

Bending right over him, Davidov whispered: "Let's swap."

"But what can we swap?" the boy whispered still more quietly.

"My pen-knife for that bit of iron you have in your pocket."

Fiodot nodded his head with such desperate resolution that
Davidov put his hand under his chin to stop it from wagging. He
put the pen-knife into Fiodot's hand, and very carefully took
charge of the grenade. The firing pin was missing, and he straightened up, breathing hard with relief.

"I see you two have got a secret between you," the teacher
said with a smile as she went past.

"We're old friends. . . . You must excuse me, Liudmila Sergeevna," he said respectfully.

"I'm glad you were present during the lesson," the girl said,
reddening.

He did not notice her embarrassment, and asked: "Tell the
headmaster to come and see me in the office this evening, but
first he must estimate what repairs are necessary to the school
and how much they'll cost. Will you do that?"

"Yes, I'll tell him. You won't be coming again, then?"

"I certainly shall when I've some free time," he assured her.
Then he asked a question which had no obvious connection
with their previous remarks. "Where do you live?"

"With Granny Agafia Gavrilovna. Do you know her?"

"Yes. Have you any family?"

"I have my mother and two small brothers in Novocherkassk. But why are you asking?"

"Well, I ought to know something about you, oughtn't I? But I'm not going to pry into your girlish secrets," he said, joking the question off.

On the veranda Fiodot was surrounded by a crowd of boys examining the knife. Davidov called the exultant owner aside and asked, as though speaking to a grownup:

"Where did you find that toy you had, Fiodot Demidovich?"

"Shall I show you?"

"Of course."

"Come on, then. Let's go there at once, I shan't have time later," Fiodot proposed in a businesslike tone.

He took Davidov's finger in one hand, and, obviously proud of having the collective-farm chairman himself in tow, glancing round at his friends from time to time, he strutted along the street. They walked in no great haste, only occasionally exchanging a brief word or two.

"You're not thinking of swapping back, are you?" the boy asked, running on a little ahead and looking up anxiously into Davidov's face.

"Why, what makes you ask? That's all settled and done with," the man reassured him.

They walked on for some minutes in a sedate silence, as behoves two men, but then Fiodot could hold his tongue no longer. Still gripping Davidov's finger, he hurried on a pace or so again, gazed up at him, and asked commiserately: "But aren't you sorry about the knife? Don't you mind having swapped?"

"Not one little bit!" Davidov answered firmly.

So they walked on again without another word. Evidently a worm was gnawing at the boy's mind; he clearly considered Davidov had had the worst of the bargain, for after a long silence he asked:

"But if you like I'll give you my sling too. Would you like it?"

With a carefree magnanimity that completely baffled Fiodot, Davidov refused the offer. "No. Why should you? You can keep the sling. We've swapped fifty-fifty, haven't we? That's a fact."

"What d'you mean by 'fifty-fifty'?"

"Why, one for one. Get the idea?"

No, Fiodot didn't get the idea at all. The frivolous attitude to a swap which this grown-up man displayed surprised the boy immensely, and made him rather wary. The precious pen-knife, gleaming in the sun, against that bit of useless iron! There was something wrong somewhere. After a moment the practical-minded boy made yet another proposal.

"Well, if you don't want the sling, shall I give you my knuckle-bones? You know what my knucklebones are like? They're almost new."

"I don't need your knucklebones either," Davidov replied, sighing and laughing at once. "Now, if it had been twenty years or so ago I should never have refused your knucklebones, brother. I'd have stripped you of them. But you needn't worry, Fiodot Demidovich. The knife is yours for ever and ever. That's a fact."

So there was silence once more. But a few moments later Fiodot asked: "Daddy, that round thing I gave you, what's it for? Is it off a winnowing machine?"

"Why, where did you find it?"

"In the shed we're going to, under a winnowing machine. There's a very old machine there, it's all in bits, and I was under it. We were playing hide and seek; I crawled under the machine to hide, and found it lying there and picked it up."

"Then it must have been a bit of the winnowing machine. But didn't you notice any little iron peg close by it?"

"No, there was nothing else."

"Well," Davidov thought, "thank God there wasn't, or you'd have done something to me that wouldn't have got straightened out even in the next world."

"But do you need that bit of the machine very much?" Fiodot asked with interest.

"Very much indeed."

"Is it wanted for another machine?"

"Well, yes."

After another brief pause Fiodot said in a deep voice: "If you need it for farming, then you needn't be sorry, you were right to swap the knife for it, and you can buy a new knife." Sagacious beyond his years, the boy smiled contentedly. Evidently he no longer felt any qualms.

By this time Davidov knew almost beyond doubt where Fiodot was taking him. When down an alley they saw the house and sheds which once had belonged to old Damaskov, Ragged Timofei's father, he asked, pointing to the reed-thatched shed:

"Did you find it there?"

"How did you guess, Daddy?" the boy asked in admiration, and let go of Davidov's finger. "Now you can get there without me, and I'll go back; I'm terribly pressed for time."

Shaking his hand as if he were a grownup, Davidov said: "Thank you, Fiodot Demidovich, for bringing me to the right place. Come and see me some time; I shall miss you. I live all alone. . . ."

"All right, I'll drop in some time," Fiodot promised in a condescending tone. Turning round sharply, he whistled with two fingers in his mouth, evidently to summon his friends, and dashed off at such a pace that all Davidov could see in the cloud of dust he raised was a pair of dirty black heels.

Davidov did not bother to go on the Damaskovs' yard, but went back to the collective-farm office. In the shady room where the management committee usually held its meetings Yakov Lukich and the storekeeper were playing draughts. He sat down at the table and wrote on a sheet torn from his notebook: "To the manager, Y. L. Ostrovnov: Please supply the teacher L. S. Popova with 32 kilos of ground wheat, 8 kilos of millet, 5 kilos of lard, and charge these against my labour days." After signing the note he rested his chin on his fist, and sat thoughtfully silent. But at last he asked Ostrovnov:

"How does that girl, the teacher Liudmila Popova, live?"

"From hand to mouth," Yakov Lukich curtly answered as he moved a draught.

"I've just been along to the school to see about repairs, and I took a look at the teacher too. She's so thin you can almost see right through her, just like an autumn leaf. She obviously doesn't have enough to eat. See that all the items I've written down here are sent to her landlady today. I'll check up on it tomorrow. D'you hear?"

He left the note on the table, and went straight out to go and find Shaly.

As soon as he had gone, Yakov Lukich jumbled the draughts

together on the board and pointed across his shoulder at the
door. "What a dog he is! First Lushka Nagulnova, then he turns
the head of Varia Kharlamova, and now he's making up to the
teacher. . . . And he has all his bitches fed at the cost of the
collective farm. He'll ruin our husbandry: it'll all go on his
women."

"He hasn't allocated anything to Kharlamova, and he's given
these items to the teacher against his own account," the storekeeper objected.

But Yakov Lukich smiled condescendingly. "I expect he ar-
ranges things with Varia in cash, and what the teacher receives,
the collective farm will have to pay for. And how much food did
I have to take to Lushka on his secret orders? That's the point!"

Down to the day of Timofei's death Yakov Lukich had supplied
him and Lukeria with ample food from the collective-farm stores,
but he had told the storekeeper: "Davidov's given me strict
orders to issue as much food to Nagulnova as she needs, and he's
threatened me: 'If you or the storekeeper utter one word it'll be
Siberia for both of you.' So you'd better keep a still tongue in
your head, my friend. Hand out lard, honey, and flour without
weighing them on the scales. It's not for you or me to judge our
bosses."

So the storekeeper had issued all the food Ostrovnov demanded, and, taking his advice, had issued less to the brigadiers
in order to conceal the deficiency.

Bored with nothing to do, Ostrovnov and the storekeeper sat
gossiping about Davidov, Nagulnov, and Razmiotnov for some
time. But meanwhile Davidov and Shaly were already hard at
work: to let more light into Damaskov's shed, Davidov climbed
on to the roof, dug the thatch away from between two of the
rafters with a fork, and called down:

"Can you see better now?"

"You've spoilt the roof quite enough. It's as light in here now as
outside," Shaly called back from inside the shed.

Davidov lightly jumped down to the soft, dungy floor. "Where
shall we begin, Sidorovich?" he asked.

"Good dancers always start their dance from the stove, but
you and I have got to start our search from the wall," the old
smith boomed.

Picking up the two stout, pointed crowbars they had swiftly made in the smithy, they walked side by side along the wall, thrusting the points into the ground, slowly moving towards the winnowing machine, which was standing by the farther wall. They were still several paces away from it when Davidov's crowbar sank into the ground almost up to his hands, and rang hollowly as it struck some metal object.

"It looks as if you've found your hidden treasure," Shaly said, laughing, and picked up a spade. But Davidov seized the spade from his hands.

"Let me start, Sidorovich, I'm younger."

At the depth of three feet he began to dig round a large bundle. It was a Maxim gun carefully wrapped in oiled canvas. They hauled it out of the hole, silently unwrapped the canvas, silently looked at each other, and silently lit cigarettes. After a couple of draws Shaly remarked:

"So they intended to give the Soviet government a good shaking up!"

"Look how efficiently they packed the Maxim: there's not a speck of rust on it; you could start firing it at once. But I'll search further, we may find something else before we're finished."

Within half an hour he had carefully set out round the edge of the hole four cases of machine-gun belts, a rifle, a box of rifle cartridges not quite full, and eight hand grenades complete with firing pins, wrapped in a half-rotten piece of oilskin. There was also an empty, home-made wooden case in the hole. Judging by its length, it had been used as a rifle case.

By sundown the two men had carried the machine gun to the smithy and had taken it to pieces, had thoroughly cleaned and oiled it. And in the twilight, in the gentle evening stillness the inhabitants of Gremyachy heard a machine gun militantly, menacingly rattling away outside the village. One long burst, two short, then one long. Then silence fell once more over the village and the steppe, at rest after the heat of the day and spicily smelling of wilted grass and warmed black earth.

Davidov scrambled up from behind the gun and said quietly: "A good machine! A damned good machine!"

"We'll go along to Ostrovnov's place at once," Shaly began, and his tone sounded furious. "We'll take out crowbars and

sound his yard and all round it. We'll make a thorough search of
his house too; we'll find out all about him."

"You're crazy, old man," Davidov replied coldly. "Who's going
to give us permission to make arbitrary searches and alarm all
the village? Really, you're crazy, that's a fact."

"We've found a machine gun in Timofei's place, so you can
bet your life we'd find a six-inch gun somewhere in Ostrovnov's
threshing floor. It's not me that's crazy; you're proving a wise sort
of fool, I tell you straight! Wait till the day when Lukich digs up
his cannon. When he opens fire on your house at point-blank
range that'll be a fact for you!"

Davidov roared with laughter and tried to embrace the old
smith. But Shaly turned sharply on his heel, spat with the utmost concentration, and, muttering curses as he went, strode off
to the village without saying good-bye.

Chapter 18

Recently old Shchukar had struck a really unlucky patch;
though to tell the truth he was always unlucky. But that day
seemed to consist entirely of little and big upsets and misfortunes,
so that by the end of it, completely worn out with his trials, he
grew more superstitious than ever. He should never have been in
such a hurry to agree with Davidov and to venture on this drive
to the district, seeing that all the signs had been so unfavourable
from the very beginning.

He drove the stallions at a walking pace no farther than two
blocks from the collective-farm office, then halted in the middle
of the road and sat hunched glumly in the driver's seat, frozen
into a profound meditation. He surely had something to meditate
over. "Before I woke up I dreamed a speckled wolf was chasing
me. But why was it speckled? And why did it have to pick on
me to chase? Isn't there anybody else in all this wide world?
When I woke up my heart was thumping so hard it all but
jumped out of my chest; great joy I had of such a pleasant dream,

damn it! And, besides, why had that wolf got to be speckled and not a natural grey? Is that a good sign, I ask you? That's the point, of course it isn't. It's a bad sign, and no good will come of this journey; I'm sure to fall in with a bad lot. And what happened when I did get up? First I couldn't find my cap, then my pouch, then my coat. And those aren't very good signs either. I shouldn't have given way to Davidov, and I oughtn't to have set out at all." He moodily turned over his woes as he gazed abstractedly along the empty street at the calves lying about in the shade of the fences, and the sparrows having dust baths in the road.

He almost made up his mind to turn back, but he recalled a clash he had had recently with Davidov, and thought better of it. Depressed by evil omens, just as he was today, he had flatly refused to drive out to the first brigade, justifying his refusal by the bad dream he had had. And suddenly Davidov's good-natured, even kindly eyes had darkened, had turned cold and prickly. Shchukar had taken fright, and, blinking imploringly, had said: "Siemion, my old friend! Do get those sparks out of your eyes. They've gone like those of a chained dog, all wicked and sharp. And you know what little respect I have for those damned insects that sit on the end of chains and bark and howl at good folk. Why should you and I cross one another? I'll go out, blast you, as you're so contrary and determined. But if anything happens to us on the road I won't answer for it."

Davidov had laughed as he listened to the old man, and for a moment his eyes had lit up with kindly merriment as in the past. He had slapped Shchukar's withered and hollow-sounding back with a heavy hand, and had said: "Now, that's something like talking, that's a fact. Let's go, old man. I'll answer to your old woman for your perfect safety, and you needn't worry about me."

As he recalled this incident Shchukar smiled and, hesitating no longer, slapped the reins down over the stallions' backs. "I'll drive to the district. To hell with those signs! If anything happens, let Davidov take the responsibility. He's good to me, there's no point in my upsetting him."

A pungent smoke from the dung bricks used in the early-morning cooking still hung about the village, a gentle breeze

stirred the insipid scent of flowering orach along the road, and
from the cattle yards came the long familiar smell of cow dung
and fresh milk. Screwing up his weak eyes, stroking his little
straggly beard with his habitual gesture, the old man looked
around him, at all the dear sights of the simple village life, and
for one moment, overcoming his torpor, he even waved his
knout to drive a flock of squabbling sparrows from under the
drozhki wheels. But as he drove past the yard of Antip Grach he
caught the smell of freshly baked bread, the titillating aroma of
the scorching cabbage leaves on which the Gremyachy women
were in the habit of laying their loaves for baking, and suddenly
remembered that he had not eaten anything since yesterday
noon. He felt so hungry that his toothless mouth filled with spittle, and he had an unpleasant sucking feeling in the pit of his
stomach.

Turning the horses sharply into an alley, he drove them back
to his yard, intending to have something to eat before his journey. He was still some distance away when he noticed that no
smoke was coming from the chimney of his hut, and he thought
with a satisfied smile: "The old woman's finished cooking and
now she's having a rest. When I'm not around she lives just like a
grand duchess. No sorrows for her, nor any sighing and groaning."

It took very little for Shchukar to pass from discontented and
sorrowful meditations straight to a feeling of benevolent self-
satisfaction. Lazily shaking out the reins, he reflected: "And why
is she able to live like that, like a bird of heaven? That's clear
enough: it's because of me. It wasn't without good reason that I
slaughtered the calf last winter. God knows it wasn't. Look how
easy my old woman finds life! She's finished cooking and now
she's having a rest. But if the calf had been allowed to grow into
a cow she'd have been up at dawn, milking the damned animal,
driving her out to join the herd, and during the day the cow
would start bellowing and rush about to get away from the flies,
and then turn up at home like a lover. Drive her out again, and
get fodder ready for her for the winter, and clean the yard for
her, and thatch her shed with reeds or straw. . . . One long
grind! I've got rid of all our lambs too, and that was even more
sensible. Drive them out to pasture and worry and worry about

them, damn them! They might wander away from the flock, or a
wolf might carry them off. And it's not in my nature to worry my
soul over such filth. I've had enough illness as it is in my long
life, and I expect my soul's all in holes, like an old leg-rag. We
haven't any pigs either, and that's another blessing. I ask you,
what the devil use would a pig have been to me? To begin
with, I can't eat lard because it gives me heartburn if I eat too
much; and then, what could I have fed it on, seeing as I haven't
more than a couple of handfuls of flour in stock? The pig
would have died of starvation and would have wrung my soul
with its squealing. And then a pig makes the whole yard stink,
you just can't breathe. But now I've got good air all round me,
the scent of grass, of fruit in the orchard, and the wild hemp. I
love good clean air, sinful man that I am. I've got two clean
little hens roving about the yard and a well-behaved little cock
with them, and that's enough livestock for me and my old woman
at our time of life. Let the young grow rich: so much wealth
doesn't mean anything to us. And Makar approves of me and
says: 'You've become a pure proletariat, Daddy, and you've done
well to give up your petty property.' But I reply with a sincere
sigh: 'Maybe it's pleasant to be regarded as a proletariat, but I'm
not agreeable to spending all my life on only kvass and thin cabbage soup. God be with the proletariat, but if they don't give us
meat or lard, say, for our labour days, to give some flavour to
the soup, then I may quite easily turn up my toes by the time
winter comes. And then what good will it be to call myself a
proletariat? I'll see by the autumn how my labour days work
out, and if they're not good enough I'll go back to petty property again.' "

He thoughtfully narrowed his eyes and said aloud: "Everything's going a new way, but it's sort of difficult to understand it
with its twists, like a good dancer. . . ."

He tied up the stallions to the fence, opened the rickety wicket
gate, and, with the slow and measured gait of the true master,
went along the path, which was overgrown with plantains, to the
veranda.

The kitchen was half in darkness; the door to the bedroom was
closed. He laid his greasy, pancake-flat cap down on the bench,
and beside it the knout he always kept with him in case he fell

in with Trofim, looked around, and called out (after all, you never know!): "Old woman! Are you alive?"

From the bedroom came a feeble voice. "Only just. . . . I've been lying here since last evening. I can't lift my head. I'm aching all over, I've no strength left, and I'm so cold I can't get warm even under the sheepskin. I think I must have relapsing fever. But what have you turned up for, old man?"

"I'm just off to the district. I dropped in to have a bite of food for the road."

"What are you going to the district for?"

Assuming an important air, he stroked his beard and replied with feigned reluctance: "I've been given an important commission; I'm driving to see the land surveyor. Comrade Davidov says: 'If you don't bring him back here, old man, you needn't bring anyone else back, except yourself.'" In a businesslike tone he added: "Get me something to eat. Time won't wait."

His old wife groaned even more wretchedly. "Oh, my dearest dear! What can I give you to eat? I haven't done any cooking today and haven't lit the stove. Go and pick some cucumbers in the garden; and there's some sour milk in the cellar. Our neighbour brought it along yesterday."

Shchukar listened to his spouse with undisguised contempt, and snorted indignantly. "Raw cucumbers, and sour milk on top of them! You're clean out of your wits, you old astrolabe. D'you want me to lose all my authority? You know very well I'm terribly weak in the stomach; after such a meal I'd be completely upset on the road. And then how could I get to the district? Carry my trousers in my hands? And I can't leave the stallions for a single moment, so what else could I do? Lose all my authority right in the street? Thank you most humbly. You eat the cucumbers yourself and push them down with sour milk, I'm not going to chance it! My position's not one to sneeze at. I drive Comrade Davidov himself around, and it's not fitting that I should risk your cucumbers. Get that, you old approbation?"

The ancient wooden bedstead creaked suspiciously, and the sound put Shchukar on his guard at once. Before he had time to finish his harangue an astonishing transformation took place in his old woman: filled with indignation and resolution, she nimbly jumped out of bed and set her arms akimbo. Her feeble

voice took on an almost metallic note as, savagely pulling her crumpled kerchief to one side of her head, she cried:

"And what else did you expect, you old block? Cabbage soup with meat in it? Or possibly you fancied some pancakes with clotted cream? Where am I to get it all from, when you've nothing in the larder but mice, and even they are dying of hunger? And how long d'you intend to go on insulting me with all sorts of impossible words? How am I an astrolabe and an approbation? Makar Nagulnov's taught you to read all sorts of unnecessary books, but do you get any joy out of it, you fool? I'm an honest wife and all my years of womanhood I've lived honestly with you, you unwiped snot; and yet in your old age you don't know how to speak to me properly."

Matters were taking an unexpected and ominous turn, so Shchukar decided to retreat into the middle of the kitchen. Falling back briskly, he said in a conciliatory tone: "Well, that's enough, that's enough, old woman. Those words aren't insulting in the least, they're sort of loving words, only in an educated way. It's all the same whether I call you my dear soul or an astrolabe. When we talk simply we say 'my dear little dear,' but when we talk like books it becomes 'approbation.' By God, I'm not lying, that's what it says in a thick book Makar gave me to read. I read it with my own eyes. You learn like I'm learning, and then you'll be saying all sorts of words just as well as me, that's a fact."

There was such a note of conviction in his voice that the old woman was mollified. Still staring at him inquisitively, she sighed. "It's rather late for me to start learning, and there's no point in it either. You'd do well to talk in your own native language too, you old polecat. As it is, the people laugh at you and think you're a big fool."

"The people laugh at anything," Shchukar said loftily; but he did not bother to argue any more.

He thoroughly crumbled a piece of stale bread into a small plate of sour milk and ate slowly, earnestly, gazing out of the window and thinking: "Why the hell should I hurry to the district? Just when a man's got it in mind to die and he ought to be washed and churched, then he has to start hurrying. But Shportnoi's not a priest, he's a land surveyor, and Davidov has no intention of dying, so why the devil should I work myself into a

fever? We'll all be in time for the next world; nobody's ever had
to stand in the line for death yet. So I'll drive out of the village,
turn into some quiet ravine where no devil can see me, and
sleep as long as I feel like it, and the stallions can have a good
feed of grass. In the late afternoon I'll drive to Dubtsiev's brigade, Kuprianovna will give me some supper, and I'll go on to the
district through the night, when it's cool. And if Davidov finds out
about it, which God forbid, I'll tell him straight out: 'Annihilate
that thrice-damned goat of yours, and then I shan't need to
sleep on the road. He fidgets all night in the hay all around me,
and how can I sleep then? It's one long disturbance.'"

Cheering up at the pleasant prospect of calling on Dubtsiev,
he smiled. But his old woman at once managed to spoil his good
humour.

"What are you chewing like that for, as if you were paralytic?
You've been sent to the district, so don't paw around here like a
beetle in dung, but drive off quick. And get those stupid bookish
words out of your head and never say them to me again, or a
stick will dance over your back, I tell you straight, you old fool!"

"Every stick has two ends," Shchukar muttered incoherently.
But, noticing the angry frown on the face of his sovereign lady,
he hastily gulped down the milk and said good-bye. "You go and
lie down, my dear; don't get up if it isn't necessary; you be ill as
much as you like and may it do you good. I'm off."

She despatched him not very graciously with "God be with
you!" and turned her back.

For some six kilometres he drove at a walking pace, dozing
pleasantly, picking his nose from time to time. Once, completely
worn out with the noonday heat, he dozed right off and all but
fell out of the drozhki. "If I go on like this I'll be falling on my
head before long," he ruminated anxiously, and turned into a
ravine.

In the depths of the ravine the scented grass stood waist high.
A little stream fed by a spring ran down from the head of the
valley along a clayey channel. The water was clear, and so cold
that even the stallions drank it only in small and rare sips,
cautiously sucking it through their teeth. It was very cool down

by the stream, and the sun high above was unable to warm the
spot properly. "Perfect bliss!" Shchukar whispered, unharnessing
the stallions. He hobbled them, turned them loose to graze, laid
his old coat down in the shadow of a thorn bush, and turned on
his back. Gazing up at the blue sky, almost a toneless white with
the heat, he gave himself over to worldly dreams.

"You couldn't cheat me out of this luxury even with a pin before the evening. I'll sleep my fill, warm my old bones in the
sun, and then drive off to Dubtsiev's to have some supper. I'll
tell him I didn't have time to eat at home, and then they're sure
to feed me, I'll stake my head on that. Dubtsiev's not the sort
of lad to fast when he's mowing. He's such a freckled rogue, he
wouldn't last one day without meat. He'd steal a sheep from
someone else's flock to feed his mowers. It wouldn't be at all
bad to tackle a piece of lamb, about four pounds of meat, say,
for supper. Especially if it was roasted with fat, or, if there's
nothing else, scrambled egg with lard, only there must be as
much as you can eat. Dumplings with cream's another holy dish,
better than any sacrament, especially when they put plenty of
them on your plate, and then a second large helping, and you
gently shake the plate so as the cream can get to the bottom, and
every dumpling's covered from head to foot."

Old Shchukar had never really been a man for belly worship;
it was simply that he was hungry. During his long and joyless life
he had rarely eaten his fill, and only in his dreams did he gorge
on all sorts of tasty dishes, as he thought them. He would dream
he was eating boiled tripe chitterlings, or rolling an enormous
pitted pancake into a tube and, soaking it in broth, transferring
it to his mouth; or, burning his mouth in his haste, he would eat
endless quantities of noodles soaked in broth with goose giblets.
There was little he did not dream of during the night, which is
always long for a hungry man; but after these dreams he woke
up depressed and sometimes even ill-tempered, and said to himself: "Dreams like that are no good whatever. They're just a
mockery. You have a good time in your sleep, you cook so much
noodles you can't finish them all, but then your old woman
pushes cold kvass soup under your nose!"

After such dreams he quietly licked his dry lips till breakfast-
time arrived, and during his miserable meal he sighed bitterly,

handling his spoon sluggishly, abstractedly chasing pieces of potato round the plate.

As he lay under the bush he wondered what there might be for supper in the brigade, then remembered rather ineptly how he had guzzled at the wake for Yakov Lukich's mother. Completely soured with thoughts of the food he had eaten, he suddenly felt such a sharp pang of hunger that his drowsiness passed in an instant, and he spat furiously, wiped his beard, and felt his sunken belly. He said aloud:

"A little bit of bread and a small mug of sour milk: is that a meal fit for a male producer? It's not food, it's wind. An hour ago my belly was as tight as a gypsy's drum, but feel it now! It's right bang up against my backbone. Oh, my dear Lord God! And you spend all your life thinking of a bit of bread and how to fill your belly, but life flows by like water through your fingers, and you don't notice that it's drawing to its end. How long is it since I was in this ravine last? The thorn bushes were in full flower then; the whole of the ravine was filled with their foaming white. When the wind blew, the white, scented flowers flew all over the place, circling like snow in a heavy snowstorm. All the road down the ravine was covered with white. But now the spring colours have faded and vanished; they've perished once and for all. My wretched life has gone black just like them, and soon now old Shchukar will have to fling his worn hoofs out in all directions; there's nothing you can do about it."

And that was the end of his lyrical, philosophical meditations. He was filled with pity for himself, he whimpered a little, sniffed and blew his nose, wiped his reddened eyes with his shirt sleeve, and began to doze off. Mournful thoughts always sent him to sleep.

The heat was at its most intense about three o'clock. A dry, hot wind blowing from the east carried burning air into the ravine, and soon no trace was left of the recent cool. As the sun hastened westward it seemed bent on pursuing Shchukar. He slept lying on his belly, his face buried in his rolled coat; and as soon as the sun struck through his ragged shirt and burned his thin body he shifted, still half asleep, into the shade. But in a few minutes the pestiferous sun was again burning his old back mercilessly, and he had to crawl on his belly to another spot. For three hours he

crawled round a good half of the little bush, without once fully
waking up. At last, tormented by the heat, swollen and wet
with sweat, he woke up, sat up, looked up at the sun from under
his palm, and thought indignantly: "There's the divine eye. Lord
forgive me! And you can't get away from it even under a bush.
It's made me circle like a hare round this bush for half the day.
And is that what you'd call a sleep? It's not sleep, it's absolute
punishment. I should have lain down under the drozhki; but even
there that demon eye would have sought me out."

Grunting and panting, he deliberately took off his worn shoes,
rolled up his trousers, and sat staring at his swollen feet, smiling
critically and mournfully shaking his head. Then he made his
way down to the stream to wash and cool his burning face with
the ice-cold water.

From that moment a string of mishaps began to plague his
life.

Raising his feet high, he picked his way over the low-growing
reeds towards the clear water in the middle. But he had not gone
far when he felt something slippery, shifting and cold, crushed
under the sole of his left foot, and he felt a gentle prick just
above his ankle. With a nimbleness unnatural to him he tore his
left foot out of the water and remained standing on his right,
like a crane in the middle of a marsh. But when he saw the
reeds to the left of him stirring and a winding track running
swiftly through them his face went green, the same colour as the
reeds, and his eyes slowly began to goggle.

Where did the old man get all his energy from? It was just
as though his long-past youth had returned: in two bounds he
was back on the bank. Sitting down on a clayey mound, he began to examine two tiny red spots on his foot, from time to time
glancing terror-stricken at the ill-omened stream.

Gradually, as his first terror passed, he recovered his ability to
think, and he whispered quietly: "Well, glory be, so it's beginning. . . . So that's what they indicated, those damned omens!
I told that stupid-head Davidov I oughtn't to risk driving to the
district today. But no, he says 'Get in and drive off.' And I've
driven right into it! He often says: 'I'm working class.' But why is
the working class always in such a hurry? If he plans to do something, you can be sure he won't let you get away without gain-

ing his end. He's gained it all right this time, the son of a bitch. Now what am I to do?"

But he suddenly had a brain-storm. "I must suck the blood from the wounds at once. Some poisonous reptile has bitten me; look how it slipped away through the sedges. A good-sized snake or maybe a grass snake; though that crawls along without hurrying, slowly, while this reptile went like lightning, it wriggled so fast. That's why it frightened me. But that's just it: who frightened who the more: me it or it me?"

There was no time to settle that complicated problem: time wouldn't wait. But with all his struggling he could not reach the spots with his lips. Holding his heel and sole with both hands, he pulled his foot towards himself with such desperate zeal that something gave a sharp crack at the ankle, and he fell over on his back with the terrible pain. For a good five minutes he lay without stirring. Coming to himself, gently feeling his left foot with his fingers, he ruminated in utter bewilderment: "It began with a bite, but it hasn't stopped there. . . . For the first time in my life I learn that a man can dislocate his own leg of his own will. Tell anybody a story like that and they wouldn't believe you. They'd say: 'Shchukar's lying again.' There's the omens for you! How far will they go? Now what am I to do? How can I harness up the stallions?"

Yet he could delay no longer. He gently got on to his feet and cautiously tried to put his left foot down. To his great joy the pain was no longer so violent, and he could move, though with difficulty. Breaking up a small piece of clay in his hands, he mixed it with spittle, thoroughly anointed the red spots, and was about to limp across to the stallions, putting his left foot down gingerly, when on the farther side of the stream, some four yards away, he saw something which made his eyes burn and his lips quiver with uncontrollable fury. Rolled into a ball, a small hedgehog was peacefully sleeping on a hummock. There could be no doubt that it was a hedgehog: orange-yellow "eyes" glowed in its head.

At the sight Shchukar went mad. His language reached a degree of pathetic indignation that surpassed all he had ever achieved before. Thrusting his damaged foot forward and solemnly stretching out his hand, he said in a quivering voice:

"You accursed crawler! You cold-blooded scum! You plague with yellow eyes! So it was you, you harmful insect, that frightened me to death! Me, a male producer! And in my stupidity I thought it was a real reptile. But what are you in fact? A crawling filth, a pah, that's all! Tread on you with my foot once more and crush you into smoke and dust, and there'd be nothing left of you. If I hadn't dislocated my foot through you, you asp, that's just what I would do with you, bear that in mind."

He took a breath and swallowed his spittle. Raising its pointed, marble, black little head, the hedgehog seemed to be listening attentively to the first speech that had ever been addressed to it. After a rest, the old man went on.

"You're goggling your shameless eyes and not even blinking, you unclean spirit! You think you'll get away with it, do you? You won't, you know; you'll get something from me in a minute that'll make you regret this labour day of yours. To think such an adaptor has turned up! I'll deal with you so that nothing but enfilades are left of you, and that's a fact."

He turned his angry gaze downward, and saw a large stone among the fine shingle brought down by the spring water from the upper reaches of the ravine. He picked it up and, forgetting the pain in his foot, strode boldly forward. A sharp pain pierced his ankle, and he fell over on his side, swearing quite unnecessarily, but still clutching the stone.

When, groaning and sighing, he got on his feet again, the hedgehog had vanished. As though it had never been. It seemed to have fallen into the ground. He threw away the stone and flung out his hands in bewilderment.

"Well, I never—where could he have got to, the anti-Christ? He must have slipped into the water again. Well, this isn't to be my lucky day, it just isn't. I shouldn't have got involved in conversation with it, old fool that I am. I should have picked up the stone without saying a word and knocked it first time on the head. But who am I to hit now he's got away, the unclean spirit? That's the question."

For a minute or two longer he stood by the stream, scratching his nape, then he hopelessly dismissed it all with his hand. Until he had gone a good distance from the stream he looked back once or twice, just in case. . . .

Beneath the wind the steppe breathed powerfully and measured with all its spacious breast, exhaling the intoxicating and always rather mournful aroma of mown grass. From the oak copses at the roadside came the cool, dead, but stimulating scent of rotting oak leaves. But for some reason the last-year leaves fallen from an ash smelt of youth, spring, and perhaps just a touch of violets. And for some reason this mingling of different scents always rather depresses ordinary man, it troubles him rather deeply, especially when he is left alone with himself. . . . But old Shchukar was not that sort of man. Making his painful leg comfortable, stretching it out on his rolled-up coat, and letting his right hang negligently over the drozhki side, he smiled broadly with his toothless mouth, contentedly screwing up his faded eyes; and his small, peeling red nose quivered as it greedily sniffed the native scents of its native steppe.

On the crest of the rise, the moment the field hut and the camp of the second brigade came in sight, he halted the lazily trotting horses and climbed out of the drozhki. He still had that dull, gnawing pain in his ankle, but he could stand on both feet more or less firmly, and he decided: "I'll show them it isn't any old water-carrier that's coming, but the coachman to the collective-farm administration. Seeing as I'm the driver for Comrades Davidov, Makar, and other important bosses, I must drive up in such a style that the people will feel envious when they see me coming."

Swearing and groaning miserably, soothing the horses, who scented their stand for the night, he rose to his full height in the drozhki, planting his feet wide apart; then he pulled hard on the reins and whooped youthfully. The stallions broke into a swinging trot. Down the slope they steadily gained speed and mettle, and before long the contrary wind was making Shchukar's shirt billow out behind him like a balloon. But he called on the horses to go faster and faster, and, frowning with the pain in his foot but merrily waving the knout, he shouted in his cracked voice: "My darlings, don't slacken your pace!"

Agafon Dubtsiev, who was in the camp, was the first to notice him coming, and remarked: "Who is that devil driving like a Tauride Tartar, standing up? Look, Pryanishnikov, who's that coming out to visit us?"

From the half-stacked rick Pryanishnikov shouted cheerfully: "It's the propaganda brigade coming: it's old Shchukar."

"He couldn't have been more welcome!" Dubtsiev said, smiling satisfiedly. "We were all going sour with boredom. The old man will stay and have supper with us. And let's agree on this, boys: we won't let him go all night."

He hauled the sack containing his personal belongings from under the cart, rummaged in it, and took out a bottle of vodka to put in his pocket.

Chapter 19

After emptying a second plate of thin wheaten gruel only poorly larded with fat, Shchukar was in a state of perfect content and gentle drowsiness. Giving the generous cook a grateful look, he said: "Thank you, all of you, for your food and vodka, and a low bow to you, Mrs. Kuprianovna. If you want my opinion, you're not a woman, you're a chest filled with gold. With your gift for cooking gruel you shouldn't be cooking for these clods but for Mikhail Kalinin himself. By God, I'm not lying. I know very well what is the main thing in life. . . ."

"Then, what is it?" Dubtsiev, who was sitting next to him, asked eagerly. "What is the main thing, Daddy, to your way of thinking?"

"Eating. I tell you as a fact that it's eating, there's no other main thing whatever."

"You're wrong, Daddy," Dubtsiev said mournfully, looking sidelong with his gypsy eyes at the others and keeping a very straight face. "You're absolutely wrong, and it's all because in your old age your little mind's grown as thin as the gruel you've just eaten. Your brain's gone watery."

Shchukar smiled condescendingly. "It isn't clear yet whose mind's the more crazed, yours or mine. But what do you think is the main thing in life?"

"Love!" Dubtsiev sighed rather than said, and rolled his eyes

so dreamily that Kuprianovna snorted as loud as a horse scenting rain, and, shaking like jelly, covered her crimson face with her jacket sleeve.

"Ha! Love!" Shchukar smiled contemptuously. "But how much is it worth, that love of yours, without good vittles? Pfooh! That's all there is to it. Keep you without food for a week and then your own wife would have nothing to do with you."

Dubtsiev held his ground obstinately. "That's what you say."

"There's nothing to argue about. I know it all in advance down to the last letter," Shchukar snapped back, and raised an admonishing finger. "I'll tell you a story, and then you'll see it all clearly and there won't be any need for further argument."

Old Shchukar had rarely had such attentive listeners. Some thirty people were sitting round the campfire, and they were all afraid of missing a single word. So at least he thought. And so, feeling in a very happy frame of mind after his supper, he was determined to talk to his heart's content. He seated himself more comfortably, crossed his legs under him like a Turk, stroked his little beard with his hand, and had just opened his mouth to begin his deliberate narrative when Dubtsiev forestalled him, saying with exaggerated sternness:

"You tell your story, Daddy, but let's have no lies! In our brigade we've got a habit of whipping liars with reins."

The old man sighed deeply, and stroked his left leg with his hand. "Don't try to frighten me, Agafon. I've already been frightened to death once today. Well, this is how it was. Last spring Davidov sends for me and says: 'Get two measures of oats from the storekeeper, get rations for yourself, and gallop with the stallions straight to the end of the Dry Valley. Our mares are out at pasture there, and you're to present yourself to them with your bridegrooms. Deaf old Vassily Babkin's the drover. Divide the drove into two. Vassily will take one and you the other. But remember, you'll be responsible for the producers: feed them up well with oats.' I have to admit that I didn't know what a producer was, I'd never heard the word before. And so I had to ask. I know 'stallion,' I know 'mare,' and of course I know what a gelding is. So I ask: 'But what's a producer?' He answers: 'The one that produces a family, he's a producer.' I ask again: 'And can a bull be called a producer too?' He frowned and said: 'Of

course.' I go on asking: 'But are you and I producers?' He
laughed and said: 'That's a question, Daddy, each must answer
for himself.' I ask him again: 'But the man who produces grain,
is he a producer or what?' But he sighed and said: 'You're
backward, old man.' To which I told him: 'It's more likely that
you're backward, Siemion, because I was born forty years before
you, and you've lagged behind.' And there we stopped."

Kuprianovna asked him in a hissing whisper: "So you're a producer too, are you, Daddy?"

"Well, what do you think I am?" Shchukar answered proudly.

"Oh, Lord!" she groaned and could say no more, for she buried
her face in her apron; only her suppressed chuckle was to be
heard.

"Don't take any notice of her, Daddy, you just carry on," Kondrat Maidannikov said graciously.

"I've never paid any attention to women all my life," the old
man answered confidently. "If I had I mightn't have lived to
such a ripe old age.

"Well," he went on, "I arrived at the drove, looked around me,
and couldn't feast my eyes enough. All around was such an
agiotage that I could have stayed in that spot all the rest of my
life. Blue flowers blossoming all over the steppe, young grass, the
mares grazing, the sun warming . . . in a word, it was an absolute agiotage."

"What was that word you said?" Beskhlebnov asked interestedly.

"You mean 'agiotage'? Well, it means when there's beauty all
around you. It means to live and rejoice in the wide world, and
there's no sorrow for you to suffer, nor lamenting. It's an educated
word," he replied with unshakable confidence.

"But where did you pick it up?" the inquisitive Beskhlebnov
asked.

"I got it from Makar Nagulnov. Him and me are great friends,
and he learns English every night, and I sit with him. He's given
me a book as fat as Kuprianovna, and it's called a dictionary. He
gives it to me and says: 'You study, old man, you'll find it useful
in your old age.' And so I'm learning little by little. But don't
interrupt me, Akim, or you'll knock the thoughts right out of my
head. And so I arrive at the pasture with my producers; but

nothing came of it, neither from my producers nor from the agio-tage. I tell you, good folk: anyone who doesn't know deaf Vaska will live an unnecessary ten years longer.

"He's such a block that compared with him Diemid the Silent's the most talkative man in all Gremyachy Log. The torture I suf-fered through Vaska's silence out in the steppe! I couldn't talk to the mares, could I? But Vaska would say nothing for days on end; he only chewed noisily, and the rest of the time he'd either sit silent or lie under a horse-cloth like a rotten log and say nothing. That was the problem he set me, and I couldn't solve it. In a word, the three days I spent there was like living in a cemetery as a guest of the corpses, and I even began to talk to myself. Ah, I thought, nothing will come of this. Before long a sociable fellow like me will be mental.

"It wouldn't have been half so bad if Vaska'd only been con-tent to be silent; but he turned out to be such a glutton that there was no keeping up with him. We cooked gruel or sour-dough dumplings, and what happened? He'd put his spoon into the pot five times while I was putting mine in once. He worked away with his enormous spoon like the piston of a steam engine: back-ward and forward, backward and forward, from the pot to his mouth, from his mouth to the pot; and before I could look twice the gruel would be down to the bottom of the pot. I'd get up hungry, but he'd be swollen up like a bullock's bladder; he'd lie down belly upward and start to belch all over the steppe. He'd belch for a good couple of hours, the unclean demon, and then he'd start snoring. And he snored so hard that even the mares grazing close by took fright and fled. He'd sleep till nightfall as heavily as a marmot in winter.

"That's how bitter my life was those days. And as hungry as a homeless dog, and in my boredom, I'd have loved a talk, but I'd no one to talk to. The second day I sat down beside Vaska, made a trumpet with my hands, and bawled right into his ear with all my lungs: 'How did you come to be deaf: was it through the war or from scrofula when you were a kid?' But he roared back at me even louder: 'Through the war. In 1919 the Reds put down a shell from a six-inch gun on an armoured train right beside me, and I've been stone deaf ever since.' So I asked him again: 'But why do you guzzle like you do, as though you had no idea what

you were doing? Is that because of the shell too?' And he answers: 'Clouds are coming over; that's good. There'll be rain before long.' You try talking to such a baldachin. . . ."

"When are you going to start talking about love?" Dubtsiev
asked impatiently.

Shchukar frowned irritably. "Can't you think of anything but
love, be it thrice damned? I'd avoid love all my life. If my dead
father hadn't forced me to I'd never have got married at all. But
now enjoy it and judge for yourself! A fine question to ask!

"Well, I'd arrived at the appointed spot, and I'd split the drove
into two, but my bridegrooms wouldn't even look at the mares:
all they did was crop the grass without stopping. They'd got no
interest whatever in their brides. Here's a fine thing, I think. So
my producers are bringing shame on me. I give them oats in full
measure too, but they don't even glance at the mares.

"A whole day passed like that, and the following two. I began
to feel quite awkward when those poor mares were around. I
walked past them with my face turned away for shame, I couldn't
look them in the eyes. I'd never blushed before in all my life,
but now I learned how to: the moment I went up to one of the
droves to drive them down to the pond for water, I began to go
as red as any girl. . . .

"Lord, the shame I felt because of my producers during those
three days! The problem was too much for me. On the third day,
d'you know what happened before my very eyes? One young
mare began to play with one of my producers, the bay with a
star on the forehead and a white sock on his left hind leg. And
she whisks round him like a fan, turning this way and that,
and gently nuzzling him with her teeth, and showing all manner
of love for him. But he lays his ears back, closes his eyes, and
sighs so miserably. . . . There's a fine stallion for you, you
couldn't find a worse. But I shake all over with fury, and wonder
what our mares must be thinking of me. I expect they were saying: 'The old devil's brought us out a lot of yokels.'

"That poor little mare lost all patience: she turned her back
on the stallion and let fly with both her hind hoofs at his flank,
so hard his innards groaned. And I run up to him, weeping bitter
tears, and give him a drubbing with the knout over his back,

roaring: 'If you're called a producer, why do you bring shame on me in my old age?'

"He trotted off some fifty yards, then he halted and whinnied so miserably that it just made my heart ache, and I began to cry with pity for him. I went up to him and stroked his nose, and he laid his head on my shoulder and sighed. . . .

"I took him by the mane and led him back to the hut, and I told him: 'We'll go home, old boy; there's no point in our hanging about here doing nothing and bringing unnecessary shame on ourselves.' So I harnessed them up and set out for the village. But deaf Vaska bawled: 'Come again in twelve months' time, Daddy, and we'll live together in the steppe and have some more gruel. By then your stallions will have come to themselves, if they aren't dead before.'

"I arrived in the village and reported it all to Davidov; and he clutched his head and shouted at me: 'You didn't look after them properly.' But I told him: 'It wasn't that I didn't look after them properly, but you've overdriven them. The stallions are never out of the collar, and you can't get oats out of Yakov Lukich even if you go down on your bended knees. And whoever drives stallions, anyway? If they're producers they shouldn't work, they should only eat fodder, otherwise you'll never solve the problem.' And believe me: they sent out two producers from the district centre—I expect you remember them—and they solved the problem of the mares in two seconds. That's what love without the necessary vittles means. Now do you understand, you stupid lot? There's nothing to laugh at, seeing as we're having a very serious talk."

Looking round triumphantly at his audience, he went on:

"And how can you expect to have any understanding of life when you live like beetles in dung, digging in the earth all the time? But I do visit the district at least once, or even more, every week. Take you, Kuprianovna. Have you ever heard the radio talking?"

"How could I when the last time I was in the district town was ten years ago?"

"That's just the point. But I hear as much as I wish every time. It's a filthy business, I can tell you." He shook his head and

laughed quietly. "Right opposite the district-committee office there's a black trumpet hanging from a post, and, my God, how it roars! It makes your hair stand on end, and your back goes all gooseflesh even in summer. I unharnessed my stallions right by that trumpet, and at first I listened with pleasure to all about the collective farms, the working class, and various other things. But after a time I'd have been glad to put my head into a horse's nosebag full of oats. And you wouldn't believe it, good folk, but I wanted to have a drink so badly that I couldn't control myself. Sinner that I am, whenever I'm sent to the district I quietly lay my hands on as many eggs as I can get out of my old woman, and as soon as I arrive I go to the market. I sell them in the dining rooms. Then I sip my vodka, and I can wait for my Comrade Davidov all day. But if I can't manage to get hold of any eggs at home, because my old woman's learnt to watch everything I do, then I go along to the district committee, and quietly ask my Comrade Davidov: 'Siemion, my dear lad, let me have enough for a pint: it's boring waiting for you with nothing to do.' And the kindly soul never refuses, and I go off at once to the dining rooms and sip and sip, and either spit for the pleasure of it in the sun or else ask someone to keep an eye on my producers and commandeer myself off to the town to see about my business."

"But what business can you have in the town?" Akim Beskhlebnov asked.

Shchukar sighed. "Hasn't any master plenty of things to see to? A bottle of paraffin to buy, or a box or two of matches? Or it might be this way: just now you asked me about my educated words and about the dictionary. In that book there's one educated word printed in large print, and these I can manage without my glasses. But opposite it, in small letters, there's the explanation, what the word means. Well, there are lots of words I understand without any explanation. For instance, what does 'monopoly' mean? That's quite clear: it means 'a pub.' An 'adaptor' is an empty sort of man, an absolute swine, and that's all. 'Aquarelle' is a good girl, as I understand it, but a 'bordure's' just the reverse, she's nothing but a hussy who spins 'entresols.' But all the same I needed my glasses. So when I went with Davidov to the district I planned to buy myself a pair of spectacles. My old woman let me have some money for that.

"I go into one hospital, but I found it wasn't a hospital at all, but a maternity home. In one room women were groaning and crying in every tone imaginable; in another babies were miaowing like little kittens. I shan't get spectacles here, I think to myself; this isn't the place for me. I go to another hospital, and there two men were sitting on the veranda playing chess. I asked them: 'Where can I buy glasses here?' They snorted with laughter and one of them says: 'The glasses you'd get here, old boy, would make your eyes drop out; this is a hospital for venereal diseases. You clear off quick, or they'll start to cure you by force.'

"Of course that frightened me to death and I trotted off as fast as my legs could carry me. But those damned fools came out through the side gate after me; one of them whistled with all his might, and the other bawled for all the street to hear: 'Run quicker, you old sinner, or the infection will catch up with you.' And at that I went off like a fine trotting horse. You never know, I think to myself; the devil doesn't joke; they may overtake me while God's asleep and then you try to explain it to the doctors if you can.

"I ran as far as the chemist's and my heart thumped madly. But the chemist hadn't any glasses either. 'Drive to Millerovo or Rostov, old boy,' he told me. 'An eye doctor's the only one who can prescribe glasses for you.' Not me, I think to myself, what the hell should I go there for? I can read the dictionary by guesswork if necessary. And so the glasses business was left completely unsettled.

"But I couldn't count all the adventures I've had in the district."

"Tell it to us all in order, Daddy. You're like a sparrow, you hop from twig to twig, and nobody can tell when you begin and when you end," Dubtsiev said.

"I am telling it all in order. The main thing is that you mustn't interrupt me. If you interrupt me again I shall lose the thread completely. Well, I was going through the district town one day, when I see coming towards me a young girl as beautiful as a doe, dressed in town clothes, with a bag in her hand. She was walking on high heels and she clattered away with them, 'tippety tap, tippety tap,' like a goat with its hoofs. But in my old age I've grown so greedy for anything new that it's simply terrible. My

boys, I've even tried to ride a bicycle. I saw a lad riding the machine and I said to him: 'My dear little boy, let me have a little
ride on your machine.' He agreed with pleasure, helped me to
perch myself on the saddle, and held me up, and I worked my
legs up and down with all my strength. Then I asked him:
'Don't hold me up, for God's sake; I want to ride by myself.' But
the moment he let go of me the handlebars broke away from my
hands and I went flying straight under an acacia. I was pricked
all over by that acacia, in all sorts of necessary and unnecessary
spots. And I tore my trousers on a stump, into the bargain."

"Tell us about the girl, Daddy; we don't want to hear about
your trousers," Dubtsiev broke in sternly. "Stop and think: what
the devil are your trousers good for?"

"Now you're interrupting me again," Shchukar glumly answered. But he decided to go on none the less. "And so that dear
delightful little doe came towards me, waving her hand like a
soldier girl, and I, sinner that I am, think to myself: 'If only I
could walk a little way with her on my arm!' I've never walked
arm in arm with anybody all my life; but I've often seen the
youngsters going about like that in the district town. But I ask
you, citizens, where could I get such a pleasure? It isn't the thing
to walk about like that in our village: the people would laugh.

"And so the question was: how could I get a walk with that
beauty? I thought of something rather clever: I bent double and
groaned for all the street to hear. She runs up and asks: 'What's
the matter, Daddy?' I tell her: 'I've been taken ill, my dear; I can't
get to the hospital nohow. I've got prickles all down my back.'
And she says: 'I'll take you, you lean on me.' And I take her by
the arm with all the nerve I've got, and we set off. I really was
enjoying myself. We got as far as the district co-operative, and little by little I began to straighten up. And before she could guess
what I was up to I kissed her on the cheek and ran off to the shop,
though I had no business there whatever. Her eyes flashed and
she shouted after me: 'Hey, Daddy, you're a hooligan and a
cheat.' But I stopped and said: 'My dear, when necessary a man
will go to even farther lengths. You just remember that I've
never walked arm in arm with a beauty before, and I've got to
die before much longer.' I went into the shop, thinking as likely

as not she'd call a militia-man. But she laughed and went her way. I ran into the shop, and couldn't get my breath. The shopkeeper asked: 'Are you running away from a fire, Daddy?' I was panting for all I was worth, but I answered: 'Still worse. Give me a box of matches.' "

He was quite prepared to go on, but his audience were tired after their day's work and slowly began to drift away. He implored them to listen to another story or two, but in vain. Soon not one man was left sitting round the embers of the campfire.

Chagrined and affronted to his very depths, Shchukar wandered off to the hay ricks and lay down, drawing his old coat over him and shivering. At midnight the dew began to rise. He woke up, trembling with the cold. "I'll go along to the Cossacks, otherwise I'll shiver to death out here like a young puppy in the frost," he decided.

He remembered from the spring ploughing that the Cossacks slept in the hut and the women outside, and it did not occur to him that there might have been changes in the past few months. So he quietly crawled on all fours into the hut, took off his boots, and lay down at the side. He fell asleep at once, warmed by a vital warmth. But after some time he woke up feeling that he was being stifled. Someone's bare leg was lying right across his chest, and he thought in great dudgeon: "What a disgusting way to sleep. He flings his legs about as if he was riding a horse bareback."

But, to his horror, when he tried to throw off that living weight he discovered it wasn't a man's leg at all, but Kuprianovna's bare arm, and he heard her powerful breathing right by his cheek. The women had taken to sleeping in the hut.

Badly shaken, he lay for some minutes without stirring, wet with sweat. Then he snatched up his shoes and, like a cat which has made a mess, quietly stole out of the hut and limped off at a trot to the drozhki. Never before had he harnessed up the stallions with such celerity. Using his knout across their backs mercilessly, he set off at a sharp trot, looking back again and again at the hut, which stood out ominously black against the dawn sky.

"Lucky thing I woke up in time. Supposing I'd slept on and the women had seen me with Kuprianovna, and her embracing

me with her great fat arm! Mother of God preserve me! I'd
have been a laughing-stock till the day of my death and even beyond."

The summer sunrise came on impetuously. The hut was lost
from sight. But beyond the rise a fresh shock awaited him: happening to glance down at his feet, he saw an almost new woman's
shoe on his right foot. Judging by its size, it was Kuprianovna's.

Going cold with fear, he prayed to the Almighty: "Merciful
God, what are you punishing me for? I must have mixed up the
shoes in the dark. But how can I ever go home to my old woman
now? My own shoe on one foot, and a woman's on the other:
that's a problem I can't solve."

But the problem did prove soluble: he turned his horses round
and drove straight back to Gremyachy, rightly deciding that he
could not present himself at the district centre either barefoot
or wearing odd shoes. "Damn the land surveyor! They'll manage
without him. We've got the Soviet government everywhere, and
collective farms everywhere, so what difference does it make if
one collective farm pinches a little hay from another?" he moodily reflected as he drove.

Some two kilometres from the village, at a point where a deep
ravine runs right up to the road, he made yet another, no less
courageous decision: he took off his odd shoes, looked about him
stealthily, and flung them into the ravine, whispering after them:
"I'm not going to be ruined by you, curse you!"

As he drove up to his yard he saw a crowd of excited women
gathered outside. "Surely my old woman hasn't kicked the
bucket?" he thought anxiously. But when, pushing through the
smiling women and entering the kitchen, he took a hurried glance
around, his legs sagged under him. Signing himself with the
cross, he whispered with difficulty: "What's all this?"

His old woman was tearfully dandling a baby wrapped in rags,
and the baby was crying convulsively.

"What on earth is all this?" Shchukar asked even louder, shaken
by the sight.

Flashing her swollen eyes furiously, his wife shouted: "They've
abandoned your child, that's what. You damned knowledge-
eater! Read the paper on the table."

His eyes went darker and darker, but somehow he managed to read the scrawl on the sheet of wrapping paper.

"Seeing as you're the father of this little child, Daddy, you feed it and bring it up."

By the evening Shchukar had almost succeeded in convincing his wife that he was in no way responsible for the child's birth. But then an eight-year-old boy, Liubishkin's son, arrived at the kitchen door. Sniffing vigorously, he said:

"Daddy, I was minding the sheep this morning when I saw you throw your shoes into the ravine. I found them and have brought them to you. Here you are!" He held out the ill-starred shoes.

What happened after that "is concealed in impenetrable gloom," as the shoemaker Lokateev, who was very friendly with Shchukar, used to say. All we do know is that for a whole week Shchukar went around with a bandaged cheek and a swollen eye. And when anyone asked him with a smile why he was all bandaged up he turned away, saying his one and only tooth was aching so badly that he couldn't even talk.

Chapter 20

Early one morning Andrei Razmiotnov was sitting in the village Soviet looking through reports from the brigades, when there was a loud knock on the door. "Come in," he shouted without looking up.

Two strangers entered the room, and at once seemed to fill it. One of them, a man dressed in a fairly new raincoat, stocky and fleshy of build, with a commonplace, round, clean-shaven face, came up to the table with a smile and held out a hand as hard as stone.

"I'm Polikarp Petrovich Boiko-Glukhov, supplies manager of the Shakhty Department for Workers' Provisions, and this is my

assistant, Khizhnak." He pointed rudely with his forefinger across his shoulder at his companion, who had remained at the door.

By the look of him this second man might well have been a head drover or cattle merchant: his worn, dirty canvas coat with hood, his wide-topped calf-leather boots, his squashed grey cap, and his decorative knout with two leather tassles—all testified to his calling. But his face was strangely at variance with his outward appearance: his inquisitively intelligent eyes, the ironic folds in the corners of his thin lips, his trick of raising his left eyebrow as though listening to something, and the general intelligence of all his features revealed to an observant eye that he had little to do with the collection of cattle or the requirements of agriculture. Razmiotnov inwardly noted these details. But he took only a hurried glance at Khizhnak's face, then shifted his gaze to his excessively broad shoulders. Involuntarily smiling, he thought: "Well, you look fine supplies-collectors, I must say. You're more like a couple of brigands. You shouldn't be collecting food supplies but standing somewhere under a bridge at night and sewing up the coats of Soviet merchants with wooden needles!" Keeping a straight face with difficulty, he asked:

"What have you come to see me for?"

"We're buying up cattle personally owned by collective farmers. We can take large and small horned cattle and pigs too. We're not interested in poultry at the moment. Possibly the situation will be different in the winter, but at the moment we're not taking poultry. We pay co-operative prices, plus an extra sum according to the animal's condition. As you can guess, Comrade Chairman, the miners' labour is hard, and we've got to feed our workers as they should be fed."

"Your documents." Razmiotnov tapped his hand lightly on the table.

The two strangers laid their certificates of authorization and other documents on the table. They were all in perfect order, with stamps, signatures, and seals. But Razmiotnov examined them long and closely; he did not see Boiko turn to his companion and wink. They smiled at each other, but at once wiped off their smiles.

"D'you think they're false?" Boiko asked, openly smiling. With-

out waiting to be invited, he seated himself comfortably on a chair by the window.

"No, I don't think your documents are false. . . . But why have you come to our collective farm?" Razmiotnov did not adopt the other's jesting tone; he regarded the conversation as serious.

"Why have we come to you? But we're not making an exception of your village, we're not intending to visit only your collective farm. We've already visited six neighbouring farms and collected about fifty head of cattle, including three pairs of old, useless bulls, calves, cows no good for milking, sheep, and some thirty pigs. . . ."

"Thirty-seven," the broad-shouldered man at the door said, correcting his chief.

"You're quite right; we've bought thirty-seven pigs, and at reasonable prices. We're going on afterwards to other villages. . . ."

"Payment down?" Razmiotnov inquired.

"At once. Of course we don't carry a lot of money around with us, Comrade Razmiotnov. These are troubled times; anything might happen. . . . So we've provided ourselves with letters of credit."

Razmiotnov roared with laughter, throwing himself back in his chair. "Are you really afraid the money might be stolen from you? Why, the two of you could empty anyone's pockets and shake the owner right out of his clothes."

Boiko smiled a restrained smile. Little dimples played on his effeminate rosy cheeks. Khizhnak remained quite unperturbed and gazed abstractedly out of the window. Only now, as he had his face turned to the window, did Razmiotnov notice a deep, long scar stretching from his chin to his left ear.

"Did you get that scratch on your face in the war?" he asked.

Khizhnak turned round sharply and smiled thinly. "Why in the war? I earned it later. . . ."

"I rather thought so. It doesn't look like a sabre cut. Did your wife scratch you?"

"No, she's a quiet sort. I got it through drinking. A friend used a knife on me."

"You look tough enough, but I did think your wife must have scratched you. If she didn't do it, you must have got it through a

woman all the same. A love affair, was it?" Razmiotnov continued his naïve questions, laughing and stroking his whiskers.

"But you're quick-witted, Chairman." Khizhnak smiled derisively.

"My position makes it necessary. . . . And that scar wasn't made by a knife, but a sword, I know enough to see that. And I can see you're as much a food collector as I'm a bishop. Your mug doesn't fit the part, it isn't simple enough, and your hands don't fit either. . . . I can see they've never held a bullock horn in your life, they're too tender. They may be pretty big, but they're too white. You should get them sunburnt at any rate, to darken them a bit, and smear them in dung. Then I might believe you're a cattle merchant. And you can't fool me by playing around with a knout: you don't pull the wool over my eyes that way."

"But you're quick-witted, Chairman," Khizhnak said again, this time without a smile. "Only you're a bit lopsided in your wits: the scar is the result of a sabre gash as you said, but I don't want to talk about it. I served with the Whites once, and I got the scar then. Who'd want to recall such a past? As for my hands, after all, I'm not a drover, I'm a merchant; my job is to pay out roubles, not to twist calves' tails. So you don't like the look of me, Comrade Razmiotnov? You see, I've only gone in for buying up stock recently. Before that I was an agronomist, but I was taken off that job for drunkenness, so I've had to change my speciality. Now do you understand, Comrade Chairman? You've forced me to be frank, and so I've had to confess all my sins to you. . . ."

"I don't need your confession any more than a dog needs a fifth paw. You go and confess yourself to the G.P.U. and get them to grant you absolution; it's nothing to do with me." Without changing his position, Andrei shouted: "Maria. Come in here!"

The young girl acting as village Soviet messenger for the day entered bashfully.

"Run and fetch Nagulnov. Tell him to come to the village Soviet at once, there's urgent business waiting for him there," Razmiotnov ordered, and turned to scrutinizing first Khizhnak then Boiko again.

Khizhnak shrugged his enormous shoulders with a puzzled

and affronted gesture, sat down on the bench, and turned away. Boiko, who was shaking like jelly with suppressed laughter, at last cried in a high-pitched voice:

"Now, that's vigilance for you, I like it. Has Comrade Khiznak fallen into it? He certainly has, like a chicken into soup."

He clapped his palms against his fat legs and bent double; his laughter sounded so genuine that Razmiotnov stared at him in open astonishment.

"And what are you laughing at, fatty? Take care you don't both of you find yourselves crying in the district centre. You can take offence or not, as you please, but I'm sending you to the district to clear up your identity. There's something suspicious about you to my way of thinking, comrade cattle merchants."

Wiping the tears from his eyes and still smiling with his full lips, Boiko asked: "But how about our documents? You've examined them and admitted they're genuine, haven't you?"

"Documents are documents, and a shop sign's a shop sign," Razmiotnov answered surlily, unhurriedly rolling himself a cigarette.

Makar Nagulnov soon arrived. He nodded to the visitors without speaking, and asked Razmiotnov: "Who're they?"

"Ask them yourself."

He turned to them, asked various questions, examined their documents, and turned back to Razmiotnov. "Well, what's the trouble. What did you send for me for? Men have arrived to buy cattle, so let them buy them."

Andrei began to boil, but he kept himself under control. "No, they're not buying anything until I've checked up on their identity. I don't like the look of them, that's the point. I'm sending them at once to the district to get a check-up on them; after that they can buy cattle if they still want to."

Boiko intervened quietly. "Comrade Razmiotnov, send your messenger out of the house. We've got to have a talk with you."

"But what secrets have you and I got to share?"

"Do as you're told," Boiko said just as quietly, but in a tone of command.

And Razmiotnov did as he was told. When the girl had left the house, Boiko drew a small red book from his jacket inner pocket and handed it to Razmiotnov with a smile.

"Read that, you keen-eyed devil! As our little masquerade hasn't come off we've got to put our cards on the table. To get down to brass tacks, Comrades: we're both members of the regional G.P.U., and we've come to your village to search for a certain individual, a dangerous political enemy, conspirator, and determined counter-revolutionary. To avoid attracting too much notice we've transformed ourselves into cattle merchants. That makes it easier for us to do our job: we can go from yard to yard talking to the people, and we're hoping that sooner or later we shall come on the tracks of this counter-revolutionary."

"Why didn't you tell me at once who you are, Comrade Glukhov? Then there wouldn't have been any misunderstandings," Razmiotnov exclaimed.

"The need for secrecy, my dear Razmiotnov. We tell you, we tell Davidov and Nagulnov, and in a week all Gremyachy Log will know who we are. For God's sake don't take offence, the point isn't that we don't trust you, but unfortunately we have to work this way sometimes. We have no right to jeopardize our operations, which are of very great importance," Boiko-Glukhov explained in a condescending tone.

"May we ask you who you're looking for?" Nagulnov inquired.

Instead of answering, Boiko-Glukhov searched through his capacious document case, and carefully laid on his palm a photograph the size of a passport photo. Razmiotnov and Nagulnov leaned across the table. An elderly, good-naturedly smiling man with broad shoulders and a bull neck gazed at them from the small oblong of paper. But his artificially affable smile was in such contrast with his wolfish brow, deep-set, moody eyes, and heavy, square chin that Nagulnov only smiled sardonically, while Razmiotnov said with a nod:

"Yes, he doesn't look a very pleasant character. . . ."

"Well, that's the man we're looking for," Boiko-Glukhov said thoughtfully, carefully wrapping the photo in a sheet of paper and putting it in his bill fold. "His name's Polovtsiev: Alexander Anisimovich. Formerly a Cossack captain in the White army, a member of Podtielkov and Krivoshlikov's punitive detachment. Later he became a teacher, hiding under a false name; then he went to live in his district town. At present he's living illegally. One of the active members of a rising now being organized

against the Soviet regime. According to information from our agents he's hiding somewhere in your district. That's all I can tell you about this fellow. You can tell Davidov about our conversation, but not a word to anyone else. I rely on you, Comrades. Well, I'll be going now. There's no need for us to meet again, unless it should be necessary, of course. Or if you come across something you think might interest us, send for me to come to the village Soviet in the day-time, only in the day-time, to avoid arousing any suspicions among the villagers concerning us. And my last word to you is: be on your guard. It would be better if you didn't go around at night at all. Polovtsiev won't resort to terroristic acts, he won't want to give himself away; but there's never any harm in caution. Don't go around at all at night, but if you have to, then never alone. Always have your weapons with you, though of course you do that already. At any rate, I heard you, Comrade Razmiotnov, spin the drum of your revolver once or twice in your trouser pocket while you were talking to Khizhnak, didn't I?"

Razmiotnov narrowed his eyes and turned away as though he hadn't heard the question. Nagulnov came to his rescue.

"Since the night I was shot at we've always been ready to defend ourselves."

Smiling a thin smile, Boiko-Glukhov said: "Not only to defend yourselves, but to attack, I'd say. And by the way, the man you killed, Comrade Nagulnov, Timofei Damaskov, called the Ragged, was connected with Polovtsiev's organization at one time, and there are members of his organization still in your village. But for some unknown reason Damaskov left it. He didn't shoot at you on Polovtsiev's orders: he was governed rather by personal motives. . . ."

Nagulnov nodded his agreement, and Boiko-Glukhov went on measuredly and calmly, as though reading a lesson.

"The fact that Timofei Damaskov broke away from the Polovtsiev group for some reason and became a straightforward bandit is proved by the circumstance that he didn't hand over to Polovtsiev's people the machine gun which had been concealed in the Damaskovs' shed since the days of the civil war and which Davidov found. But that's not the point. I'll say a few words concerning our task: we've got to capture Polovtsiev alone,

and at all costs alive. At present we need him alive or not at all.
We can render the rank-and-file members of his group harmless
afterwards. I must add that he is only one link in a long chain;
but he's not an unimportant link. That's why the task of discover-
ing and arresting him has been entrusted to us and not to any
member of the district G.P.U.

"So that you shan't feel offended with me any longer, Comrades, I'll tell you that only the head of your district department
knows we're in your district. Not even Nesterenko knows. After
all, what contact does the district-committee secretary need to
have with petty cattle merchants? Let him get on with the Party
work in his district, while we get on with our own business. And
I must say that in the collective farms we've visited so far we've
been perfectly able to pass ourselves off as merchants, and you,
Razmiotnov, were the first to suspect Khizhnak, and in con-
sequence me too, of not being genuine. Well, that's a tribute to
your vigilance. Though either way I'd have had to tell you who
we really are before many days had passed, because my pro-
fessional intuition tells me Polovtsiev's hanging around somewhere in your village. We shall try to find out whether anyone
here served with him during the German or the civil war. We
know the regiments in which he served, and most likely he's
staying with someone who was with him then. Well, that's it.
We'll meet again before we leave Gremyachy, but so long for the
time being." He went to the door, but halted and turned to look
at Nagulnov. "I suppose you're not interested in what's happened
to your wife?"

A crimson patch appeared on Makar's cheeks and his eyes went
dark. He coughed, and quietly asked: "Do you know where she
is?"

"She's in Shakhti."

"What's she doing there? She doesn't know anybody in that
town, no relations or even acquaintances."

"Your wife's working."

"In what capacity?" Makar laughed sarcastically and joylessly.

"She's working in a mine, unloading trucks. Members of our
G.P.U. helped her to find a job. But of course she has no idea
who assisted her to set herself up. . . . And I must say she's working very well, I'd even say excellently. She behaves modestly,

she's not making any new acquaintances, and so far none of her old acquaintances have called on her."

"But who'd be likely to?" Nagulnov asked quietly. Outwardly he seemed quite calm; only his left eyelid twitched a little.

"Well, who knows? Some of Timofei's friends, possibly. Or do you completely exclude that possibility? All the same, it does look as if she's changed her life, thought better of it. And so you needn't be anxious about her, Comrade Nagulnov."

"And why do you think I'm likely to be anxious about her?" Nagulnov asked even more quietly. He got up from his chair and leaned a little forward over the table, supporting himself with his long hands on its edge. His face went deathly white; the fleshy knobs worked below his cheekbones. Choosing his words, he said more slowly than usual: "Comrade orator, have you come here to do a certain job? Well, go and get on with it. And you needn't give me any of your comfort: I don't need your sympathy. Nor need you have any fears for us: whether we go about by day or night is our business. We'll get through somehow without your ridiculous exhortations, and without nannies. Get that? And now clear out. You've already talked too much as it is: you've turned yourself inside out. A fine thing: you call yourself a Cheka-man, but for my part I can't make up my mind whether you're really a responsible officer of the regional G.P.U. or just an ordinary cattle merchant: a sermonizer or, as we would say, a bully."

The taciturn Khizhnak looked at his disconcerted superior with a touch of malicious pleasure. But Nagulnov came round from behind the table, adjusted the belt to his tunic, and went to the door, erect and spruce as always, possibly even exaggerating his military bearing a little.

When he had gone, there was an awkward silence.

"I suppose I shouldn't have said anything about his wife," Boiko-Glukhov said, scratching his nose with his little finger. "It's clear he's still gone on her."

"You're right, you shouldn't have," Razmiotnov agreed. "Makar's a prickly customer and he's not over-fond of people in muddy boots tramping about in his clean soul. . . ."

"Oh, it's nothing; he'll get over it," Khiznak said in a conciliatory tone, turning to the door.

To smooth matters over, Razmiotnov asked: "But tell me, Comrade Glukhov: what about your acting as cattle merchants: how far will you go? Will you really buy cattle or are you simply intending to go from yard to yard talking about buying and prices and so on?"

Boiko-Glukhov was amused at the naïve question, and the dimples played again over his fat cheeks. "You're a real farmer, that's obvious. Of course we shall buy cattle, and we'll pay in full with ready money. But don't you worry about that; we shall drive any cattle we buy to Shakhti, and the miners will enjoy the meat. And when they eat it they won't even thank us, for they won't have any idea what an important state institution has provided them with their nourishment! That's the way things have to be done, my boy."

After seeing the visitors to the door Razmiotnov sat for a long time at the table supporting his cheeks on his fists, his elbows spread wide apart. One thought would give him no peace: "Which of our villagers could belong to that damned officers' conspiracy?" He went over all the adult Cossacks in the village, and did not feel that he could genuinely suspect any one of them.

He rose from the table to have a stretch, paced up and down from door to window three times, and suddenly halted in the middle of the room as though he had run up against an invisible obstacle. Anxiously he thought: "That fatty's really upset Makar's feelings. What the hell did he have to go and talk about Lushka for? Supposing Makar starts hankering after her and slips off to Shakhti to see her? He's a bit two-faced these days: he doesn't show any sign, but I've got a feeling he's drinking a bit when he's alone at night. . . ."

Andrei lived in a state of anxious anticipation for several days: would Makar do anything? And when on Saturday evening Nagulnov mentioned in Davidov's presence that he was thinking of riding to Martinovsk district centre with the approval of the district committee, to see how one of the first Motor-Tractor Stations to be organized in the Don was progressing, Razmiotnov groaned inwardly: "Makar's done for. He's going off to Lushka. Hasn't he any pride as a man left?"

Chapter 21

Back in the spring, when the last snow, streaming with crystal moisture, was beginning to vanish even on the northern side of the wattle fences, a pair of wild blue pigeons took a fancy to Razmiotnov's yard. They circled over the house for some time, sinking lower and lower with each turn, then dropped to the ground near the cellar, and, effortlessly rising again, settled on the house roof. They perched up there for quite a long time, peering and cocking their heads this way and that, looking about them and getting their bearings in this new spot. Then one of the two, lifting its raspberry-coloured feet with a fastidious air, strutted over the dirty whitewash spattered round the chimney, drew in and threw back its head a little, and cooed uncertainly, its rainbow collar glistening round its swollen pout. But its mate slipped off, flapped her wings noisily a couple of times in flight, and, describing a semi-circle, alighted on the projecting window frame of Razmiotnov's best room. What else could that twice-repeated flap of her wings have been but an invitation to her friend to follow her example?

Razmiotnov came home to dinner at midday, and noticed the pigeons as he passed through the wicket gate. The female was strutting hurriedly on her brilliantly coloured feet round the edge of a little puddle of melted snow water, pecking as she went, while the male pursued her, taking little runs. Then he, too, halted for a moment, circled, bowed, almost touching the ground with his beak, cooed furiously, and once more set off in pursuit, spreading his tail fanwise, dancing and bowing down to the still damp, cold, and wintrily unpleasant ground. He kept stubbornly to the left, trying to edge the female away from the puddle.

Stepping warily, Razmiotnov passed them only a couple of paces away. But they did not even attempt to fly off; they only drew a little aside. As he stood at the foot of the steps to his house, Andrei decided with ardent, boyish joy: "They're not guests, they're the masters arrived." And he whispered, or

possibly only thought, with a bitter smile: "They're settling in
to bring me some belated happiness. It must be that. . . ."

He gathered up a full handful of wheat in the barn and scattered it beneath the window.

All morning he had been gloomy and ill-tempered; things
were going badly with the preparations for autumn sowing,
with the seed cleaning; Davidov had been summoned to the
district that morning; Nagulnov had ridden off to the fields to
look at the soil prepared for sowing; and by noonday Andrei himself had managed to quarrel violently with two brigadiers and
the warehouseman. But now, as he sat down to his meal and, forgetting the soup going cold in his plate, began to watch the
pigeons, his face seemed to light up beneath its tan from the
spring winds. But his heart grew even heavier.

Twenty years before, he too, young and as handsome of bearing as a pigeon, had circled round his loved one. Then they had
married, but he had had to do his army service, and go off to the
war. . . . With what terrible, with what frightening, speed life
had fled past! As he recalled his wife and young son he thought
sadly: "I didn't see much of you when you were alive, my dears,
and I don't often visit you even now."

On that sunny April day the male pigeon had no thought of
food. And Andrei Razmiotnov did not feel like food either.
With unseeing eyes, not merely misted but wet with tears, he
gazed through the window. And he saw not the pigeons, not
the gracious spring tints in the yard outside, but the sorrowful
features of the only woman he had ever loved, whom he had
loved more than life itself, but whom he had not been granted
to love through the long years of his life; he saw the woman
whom death had taken from him twelve years before, maybe
on a sunny spring day like the one in the yard outside.

He chewed his bread with his head sunk low over the plate,
for he did not want his mother to see the tears rolling down his
cheeks, salting the already over-salted soup. Twice he picked up
his spoon, but each time he let it drop back on to the table,
unable to hold it with his strangely strengthless, violently trembling hand.

There are times in our life when a man whose soul is wounded
responds not only to human happiness, but even to the brief

happiness of the birds, not with a condescending smile, but with a heavy, overbearing bitterness provoked by the torment of memory. Andrei rose abruptly from the table and, turning his back to his mother, put on his quilted coat. Crumpling his fur cap in his hands, he said:

"God save you, Mother; I don't feel much like food today."

"If you don't want the soup, would you like some gruel with sour milk?"

"No, thank you."

"Have you got something on your mind?" his mother asked him warily.

"I haven't got anything on my mind. I've had my troubles, but they've been grown over long since."

"You always did keep things to yourself, Andrei, my boy. You never did tell your mother anything, you never complained. . . . You've got a stone for a heart, that's clear. . . ."

"You bore me, Mother, and you can't shift the blame on to anyone else. As you brought me into the world, so I am; and there's nothing to be done about it."

"Well, then, go your own way," the old woman said, chewing her colourless lips in her chagrin.

He went out through the wicket gate and turned, not right to go to the village Soviet, but left, out into the steppe. With a long, unhurrying stride he walked straight ahead, by pathless fields, to the other Gremyachy Log, where the dead had dwelt in close proximity from time immemorial. The cemetery was fenced off. In those difficult days the dead did not get much respect from the living. The old, blackened crosses stood crookedly; some of them were overthrown. Not one grave was tended, and the wind blowing from the east gloomily stirred the last year's scrub on the clayey mounds, and tenderly, as though sorting it over with fine feminine fingers, rustled the twigs of the faded, darkened wormwood. The mingled scents of decay, rotting grass, and thawed-out black earth hung heavily over the graves.

At any season of the year a cemetery is a mournful spot for the living, but in early spring and late autumn such places are haunted by a distinctive, piercing sorrow.

Along a path which calves had trodden out Andrei went

northward beyond the bounds of the cemetery, to the spot where
suicides had formerly been buried, and halted beside a familiar
grave with sunken edges. He took his fur cap from his bowed
grey head. Only the skylarks disturbed the pensive silence that
hung over this scrap of earth forgotten by man.

Why had he come here on this day of spring, a day radiant
with sunlight, filled to the brim with exuberant life? Simply in
order to stand with his strong, stumpy fingers clasped together
and with teeth clenched, and to stare with half-closed eyes at the
misty rim of the horizon, as though in that smoky haze he sought
to discern his still remembered youth, his fleeting happiness?
Possibly. For though the past is dead it is precious to the heart,
and it is always good to contemplate, whether in a cemetery or
in the mute darkness of sleepless nights.

From that day onward Razmiotnov took the two pigeons
which had quartered themselves on him into his constant care.
Twice every day he scattered a handful of wheat under the
window and stood on guard, driving off the impudent chickens,
until the pigeons had had their fill. He would sit long of an
early morning on the step of the granary door, smoking and
silently watching the new inhabitants as they dragged straw
and twigs behind the window frame and added tufts of faded bullock hair from the wattle fence. Soon they had a roughly shaped
nest ready, and he sighed with relief: "They've settled down.
They won't fly away now."

For a fortnight the female did not come out to feed. "She's
starting a family. The business is beginning to show a profit."
He smiled.

With the arrival of the pigeons his cares were perceptibly
increased: he had to put out food for them, and to change the
water regularly in a bowl, for the puddles in the yard soon dried
up. In addition, he was forced by necessity to undertake guard
duty to protect the two defenceless birds.

One day, coming home from the fields, as he drew near to his
house he saw the old cat, his mother's favourite, creeping along
the house roof, her body pressed close against the straw thatch.
She sprang lightly down to the half-open window shutter, slowly
waving her tail, making ready to spring. The female pigeon was
sitting perfectly still in the nest, with her back to the cat, seem-

ingly unaware of her danger. Yet death was barely eighteen inches away.

Razmiotnov ran into the yard on tiptoe, snatching his pistol from his pocket as he went, holding his breath and not turning his eyes away from the cat. When she crouched down, nervously pawing with her front paws, a shot cracked out, and she fell headlong down to the house ledge.

At the sound of the shot Andrei's mother ran out.

"Where's our iron spade, Mother?" he asked in a matter-of-fact tone, as though nothing had happened. He picked up the dead cat by the tail and made a squeamish face. The old woman clapped her hands and began to lament at the top of her voice:

"You damned murderer! You've no pity for any living thing. It's all one to you and Makar whether you kill a man or a cat. You can go without killing as little as you can go without tobacco; all life makes you sick."

"Now, now! No panic!" her son sternly broke in. "We've finished with cats for ever. And don't let your tongue wag too much about me and Makar. He and I get very sensitive when we get called names. It is because we feel pity that we kill all sorts of muck, whether on two or four legs, which won't let other things live. All right, Mother? Now go back into the house. You can go and get worked up in the house, but as Chairman of the village Soviet I categorically forbid you to get agitated and swear at me in the yard."

She would not speak to him for a whole week, but her silence only played into his hands: during that week he shot all the neighbours' cats and kittens and so ensured that his pigeons were safe for a long time to come. One day Davidov dropped in at the village Soviet and asked:

"What are you doing all this shooting all over the village for? Not a day passes without my hearing pistol shots. What are you upsetting the people for, I ask you? If you want to let off your gun, go out into the steppe and bang away there: it's awkward your doing it in the village, Andrei. Fact!"

"I'm slowly but surely wiping out all the cats," Razmiotnov answered surlily. "You see, they won't let anything else live."

Davidov lifted his bleached eyebrows in astonishment. "What cats?"

"All sorts. Brindled, and black, and tabbies. Any cat that comes within my sight belongs to me!"

Davidov's upper lip quivered: a sure sign that he was wrestling with an attack of laughter. Recognizing the sign, Andrei frowned and raised his hand in an anxious, warning gesture.

"Wait a bit before you laugh, sailor boy! First find out what it's all about."

"Well, what is it all about?" Davidov asked, making a face and all but crying with suppressed merriment. "I suppose it's something to do with non-fulfilment of the pelt-collection plan? The collection's not moving fast enough, so you're helping it along? Oh, Andrei, I can't . . . do tell me quick, or I'll die on the spot. . . ." He dropped his head into his hands; his shoulders quivered spasmodically.

Razmiotnov jumped up as though stung by a wasp and shouted: "You fool! You citified fool! Pigeons are starting a family on my house, if you wish to know, and you go and talk rot about pelt collection! What the devil do I care for all that shopkeeping rot? Pigeons have taken a fancy to settle down on my house, and I'm protecting them as they deserve to be. And now you can laugh as much as you like."

He was prepared for an outburst of laughter, but not for the impression his words actually made. The chairman hurriedly wiped the tears from his eyes and asked with quickened interest:

"What pigeons? Where did you get them from?"

"'What pigeons, what cats, where did I get them from?' What the hell are you asking me all these idiotic questions for, Siemion?" Andrei indignantly retorted. "They're just ordinary pigeons, with two legs, two wings, and each has got one head and a tail at the other end. And they both wear feathers for clothing. But they haven't anything on their feet, they're poor, so they go around barefoot even in the winter. Had enough?"

"I'm not asking about that: what I want to know is are they pedigree birds? When I was a boy I reared pigeons myself, that's a fact. So I'm interested to know what breed of pigeons they are: tumblers, or pouters, or are they jacobins or fantails? And where did you get them from?"

Now Razmiotnov smiled as he stroked his whiskers. "They've flown to my place from some other yard, I expect, so they're

yardies by breed; and as they arrived without being invited, they might also be called 'wanderers' or 'strangers,' since they're living on my food and don't bother to forage for themselves. In a word, you can call them what breed you like."

"What colour are they?" Davidov asked seriously.

"Just ordinary, sort of bluish."

"Yes, but what blue?"

"Like a ripe plum before it's picked, with a bloom on it."

"So they're only stockdoves," Davidov commented in a disillusioned tone, but he at once rubbed his hands cheerfully. "Though there are some stockdoves, my boy, as good as any breed of pigeon. I must see them. It's very interesting, and that's a fact."

"Come along and have a look; let me invite you."

Some days after this conversation a group of boys stopped Razmiotnov in the street. The boldest among them, keeping a respectful distance, asked in a squeaky voice:

"Daddy Andrei, is it true you're cooking cats?"

"Wha-a-at?" He turned on them menacingly.

They scattered in all directions like a flock of sparrows; but in a moment they gathered together again in a solid bunch.

"Who told you that?" Andrei asked fiercely, hardly able to control his indignation.

But they did not answer. Hanging their heads and exchanging glances, they drew patterns with their bare feet in the cold road dust, the first of the year.

At last the same lad ventured to pipe up again. Drawing his head down between his thin shoulders, he squeaked: "Mummy says you're shooting the cats. . . ."

"Well, so I am, but I'm not cooking them. That's a different matter, my boy."

"But she said: 'Our Soviet chairman's shooting them as if he was going to cook them, you might say. He ought to come along and kill our cat, for she's killing off all the pigeons.'"

"That's quite a different question, sonny," Razmiotnov exclaimed, showing much more interest. "So your cat's killing the pigeons, is she? Whose son are you, my boy? What's your name?"

"My daddy's Yerofei Vasilich Chebakov, and my name's Timo-fei."

"Well, take me along to where you live, Timofei, my boy. We'll put a stop to your cat's goings-on at once, especially as your mummy herself would like me to."

However, the magnanimous readiness to save the Chebakovs' pigeons brought Razmiotnov neither success nor additional glory. Rather the opposite. Accompanied by a horde of chattering lads, he strode deliberately to the Chebakovs' yard. But he had hardly turned the corner of the street, shuffling along warily in his boots in his anxiety not to tread on the bare feet of the children dancing around him, when an old woman, who proved to be Yerofei's mother, came out on to the veranda. She was well built, buxom and majestic, and she frowned threateningly as she pressed an enormous, plump ginger cat to her chest.

"Your health, old lady." Andrei greeted her in a friendly tone out of respect for her age. He touched his grey fur cap with the fingers of his right hand.

"Thank God, I'm well. What do you want, village ataman?" the old woman answered in a deep voice.

"Why, I've come about the cat. The children say he's killing off all the pigeons. Hand him over and I'll bring him to trial at once. And I'll sign the death warrant: final sentence without right of appeal."

"And by what right will you do that? Has the Soviet government made a law that all the cats are to be destroyed?"

"What on earth do you want a law for?" Razmiotnov answered, smiling. "If the cat's behaving like a bandit and killing off all kinds of birds, then he's earned the extreme sentence, and that's the end of it. We've only one law for bandits: 'governed by revolutionary legality,' and that's enough. So there's no excuse for delay. Hand over the cat, old lady, and I'll deal with him short and sharp. . . ."

"But who's going to catch the mice in our granary? Perhaps you'd like to take on the job for us?"

"I've got my own job to do; but you've got nothing to do, so you deal with the mice, instead of saying senseless prayers to God and bowing down to an icon."

"You're young to teach me," the old woman thundered. "I can't

make out how our Cossacks ever came to elect such a lousy scum as Chairman. Why, do you know that in the old days there wasn't one village ataman who could talk to me and manage me? As for you, I'll put you out of the yard so quick that you won't come round till you find yourself in the street."

At the sound of the woman's sonorous voice a speckled whelp leaped out from under the granary and gave tongue to a ringing, ear-splitting howl. Razmiotnov stood below the veranda, calmly rolling a cigarette. Judging by the size of it, he had no intention of abandoning the position he had taken up. A good seven inches long and as thick as his index finger, that cigarette was intended to last through a prolonged conversation. But things didn't happen that way.

"You're right, old lady," he said calmly and deliberately. "The Cossacks were stupid to choose me for their chairman. It's not for nothing that there's a saying: 'The Cossack's got his mind in his ass.' I agreed to take on all this bother just because I hadn't got much mind. But don't worry: before long I shall be resigning my position as Chairman."

"You should have done that long since."

"That's just what I say. But meanwhile, old lady, say good-bye to your cat and hand him over to me as Chairman."

"You've already shot most of the cats in the village; soon there'll be so many mice around that you'll be the first to have his nails chewed off by them during the night."

"Never on your life," Razmiotnov retorted firmly. "My nails are so hard that even your little puppy there would break his teeth on them. But all the same, hand over your cat: I haven't time to argue with you. Sign the cross over him and give him to me with a good heart."

The old woman held up the gnarled brown fingers of her right hand suggestively, while her left pressed the cat to her bosom so obviously that the animal squealed like mad and began to scratch and snort furiously. The lads standing in a solid bunch behind Razmiotnov giggled maliciously. Their sympathies were clearly with the chairman. But they were silent as though by command when the old woman, soothing the agitated animal, shouted:

"Clear out of here at once, you unclean spirit, you damned

heathen! Clear out while the going's good or I'll give you something you won't forget."

Andrei slowly and diligently ran his tongue along the edge of the rough newspaper and rolled his cigarette, looking up craftily from under his brows at the militant old woman. He even went so far as to smile jauntily. There's no point in denying that for some reason he got a tremendous kick and satisfaction out of wordy battles with all the village old women except his own mother. Despite his age he still possessed the impudence and the wild, coarse sense of fun of the young Cossack. He remained faithful to his bad habits: lighting his cigarette and taking two draws in succession, he said affably, in fact in a tone of sheer delight:

"What a damned fine voice you've got, old lady Ignatievna. I could listen to you for ever and never get bored. I wouldn't take food or drink. I'd only have you shout from morning till eve. Say what you like, it's a voice in a million. Deep, rolling, perfectly like an old village deacon or one of our collective-farm stallions. From now on I shan't call you Mrs. Ignatievna but 'Mrs. Stallion.' Let's make a bargain: if we want to summon the people to a meeting we'll get you to bawl at the top of your voice in the square. We'll grant you labour days from the collective farm for the job. . . ."

He was not allowed to finish the sentence: the old lady flew into a rage, seized the cat by the scruff of its neck, and swung it with masculine strength. He dodged to one side in alarm, and the cat, his four paws sprawling in all directions, rolling his green eyes and miaowing fearfully, flew past him, alighted springily on the ground, and, letting his enormous tail drag behind him as if he were a fox, tore off at full speed into the garden. The puppy dashed after him, yapping hysterically, its ears flapping, and the boys tore after the puppy, whooping wildly. The cat flew over the fence as though carried on the wind; the puppy, incapable of surmounting such an obstacle, tore off in an instant to a familiar gap in order to get round it, and the boys, nimbly climbing up the rotten wattle fence, at once sent the whole lot crumbling.

The cat flashed through the beds of cucumbers, tomatoes, and cabbage like ginger lightning, and Razmiotnov, delighted be-

yond all measure, squatted down and clapped his hands on his thighs as he shouted:

"Hold him! Don't let him get away! Catch him! I know him!"

Happening to glance up at the veranda, he was amazed to see that the old woman was laughing her head off, holding her violently shaking, heavy breasts with her hands. She wiped her eyes with the ends of her kerchief and, still simmering with laughter, said in a thick voice:

"Andrei Razmiotnov, either you or your village Soviet, I don't care which, will pay for the food you've spoilt. By this very evening I'll reckon up how much the bandits you brought with you have trodden down, and then you can empty your purse."

He went to the veranda and looked up at her with eyes full of entreaty. "Old lady, you'll have payment in full either from my pay as Chairman or from our garden in the autumn. But in exchange let me have the pigeons your cat has been chasing. My pair will be bringing up their young soon now. And then, with the pair you give me, I shall have quite a prosperous pigeon-rearing business."

"Take them, in the name of Christ; take the lot if you wish. They don't bring in anything: they only starve my chickens with eating their food."

Turning to face the garden, Andrei shouted: "Boys, cease fire!"

Some ten minutes later he was on his way back home. But he did not go through the streets; he went down by the river, so as not to attract the attention of the gossipy Gremyachy women. A fresh, almost cold wind blew from the north. He had put a pair of warm pigeons with heavy crops into his fur cap and had covered the cap with the edge of his quilted coat, and now looked around him stealthily, with an embarrassed smile, while the wind, the cold wind from the north, played with his greying forelock.

Chapter 22

A couple of days before the open meeting of the village Communist group six women members of the collective farm called
on Nagulnov. It was early in the morning, and they did not like
to crowd into the house in a bunch. So they sat down in a businesslike fashion on the steps leading to the veranda and on the
ledge round the house wall. Adjusting her clean, deep-blue kerchief on her head, Kondrat Maidannikov's wife asked:

"Well, women, am I to go in and see him?"

"You go, as you've offered," Dubtsiev's wife, who was sitting
on the bottom step, answered for them all.

Makar was in his room, shaving, awkwardly bent double as
he sat in front of a small fragment of mirror set up against
a flower pot. The old, blunt razor removed the coarse black
bristles from his cheeks with a noise like an electrical discharge,
while he frowned with misery, groaned, and occasionally bellowed hollowly, wiping the tears from his eyes with the sleeve
of his undershirt. He had already managed to cut himself in
several places, and the thin lather on his cheeks and neck was no
longer white, but unevenly rosy. The face reflected in the dim
glass expressed various feelings: humble submission to fate,
restrained torture, and raging fury. At times in its look of desperate resolution it recalled the face of a suicide planning to end
his life at all costs with the aid of a razor.

As she entered the room, Maidannikov's wife said a quiet
"Good morning." Makar swiftly turned his gloomy, contorted,
and blood-stained face to look at her, and the poor woman cried
out in alarm and dropped back to the door:

"Oh, my goodness! What are you all smothered in blood for?
You ought to go and wash yourself; the blood's pouring out of
you as if you were a slaughtered pig."

"Don't be alarmed, you devilish fool: sit down!" he said in
greeting, smiling graciously. "The razor's blunt, and so I've cut
myself. I ought to have thrown it away long ago, but I don't like
to. I've got used to torturing myself with the damned thing.

It's been through two wars with me; for fifteen years now it's helped to make me look handsome. So how can I throw it away? Do sit down: I'll be finished in a minute."

"You say the razor's blunt?" she asked, not knowing what else to say, as she timidly sat down on the bench and tried to avoid looking at him.

"Terribly. Though the blast . . ." He bit off the syllable, coughed once or twice, and ended in a gush of words: "Though I could bandage my eyes and scrape myself without looking. But what have you turned up at this unearthly hour for? Has something happened at home? Has Kondrat had a stroke?"

"No, he's quite well. And I haven't come by myself. There are six of us to see you."

"What on earth about?"

"The day after tomorrow you'll be taking our husbands into the Party, and we wanted to put the school in order for the day."

"Did you think of this yourselves, or did your husbands suggest it to you?"

"Why, d'you think we haven't any minds of our own? You don't think much of us, Comrade Nagulnov."

"Oh, all right; if you thought it up yourselves, that's all right."

"We want to paint and whitewash the school inside and out."

"A very good idea. I approve wholly and entirely; only bear in mind that we shan't allow you any labour days for this job. This is a social activity."

"What have the labour days got to do with it when we're doing it of our own choice? Only you must tell the brigadiers not to send us out on other work. There are six of us; put our names down on a bit of paper."

"I'll tell the brigadiers. But there's no point in writing your names down; there's enough bureaucracy and paper-writing about without your adding to it." She got up, and was silent for a moment, looking at him sideways. Then she smiled. "You know, my husband's just as queer as you, and possibly even worse. The people tell me that all the time he's out in the fields he shaves himself every day, and when he comes home he's continually trying on his shirts. He's only got three altogether, but he stands there trying on first one then another, unable to make up

his mind which one to join the Party in on Sunday. I laugh and
tell him: 'You're just like a girl before her wedding.' But he gets
terribly cross, though he doesn't show it. Only once, when I
laughed at him, he narrowed his eyes. And then I know he's
about to let fly a lot of filthy language, and I get out quick: I
don't want to upset him completely."

Makar smiled wryly and turned up his eyes. "My dear, this
business is more serious for your husband than for any girl
about to get married. A wedding's just spit. They exchange rings
and dash off home, so to speak, and that's the end of it. But the
Party, my girl, is a sort of business . . . in a word . . . a sort
of business. . . . But you wouldn't understand it anyway. You'd
swim through Party considerations and ideas like a cockroach
in soup; I don't know why I'm gassing away to you now unnecessarily, grinding water in a mortar. In a word, the Party's a serious
business and that's my last word. Is that clear?"

"That's clear, Makar dear; only you must tell them to bring
ten loads of clay."

"I'll tell them."

"And chalk for whitewashing the walls."

"I'll tell them."

"And a pair of horses with lads to mix the clay."

"And perhaps you'd like us to get you a dozen plasterers from
Rostov too?" Makar asked sarcastically, turning all his body
round like a wolf to look at her, and holding the razor in his outstretched hand.

"We'll do the plastering ourselves, but do let us have the horses;
otherwise we shan't get the work done by Sunday."

Makar sighed. "You know how to sit on our necks, you
women! All right, we'll let you have horses too, we'll put everything at your disposal, only do go away, for God's sake. Through
you I've cut myself twice more than necessary. If you remain here
talking to me for another minute or two, there'll be nothing left
of me. Get that?"

Makar's masculine voice sounded a note of such miserable
entreaty that she turned round in a hurry, said: "Oh, well, so
long," and went out. But a moment later she opened the door
again. "You must excuse me, Makar . . ."

"Now what d'you want?" he asked with undisguised annoyance.

"I forgot to say 'thank you.'"

The door was slammed noisily behind her. Makar started and once more sent the razor deep into his flesh. "Thank you, thank you all, you devilish idiots. But you've got nothing to thank me for," he shouted after her. But he went on laughing noiselessly for some time after her departure. And this little incident made the normally gruff Makar so cheerful that he smiled to himself all day, every time he recalled her visit.

The days turned unusually fine, sunny, and windless. By Saturday evening the outside of the school was shining with the irreproachable white of its walls, while the floors inside, washed and scoured with brick-dust, were so spotlessly clean that everybody who went in involuntarily began to walk about on tiptoe.

The Party meeting was timed to begin at six o'clock, but by four in the afternoon more than fifty people had gathered in the school. And at once, although all the doors and windows were flung wide open, the classrooms were filled with the spirity, pungent smell of masculine sweat and of the cheap pomade and equally cheap soap used by the women and girls in their Sunday best, who were all bunched together in a single group.

It was the first open Party meeting for the reception of new members that had been held in Gremyachy Log, and by six o'clock all the adults in the village, with the exception of those too ill to get up, were either in the school or gathered outside. Not a soul was left out on the steppe, in the field camps; everybody had come back to the village. Even the herdsman Agei abandoned the village herd to the care of his assistant, and turned up in a change of clothes, his beard neatly combed, and wearing ancient, worn-out boots with excessively wide tops. So unusual was the sight of him in boots and all dressed up, without his knout and his canvas wallet hanging from one shoulder, that many of the older Cossacks didn't recognize him at first and greeted him as if he were a visitor from another village.

At six o'clock precisely Makar Nagulnov stood up behind the

table covered with red satin cloth, and surveyed the solidly packed rows of collective farmers crowded on the school desks and standing in the gangways. The dull murmur of voices and a woman's squealing laughter in the very back row did not stop. So he raised his hand high.

"Now, then, take yourselves in hand a bit, those of you who're kicking up so much noise, and especially the females. I ask you to keep as quiet as possible, and I declare this open Party meeting of the Gremyachy group of the All-Union Communist Party (Bolshevik) duly open. The first to speak will be Comrade Nagulnov, that's myself. There's only one item on the agenda: the taking in of new members into the Party. We've had several applications, and among them one from our fellow villager Kondrat Maidannikov. You all know him as well as if he was naked. But regulations and the Party constitution lay it down that his case has to be considered. So I ask you all, both the Party and also the non-Party comrades and citizens, to give us your true opinion about Kondrat, who thinks what, who's for, and who's against, if anyone is against. Any statement opposing his acceptance is called an objection. You must say 'I make an objection to Comrade Maidannikov,' and then give your reasons why you think Maidannikov is unworthy to be in the Party. We need definite facts, we can only take facts into consideration; it's a bad business to wander round and round and maunder about a man without facts. We shan't take any tongue-wagging of that sort into account. But first of all I shall read Kondrat Maidannikov's short application; then he'll give us his autobiography: in other words, he'll describe his past, present, and future life. And then it'll be your turn to speak, those of you who feel like it, concerning Comrade Maidannikov. Is that all clear? So now I'll go into action. I'll read his application."

He read the application for membership, smoothed out the sheet of paper on the table, and laid his long, heavy palm on it. That sheet torn from a school exercise book had cost Maidannikov many sleepless nights and much tormenting celebration. And now, only rarely glancing up at the Communists sitting behind the table and round at his neighbours with a timid glance not at all like him, Kondrat grew so agitated that great beads of sweat

stood out on his forehead, and his face looked as though it had been sprinkled with rain.

In a few words he told of his life, painfully searching for words, making long pauses, frowning and simultaneously smiling a twisted, miserable smile.

Liubishkin could not stand it and said in a loud voice: "What are you so ashamed of your life for? What are you so anxious about, like a horse fretting at the tether post? Your life's good enough, Kondrat; speak up bolder."

"I've said all I've got to say," Maidannikov quietly replied, sitting down and wriggling his shoulders as if he were cold. He felt as though he had just come out unclothed from an overheated hut into the frost.

There was a momentary silence; then Davidov rose to his feet. He spoke briefly but warmly of Maidannikov, who, by his hard work, set an example to the other collective farmers, and ended on a tone of conviction. "He's thoroughly worthy to be in the ranks of our Party, and that's a fact."

Several others spoke in warm and friendly tones concerning Maidannikov; again and again they were interrupted by cries of approval. Pale with agitation, Kondrat had to sit and listen to many flattering remarks about himself, and the opinion of the meeting seemed to be unanimous. But unexpectedly old Shchukar not so much stood as wriggled up, and began a speech.

"Dear comrades and old women! I'll strip Kondrat naked. I'm not like others: with me friendship is friendship, but tobacco's another question. That's the sort of man I am! Kondrat's been described here this evening as if he wasn't a man but a holy saint. But I ask you, citizens: what sort of saint can he be when he's just as sinful as all the rest of us?"

"You're getting things mixed up like you always do, Daddy. We're not accepting Kondrat into paradise, but into the Party," Nagulnov admonished the old man good-naturedly.

But Shchukar was not the sort to be put out of his stride by a single retort. His one eye glittering evilly (for the other was bandaged with a crimsoned, very dirty handkerchief), he turned on Nagulnov. "Ah, my dear Makar, you're quick to pick good people up. What are you trying to close my mouth for, not letting

me speak? I'm not talking about you, I'm not stripping you bare. So you shut up, for the Party says that we're to develop criticism and self-criticism with all our powers. And what is self-criticism? To put it in good Russian: it's self-acting criticism. That means you should pinch a man wherever you like, but in any case until it hurts. Pinch him, the son of a bitch, so that he's wet from head to foot with sweat. That's what 'self-criticism' means."

"Hold your horses, Daddy," Nagulnov firmly interrupted. "Don't twist the word to make it suit you. Self-criticism means to criticize yourself, that's what it means. So now draw in your horns and sit quietly."

"No, you draw your horns in, and don't push my criticism back down my throat," Shchukar cried in a high falsetto, growing excited. "You're altogether too clever, Makar. Why the penny candle should I give myself a whipping? And what benefit shall I get out of trying to persuade myself? There are fools enough in the Soviet regime. The old fools have come over, and you couldn't add up how many new ones have been born. Under the Soviet regime they're not sown, they're like seed that's fallen by the wayside, there's no stopping that harvest. Take you, for instance, my dear Makar . . ."

"You can leave me out. I'm not the subject under discussion," Nagulnov said sternly. "Get to the point about Kondrat Maidannikov. But if you haven't anything to say, shut your mouth and sit quietly and orderly like all decent people."

"Then are you orderly or not?" Shchukar sorrowfully asked.

To which someone sitting at the back commented in a deep voice: "You orderly old man, you should tell us all about yourself, whom you've had children by in your old age, and why you've only got one eye to see with. You're cuckooing away about other people like a cock on top of the wattle; but you're not saying anything about yourself, you cunning old devil."

A roar of laughter echoed through the school, but it died away when Davidov stood up. His face was clouded; his voice sounded indignant. "Comrades, this isn't a comic act we're putting on here but a Party meeting, that's a fact. If anyone wants his bit of fun let him go and spend the evening with the women sitting around and gossiping. Will you get to the subject, old man, or do you intend to go on being funny?"

It was the first time Davidov had ever spoken to Shchukar like that, and the old fellow lost his temper completely. Standing behind the desk, he danced up and down like a young cock before a fight; even his wispy beard quivered with rage.

"Who's being funny, me or that half-wit who's sitting at the back and asking idiotic questions? And what sort of open meeting d'you call it when a man isn't allowed to say one word openly? I am talking about the subject of Kondrat's application. I say I'll strip him naked. Such as him aren't needed in the Party, that's all I have to say."

"Why not, Daddy?" Razmiotnov asked, laughing quietly.

"Because he's not worthy to be in the Party. And what are you laughing at? If you don't see why Kondrat isn't worthy to join the Party I'll explain it to you categorically, and then you'll stop cackling like an old ram eying the sheep. You should set others an example, but what are you doing? You're the chairman of the village Soviet: both old and young should take their example from you. But how are you behaving? You're blowing all over the meeting with your idiotic laughter. What is there to laugh at when Kondrat's fate is being weighed in the balance? Take yourself in hand. Who's the more serious of us two, you or me? I'm sorry, my lad, that Makar's forbidden me to use various foreign words in my speech, or I'd put it over on you so that you'd never make head nor tail of what I was talking about. I'm against Kondrat being in the Party because he's a petty property owner; and you won't squeeze anything else out of him even if you put him in a press. To put it scientifically, he'd make oilcake, but never a Communist."

"But why won't I make a Communist, Daddy?" Kondrat asked in a voice quivering with injury. "Explain to me and the other citizens why I'm not worthy. Only speak the naked truth, without any of your fairy tales."

"When have I ever lied? Or made up any sort of fairy tale?" He sighed so loud that it must have been heard all over the school. "All my life I've only spoken the mother truth straight to the good folk's faces, and for that very reason, my dear Kondrat, I'm a disagreeable aliment to some people in this world. Your late father used to say: 'If Shchukar lies, who ever speaks the truth?' Pity he's dead, or he'd confirm his own words: may he

inherit the heavenly kingdom!" He crossed himself and had it in mind to let drop a tear or two; but for some reason he thought better of it.

"My father's got nothing to do with it. What exactly are you accusing me of?" Maidannikov insisted.

Judging by such remarks as could be distinguished, the restrained hum of disapproval that arose in the meeting was clearly directed against Shchukar; but that didn't disturb him in the least. Peaceably waving his arms, he said: "In one minute I'll explain everything. But you, citizens and good old women, keep your hum to yourselves. You won't stop my flow of thought whatever you say. Just now I heard someone behind me hiss like a snake: 'He's got nothing else to do, so he . . .' and so on. But I know who that whisper belongs to. That, dear citizens and old women, was Agafon Dubtsiev hissing behind me, like a savage snake from hell. He's trying to make me lose the thread of my thought so that I say nothing about him. But I shan't do him such a favour: he's chosen the wrong man for that. Agafon is another that's trying to crawl into the Party, like a grass snake into a cellar, to get its fill of milk. But today I shall skin him alive, even worse than Kondrat. I know something about him that'll make you all groan when you hear it."

Nagulnov tapped his pencil on a glass and said angrily: "Old man, you've already lost the thread of your confused ideas, so stop the cackle. You're taking up the time of the meeting."

"So you're trying to stop my mouth again, Makar, old boy?" Shchukar whined in a lachrymose tone. "Just because you're the group secretary! There's nothing in the Party constitution which says old men are forbidden to speak, I know that for certain. You've offended me to death, Makar."

He let fall an ardent tear after all, wiped his eyes on his shirt sleeve, and went on with all his previous fervour as though nothing had happened.

"But as for me, I don't care who it is, I won't shut up for him. And I shall deal with you, Makar, at a closed Party meeting, and in such a fashion that you'll never get away from me; you've attacked the wrong man now. I'm a desperate man when I let myself go; I don't care who it is. But you ought to know and understand that. After all, you and I have been close friends a

long time, so be ready for me and my criticism and self-criticism. I'll never let anyone go: bear that in mind anyone who thinks of bringing mud on the Party."

Raising his left eyebrow, Nagulnov turned to Davidov and whispered: "Shall we have him put out? He's breaking up the meeting. Why on earth didn't you send him off somewhere for the day? The old boy's got the reins under his tail, there'll be no stopping him now."

But Davidov hid his face behind a newspaper, and only shook his head. Nagulnov, thoroughly annoyed, shrugged his shoulders, and turned his angry gaze on Shchukar again. The old man went on, hurrying and stumbling over his words.

"Seeing as it's an open meeting, you, Kondrat, should be just as open and tell us: when you joined the collective farm and were ordered to hand over your pair of bullocks to the farm, did you cry over them or didn't you?"

"That question's nothing to do with it," Diemid Ushakov shouted.

"It's a darned foolish question," Ustin Rykalin said in support of Diemid.

"No, it isn't a foolish question, it's got everything to do with it. And you do-gooders, you shut your mouths," Shchukar bawled, trying to shout them down and going livid with the effort. He waited till there was silence, then said again, now quietly and craftily: "Maybe you don't remember, my dear Kondrat; but I do, that when you drove your bullocks to the communal yard in the morning your eyes were as big as a fist and as red as a rabbit's, or, let's say, like those of a drowsy old dog. And now answer as though you were confessing to the priest, was that so or not?"

Maidannikov rose, pulled down his shirt with an embarrassed gesture, gave old Shchukar one brief angry glance, and answered with restrained firmness: "That was so. I don't try to hide it, I did cry. I was sorry to part with them. Those bullocks hadn't been left to me by my father: I'd earned them myself with my own labour. I didn't come by them all that easily. But that's a thing of the past, Daddy. And what injury does the Party suffer by my past tears?"

"What d'you mean, 'what injury'?" Shchukar cried indignantly.

"Why, where were you going with your bullocks? You, my friend, were going to socialism, that's where you were going. But after socialism what shall we have next? We shall have complete communism, that's what we'll have, I tell you that straight out. Everybody sitting here knows that Makar Nagulnov and I are tremendous friends, and I get all sorts of knowledge from him by the handful; at night I read all sorts of thick books, serious books, and no pictures in them. My memory's gone just like trousers with torn pockets: whatever I put into it falls through and that's the end of it. But when I get a little pamphlet into my hands you can't tear it away from me. I remember everything it says. I've read lots of pamphlets and I know them by heart and I can argue with whoever you like, right till the third cock, that after socialism communism will be calling on us. I tell you that categorically. And that's where I'm troubled by doubt, Kondrat. You entered into socialism washing your face with tears; so how will you present yourself to communism? You'll wade up to your knees in tears, that's as true as God's sacred. But I ask you, citizens and dear old women, what need has the Party of him, a tear-shedder?"

He sniggered merrily and covered his toothless mouth with his hand.

"I can't stand the serious sort of people, either in the Party or generally. What the devil do we need them there for, these gloomy devils? To make good folk miserable, to distort and ruin the Party constitution with their looks? I say you want to take cheerful, lively people like me into the Party; but they take in only the serious sort. There's Makar, for instance. Since 1918 he's grown as stiff as if he'd swallowed a steel rule, and even today he goes around as serious and important-looking as a crane in a marsh. You never hear him joke: he never says a cheerful word. He's not a man: he's nothing but naked boredom in trousers."

"Old man, don't start talking about me and my person, or I'll take steps," Nagulnov sternly warned him.

But Shchukar, smiling beatifically, and quite unable to master his oratorical itch, continued fervently. "I'm not talking about you at all. As for Kondrat, you can have him for twenty roubles; he's mounted a pencil and now he's well away: he's always writing things down and reckoning things up, as though if he wasn't

around there'd be nobody capable of taking a note. His job is to twist the oxen's tails, but like a fool he's pushing his way in, when there are far more educated people in Moscow. But in my view, citizens and dear old women, he's doing all this becuase he suffers from a great lack of mental consciousness. Our Kondrat hasn't yet developed politically, and if he hasn't done that, let him sit quietly at home and develop himself little by little. But don't let him crawl into the Party yet awhile. He can feel as injured as he likes till he bursts, but I'm categorically against him and give him my full objection."

Suddenly Davidov heard Varia Kharlamova's high-pitched, quivering voice calling from the next classroom. It was some time since he had seen her, or heard her pleasant voice. "May I speak?"

"Come in here so that we can see you," Nagulnov proposed.

Boldly pushing through the solidly packed Cossacks, droopy Varia went up to the table, tidying the hair on her nape with a light touch of her sunburnt hands. Davidov stared at her in astonishment, hardly able to believe his eyes. During the last month or two she had changed almost beyond recognition: she was no longer a gawky adolescent, but a shapely young woman, carrying her head proudly with its heavy knot of hair caught in a triangular blue kerchief. She stood half turned to the chairman's table, waiting for silence and looking over the heads of the people, screwing up her young and beautiful eyes as though gazing into the distant steppe. "How much handsomer she's grown since spring," Davidov thought. Her eyes glittered with excitement, and her rosy face shone with sweat. But now, confronted with so many eyes fixed on her, her courage failed her; her big hands spasmodically crumpled her lace handkerchief, her face flooded with a deep flush, and her husky voice quivered with agitation as she turned to Shchukar.

"You're all wrong, Daddy. You're saying bad things about Kondrat Maidannikov, but nobody will believe you when you say he isn't worthy to be in the Party. I worked with him during the ploughing in the spring, and he ploughed best of all and most of all. He's putting all he knows into the collective-farm work, and yet you're against him. . . . You're an old man, but you reason like a silly child."

"That's the way, Varia, pepper him. He tinkles away like a bell round a calf's neck, and you'll never hear him say a good word about others," Pavel Liubishkin said in a ripe bass voice.

"She's talking sense. Kondrat's got more labour days to his credit than anyone else in the collective farm," old Beskhlebnov intervened.

Someone outside in the passage cried in a tenor voice: "If a man like Kondrat isn't to be accepted in the Party, then let old Daddy Shchukar join. Under him the collective farm will go flying up at once. . . ."

Shchukar only smiled condescendingly into his unkempt beard and stood at the desk as though bolted to the floor, not even turning round to face the speakers. When silence fell again, he calmly said: "Varia has no right to be here at all, seeing she isn't of age. She ought to be playing with her doll somewhere under a shed. But the magpie's turned up here to teach sense to wise old men like me. The egg's started to teach the hen. And the others are just as clever: they judge by the labour days—why, Kondrat's got so many you couldn't load them on to a cart. But I ask you: what have the labour days got to do with it? He's only got them through greed: the small owners are always greedy, if you wish to know. Makar's explained that to me more than once. And now we've found another fool: take Shchukar into the Party and the collective farm will cheer up at once. There's nothing funny in that remark: only someone who's cracked could laugh at it. Am I literate? Completely. Do I accept the Party constitution? I accept it very much. Do I agree with the programme? I do agree and I've got nothing against it. I can go from socialism to communisn, and not simply at a marching pace. I can tear along at top speed, of course within my possibilities as an old man, not too fast, otherwise I'd peg out. And I'd have joined the Party long ago, and I might have been going about with a document case under my arm, but, dear citizens and dear old women, I declare to you as if I was before the Lord God Almighty that at present I'm not yet worthy of our Party. And why not, I ask you? Why, because religion's eaten me up, may it be triply damned! As soon as anything happens over my head, up in the sky, a heavy clap of thunder, say, I start whispering: 'Lord have mercy on me, a sinner.' And I make the sign

of the cross, I pray to Jesus Christ and the Virgin Mary, and the Madonna, and to all the saints I can remember in the heat of the moment. I pray and pray and even squat down on my heels when I hear a thunderclap. . . ."

He was so carried away by his story that he started to cross himself and raised his hand as far as his brow. But he recollected himself in time and, scratching his forehead, giggled disconcertedly.

"But what was I saying? With fear in my eyes, as you can imagine: 'The devil knows what he, Elijah the Thunder-bearer, may think of. He may get it into his head to strike me with lightning on my bald patch, just for fun; and then lie down, Shchukar, and throw out your hoofs all four ways.' But that isn't what I want at all. I want to go on until we get to communism, I want to make my way to a pleasant life, and so sometimes I pray and give the priest a coin, not more than a silver kopek, so that God may not be unnecessarily angry with me. You'd think that that way it might be safer, you dream the priest will pray for your health, you fool! But if you get to the bottom of it all, you're as necessary to the priest as a loose woman is to a dead man, or, to put it in learned language, a bordure: that means the same. . . . And so I have to tell you: how can I with my anathematic religion creep into the Party? Only to distort it, and myself, and the programme too? No thanks: save me from such a sin. That's not how it should be with me, I declare categorically."

"You've gone off the rails again, Daddy," Razmiotnov cried. "Turn back on to the road, don't go wandering down side tracks."

Shchukar raised his hand in admonition. "I'll be finished in a moment, Andrei. Only don't put me off with your idiotic shouts. You sit and listen quietly to the intelligent speeches: you'll find them useful. I never do go off the rails, that never happens to me; but you and Makar are taking turns to shout at me like a deacon and the choir, and as a result I can't help losing the thread of my thoughts. Well, as I was saying: though I'm non-Party I'll get to communism all the same, and not crying like Kondrat, but dancing, cheerfully, because I'm a pure proletariat and not a small owner, I tell you that straight. I've read somewhere that the proletariat has nothing to lose but his chains. Of course I haven't any chains, except an old chain which I used to use to fasten up the

dog with—that was when I was living in comfort. But I've got my old woman, and I tell you, brothers, she's worse than any chains and penal servitude leg-irons. But I've no intention of losing my old woman, either: she can go on living with me, God bless her. But if she starts to get in my way and stands across my direct road to communism, I shall shoot past her so fast she won't have time even to groan. I'm a desperate man when I let myself go, so let no one stand across my road. I'll either trample him to death or I'll shoot past him so fast that nobody will have time to blink."

"Bring it to an end, old man, or I'll have to stop you," Nagulnov resolutely informed him, smacking his hand down on the table.

"I'll be done in a minute, Makar, my dear. Don't bang too hard or you'll knock your hand off. And as I was saying: if you're all in favour of Kondrat, then I don't object either. God bless you, take him into our Party. He's a respectable, hard-working lad, and I've always said so. In a word, Kondrat is fully worthy of being a Party member. And that's all I've got to say."

"So you began by killing him and end with blessing him?" Razmiotnov asked. But the remark could hardly be heard above the general roar of laughter.

Satisfied beyond all measure with his speech, Shchukar wearily sat down on the desk, wiped his sweaty bald spot with his sleeve, and asked his neighbour, Antip Grach: "Did I . . . you know . . . criticize properly?"

"You should go and join a circus, Daddy," Antip whispered.

The old man squinted distrustfully at Antip, but did not notice the smile lurking in the tow of his beard, and asked again: "Why d'you think I ought to do that?"

"You'd shovel up money with a spade; there's work you can do there—get going. Amuse the people with your merry tales, tell even more lies, be even more queer, that's all the work you're fit for. It's not dusty, but it brings in the money."

Shchukar clearly brightened up, fidgeted on the bench, and smiled. "Why, my dear Antip! Bear in mind that Shchukar would never be at a loss. He never wastes a word, he always speaks to the point, he's not the sort to ramble. In the worst resort, when old age finally lays its hands on me, I could go and join a circus. I

was good at that sort of thing even when a boy, but now I'm first-class. It's a mere flea-bite to me."

He chewed thoughtfully with his toothless gums, and was silent, turning something over in his mind. At last he asked:

"But you don't happen to know how much they pay in a circus, do you? Is it by the job, or how? In a word, what's the wages? Kopeks can be scraped up with a shovel, but they're no use, though a miser regards even a kopek as good money."

"They pay according to the trick and the number, and how you go down with the people," Antip whispered conspiratorially. "The looser and the more on the go you are, the more pay you get. All they do, brother, is eat and drink and travel around from town to town. They have an easy life, like the birds, you might say. . . ."

"Come outside and have a smoke, Antip," Shchukar suggested, at once losing all interest in the meeting.

They left the classroom, pushing their way with difficulty through the crowd. They sat down on the ground, still warm with the sun, under the wattle fence, and lit up.

"But have you ever seen these circuses you speak of, Antip?"

"Plenty of times. When I was in the regular army at Grodno I saw plenty of them."

"Well, and what are they like?"

"Just ordinary."

"Did they look well fed?"

"Like pigs."

Shchukar sighed. "So they never go without vittles winter or summer?"

"That's right."

"And where d'you have to go to join them?"

"Only in Rostov. They never come any nearer."

"But that's not all that far. Why didn't you tell me before? I might have fixed myself up with a job among them long ago. You've robbed me of a modest crust of bread. You're not a man: you're a blunt mattock."

"But we've never had any reason to talk about it before," Antip said in self-justification.

"You should have brought it to my notice long ago, and I'd

have been getting my food among the artists long ago. And
whenever I came to see my old woman you'd have had half a litre
of vodka for your good advice. I'd have been full and you'd have
been drunk, and everything would have been perfect. I must
talk it over with the old woman this very day, and perhaps next
winter I'll set out to make some money. I'll get a little cow, buy a
dozen sheep or so, and a young pig, and that'll cheer things up a
bit." He dreamed aloud, encouraged by Antip's sympathetic silence. "But I have to admit I've got bored with the stallions,
and, besides, winter driving isn't for me. To put it frankly, my
health isn't what it was. You sit an hour in a sled and get so cold
your pipes freeze to one another inside you. And if that goes on
for long you get a blockage, if everything gets frozen up inside
you with the frost, or inflammation of the sciatic nerve, like it was
with Khariton, who died. And I don't want anything like that.
I've lots of things to do yet, and I'll get through to communism
even if I split in two."

Antip was getting tired of his fun at the expense of the child-
ishly credulous old man, and he decided to bring the joke to an
end.

"But I should think about it a lot, Daddy, before you put your
name down to be an artist. . . ."

"There's nothing to think about," Shchukar declared confidently. "Once there's money being given away, I'll be there by
the winter. It's easy enough to amuse good folk and tell them all
sorts of stories."

"But you mightn't always want to have the money. . . ."

"Why not?" Shchukar sounded anxious now.

"They beat them, these artists. . . ."

"Beat . . . them? But who beats them?"

"The people who pay money for the tickets beat them."

"But what for?"

"Well, if the artist doesn't please them with something he says,
or if his tale bores them, they beat him. Sometimes they beat
the artist so bad that the poor devil's taken straight from the
performance to the hospital and sometimes even to the cemetery.
Before my very eyes in the old days they bit off the ear of one
artist in the circus and twisted his hind leg round back to front.
And he went home like that, the poor wretch. . . ."

"Hold on! What d'you mean by his hind leg? Had he got four legs, then?"

"You can see all sorts of things there. They keep all sorts of freaks just for fun. But this time I was making a mistake. I ought to have said: his left, his front leg; what they did was to twist his left leg round so that he walked ass forward, and you couldn't tell which way he was going. And how he yelled, the wretch! He could be heard all over town. He howled like a locomotive; it clean made my hair stand on end."

Shchukar stared long and searchingly at Antip's face; it was serious, in fact positively gloomy, evidently because of these unpleasant memories. He decided to believe what he had heard and asked indignantly: "But where were the police, damn them?"

"The police themselves took part in the beating. I myself saw a policeman holding a whistle in his left hand and blowing it, and shaking the artist by the neck with his right."

"That sort of thing could happen under the Tsar, Antip; but under the Soviet regime the militia aren't allowed to take part in a fight."

"Of course the militia don't touch ordinary citizens; but they beat the artists all the same, they're allowed to do that. That's been the order of things all through the ages, and there's nothing to be done about it."

Old Shchukar half closed one eye suspiciously. "You're lying, you devil! How do you know they beat the artists these days? You haven't been in a town for thirty years, you never show your nose outside our village, so how can you know?"

"I've got a relation living in Novocherkass, and in his letters he tells me all about life in the towns," Antip assured him.

"Surely your relation . . ." Shchukar was shaken again, and sighed deeply, while his face grew gloomy. "So there's a snag, Antip. . . . It seems to be a risky business, being an artist. If the people go so far as to beat a man to death I'm not interested. They can enjoy themselves without me."

"Well, I warn you just in case. You can talk it over first with the old woman."

"The old woman doesn't come into this," the old man replied curtly. "If anything happened it wouldn't be her sides that would feel the stick. What am I to talk it over with her for?"

"Then decide for yourself." Antip scrambled to his feet and stubbed out his cigarette.

"I'm not in any hurry, it's a long time yet to winter, and I must admit I'd be sorry to leave the stallions; and the old woman would start yearning for me if I left her. No, Antip, let the artists manage without me. If you're going to be thrashed with whatever comes to hand every day, I thank you most humbly. You try those jam tarts yourself. Everybody's been down on me ever since I was a kid. Geese, and bulls, and dogs, and I don't know what else. It's even gone so far as children throwing things at me. And then in my old age to become an artist and be beaten up or have a limb turned round the wrong way. I thank you most humbly. Let the artists think for themselves. Evidently they're all young and healthy, the devils. But I'm getting old. What if the vittles are good, let them give me a couple of good whackings and I'd be yielding my soul to God. And what the devil use would that modest piece of bread be to me then? I don't want to be an artist, and don't try to get me to go there any more, you black devil, and don't get me all worked up. Just now you mentioned that one artist had his ear bitten off by some senseless idiot, and had his leg twisted round, and was beaten up, and now my ears are aching, and my leg feels as if it's broken, and all my bones are aching as if I'd already been beaten up, bitten by the ear, and dragged around just as they liked. . . . I'm terribly sensitive to such beastly stories. So you go back to the meeting by yourself, and I'll take a little rest out here and get calmed down. And then I'll come and make my objection to Dubtsiev. I couldn't speak now, Antip; there's a shiver running down my spine, and I've got a trembling in the knees like an ague, I couldn't stand firmly on my feet, damn it."

He began to twist a new cigarette. And his hands were genuinely trembling, the coarsely rubbed tobacco slipped out of the trough of the scrap of newspaper, his face furrowed lachrymosely. Antip looked at the old man with assumed pity.

"I didn't know you were such a sensitive soul, old man, or I wouldn't have told you about the artists' bitter life. No, Daddy, you're not fitted to be an artist. You just sit up on the stove and don't go chasing after an extra rouble. And, besides, it wouldn't

be right to leave your old woman alone for so long, you should have pity on her old age. . . ."

"That's just it: she'll be delighted when I tell her I refused to become an artist for her sake. There'll be no end to her gratitude to me."

He smiled touchingly, and nodded his head, anticipating the satisfaction he himself would feel and would give his old woman when he told her the pleasant news.

"And talk of the devil, here is your old woman," Antip Grach said, now openly smiling and grunting with pleasure.

Shchukar looked up. The beatific smile was wiped from his face as though by a wet sponge. His wife was coming straight towards him, a fierce, resolute look on her face. "Oh, damn her . . ." he whispered in dismay. "Where's she turned up from, the devil? She was lying ill in bed and couldn't lift her head. What evil is the unclean spirit bringing her here for?"

"Come on home, Grand-dad," the old woman ordered in a voice that would allow of no objection.

Sitting on the ground as though bewitched, Shchukar stared up at her like a rabbit at a snake. "The meeting isn't over yet, my dear, and I've got to make a speech. Our village authorities have enthusiastically asked me to speak," he said at last in a quiet voice, beginning to stutter.

"They'll manage without you. Come on. I've got a job for you to do at home."

She was almost a head taller than her husband, and twice as heavy. She authoritatively took him by the arm and, with one tug, easily dragged him on to his feet. He came to himself and angrily stamped his foot.

"Well, I'm not going. You've no right whatever to deprive me of my right to speak. This isn't the old regime now."

Saying no more, she turned and strode off homeward. Dragged by her hand, occasionally resisting, Shchukar trotted along beside her. All his bearing indicated a blind submission to fate.

Antip Grach stood gazing after them, chuckling. But as he went up the school steps he thought: "Though after all, God grant the old fellow doesn't die yet awhile. Life would be less interesting without him in the village."

Chapter 23

As soon as Shchukar had gone, the meeting grew more business-like, no longer interrupted by sudden gusts of laughter. Several speeches were made in favour of Dubtsiev's candidature. All the farmers applying to join the Party had been subjected to thorough consideration; all three had been unanimously accepted by open vote as candidates for Party membership, with a six-month trial period, when old Shaly asked permission to speak. A silence like that which presages a storm fell over the meeting. He rose from a desk close to the window, leaned his broad back against the sill, and asked:

"May I ask our farm manager, Yakov Lukich, one question?"

"You can make it two if you wish," Makar Nagulnov decided, half jesting, half on his guard.

Yakov Lukich reluctantly turned to face the smith. A tense look froze on his face. "Here we have men joining the Party; they don't want to live just outside it, but right in it, to share its sorrows and joys," Shaly began in a thick, deep tone, keeping his swollen eyes fixed on Yakov Lukich. "So why don't you apply to join, Lukich? I want to ask you straight out: why are you keeping out? Or aren't you concerned at all that the Party, like fish against ice, is struggling to take us on to a better life? What about you? You're trying to keep out of the hot jobs and you're sitting in the shade; you're waiting till you've been given your piece, till someone comes and puts it in your mouth, is that it? But why should that happen to you? You manage pretty well— all the people can see that very clearly. All the village sees it, if you wish to know."

"I work for what I get and I've never asked you for anything yet," Ostrovnov replied energetically.

But Shaly flung his hands out violently, as though pushing this feeble argument aside, and said: "There are all sorts of ways of getting hold of bread to feed yourself. You can hang your wallet across your shoulder and go begging in Christ's name, and

that'll keep you from dying of hunger. But that's not what I'm talking about, and don't try to wriggle out of it, Lukich, like a snake from under the fork. You understand what I'm talking about. In the old days, when we were individual farmers, you were a hard taskmaster, you were like a wolf. You never let go; you took on any job in order to get hold of an extra kopek wherever you could. But now you're working any old how, just to throw dust in our eyes. But that's not what I want to speak about: the time hasn't yet come for you to account to the people for your slack work and crooked ways. When the time does come, you'll account to them. But now tell us straight: why don't you join the Party?"

"I'm not educated enough to join the Party," Ostrovnov answered quietly, so quietly that only those sitting close to him heard what he said.

Someone at the back demanded: "Speak up! We can't hear what you're muttering to yourself. Say it again."

Yakov Lukich sat for some moments without speaking, as though he hadn't heard the demand. In the expectant silence the frogs could be heard croaking down by the dark and drowsy little stream, and somewhere in the distance, probably around the old windmill outside the village, an owl hooted; in the greenery of the acacias outside the school windows the waxwings chattered.

He could not go on sitting silent, and he repeated in a much louder voice: "I'm not educated enough for the Party."

"So you're educated enough to be manager, but not to join the Party?" Shaly asked again.

"That's farm management, but this is politics. If you can't see the difference between them, I do," Yakov Lukich said in a clear, ringing voice, recovering from the unexpected challenge.

But Shaly would not yield: he said with a sneer: "But our Communists occupy themselves with both farm work and politics, and—you'll realize how extraordinary this is—look at the results. It looks as though the one doesn't get in the way of the other. You're twisting somewhere, Lukich, you're not speaking your mind. You want to avoid the truth, so you're twisting."

"I've got nothing to twist about," Ostrovnov answered thickly.

"Oh yes you have. For some secret reason of your own you don't wish to join the Party. But maybe I'm mistaken: in that case you correct me; go on, correct me."

The meeting had lasted more than four hours. Despite the coolness of the evening, it was unbearably stifling in the school rooms. A few table lamps burned dimly in the corridor and in the classrooms, but they seemed to make the place even more stuffy. Yet the people, though streaming with sweat, sat on without fidgeting, silently, tensely following this unexpected duel between the old smith and Ostrovnov, and sensing that behind it was concealed something not expressed in words, something complicated and obscure.

"But what secret reasons could I have? Since you see through everything in the world, you tell me," Ostrovnov proposed, recovering his equanimity and turning to the attack.

"You speak up and tell us about yourself, Lukich. Why should I have to speak for you?"

"I've got nothing to say to you."

"But you haven't got to say it to me in any case; say it to the people."

"You're the only one who's asked me to speak."

"But that's enough for you. So you don't want to speak? All right, we'll wait: you'll talk all the same tomorrow, if you won't today."

"What on earth are you attacking me like this for, Ippolit? Why don't you join the Party yourself? You speak for yourself; I've got nothing to confess, you're not a priest."

"But who told you I shan't join the Party?" Shaly asked slowly, emphasizing every word, but without changing his position, still leaning against the window sill.

"You're not a member of the Party, and it's quite clear you're not joining."

Clearing his throat, the smith thrust himself away from the sill with his shoulders, the villagers opened a path for him, and with a deliberate rolling gait he went up to the chairman's table, saying as he went: "I haven't joined so far, that's true, but I'll join now. Seeing that you're not joining, Yakov Lukich, I've got to join. But if you'd put in an application today I'd have held mine

back. There isn't room for you and me in the one Party. You and
I belong to different parties. . . ."

Ostrovnov made no comment; an uncertain smile hovered on
his lips. But Shaly went up to the table, met Davidov's beaming,
welcoming gaze, and, holding out an application scribbled on a
small sheet of old, yellowing paper, said:

"I've got no one to recommend me. I'll have to get myself out
of that somehow. Which of you will support me, lads? Write it
down for me."

But Davidov was already writing his recommendation in a
hurried, sprawling hand. Then Nagulnov took over the pen.

So Ippolit Shaly also was accepted unanimously as a candidate
for Party membership. After the vote had been taken the members of the Gremyachy Communist group stood up and clapped,
and everybody in the meeting also stood up and clapped rag-
gedly, awkwardly, with their work-worn, calloused hands.

Shaly stood blinking, struggling with his feelings. But when
Razmiotnov whispered into his ear: "You ought to say something, something that'll move the people, Ippolit," the old man
obstinately shook his head.

"There's no point in wasting words. And besides, I haven't
any words of that kind in my pocket. Look how they're clapping. It strikes me they understand already without any words
from me."

At that moment Davidov happened to glance at Nagulnov beside him, and was astonished: he had never seen the group secretary look like that before. Makar was openly, broadly smiling.
Standing drawn up to his full height behind the table, he adjusted his tunic a little nervously, fidgeted unnecessarily with his
military belt, shifted from foot to foot, and, most significant of all,
he smiled, revealing his small, white teeth. His lips, normally
always pressed tightly together, were quivering at the corners
in almost a childlike, touching smile. That smile was so rarely
to be seen on his ascetically stern features that Ustin Rikalin
forgot himself, and exclaimed in the utmost amazement:

"Just look, everybody! Look at our Makar. I do believe he's
smiling. This is the first time I've ever seen such a miracle."

Making no attempt to hide his smile, Nagulnov retorted: "So

someone's noticed it, have they? But why shouldn't I smile? I'm
feeling good inside, that's why I'm smiling. That smile hasn't
been bought. And who's going to forbid me, anyway? Dear
citizens and fellow villagers, I declare this open Party meeting
closed. We've completed the agenda." Gathering himself together and straightening his already stalwart shoulders still more,
he stepped away from the table, and cried: "As Secretary of the
Party group I ask all the dear comrades who've just been accepted in our great Communist Party to come up to the table.
I want to congratulate you all on the great honour." Then, compressing his lips and returning to his normal mood, he added
quietly but in a tone of command: "All of you come to me."

Kondrat Maidannikov was the first to move forward. The people sitting behind him could see that his shirt was wet with
sweat and sticking to his back from the shoulders to the loins.
"He looks awful, anyone would think he'd scythed a whole hec-
tare of corn," one of the old women mumbled sympathetically.
But someone else chuckled quietly: "Kondrat's been properly
cooked."

Bowing his head, Nagulnov took the hand Kondrat thrust out
to him in his own long, moist hands, and squeezed it with all his
strength, saying in an exultant, quivering voice: "Comrade!
Brother! I congratulate you. We hope, all of us Communists
hope, you'll be an exemplary Bolshevik. But you couldn't be
anything else."

Ippolit was the last to come up, waddling like a bear and
smiling a wan smile, embarrassed with so many people staring
at him. He held out his black, work-worn, enormous hand. But
Nagulnov stepped forward to meet him, and gave the old smith's
broad, bowed shoulders a powerful hug with both arms.

"Well, Daddy Ippolit, things have turned out really fine. I congratulate you with all my heart. And the other Communist lads
here congratulate you too. Go on living and never fall ill; hammer away for another hundred years for the benefit of the Soviet
government and our collective farm. Have a long life, old man,
that's what I wish you. Nothing but good will come to the people
from your living for a long time yet, that's something you can be
sure of."

Huddling together and jostling one another awkwardly, the

four men taken into the Party shook hands with the other Communists. The meeting began to break up, to the sound of excited
chatter. But Davidov shouted:

"One minute, citizens. Allow me to say a few words."

"All right, Chairman, only cut it short, or we'll be choked to
death in here. The smell and heat's as strong as a good Russian
bath," one of the crowd warned him with a laugh.

The villagers began to sit down again in their places. There
was a quiet hum of voices for a few moments, then all was still.

"Citizen collective farmers, and especially the women farmers.
Today for the first time we have every member of our collective
farm gathered here," Davidov began. But Diemka Ushakov
shouted into the room from the passage:

"Why, Davidov, you've begun your speech just like old
Shchukar. He said: 'Dear citizens and old women,' and you say
almost the same: you're starting your dance from the same stove.
They're all learning the same lesson, including Shchukar. Shchukar's started to use Davidov's words: 'That's a fact,' and before
long Davidov will be saying: 'Dear citizens and dear old
women.' "

Such a burst of thunderous laughter rolled through the school
that the flames danced in the lamp-glasses, and one even went
out. Davidov laughed too, covering his gap-toothed mouth with
his hand, as was his habit. Only Nagulnov cried indignantly:

"Why, what are you up to? Can't the meeting take anything
seriously? Have you lost all your sense of responsibility together
with your sweat?"

But his shout only seemed to cause even more merriment, and
the roar of laughter rolled again through all the classrooms and
along the corridor. Makar waved his hand with a hopeless gesture, and turned with a bored look on his face to gaze out of the
window. All the same, he didn't find it easy to maintain this
demonstrative indifference, judging by the way the knobs of
flesh worked on his cheeks and his left eyebrow twitched.

But a moment or two later, when the room was quiet again, he
jumped up from his chair as though stung: from the back rows
came old Shchukar's loud, jarring voice:

"But I ask you, dear citizens and old women, why did I start
my speech like that?"

The words were hardly out of his mouth when the laughter broke out like gunfire, extinguishing two more lamps. In the semi-darkness someone accidently broke a lamp-glass, and swore violently. A woman's voice said in a tone of reproach:

"Now, now, hold it back! You're delighted because you can't be seen in the dark, and so you're swearing, are you, you fool?"

The laughter died down a little, and in the darkness Shchukar's jarring, indignant tones were heard again. "There's one fool swearing unnecessarily in the dark for some reason, and others are laughing their heads off, goodness knows why. This isn't serious, this is fun. Such people shouldn't come to meetings. I'll explain why I started by saying: 'Dear citizens and old women.' It's because the old women are sure and reliable. Any old woman, it doesn't matter which, is just like the State Bank; she lives without fraud or trickery. But as for the young women and girls, I don't even look at them. And why not, I ask you? Why, because it wasn't some respectable old woman that foisted a baby on me, that's not an old woman's trick; and even the most active old woman has guts too thin to bring a child into God's world. But some young hussy thought she'd be generous to me and of her own accord decided to reckon me in the list of fathers. That's why I can't stand these various and such like bits of skirt. After this business with the baby how can I say, for instance: 'My dear young women and spotless girls,' and offer tender words to them on a plate. Well, I ask you: never on my life!"

Nagulnov raised his eyebrows and asked in astonishment: "And where've you sprung from, Daddy? Your old woman carted you off home, so how is it you've managed to turn up here again?"

"Well, and supposing she did?" Shchukar answered loftily. "What's that to do with you? That's our family affair, not the Party's. Is that clear?"

"Not in the least. If she took you off home you ought to be at home still."

"I've been home, but I've got away again, my dear Makar. And I'm in debt to no one, neither to you nor to my old woman, by anti-Christ! So don't keep on at me, for God's sake."

"But how did you manage to steal away from home?" Davidov

asked, half laughing. He screwed up his eyes and covered his mouth with his hand as he waited for an answer.

Encouraged by the question, the old man forced his way towards the table, furiously working his elbows and thrusting aside the people standing in the gangways.

"Daddy, what are you walking on the people's heads for?" Nagulnov shouted at him. "Speak from your place; we give you permission. Only cut it short."

Halting halfway to the table, Shchukar hotly shouted back: "You teach your own woman where she should speak from. I know my place. You always climb up on to the platform, Makar, or you speak from the chairman's table and go round and round in circles from there. But why should I speak to the people from some dark corner? I can't see a single face from here, only necks, backs, and what good people sit down on. Who have I got to speak to and make my statements to, in your view? To the necks, backs, and so forth? You come to the back yourself and make your speeches from here; when I speak I want to look people in the eyes. And now shut up for a bit; don't throw me off my pace. You start letting fly all sorts of objections to me like from a sling before I've even had time to open my mouth. No, brother, that won't work between me and you." Standing in front of the table and staring hard at Makar with his one eye, the old man asked: "Have you in all your life ever known a woman to take a man away from his business for any real reason? Answer me honestly."

"Not often, but I've known it to happen: if there's a fire or some other disaster, for instance. Only don't drag the meeting out, old man; let Davidov have his say, and afterwards come along to my place and we'll talk till sunrise if you like."

The inflexible Nagulnov was obviously prepared to make concessions in order to butter up Shchukar and to prevent his holding up the meeting. But he achieved a quite unexpected effect: the old man broke into a grizzle, wiped the tears from his eyes with his sleeve, and through those genuine tears declared:

"As for me, it's all one whether I spend the night with you or the stallions; but one thing's quite sure: I simply can't go home tonight, for I'd have to face such a Turkish battle with my old

woman that I might turn up my toes right on the doorstep, and very easily too."

He turned his face, as furrowed as a baked apple, to look at Davidov, and went on in a voice that took on sudden strength:

"You asked me, Siemion, how it happened that after being taken home I slipped away again. D'you think that was so easy? I must tell the meeting all about my mischievous old woman, because the people ought to give me their sympathy, and if I don't get it, old Shchukar might just as well lie down on the damp ground and die with the blessing of the Lord God to the devil's dam. I'll tell you the sort of Punch and Judy show my life is. An hour or so ago I was sitting with Antip Grach in the yard, talking about artists and our present life, when my sweetheart turns up. She comes, the triply damned, takes me by the hand, and drags me after her, like a well-fed horse dragging a harrow with the teeth uppermost. She drags me along quite easily, not even groaning or gasping under the strain, though I was dying in both my legs.

"And if you'd like to know, you could plough with my old woman harnessed up, and shift loaded wagons, and she could drag me wherever she liked, she's so strong, damn her! By God I'm not lying. Other people may think what they like, but I know her strength to the last degree; I've felt it on my own back. . . .

"And so she dragged me along behind her, and what could I do? Force would break a straw. I hurry after her, and keep asking: 'What need was there for you to drag me away from the meeting like a new-born child from its mother's breast?' But she says: 'Come along, old man; one of the shutters has broken away from its hinge; you must mend it, or during the night the wind will blow and smash our window.' What d'you think of that for a yarn? Well, I'm damned, I thought. 'Why,' I ask her, 'it'll be daylight tomorrow, so can't I rehang the shutter then? You must be half crazy, you old poker.' But she says: 'I'm ill, and I'm bored with lying alone ill in bed. You won't object to sitting with me for a little while, will you?' And that was story number two! To that one I replied: 'Send for one of the old women: she'll sit with you until I get back from the meeting after making my objection to Agafon Dubtsiev.' 'I only want to share my boredom

with you, I don't want any old woman.' And that was number three: three filthy answers.

"What's your opinion: should a man put up voluntarily with being mocked at like that, or should he evacuate himself from such hopeless stupidity? That's just what I did: I voluntarily evacuated myself. I went into the hut with her; but it didn't take me long to slip out onto the porch, and then onto the veranda. And I put the chain across the door and came back to the school at a trot. The windows of our hut are small and narrow, and, as you know, my old woman's fat and rather big. She couldn't ever get through the window: she'd get stuck like a well-fed pig in a hole in the fence. I've known that to happen before now: she's got stuck in the window more than once. And so now she's sitting at home, she's sitting, my darling, like a devil in the old days, before the revolution, would sit in the wash basin; but she can't get out of the house. If anyone feels like it he can go and release her from captivity; but not me—I simply can't go and let her see me. I'll go and live with someone else for a few days until she cools down a bit. She might do me in in a wild moment, and then what? And then the prosecutor would write that all was quiet in Warsaw, and that'd be the end. No, thank you very much, you try that fritter for yourself."

"Have you finished, old man?" Razmiotnov asked calmly.

"I don't feel like finishing with you. I've got back too late to make my objection to Agafon, you've taken him into the Party all the same. And maybe that's all for the best, maybe I'm even agreed with you on that. I've told you all about my old woman, and I can see by your eyes that all of you sitting at the chairman's table feel great sympathy for me. And I don't want anything else. I'm satisfied to have had this talk with you; after all, I'm not expected to talk only to the stallions, am I? Even if you haven't got much understanding, at any rate you've got more than my stallions. . . ."

"Sit down, old man, or you'll start another speech," Nagulnov ordered.

Contrary to everybody's expectation, Shchukar went to his seat without any of his usual backchat; but he wore such an extraordinarily self-satisfied smile and his one eye glittered so triumphantly that everybody could see he was not the vanquished but

the victor. His path back to his seat was lined with friendly smiles, for despite everything the Gremyachy people were fond of the old man.

But Agafon Dubtsiev could not resist the opportunity to spoil the old man's cheerful mood. As, strutting importantly, Shchukar went past him, Dubtsiev whispered sinisterly, his face the picture of gloom: "Well, so you've come to the end, old man? . . . Let's say good-bye."

Shchukar stood rooted to the floor, chewed his lips for a moment or two in silence, then pulled himself together and asked in a shaking voice: "You . . . I mean . . . what have we got to say good-bye for?"

"Why, because you've only a little while left to live in this world. . . . Only time enough for a couple of looks and four sighs. A shaven girl wouldn't have time to plait her hair before you're covered with a board. . . ."

"But . . . what makes you think that, Agafon?"

"Why, it's quite simple. They're making plans to kill you."

"Who are?" Shchukar could hardly get the words out.

"Kondrat Maidannikov and his wife. He's already sent her home to get the chopper."

The old man's legs trembled under him, and he sat down helplessly beside Agafon, who obligingly made room for him. Then he asked in bewilderment: "But what have they decided to finish me off for?"

"Can't you guess?"

"Because I made an objection to him?"

"Exactly. The critic is always killed off, sometimes with a chopper, sometimes with a gun. Which would you like: to die from a bullet or by a chopper?"

" 'Like!' That's a good word! Whoever would like either?" Shchukar replied indignantly. "You tell me rather what I'm to do now. How am I to defend myself from such a stupid fool?"

"Report it to the authorities while you're still alive, that's all."

"That is the only thing to do," Shchukar agreed after a moment's reflection. "I'll go and complain to Makar at once. But isn't that damned Kondrat afraid of being sent to penal servitude over me?"

"He said he didn't expect they'd give him more than a year

for killing Shchukar, or two at the worst; and he could manage
to get through a year or two, that'd be easy. 'They won't give
me a heavy sentence over such an old man,' he said. 'They give
just nothing at all for such rubbish.' "

"He can lick his lips, the son of a bitch. But he'll get ten years
if he gets a day, that I know for a fact," the old man howled in a
fury.

At once Nagulnov gave him a stern warning. "If you bawl
out like a half-slaughtered goat you'll be put out of the meeting
at once."

Shchukar could not utter a word in reply. He sat with his
elbows on his knees and with drooping head. He was thinking
hard; his forehead was wrinkled painfully. Suddenly he started
up, pushed his way through the people, and trotted up to the
chairman's table. Dubtsiev saw him bend over Nagulnov and
whisper something into his ear, then point to Dubtsiev and afterwards to Kondrat Maidannikov.

It was difficult, indeed almost impossible, to amuse Nagulnov;
but now he could not refrain from smiling at the corners of his
mouth. Looking across the room at Dubtsiev and shaking his
head reproachfully, he made Shchukar sit beside him, and whispered: "You sit here and don't move, or you'll talk yourself into
committing a sin."

Shchukar sat down exultant and reassured, and, happening to
catch Maidannikov's eye a little later, he spitefully stuck up two
fingers at him behind his left elbow. Kondrat raised his eyebrows
in amazement, while the old man, feeling that he was perfectly
safe at Makar's side, promptly stuck his fingers up again.

"What's the old fellow doing that to you for?" Kondrat's neighbour, Antip Grach, asked him.

"The devil knows what he's got into his head," Kondrat answered in a piqued tone. "I'm beginning to think he's going a
little soft in the brain. And about time too: he's had a long life,
and he's had to live through quite a lot. He and I always got on
well, but it looks as though he's got something against me now.
I'll have to ask him what's upset him." Then he happened to
glance round at the spot where Shchukar had been sitting, and
laughed quietly. He nudged Antip with his elbow. "Now I see it;
he was sitting next to Agafon. Agafon must have whispered

something to him about me; he's thought up some slanderous story, and now the old man's furious with me. But I haven't the least idea what it's all about. He's gone just like a little child, he believes everything he's told."

Meanwhile, standing by the table, Davidov was waiting patiently for the always deliberate villagers to sit down again in their places and for the conversation to die away.

"Come on, Davidov, get on with it, don't drag it out!" Diemka Ushakov cried impatiently.

After exchanging a few words in a whisper with Razmiotnov, Davidov hurriedly began his speech. "I shan't keep you long, that's a fact. I'm going to speak specially to the collective-farm women, because the question I'm about to ask you concerns them more. Today all the collective farm is present at our Party meeting, and we Communists have discussed it among ourselves and want to propose the following idea. In our factories we've long since set up kindergartens and nurseries, where the little children are looked after and fed, and play every day, from morning till evening, under the care of experienced nannies and governesses. That's a fact, Comrades. And meanwhile their mummies go to work and don't have to worry at all about their children. Their hands are untied, they're freed from cares about their children. Why shouldn't we organize something of the sort for our collective farm? We've got two kulak houses standing empty; we've got milk, bread, meat, wheat, and other things in the collective farm, and that's a fact. We'll provide victuals for out little citizens, all they need, and care too. So what's the difficulty, damn it? The harvest is almost upon us now, and as our women go out to work in the fields you know how important the matter is for us. I'm prepared to say the situation's serious, and you know that as well as I do. Well, women of our collective farm, d'you agree with our proposal? Let's vote on it, and if the majority agree we'll decide at once so as not to have to call another meeting. Those in favour please hold up their hands."

"Who'd be against such a blessing?" cried Mrs. Turlinia, who had a large progeny of children. She looked round at her neighbours, but, even so, was the first to raise her hand.

A solid shower of hands rose from the collective farmers and their women sitting at the desks and crowded in the gangways.

Not one voted against. Davidov rubbed his hands and smiled with satisfaction.

"The proposal to organize a kindergarten is passed unanimously. I'm very glad of that, comrades and citizens, and it shows we've hit on the right idea. We'll set to work to put the plan into operation tomorrow. Mothers, bring your children along to the collective-farm office and put your names down from six o'clock tomorrow morning as soon as you've finished your cooking. Discuss it among yourselves, women comrades, and choose a woman who can cook, someone who's neat and clean and can cook well, and then two or three other collective-farm women who're neat and tidy and good with children, for nurses. I shall ask the district to let us have someone who can take charge, a woman who's educated and can keep accounts. We've been adding it all up and decided that we'll allow one labour day for every day of work to each of the collective-farm nurses and the cook, but we'll have to pay the women who take charge in accordance with the state-wages table. That won't ruin us, and that's a fact. In any case, we needn't regret it: the expenses will be covered by the increased receipts from our own work; I'll prove that to you later. We shall take children between the ages of two and seven. Any questions?"

"But isn't it rather a lot to allow one labour day? It's not hard work looking after children; it's not the same as digging with forks in the fields." The speaker was Yefim Krivosheyev, one of the last individual farmers to join the collective farm.

But such a storm of indignation rose from the women around him that he was almost deafened, and knitted his brows and waved his hands as though beating off bees. Finally, realizing that the situation was looking rather bad, he jumped onto the desk and merrily roared at the top of his voice:

"Have mercy, my dears! Mercy, for Christ's sake! I was only thinking aloud. I spoke without thinking. Let me get to the door and please don't wave your fists so close to my nose. Comrade Davidov, save your new collective farmer. Don't leave me to die a heroic death. You know what our women are like."

But the women went on shouting and yelling: "You old so and so, have you ever had to deal with children?"

"Make him the cook, the big-beard!"

"Or a nurse!"

"He'd expect more than two labour days for every day he spent with them. But now he's being miserly, the old wolf-head."

"Women, teach him to stop talking nonsense and to learn the truth."

They were decidedly not prepared to let him get away with it; laughing and whistling, a swarm of women dragged him down off the desk, a swarthy hand clutched his chestnut beard in its grip, and his new satin shirt split with a ripping noise down its seams. Nagulnov jumped to his feet and called the women to order, but in vain. The rough-and-tumble continued, and Yefim, livid with laughter and embarrassment, was energetically dragged out into the passage. Both sleeves were torn off his shirt to be left lying on the classroom floor, while the shirt itself was stripped of buttons and torn to rags.

Panting with laughter, Yefim cried through the roar of the Cossacks' laughter: "The strength our women anathemas have got! This is a tragedy for me. It's the first time I've ever raised my voice to say anything against them, and look at the mess I've made of it. . . ." He bashfully drew his ragged shirt over his swarthy belly, and complained: "How can I go home to my wife in this lace? She'll turn me out of the house. I'll have to go and fix myself up with old Shchukar and some widow in temporary quarters, that's the only hope for him and me now."

Chapter 24

The meeting broke up long after midnight. The people strolled off along the streets and alleys, talking animatedly; the wicket gates creaked, the door latches rattled in the nocturnal silence; here and there a laugh arose occasionally, and, unaccustomed to so many people being around and making so much noise at that time of night, all the dogs of the village woke up and started barking and baying furiously.

Davidov was one of the last to leave the school. After the thick, poisonous atmosphere which had filled every room, the air in the street was cold, and intoxicating in its freshness. He even thought he could catch the smell of home-made beer as he gulped in great mouthfuls of the gentle breeze.

Ahead of him two men were walking along. As he caught their voices he could not help smiling. Old Shchukar was saying fervently:

"But I, like an old fool, I believed him, the devilish tongue-wagger. He said Kondrat was seriously planning to kill me for my criticism and self-criticism, and I was terribly scared. I thought to myself: 'In Kondrat's hands a chopper would be a trifle. One wave with it in hot blood and he'd split my head in two as if it was a watermelon.' How could I have been so ready to believe that devil of an Agafon? All his life he's let his tongue wag like a worn mitten on a stick. It was he who taught the goat Trofim to charge at me and stick its horns in whatever part of me it could reach. I know that's so without a doubt. I myself saw him teaching it the beastly trick, only it didn't occur to me at the time that he was setting the goat against me and teaching it to shorten my life."

"Don't believe anything he says, always take it with a pinch of salt. Agafon's terribly fond of playing that sort of trick, he'd turn anything into a joke," Nagulnov replied in a reassuring tone.

They turned into Nagulnov's yard, and Davidov thought of joining them, but changed his mind. Instead he went down the next alley. A little way along it he saw Varia Kharlamova leaning against the fence. She came to meet him. The late, waning moon shed only a dim light, but he discerned an embarrassed, cheerless smile on the girl's face.

"I've been waiting for you; I know you always come home this way. It's a long time since I saw you last, Comrade Davidov."

"It certainly is a long time since we last met, droopy Varia!" he said in a tone expressive of his pleasure. "And meanwhile you've grown up, and you've grown beautiful too, that's a fact. Where've you been all these days?"

"Weeding, and hoeing, and mowing, and busy at home too. . . . But you've never come to see me; I don't suppose you've ever even thought of me. . . ."

"You do take offence easily. Don't blame me; I simply never have any time; I'm always on the go. I go a week without shaving, we eat once a day: that's how hard we're being driven these days before the harvest. But what were you waiting for me for? Is there something you want to talk to me about? You seem sad, somehow. Or am I wrong?" He gently squeezed the girl's firmly swelling arm above the elbow, and looked into her face sympathetically. "You haven't got some trouble on your mind, have you? Tell me."

"Are you going home?"

"Where else should I go at this late hour?"

"It doesn't matter where: all doors are open to you. But if you're going home you're going my way. Would you see me as far as our wicket gate?"

"Why bother to ask? You really are queer, straight you are! Whenever was a sailor, or even an ex-sailor, known to refuse to see a good-looking girl home?" he exclaimed in a joking tone, taking her by the arm. "Let's step off together. One, two; one, two. So you have got something on your mind? Tell me all about it, don't keep anything back. The chairman should know everything, that's a fact. Everything, down to your very deepest secrets."

Unexpectedly he felt her arm quiver under his fingers; her step grew uncertain, almost stumbling, and he heard a little sob.

"Well, you certainly have gone soft, my dear Varia. What's the matter?" he asked quietly, anxiously, dropping his jesting tone. He stopped and tried to look into her face again.

She buried her tear-stained face on his broad chest. He stood without stirring, his brows knitted; then he raised them in amazement. He heard her say through her choking sobs:

"I'm going to be engaged . . . to Vania Obnizov. . . . Mummy's always at me day and night: 'Take him for husband. They're well off.'" Suddenly all the bitter sorrow that evidently had been gathering in her heart for a long time broke out in a suffering cry: "Oh God, what am I to do?"

Her arm lay across his shoulder for a brief moment; then it slipped down and hung limply.

This was unexpected news, and he would never have believed that it could plunge him into such consternation. Bewildered,

dumbfounded by the announcement, feeling a sharp pain at his heart, he silently squeezed her hands and, stepping back a little, gazed into her drooping, tear-stained face, not knowing what to say. Only then did it begin to penetrate his consciousness that without knowing it he had loved this girl for possibly quite a long time, and with a love quite new to him, despite all his mature experience. It was a pure and unfathomable love, but at this very moment of recognition he also began to realize that he had simultaneously made the acquaintance of two mournful friends and companions of almost all true love: separation and loss.

Pulling himself together, he asked in a rather husky voice: "But how about you? What do you think, my little doe?"

"I don't want to marry him. D'you understand? I don't want to."

She raised tear-washed eyes to him. Her swollen lips quivered wretchedly, appealingly. And his heart quivered too, as though in response. His mouth went dry. He swallowed hard, and said:

"Well, then, don't marry him; that's a fact. No one can force you to."

"But don't you see, Mother's got six of us to look after, and I'm the oldest. And Mother's ill, and I couldn't feed all that horde by myself. Even if I killed myself with work. How is it you don't see that, my dear?"

"But supposing you do get married, what then? Will your husband give a hand?"

"He'd squeeze the last drop out of himself in order to help. He'd work the skin off his hands. You don't know how much he loves me. He loves me terribly. Only I don't want his help, or his love. I don't love him in the least. I just can't stand him. When he takes my hand in his sweaty hand I feel sick. I'd rather . . . Oh, but what's the good of talking? If Father was alive I wouldn't stop to think twice. I might have finished the secondary school by now. . . ."

Davidov was still gazing fixedly at her tear-stained face, pale in the moonlight. The corners of her swollen lips were turned down bitterly, her eyes were downcast, the lids had a blue tinge. She stood silent, crumpling a handkerchief in her hand.

"But supposing we could help your family?" he asked uncertainly, after thinking a moment.

He had hardly said the words when her eyes, dry in a moment, glittered not with tears but with anger. Dilating her nostrils, she exclaimed in a masculine, coarse, jarring tone:

"You can go to the devil with your help. Get that?"

There was another brief silence. Then, a little annoyed at her unexpected outburst, he asked: "But why?"

"Just because."

"But why, all the same?"

"I don't need your help."

"I don't mean help from me personally; the collective farm will help your mother, as she's been a widow for many years. D'you see? I'll have a talk with the collective-farm committee, and we'll make the decision. Now do you understand, droopy?"

"I don't want any collective-farm help either."

He shrugged his shoulders with chagrin. "You're a queer girl, that's a fact. First she needs help and is ready to accept the first young man that comes along as a husband, then she doesn't need anybody's help. There's something about you I don't understand. . . . One of us two has a screw loose today, that's a fact. What is it you do want, in the last resort?"

His voice, calm, reasonable, or so perhaps it seemed to her, plunged her into utter despair. She broke into a passionate weeping, pressed her hands to her face and, turning her back on him, started to walk and then to run along the alley, bent forward and keeping her hands pressed to her face.

He overtook her at the corner, seized her by the shoulder, and said spitefully: "Now, droopy, don't try to be so clever! I ask you straight out: what's it all about?"

The wretched girl threw wide the gates confining her desperate despair, her bitter sorrow. "You blind fool! You damned blind fool! You can't see a thing! I love you. I've been in love with you ever since spring. But you . . . you go about as if you had a bandage over your eyes. All my girl-friends are laughing at me, and I expect everybody else in the village too. Well, aren't you blind! The tears I've shed because of you, you enemy! The nights I've been unable to sleep. But you don't see a thing. How can I accept help from you or charity from the collective farm, when I love you? And you, you devil, you can turn your tongue

to saying such things? Why, I'd rather die of hunger than take anything from you. Well, now you know everything. Have you got what you wanted? What you expected? Now clear off to your Lushkas, I don't need you. I've got no need whatever of such a cold stone, such an unseeing, blind bat."

She struggled to tear herself out of his hands, but he held her firmly. He held her strongly, but he said nothing. They stood thus for several minutes; then she wiped her eyes with the end of her kerchief and said in a faded, everyday, weary voice:

"Let me go; I'll go home."

"Talk more quietly; someone might hear you," he said.

"I'm already talking quietly."

"You're being imprudent . . ."

"Enough of that! I've been prudent for half a year, and I can't any more. Well, let me go, I tell you. It'll be getting light soon, I've got to go and milk the cow. D'you hear?"

He was silent, standing with his head sunk on his chest. But with his right hand he still firmly embraced her gentle shoulders, very conscious of her warm young body, breathing in the spicy scent of her hair. It was a strange feeling he experienced during those moments: neither agitation, nor fire in his blood, nor desire. Only a quiet sorrow, like a haze, invested his heart, and for some reason he found it difficult to breathe.

Shaking off his torpor, with his left hand he felt for the girl's rounded chin, gently raised her head, and smiled. "Thank you, my dear. My dear, droopy Varia."

"But what for?" she whispered almost inaudibly.

"For the happiness you're giving me, for swearing at me, for calling me blind. But don't think I'm blind beyond all hope of healing. You know, I had begun to think . . . it frequently came to my mind that I'd left my happiness, my personal happiness, behind the stern . . . in the past I mean. . . . Though even in the past it was always measured out to me . . . it would have made a cat weep. . . ."

"And to me even less," she said quietly. Then, a little louder, she asked: "Kiss me, my chairman, for the first and last time, and then let's part; for dawn's coming already; it wouldn't be good for us to be seen together, it would be shameful. . . ."

Rising childlike on her toes, she pursed up her lips, and threw back her head. But Davidov, with the restraint and gravity of a child, kissed her on the brow and said firmly:

"Don't grieve, Varia, everything will be all right. I won't take you any further now, I'd better not, that's a fact. But we'll see each other tomorrow. You've set me a riddle. But I'll have the answer by the morrow, I'll solve the riddle, that's a fact. Tell your mother she's to remain at home tomorrow evening; I'll come along to your place at sunset, we'll talk it over. So you be at home too. So long, my little doe. Don't be upset because I leave you like this. . . . I too have got to think over a bit what's to happen to you, and to me. Isn't that so?"

He did not stop for her reply. He turned silently, and silently walked towards his home, with his usual measured, unhurried gait.

Thus he would have parted from her, leaving her neither his nor another's. But she very quietly called to him. He halted reluctantly, and asked in an undertone:

"What do you want?"

As she came up to him he gazed at her with some feeling of anxiety, thinking: "What new decision has she managed to take in these few moments since I left her? Her sorrow may upset everything, that's a fact."

She came up impetuously, pressed against him, breathing into his face, and said in a burning whisper: "My dearest, don't come along to our place, don't say a word to Mother. If you like I'll live with you . . . well . . . like Lushka did? We'll live together a twelve-month, and then you can throw me over. And I'll take Vania for a husband. He'll have me anyhow; even after you he'll have me. The day before yesterday he even said so: 'You'll always be dear to me whatever you do,' he said. Would you like that?"

Without stopping to reflect he pushed her away violently and said contemptuously: "You fool! You hussy! You slut! Do you realize what you're saying? You've gone clean crazy, that's a fact. Come to your senses and go home and sleep it off. D'you hear? But I'll come along tomorrow evening, and don't get it into your head to hide from me. I'll find you wherever you are."

If she had gone away affronted and silent, they would have parted with words of anger. But she quietly asked in a troubled tone: "But what am I to do, Siemion, my dearest?"

And for a second time that night his heart quivered, but now not with pity. He put his arms round her, passed his hand several times over her drooping head, and asked: "Do forgive me; I lost my temper. . . . But you're fine. So you thought you'd sacrifice yourself to me? Now go, do really go, dear Varia; have a little sleep, and we'll see each other in the evening. All right?"

"All right," she answered humbly. Starting back from him in alarm, she exclaimed: "Lord! Why, it's quite light. I'm done for. . . ."

The dawn had crept on unnoticed, and Davidov too, as though he had just awakened, saw the distinct outlines of the houses, the sheds, the roofs, the solid dark-blue clumps of trees in the silent orchards, and, to the east, hardly visible, the purple streak of the sunrise.

There was much truth in what he had said to Varia: that his happiness had been left astern. But had he ever known happiness at all in his restless life? Probably not.

Till late in the morning he sat by the open window at home, smoking cigarette after cigarette, going over his amorous adventures in his mind, and realizing that all his life he had known no experience which he could recall with gratitude, or sorrow, or even, in the worst case, with a pang of conscience. He had had brief liaisons with various women, associations that bound neither side to anything, but that was all. They had come together lightly enough, and had parted again without difficulty, without suffering or miserable words; and within a week they had been meeting as strangers, and had exchanged chilly smiles and a few meaningless remarks only for the sake of decency. Calf love! Even to recall those affairs made him feel ashamed, and as he journeyed in thought through all the amours of his past his brow furrowed squeamishly; he tried to skate quickly over something which stained his past as a grease spot stains a sailor's clean uniform. To forget those unpleasant incidents the more quickly, he lit another cigarette, thinking: "Well, now try taking

stock! The only result you get is rubbish, that's a fact. So the marks you receive are a nought with no digit, sailor boy! Well, you've had your good time with women, like any other dog!"

But already by eight in the morning he had decided. "All right, I'll marry Varia. It's time the sailor finished with his bachelor existence. That way things should go better. I'll fix her up in the agricultural school; in a couple of years we'll have our own agronomist in the collective farm, and then we'll be pulling together. And after that, well, we'll see."

Once he had taken a decision he was not in the habit of delaying or burying it: he washed and went off to Varia's house.

He met her mother in the yard, and greeted her respectfully. "Hello, Mother, how are you?"

"All right, Chairman. We manage somehow. What have you called for? What necessity has brought you here?"

"Is Varvara at home?"

"She's asleep. You sit on in your meetings till broad daylight."

"Let's go into the house. Wake her up. I want to talk to you both."

"Come in, you're welcome."

They went into the kitchen. Looking at Davidov anxiously, the mother said:

"Sit down, I'll get her up at once."

A minute or two later Varia came out from the bedroom. Evidently she hadn't slept, either, that morning: her eyes were swollen with tears, but her face was youthfully fresh and radiant with an inward, gracious warmth. Glancing at him from under her eyebrows, searchingly and expectantly, she said: "Hello, Comrade Davidov. So you've come to visit us this morning?"

He sat down on the bench, took a quick glance at the children sleeping huddled together on the cheap bed, and answered: "I've not come on a social visit, but on business. Listen, Mother . . ." He stopped short, searching for words, gazing at the elderly woman with his tired eyes. She stood by the stove, fidgeting anxiously with the folds of her shabby dress.

"Listen, Mother," he started again. "Varvara loves me, and I love her too. And this is our decision: I'll send her to the regional centre to study to be an agricultural specialist. There's a technical school there; in two years she'll have won her diploma, and

she'll come back to work here in Gremyachy. And this coming autumn, when we've got through the summer work, we'll have a wedding. People have come from the Obnizovs to arrange a marriage before me; but don't force the girl, she'll seek and find her own fate; that's a fact."

With a suddenly severe look on her face, the woman turned to her daughter. "Varia?"

But the girl could only whisper: "Mummy!"

Rushing across to her mother, bowing very low, weeping tears of happiness, she began to kiss her mother's hands, wrinkled and toil-worn with many years of labour. Turned to the window, Davidov heard Varia whisper between her sobs:

"Mother dearest, oh, my dear! I'd follow him to the very end of the world. Whatever he says I shall do. I'll study and learn, or I'll work, I'll do anything. Only don't make me take Vania Obnizov for a husband. . . . I shall be finished with him as . . ."

There was silence for a moment, then he heard her mother's quivering voice. "I can see you two have come to an agreement without your mother's consent. Well, all right! God be your judge, sailor, I don't wish Varia any ill, but I ask you: don't bring shame on my daughter. She's all the hope I have. You see, she's my oldest child, she's in place of the master. And I, with my sorrows, with my little children, my great need . . . You can see what I've become. I'm an old woman before my time. But as for you sailors, I saw during the war what you're like. . . . Don't bring ruin on our family."

He turned round sharply and stared hard at her. "And you, Mother, don't run sailors down! We fought and beat your darling Cossacks. Some day people will write all about that, you see! But as for our honour and our love, we've known how to be honest, and faithful, and we still know how to be, more truly than any civilian scum. You needn't worry about Varia: I shan't do her any wrong. But in regard to what we've to do, I want to ask you one thing: if you agree to our coming together, I'll drive her to Millerovo tomorrow and fix her up in the technical school. And then, until we're married, I'll come and live with you myself. It'll be easier for me to be with you than with strangers. And one other thing: somehow or other I ought to support your family now, and help you, oughtn't I? Without Varvara around

you'll overtax your strength trying to look after the children. So
I'll take the job of looking after you on my shoulders. And you
needn't worry, they're pretty broad; they'll stand it. That's the
arrangement I propose. Well, what d'you think? Shall we agree
on that?"

He took a great stride towards her and put his arms round her
thin shoulders. But when he felt his future mother-in-law's kiss
on his cheek, and realized that her lips were wet with tears, he
said angrily: "You women do have a lot of tears to waste. Why,
you'd wear a channel in the hardest rock! Now, now, old lady,
we'll manage somehow, shan't we? I tell you as a fact we shall
manage."

He hurriedly took out a carelessly crumpled packet of notes
from his pocket, pushed it under the cheap little tablecloth on
the table with an embarrassed gesture, smiled awkwardly, and
muttered: "That's something I've saved up from past work. I only
need a little for tobacco. I don't drink much, and you need some
money so that Varvara can buy something for the road. And
you can get something for the kids too. Well, that's the lot. I'll
be off now, I've got to ride to the district today. I'll be back this
evening, and then I'll bring my trunk along. And you, Varvara,
get ready for the journey. We'll be leaving for the regional centre
tomorrow at dawn. Well, look after yourselves, my dears." He
put his arms round both Varia and her mother, turned resolutely
on his heel, and went to the door.

His step was as firm and confident as ever, with a slight sailor
roll. But if any of his acquaintances had watched him closely
they would have seen a new quality in his gait.

During the day he rode to the district-committee office and
obtained Nesterenko's permission to drive to the regional town
to arrange things with the Party committee.

"Only don't stay there long," Nesterenko warned him.

"I shan't stay there an hour longer than necessary; but you
might phone the regional secretary and ask him to see me, and
to help in fixing up Varia Kharlamova in the technical school."

The secretary narrowed his eyes quizzically. "Don't try any
tricks on me, sailor. You watch out, you'll have only yourself to
blame if you take me in and don't marry the girl. We shan't let
you play the Don Juan a second time. Things were simpler in

regard to Lukeria Nagulnova: after all, she was a divorced woman. But this is a very different kettle of fish."

Davidov gave Nesterenko an evil look and broke in without letting him finish. "Damn it all, you've got a rotten idea of me, Secretary, and that's a fact. But I've already spoken to her mother and got engaged in accordance with all the rules. What else do you want, and why don't you trust me?"

Nesterenko asked in a quiet voice: "This is my last question to you, Siemion. You haven't been with her, have you? And if you have, why don't you want to marry her properly before she goes off to the school? You're not expecting anyone from Leningrad to arrive here, are you, such as a former wife or that sort of thing? Do realize, you blasted blockhead, that I'm worried about you, well, say, like a brother would be. And it would be a very bitter thing for me to be disillusioned in regard to your decency. . . . I'm not prying into your soul out of idle curiosity, not at all. You're not to take offence, d'you hear? Well, now, this is my very last word: you're not wanting to fix her up in the school in order to get shut of her, are you? So that she's no longer around? . . . You watch out, my brother!"

Wearily flexing his legs, which were stiff from the ride, Davidov dropped heavily into an ancient chair standing beside the armchair in which Nesterenko was sitting, stared stupidly at the willow wattle arms of the cheap chair, and then listened to the chirruping of the sparrows in the acacias. Glancing at Nesterenko's yellow face, at his shabby tunic with its neatly repaired sleeves, he replied: "I was wrong to tell you what I did out of friendship when I made your acquaintance in the spring. I was wrong, I say, because it's obvious you're never prepared to believe anybody. Well, you can go to hell, Secretary. It looks as if you only trust yourself, and then only on your days off. You always have some idiotic suspicion of everybody else, even of people you swear friendship to. If that's your nature, how can you direct the district Party organization? You learn first to trust yourself as you ought, and then you can be as suspicious as you like of everybody else."

Nesterenko pulled a painful, twisted smile. "So you have taken offence, though I asked you not to?"

"Yes, I have."

"Then you're not worth a brass penny."

Still more wearily, Davidov got up out of the chair. "I'll go now, otherwise you and I will be quarrelling. . . ."

"I wouldn't like that to happen," the secretary answered.

"Nor I."

"All right, then, hang on for another five minutes or so, and we'll let our differences simmer down."

"All right, I'll stop." Davidov dropped back into the chair and said: "I've not done the girl any wrong, that's a fact. She ought to study. She's got a large family at home, and she's the oldest, she's carrying all the burden. Get that?"

"Yes," Nesterenko replied, but he still gazed at Davidov with stern, hostile eyes.

"I'm thinking of marrying her when she's finally fixed up in the school and I've got on top of the autumn work. To put it briefly, a peasant wedding, after the harvest." He smiled wryly. Noticing that the secretary's stern expression was beginning to soften and he was listening closely, Davidov went on more readily, losing his previous constraint and embarrassment. "I've never been married before, not in Leningrad nor anywhere else; this is the first time I'm taking such a risk. And about time too: I shall be in my fortieth year soon."

"I suppose after thirty you count every year as ten." Nesterenko smiled.

"But what about the civil war? I'd certainly count every year burnt up in that as ten."

"Rather a lot . . ."

"You take a good look at yourself and then you'll agree it's just right."

The secretary rose from the table and walked up and down the room, rubbing his cold hands together. He answered in an uncertain tone. "That's as it may be. . . . But we're not talking about that, Siemion. I was glad when you explained that this time you haven't tripped up as you did with Lukeria Nagulnova; this time it looks like being something reliable. Well, in that case I support your wise undertaking, and I wish you happiness."

"Will you come to the wedding in the autumn?" Davidov asked, warming again to the secretary.

"I'll be the first guest," Nesterenko said, and once more, as of

old, his face beamed with unfeigned pleasure, and the old impudent sparks glittered in his faded eyes. "I mean first not in the sense of importance, but because I'll be the first to arrive as soon as I hear of it."

"Well, keep fit and well. You'll give the regional secretary a ring?"

"This very day. Off you go, and don't stay there too long."

"I'll go hot-foot."

They exchanged a strong handshake.

As Davidov went out into the dusty, sunny street he was thinking: "But somehow he doesn't look at all himself, not what he was before. He's pretty queer, that's obvious. His yellowish colour, his cheeks sunk like a corpse's, his faded eyes. . . . Maybe that's why he went for me like he did?"

He had almost reached his horse when Nesterenko leaned out of the window and called to him quietly: "Siemion, come back for a moment or two."

With some reluctance Davidov climbed the steps back to the district-committee veranda. Nesterenko, still more bowed and seeming to have shrunk, looked at him for a moment, then said:

"Maybe I did speak rather roughly, but don't take any notice of it, brother; I've got plenty of troubles of my own. To my malaria I've now added tuberculosis; the devil knows where I picked it up. It's giving me a hell of a time; I've got holes in both lungs. I'm going into a sanatorium tomorrow, the regional committee's sending me. I didn't want to leave the district before the harvest, but it can't be helped, I'm not going just for fun. But I'll try to be back for your wedding. I suppose you think I'm weeping on your shoulder! Don't get me wrong. I just felt like sharing with a good friend the sorrow that's overtaken me, and so unexpectedly."

Davidov passed round the table and, without saying a word, gave Nesterenko a strong embrace, kissed him on his moist, hot cheek, and said: "You go and get cured, old friend. Only the young die of that disease, and that sort of thing won't carry you or me off."

"Thank you," Nesterenko said, almost inaudibly.

Davidov went out into the street with great strides, mounted his horse, warmed him up with his whip, and swiftly galloped

away, furiously cursing himself through clenched teeth: "You're always asleep, you lop-eared devil!"

He returned to the village in the afternoon, rode straight to the Kharlamovs' house, dismounted at the wicket gate, and walked slowly into the yard. As he went up to the steps he was grimacing for he was saddle sore after his unusually long ride. Evidently he had been seen arriving, for he was welcomed by his future mother-in-law at the door. She seemed changed, more forthcoming, as though in half a day she had grown completely used to him as her son-in-law.

"Why, my dear little son," she exclaimed, "I'm afraid you're chafed, aren't you? And how quickly you've got back! The ride to the district and back is quite a step," she added with somewhat exaggerated sympathy, watching him as he walked uncertainly, bandy-legged, to the door. Without doubt she was laughing inwardly at her future son-in-law because of the way he dashingly waved his whip though he could hardly bend his legs. She, an old Cossack woman, should know better than most how the "Russian" horsemen rode their mounts!

"Now, you needn't fuss, Mother. But where's Varvara . . . ?"

"She's gone to find a dressmaker somewhere. After all, she must get her old clothes into some sort of readiness, mustn't she? Well, my lad, you've found a bride all right! Except for one very old skirt, you could rip her to pieces and you wouldn't find anything more. Where were your eyes?"

"It wasn't a skirt I came to get engaged to today, but a daughter," he replied, licking his parched lips. "Have you some cold water I can drink? Skirts are things that can be bought, we can wait a little for the skirts. When will she be back?"

"Christ alone knows. Come into the house. Well, have you fixed things up with your authorities for Varia to go and study?"

"What else did you expect? Tomorrow we're driving to the regional centre, so get your daughter ready for a long journey. Now what's the matter? Going to cry over it? You're too late."

She was, indeed, crying bitterly, disconsolately. But soon she mastered her weakness, wiped her eyes on her not very clean apron, and said in a vexed tone, though still quietly sobbing: "Go into the house. Go inside, my dear. We can't talk over such serious matters in the yard."

He went into the hut and sat down on a bench, flinging his whip under it. "Mother, what have you and I got to talk about?" he asked. "The matter's all clear and settled. Let's agree on this: I've got terribly tired these last few days; give me a drink of water, then I'll have a sleep for an hour or so, here in the hut, and after that we can talk. Get one of our lads to take my horse back to the collective-farm stables."

She cheered up a little and said: "Don't worry about the horse, the boys will see to it. And if you'll wait a bit I'll bring you some cold milk. I'll bring it at once from the cold cellar."

His fatigue and his sleepless nights had worn him out, and he could not keep awake long enough to drink the milk. When she returned, carefully carrying a jug sweating with condensation, he was fast asleep where he sat, his right hand hanging limply, his mouth slightly open. She did not disturb him. Carefully raising his hanging head, she pushed a small, blue-embroidered pillow under it.

Torpid with the heat of the room and his weariness, he slept a good couple of hours without stirring, and only woke up when he felt a childish tickling which proved to be caused by the gentle touch of a girl's warm hand. He opened his eyes and saw Varia sitting by the bench, smiling at him happily, while five boys, all the Kharlamov progeny, were crowded round him. The youngest, and evidently the boldest, trustfully took his large hand in his little fist and, pressing it to his body, asked timidly:

"Daddy Siemion, is it true you're going to live with us?"

"That's right, little son. And what else could we do? Varia's going away to study, so who's going to feed, clothe, and shoe you? That's my job now, that's a fact." He laid his hand in fatherly fashion on the child's warm, bristly head.

Chapter 25

Long before dawn next day Davidov went and woke up Shchukar in the hayloft, helped him to harness the stallions, and drove

to the Kharlamovs' yard. Through a chink in the not quite closed
shutter he saw that a lamp was burning in the kitchen. Varia's
mother was cooking, the boys were all asleep, lying across the
breadth of a broad wooden bed, and Varia, dressed for the
journey, was sitting looking as though she didn't live in that
house, but was simply a visitor who had dropped in for a moment or two.

She greeted Davidov with a welcoming, beaming smile. "I've
been ready and waiting for you a long time, my chairman."

Her mother added: "She started to get ready immediately
after the first cock. She's young and green! And as for stupid,
that goes without saying. Breakfast will be ready in a minute.
Come in and sit down, Comrade Davidov."

The three of them hurriedly ate some soup left over from yesterday, some fresh baked potatoes, and had a glass of milk.
Davidov rose from the table, thanked the mother, and added:
"Time we were off. Say good-bye to your mother, Varia, only
don't take long over it. There's no need to make the place damp,
you're not leaving her forever. Whenever I drive to the region,
Mother, I'll take you with me to see your daughter. Now I'll go
out and see to the horses." At the door he turned and asked
Varia: "Are you taking some warm clothes with you?"

She replied with a touch of embarrassment: "I've got a quilted
jacket, only it's rather old. . . ."

"It'll do; you're not going to a ball, that's a fact."

An hour later they had left the village far behind. Davidov
sat with Shchukar; Varia had the seat opposite. From time to
time she took Davidov's hand, gave it a little squeeze, then was
lost again in her thoughts. During her short life she had never
left her village for any length of time, she had visited the district
town only on rare occasions, she had never seen a railway, and
this first journey to the regional town made her heart flutter with
excitement and rapture. To part from her family and her friends
was bitter all the same, and tears welled into her eyes now and
again.

When they crossed the Don by the ferry and the stallions began to climb the hill on the farther side, Davidov jumped out of
the drozhki and began to walk along beside the seat where she
was sitting. His leg-boots sent a copious dew scattering from the

low-growing wormwood of the wayside: it was still colourless
before the sunrise, but it glittered just as much as it would later
in the morning, when the sun would be making it sparkle with
all the colours of the rainbow. He glanced at Varia occasionally,
gave her an encouraging smile, and said quietly: "Now, Varia, get
those eyes of yours dry again. Why, you're my big girl now;
grownups shouldn't cry, there's no need for tears, my dear."

And she obediently wiped her wet cheeks with the corners of
her blue kerchief and whispered something inaudibly, respond-
ing to him with a timid, humble smile. Over the chalky spurs of
the Donside hills mist was lying, and the ridge was still hidden
in its folds.

In that early-morning hour the steppe plantains, the fading
twigs of the yellow melilot, the corn which was ripening up the
hillside, gave off none of their customary scents of the day-time.
Even the all-pervading wormwood had lost its smell. All the
scents were absorbed in the dew which lay on the grain and the
grasses as plentifully as if rain had fallen recently, the brief,
heavy rain of July. And so in this quiet twilit hour two simple
scents dominated all the steppe: from the dew and the roadside
dust.

Shchukar, wearing an old canvas coat belted with an even
more ancient woven red belt, sat huddled up with the cold; he
was silent an unusually long time for him, and urged on the
horses, which were already moving at a spanking trot. But when
the sun rose he came to life. "People in the village are saying
you're thinking of marrying Varia, Siemion, my boy. Is that true?"

"It's quite true, Daddy."

"Oh well, that's life; you can wriggle as much as you like, but
you can't avoid wedlock sooner or later. I'm talking about men,
of course," the old man uttered with an air of profound wisdom.
"My dead parents married me off when I was only just eighteen.
But even then I knew what a devilish game wedlock was. So I
twisted and twisted to get out of it. I knew very well what getting married meant: it wasn't the same as getting drunk on
mead. So I pretended I was mad and ill, and had fits. My father
—he was a hard man—he gave me a good whipping lasting two
hours for my acting mad, and he stopped only when he broke
the stock over my back. For pretending I had fits he beat me

with leather reins. And when I played sick he began to roar that I was all rotten inside, and without saying another word he went into the yard and brought back a sledge-shaft pole. That's what my father was like, may he inherit the heavenly kingdom! He brought the shaft into the house and said to me quite kindly: 'Get up, little son, and I'll cure you.' Well, I thought, if he's gone to all that trouble to pull out the center pole he won't think it too much trouble to beat the soul out of me. So I wriggled out of bed as if I'd been splashed with boiling water. And I got married. What else could I do with him, that stupid father of mine? After that my life went all to sixes and sevens, sideways and backwards and upside-down. My old woman must weigh a good two hundred and eighty pounds now, but when she was nineteen she was . . ." He chewed his lips thoughtfully, turned his eyes upward, and ended firmly: "Not a pound less than 500, that's as true as I'm here."

Davidov asked quietly: "But isn't that rather a lot?"

To which Shchukar answered in a tone of sweet reasonableness: "But what difference does it make? A stone more or less, what does it matter? Life was one long hell: that married life of mine was so terrible I could have hung myself. Only that wasn't the sort of man she'd got hold of. In my desperation I thought: 'You hang yourself first, and I'll come after. . . .'"

He shook his head merrily and sniggered, evidently enjoying his memories. Seeing that his companions were listening intently, he readily went on:

"Ah, dear citizens . . . and you, Varia. When I was young my love with my old woman was a raging fury. But I ask you: why a fury? Because she's spent all our life together in a bad temper, and a bad temper and fury are one and the same. I read that in Makar's thick dictionary.

"And so sometimes I'd wake up at night and my woman would be crying her eyes out, or laughing, but I'd think to myself: 'Cry on, my dear; women's tears are the divine dew. I don't have such a honied life with you either, but I don't cry over it.'

"And so, when we'd been married five years I'll tell you what happened. My neighbour, Polikarp, came back from active service. In the army they'd taught him to twist his whiskers, the fool, and so when he came home he began to twist his whiskers

around my wife. One evening I looked out and they were standing at the fence, my wife on one side and he on the other. I
went back into the house and pretended to be blind, as though I
hadn't seen anything. Next evening they were there again. Well,
I thought, this is no joke. The third day I deliberately went out.
I came back just as dusk was falling and there they were again.
I'd got to do something about it. I wrapped a three-pound weight
in a towel, stole through the yard up behind Policarp—I went
barefoot so as he shouldn't hear me—and while he was twisting
his whiskers I cracked him one on the nape with all my force. He
dropped like a log.

"Some days later I happened to meet him in the street. He
had his head bandaged up. He said to me sourly: 'You fool! You
might have killed me.' But I said to him: 'It isn't certain yet
which of us is the fool, the one who dropped or the one who remained on his feet.'

"After that my old woman was more careful. They stopped
standing by the fence. Only before long she learnt the trick of
grinding her teeth at night. She woke me up with her grinding,
and I'd ask her: 'Doesn't it make your teeth ache, my dear?' And
she'd answer: 'Shut up, you fool!' I'd lie and think to myself: 'It
isn't certain yet which of us is the bigger fool, the one who
grinds her teeth or the one who sleeps quietly and calmly, like a
peaceable baby in a cradle.'"

Afraid of upsetting the old man, his audience sat very quiet.
Varia shook with silent laughter. Davidov turned his back on
him, hid his face in his hands, and coughed rather more often
than necessary. But Shchukar did not notice anything, and continued enthusiastically with his story.

"That's what it's like sometimes, love with fury! To put it in
a nutshell, good rarely comes of wedlock, or so I judge with my
old man's mind. Take the following case: in the old days there
was a young teacher lived in our village. He was engaged to a
merchant's daughter who lived here. He went about so togged
up, as fine, as handsome—I'm talking about his clothes—as a
young cock, and mostly he didn't walk, he rode a cycle. They'd
only just come into use, and everybody in the village thought his
cycle was a monstrosity. I needn't tell you what the dogs thought
of it. That teacher only had to appear in the street with his glit-

tering wheels for the damned dogs to go clean off their nuts. But he'd pedal faster and faster trying to get away from them, bending double over his machine and spinning his legs round so fast you couldn't see them for speed. I don't know how many little dogs he ran over, but he had to put up with a devilish time from them.

"One morning I was going across the square when I ran right into a dogs' wedding. A bitch was tearing along in front, and after her, as was quite natural, a pack of dogs, thirty of them at least. In those days our villagers, may they be damned, kept so many dogs you couldn't count them. There were two or three in every yard, and every one of them worse than a savage tiger: they guarded all their masters' chests and cellars. But what good came of it? And here was this wedding tearing towards me. I, not being a fool, dropped the bridle I was carrying and flew up a telegraph pole like a wild cat and stayed there, clinging to it with my legs. But then to cap it all this teacher comes along on his machine, and they turned and went for him. He jumped off the machine, and stood there dancing in one spot. But I shouted to him: 'You fool, climb up this post to me, or they'll tear you to pieces.' He climbed up after me, the poor devil, but he was a little too late: the moment he put his arms round the post they tore off his new trousers, and his military jacket with gold buttons, and all his underwear. And the most savage of the dogs managed to get his teeth into the raw flesh in a rather exposed spot.

"They had all the fun they wanted with him, and then ran off on their doggy business. But he sat clinging to the post, and all he had on was his peaked cap with its cockade, and even the peak had got broken when he climbed up the post.

"He and I dropped down from our refuge, him first and me after. And there he stood naked, and all I had on was a simple shirt and one pair of canvas trousers. He asked me: 'Daddy, let me have your trousers for a little while, I'll let you have them back in half an hour.' I said to him: 'My dear man, how can I let you have them when I've got nothing on underneath? You'll ride off on your machine, but I can't go circling round and round the post with no trousers on in broad daylight, can I? I'll let you have my shirt for a while, but I can't let you have my trousers, really

I can't.' He put on my shirt, thrusting his legs into the sleeves, and went off, the poor devil, hobbling along very quietly. Well, the merchant's daughter, his future wife, saw him in my shirt. And their love came to an end that very day. He had to arrange a quick transfer to another school. And so in less than a week he was put to shame, was terrified by the dogs, and his future wife jilted him. And all their love went to the devil: that young man caught galloping consumption and died. That's what it does for you, the accursed thing called love. And so, Siemion, you should think a hundred times before you get married to Varia. They're all tarred with the same brush, and it's no wonder me and Makar hate them now."

"All right, Daddy, I'll think it over," Davidov assured him. But, taking advantage of a moment when Shchukar was lighting a cigarette, he drew Varia to himself and kissed her on her temple, just where a fluffy curl was stirring in the wind.

Exhausted with his story-telling, or possibly by his memories, the old man began to doze soon after, and Davidov took the reins from his helpless hands. Shaking off his drowsiness, Shchukar muttered:

"Thank you, my Siemion; you wave the knout at the stallions, and I'll have a little sleep. As soon as the sun begins to warm me I begin to be troubled with sleepiness." Frail and small, he stretched himself out in the drozhki between Varia and Davidov, and soon he was snoring and whistling softly.

As the sun warmed the steppe, it began to breathe off all the aromas of its various grasses; the smell of warmed road dust blended insipidly with the scent of mown grass; the thread of the distant hazed horizon began to appear as a misty azure, and Varia looked over the unfamiliar country of the farther side of the Don, which still was her own boundless steppe, with eyes that drank it all in.

They stopped for the night close to a haystack, having covered more than sixty miles in the day. They supped on the modest provisions they had brought from home, and sat on for a while beside the drozhki, silently gazing at the starry sky. Then Davidov said:

"We'll have to be up early again tomorrow, so let's get to sleep. You, Varia my dear, will lie in the drozhki. Take my coat to

cover yourself with. Daddy and I will fix ourselves up by the haystack."

"That's a sound decision you've taken, Siemion," Shchukar
said approvingly in his most educated tone, highly satisfied that
Davidov and he were to sleep close together. It has to be admitted that the old fellow was rather afraid of spending the night
alone on this strange, unpopulated steppe.

Davidov lay down on his back, put his arms under his head,
and gazed up at the light night sky above him. He found the
Great Bear, sighed, and then caught himself smiling at something or other.

The ground, which had been warmed by the fiery heat of the
day, did not cool off until midnight, but then it turned really
cold. Not very far away was a pond or a steppe stream, and the
smell of slime and reeds came from it. A quail rattled away quite
close at hand. The frogs croaked hesitantly, only a few at a time.
"I sleep, I sleep," a little owl called drowsily in the night.

Davidov was just dozing off when a mouse rustled in the hay,
and old Shchukar jumped up with extraordinary agility, shook
him, and said:

"Siemion, did you hear that? We've chosen a fine spot to sleep
in, there's no denying it. This stack must be full of hedgehogs
and snakes. D'you hear them rustling around, damn them? And
owls are calling as if it was a cemetery. Let's get away from this
God-forsaken spot and drive to some other place."

"Go to sleep, stop imagining things," Davidov sleepily answered.

The old man lay down again, but fidgeted restlessly, tucking
his coat close round him and muttering: "I told you we ought
to take a wagon, but no, you wanted to drive in state in a
drozhki. And now enjoy it. We could have brought a whole
wagonload of our own hay with us, and then all three of us could
have slept in the wagon. But now we're rotting like homeless
dogs under other people's stacks. It's all right for Varia, she's
sleeping up above, under cover, like a young lady. But down
here there's something rustling by our heads, something else
rustling by our feet, and the devil knows what it is that's doing it.
You wait: a serpent will crawl up to you, take a bite at your secret parts, and that'll put an end to your dream of a wedding.

And if he bites you in one certain spot, you'll be turning up your toes. And then your Varia will fill a trough with her tears, but what'll be the good? There's no reason why any serpent should bite me; my meat's old and stringy. It's bound to bite you, and not me. . . . Let's get away from this spot."

"You're very fidgety, Daddy," Davidov said angrily. "Where can we drive to in the middle of the night?"

"So you won't shift from this spot, my dear Siemion?"

"No. Go to sleep, old man."

Sighing deeply and crossing himself, Shchukar answered: "I'd be very glad to sleep, Siemion, but I'm terribly frightened. My heart's thumping away inside my chest, and that damned owl goes on calling and calling; if only she'd choke. . . ."

To these lamentations Davidov dropped off to sleep.

He was awake before dawn. As he opened his eyes he saw Varia sitting beside him, leaning sideways against the haystack with her knees tucked up under her chin. She was gathering the tangled strands of hair off his forehead. The touch of her fingers was so gentle and cautious that he hardly felt it even when he awakened. He looked round for Shchukar, and found him sleeping in the drozhki, under Davidov's coat.

Looking as rosy and fresh as the July morning, she said very quietly: "I've already been down to the pond and had a wash. Wake up old Daddy Shchukar and let's be off." She gently pressed her lips against his scrubby cheek and sprang lithely to her feet. "Will you go and wash, Siemion? I'll show you the way to the pond."

He answered in a voice hoarse with sleep: "I've overslept my washing time, my dear; I'll have to get one somewhere on the road. But did that old marmot wake you up very early?"

"He didn't wake me up. I woke up at first light and found him sitting beside you with his arms round his knees, smoking. I asked him: 'Why aren't you asleep, Daddy?' And he said: 'I haven't slept a wink all night, my dear, this place is full of snakes. You go and take a walk over the steppe, and I'll doze off for an hour or so quietly in your place.' So I got up and went and washed."

They arrived at Millerovo late in the morning. In half an hour Davidov had arranged everything in the regional committee,

and came out looking cheerful, a contented smile on his lips.

"The secretary's decided everything as it ought to be, swiftly and efficiently. My dear droopy, you'll be put in the care of the girls belonging to the Young Communist organization. And now we'll drive along to the technical school. I'll have you fixed up in a new home double quick. We've already reached agreement with the vice-director. Until the entrance exams start, one or two teachers will take special charge of you, and by the autumn you'll be shod for me on all four hoofs, that's a fact! I've already arranged on the phone for the girls of the regional committee to call and see you." He rubbed his hands together vigorously, and asked: "And, Varia my dear, d'you know who they're sending to Gremyachy as secretary to the Young Communist group? Ivan Naidionov, the youngster who came to the village last winter with the propaganda column. He's very efficient: I'll be terribly glad to have him there. Our group will really get moving then, I tell you that as a fact."

Within two hours everything was arranged at the technical school too. The moment of parting arrived. Davidov said firmly: "So long, my dear droopy Varia; don't give way to longing for home, and study well, and we in the village won't be altogether lost without you."

He kissed her on the lips for the first time, turned, and walked away along the corridor. At the door he looked back, and suddenly such a keen feeling of pity came over him that for a moment the boarded floor swayed under his feet as if it were a ship's deck: Varia was standing with her forehead pressed against the wall, her face in her hands. Her blue kerchief had slipped down over her shoulders, and all her being expressed such helplessness and sorrow that he only groaned and hurried out.

He was back in Gremyachy late in the evening of the third day after his departure. Despite the hour, Nagulnov and Razmiotnov were both waiting in the office for him. Makar greeted him glumly and said as glumly:

"You don't seem to be living here at all these last few days, Siemion. First you ride to the district, then you drive right to the regional committee. What need was there for you to go to Millerovo?"

"I'll report on it all at the proper time. But what news is there at your end?"

Instead of answering the question directly, Razmiotnov asked: "Did you notice the corn as you drove? What's it like: is it ready for reaping, d'you think?"

"In some places the barley can be reaped now, if the right spots are chosen; and that applies to the rye too. In my view the rye can be reaped right to the last ear. But our neighbours seem to be slow in starting."

Half to himself, Razmiotnov said: "Then we won't be in a hurry either. It's all right to cut it green when the weather's fine: it ripens as it lies. But if rain should come, then we lose good food."

"We can wait till Trinity if necessary," Nagulnov agreed. "But after that we'll have to give it everything we've got, otherwise the district committee will have you on the carpet, Siemion. And they'll have Andrei and me as hors d'oeuvres. But I've got some news too: I've a war-time friend in the Soviet farm, and I rode over to see him yesterday. He invited me long ago, but I just couldn't manage it before. But it occurred to me yesterday to slip off and spend the day with him; I'd see an old friend and take the opportunity to watch tractors at work. I've never seen one, and I was rather curious. They've got a couple ploughing away there, and I spent all day in the fields. My word, boys, but that Fordson tractor's some job. It ploughs at a gallop. But as soon as it comes to virgin soil, at a turn, say, it hasn't strength enough for the job, unfortunately. It rears up on its hind wheels like a mettlesome horse before an obstacle; it sticks and sticks and churns its wheels into the ground, and is only too glad to get back onto the ploughed land. It just can't manage virgin soil. But all the same it wouldn't do any harm to have a couple of horses like that on our collective farm: so I thought, and I've been thinking so ever since. I'm very envious when it's a question of using machinery in agriculture. I got so interested I didn't even have time for a drink with my friend. I rode straight back from the fields."

"And did you think of riding to the Martinov Motor-Tractor Station?" Razmiotnov asked.

"What difference is there between a tractor station and a Soviet farm? They've both got tractors. And, besides, it was

rather a long ride to the station. And we ought to be reaping any day now."

Razmiotnov half closed his eyes slyly. "To tell the truth, I sinfully thought that on the way back from Martinov you'd turn aside to Shakhti to see Lukeria."

"That didn't even enter my head," Nagulnov said firmly. "But you'd have done it; I know you, you old bleached whiskers!"

Razmiotnov sighed. "If she'd been my former wife I'd not only have ridden to see her, I'd have been her guest for at least a week." He added jokingly: "I'm not such a paillasse as you."

"I know you!" Nagulnov repeated. He sat thinking for a moment, and added: "That devilish hussy! But I'm not such a skirt-chaser as you."

Razmiotnov shrugged his shoulders. "I've been a widower thirteen years. What else would you expect?"

"That's just why you go chasing skirts."

There was a momentary silence, but then Razmiotnov said very quietly and seriously: "And possibly all these past thirteen years I've had only one love. Do you know that?"

"What, you? Of course I believe you!"

"Only one."

"You mean Marina Poyarkova?"

"It's nothing to do with you who it is; don't try to ferret out another man's secrets of the heart. Maybe some day, when I'm drunk, I'll tell you who I loved and still love. But you see . . . You're a cold-blooded lot, Makar, a man can't talk to you about intimate things. What month were you born in?"

"December."

"Just as I thought. Your mother must have given birth to you right by a hole in the ice; she must have been going to fetch some water and had her travail come upon her right there. That's why you always spread such a chill around you. How could anyone tell you his love secrets?"

"But I can see you were born on a hot plate!"

"Very hot," Razmiotnov agreed readily. "That's why I give off heat like a hot day in a year of drought. But you're completely different. . . ."

"I've had enough of this," Nagulnov said in a tone of annoyance. "We've talked enough about women. We'd do better to dis-

cuss which of us is to go to which brigade for the harvesting."

"No," Razmiotnov objected, "let's finish the conversation now we've begun; we've got plenty of time to decide who's to go where. You think calmly over what you said, Makar. You called me a skirt-chaser, but how can you say that of me, when shortly I shall be inviting both of you to a wedding?"

"What wedding?" Nagulnov asked sternly.

"My own. My mother's quite old: it's difficult for her to manage the house. She says I've got to get married."

"And do you listen to her, you old fool?" Nagulnov could not conceal his intense indignation.

Razmiotnov replied with the utmost humility: "What else am I to do, my dear?"

"Well, then, you're a triple fool." Scratching the bridge of his nose in perplexity, Nagulnov exclaimed: "Siemion, you and I will have to take a house and live together to keep life from getting boring. And over the gate we'll put up a notice: 'Only bachelors live here.'"

Davidov was not slow to answer: "You won't get far with that idea, Makar. I'm already engaged: that's why I drove to Millerovo."

Nagulnov turned his searching gaze from the one to the other, trying to decide whether they were joking. Then he slowly stood up, dilating his nostrils and turning rather pale with his agitation. "Have you both gone clean crazy? I ask you for the last time: are you serious, or is this a joke you're playing on me?" Without waiting for an answer he spat down at his feet with all his force and left the room without saying good-bye.

Chapter 26

Polovtsiev and Lyatievsky had returned to Yakov Lukich's small best room after a time, but were growing more and more mentally numbed with boredom; the enforced inactivity was steadily undermining their morale. During recent weeks the visits of

liaison couriers had dropped off considerably, and they had long
since lost all faith in the encouraging promises which the local
headquarters of the conspiratorial organization sent them in
plain, well-sealed packets.

Possibly Polovtsiev was coming through this protracted isolation better than Lyatievsky; certainly to outward appearances
he seemed to possess more equanimity, whereas the Pole had
occasional moments when he lost his control. For days on end he
would not say a word, but sat staring at the wall with faded
eyes. Then he would grow unusually, uncontrollably garrulous,
and at such times, despite the summer heat, Polovtsiev drew his
cloak over his head, feeling an almost irresistible desire to draw
his sabre and cleave Lyatievsky's head from the neat parting of
the hair down to the shoulders. At last, as dusk was falling one
evening Lyatievsky slipped unnoticed out of the house, and returned only as daylight was coming. With him he brought an
armful of dewy flowers.

Polovtsiev had been alarmed at his absence, and had not slept
all night, lying in a state of fearful agitation, listening to every
sound that penetrated from outside. Smelling of the nocturnal
air, excited and cheerful after his escapade, Lyatievsky brought
in a pail of water and carefully arranged the flowers in it. In the
stale air of the room the perfume of petunias, tobacco plant,
violets, and other flowers was almost stupefyingly intoxicating.
Polovtsiev's reaction was quite unexpected: as the strict Cossack
captain breathed in the half-forgotten scent of the flowers he
suddenly broke into tears. He lay on his stinking pallet in the
darkness of the early morning, pressing his sweaty hands to his
face. At last, so choking was his sobbing that he turned violently
to the wall and thrust the corner of the pillow into his mouth.

Lyatievsky padded quietly about the warm floorboards in his
bare feet. He was moved by a queer feeling of delicacy, and he
whistled operetta arias under his breath and pretended that he
heard nothing, noticed nothing.

Polovtsiev dropped off into a short, oppressive sleep and
awakened late, about eleven o'clock in the morning. He felt like
reprimanding Lyatievsky for taking the risk of leaving the house.
But he said: "The water in the bucket ought to be changed.
Otherwise they'll fade."

"It shall be done this very minute," Lyatievsky cheerfully replied. He brought in a pitcher of cold well water and splashed the tepid water out of the bucket over the floor.

"Where did you get the flowers?" Polovtsiev asked. He felt awkward as he recalled his breakdown, and ashamed of his tears, and he would not look at Lyatievsky.

" 'Get' is too gentle a word, Mr. Polovtsiev," Lyatievsky answered with a shrug of his shoulders. " 'Stole them' is coarser, but it's nearer the truth. As I wandered past the school house I was attracted by a divine perfume, and I climbed the fence into the headmaster's garden and reduced two beds by fifty per cent, so as to bring some beauty into our wretched existence. I promise to keep you supplied with fresh flowers."

"No, don't get any more."

"So you haven't quite lost certain human feelings?" Lyatievsky said quietly, suggestively, staring hard at Polovtsiev.

But his companion made no comment; he pretended he hadn't heard.

Each had his own way of passing the time. Polovtsiev sat at the table for hours, playing patience, fastidiously handling the greasy cards with his stumpy fingers, while Lyatievsky lay on his bed and read for possibly the dozenth time the only book they had—a novel by Sienkiewicz—enjoying every word.

Sometimes Polovtsiev put down his cards and squatted on the floor, tucking his legs beneath him Kalmik fashion. Spreading a strip of canvas, he would dismantle and clean the spotlessly clean hand machine gun, rubbing and oiling every part with warm oil. Then he would unhurriedly assemble it, taking pleasure in its perfection, cocking his bullet head from side to side. Then, with a sigh, he would wrap the machine gun in the scrap of canvas, carefully put it under his bed, and oil and recharge the discs. Going to the table and sitting down, he would draw his officer's sabre out from under the mattress, try the blade edge on his thumbnail, and run a dry whetstone once or twice along its dully gleaming steel. "Like a razor," he would mutter in a satisfied tone.

At such moments Lyatievsky put down his book, screwed up his one eye, and smiled ironically. "You astonish me; you astonish me beyond all measure with your stupid sentimentality. Why

play with your weapons like some fool of a girl with an embroidered handbag? Don't forget it's 1930 now, and the age of
sabres, pikes, pole-axes, and similar scrap iron is long past. My
dear fellow, in the last war it was the artillery decided everything, not soldiers on horses—or off them. And the artillery will
determine the results of all future battles and wars. As an old
artillery-man I can state that with the utmost confidence."

As always, Polovtsiev glowered at him and said through his
teeth: "So you're thinking of starting a rising by relying from the
beginning on the fire of howitzer batteries? Or will it be begun
by soldiers with swords? You give me just one six-inch battery to
start with, and I'll gladly hand over my sword to Yakov Lukich's
wife to look after. But until then you can hold your tongue, you
most noble phrasemonger. I'm sick of your homilies. Go and tell
the young Polish ladies of the part the artillery played in the
last war, not me. You've got a habit of talking to me in a contemptuous tone, but it doesn't come off, you representative of the
Great Poland. Your tone and your homilies stink. Wasn't it your
country that people talked about in the twenties, when they
said: 'Poland has not yet perished, but she's already given up the
ghost'?"

In a tragic tone Lyatievsky exclaimed: "My God, what intel-
lectual poverty! Cards and sabres, sabres and cards. . . . In the
past six months you haven't read a single word of print. What a
savage you've become! And yet you were a teacher in a high
school once."

"I was a teacher from necessity, my dear sir. Out of bitter
necessity."

"There's a story your Chekhov tells about the Cossacks, I believe: a boorish and stupid Cossack landowner lives in a village,
and his two grown-up brutes of sons can find nothing else to
do, so one of them throws farmyard cocks up into the air and the
other fires at them with a gun. And that goes on day after day:
they have no books, no cultural needs, not the ghost of any in-
tellectual interest. . . . I sometimes think you must be one of
those two sons."

Instead of replying, Polovtsiev breathed on the dead steel of
his sabre, watched the bluish vapour spread and then slowly
fade, wiped the blade with the edge of his grey Tolstoyan shirt,

and carefully, even tenderly, replaced it noiselessly in its shabby
scabbard.

These sudden conversations and brief verbal duels did not always end so peacefully. The room rarely had an airing, and it
was stifling; the increasing heat of the summer made their difficult existence even more oppressive, and more and more frequently Polovtsiev would spring out of the damp smelly bed
and bellow thickly: "It's a prison. I shall be finished off in this
prison." Even in his sleep at night he often uttered that unpleasant word, and at last Lyatievsky lost all patience and told him:

"Mr. Polovtsiev, anyone would think you had only one word
left in your far from rich vocabulary—the word 'prison.' If you
yearn so much for that godly institution, I suggest you go this
very day to the district G.P.U. and ask them to put you inside
for twenty years at least. I assure you they won't refuse you."

"I suppose you'd call that a Polish witticism?" Polovtsiev asked,
twisting his lips into a smile.

Lyatievsky shrugged his shoulders. "Don't you think it good?"

"You're just a cur!" Polovtsiev said indifferently.

Lyatievsky shrugged his shoulders again, and sneered:

"Maybe. But I've lived with you so long now that I may be ex-
cused for losing all semblance of humanity. . . ."

After this clash they did not speak to each other for three
days. But on the fourth day they had to talk, despite themselves.

Early that morning, before Yakov Lukich went off to the collective-farm office, two strangers entered his yard. One was
wearing a fairly new mackintosh, the other a stained canvas coat
with hood. The first had a capacious, tightly packed document
case under his arm; on his shoulder the second carried a knout
with ornamental leather fringes to the handle. Yakov Lukich was
at the window and saw them coming and, in accordance with
the long-standing arrangement, hurriedly went into the passage,
knocked twice, with a brief interval between, on the door of the
room in which Polovtsiev and Lyatievsky lived, then walked
sedately out onto the veranda, stroking his whiskers.

"Have you come to see me, good folk?" he asked. "Or have

you taken a fancy to something from the collective-farm corn bins? And who may you be? Visitors?"

The thick-set fellow with the document case smiled affably, and two effeminate dimples appeared in his fat cheeks. He touched the peak of his shabby cap and answered: "Are you the master of the house? Good morning, Yakov Lukich. Your neighbours directed us to you. We're cattle collectors, we're working for the miners, collecting cattle for them, for their daily nourishment, as we say. We pay well—higher than state prices. We pay higher just because we have to keep the miners fed properly and without let-downs. You're the collective-farm manager, so you should realize that we need the food. But we're not after anything from the collective-farm bins; we're buying up cattle owned privately, whether by collective or individual farmers. We've been told you have a calf born last summer. Would you sell it? We shan't haggle over the price provided it's fat."

Yakov Lukich was silent; he thoughtfully scratched his left eyebrow, mentally calculating how much extra he would get out of these collectors without having to go to market. Then he answered as most farmers who know how to bargain would answer: "I haven't any calf for sale."

"But, all the same, perhaps we could look it over and agree on a price? I tell you again we're prepared to pay extra."

After another moment of thought, Yakov Lukich, stroking his whiskers in order to drag out the proceedings, said as though talking to himself: "I have got a calf, that's true, and she's certainly fat, she absolutely glistens with it. But I need her myself. My cow's getting old, I need a calf to replace her, and she's a very good breed for milk and cream. No, Comrades, I'm not prepared to sell her."

The stocky man with the document case sighed with a disillusioned air. "Oh well, you know best. Then you must excuse us, we'll look for our goods elsewhere." Once more touching his peak awkwardly, he turned to leave the yard.

The big, broad-shouldered drover shuffled after him, swinging his knout, running an abstract gaze over the yard, the house, the windows, the shut door of the barn loft.

And now Yakov Lukich's heart, always keen on good business, ran away with him. He let the visitors reach the wicket gate,

then called to the thick-set man: "Wait a bit, Comrade collector. How much would you pay per kilo of live weight?"

"Whatever price we agree on. But I've already told you we shan't haggle, and we have money to dispose of entirely as we think. It's counted out to us, but not measured," he answered, slapping his fat hand boastfully against his document case and waiting expectantly by the gate.

Yakov Lukich came down from the veranda with a resolute step. "Let's go and look at the calf before she's driven out to the herd. But bear in mind I'm not letting you have her cheap; I'm only selling at all out of respect for you, because I can see you're reasonable and not too niggardly. I don't want miserly merchants in my yard."

The two men examined and felt the calf thoroughly, almost captiously. But at a certain stage the thick-set man began the boring haggling over the price, and the man with the knout walked about the yard, whistling in his boredom, glancing into the fowl-house, the empty stable, and all sorts of places which he didn't need to look into. And in a flash Yakov Lukich realized: "These two aren't merchants, oh no!"

At once lowering his price by a full seventy-five roubles, he said: "All right, I'll stand the loss, seeing it's for our miner comrades. But you must excuse me now, I've got to go to the office. I can't spend any more time with you. Will you take the calf at once? In that case, money down on my palm!"

Standing at the entrance to the cowshed, the stocky man, spitting on his fingers, took a long time to count out the notes. He added fifteen roubles to the price he had offered, shook the dispirited Lukich's hand, and winked. "How about cracking a bottle over it, Yakov Lukich? Our job as collectors demands that we should seal the bargain with a drink." He drew a vodka bottle slowly out of his side pocket; it shone dully in the light of the early-morning sun.

Assuming a cheerfulness he did not feel, Yakov Lukich answered: "This evening, dear friends, this evening. I'll be very glad to welcome you and have a drink with you then. We can find the sort of happiness you have in that bottle in our own house: we're not all that poverty-stricken. But now you must excuse me: my health won't allow me to drink vodka in the morn-

ing, and nor does my job. I've got to go off to my collective-farm
duties. Come along after sunset and then we'll drink to my calf."

"You might at least invite your visitors in and treat us to a
drink of milk from the calf's mother," the thick-set man commented, beaming with a good-natured smile and dimpling his
chubby cheeks. He took Yakov Lukich's elbow in his hand in a
gesture of entreaty.

But Yakov was unyielding: all his will was directed towards
repelling any such suggestion. Smiling with a touch of contempt,
he replied: "We Cossacks are good hosts; but we go visiting not
when we feel like it, but when we're invited. Maybe your ways
are different. But if that's so, if you don't mind we'll follow the
custom of our village. Do we agree to meet this evening? If so,
there's no need to waste more time talking about this morning.
Good morning."

Turning his back on them, and not even glancing at the calf,
which the big fellow was unhurriedly roping by its horns, Yakov
Lukich went back to the steps with a sluggish waddle. Groaning
and coughing unnecessarily, with his left hand planted against
his loins, he climbed the steps. But when he reached the door he
pressed his hand to his chest by no means unnecessarily, stood
still for a good minute with his eyes closed, and whispered with
blanched lips: "May you be thrice damned!" The pricking pain
around his heart soon stopped, and his head ceased to swim. He
stood for a moment or two longer, then respectfully, but insistently, knocked at the door of the best room.

He opened the door, but hardly had time to get out the words:
"Your excellencies, there's trouble . . ." Like a flash of lightning
in a thunderous night he saw a pistol barrel pointed at him,
Polovtsiev's heavy jaw thrust out above it, and his hard, unwinking stare; he saw Lyatievsky sitting on the bed in an unconcerned attitude, but with his shoulders pressed against the wall,
the hand machine gun on his raised knees, with the barrel of that
gun also pointed towards the door at the level of Lukich's chest.
All this he saw in a moment of blinding vision, and even Lyatievsky's smile and the feverish glitter of his one eye as the question
reached his ears from far, very far off, as it seemed.

"Who were those two you brought into the yard, my dear
host?"

The badly shaken Yakov Lukich did not recognize that voice: it was as though a third, invisible person had asked it in a broken whistling whisper. But a force greater than himself brought about a complete change in him: his arms stretched down his trouser seams, bent at the elbow; yet he seemed to sag and shrink. When he replied, although his words were disconnected, broken by pauses, he spoke in a language different from any he had ever used before to his guests. "I've not brought anybody here; they turned up uninvited. And how much longer, my good sirs, do you intend to shout at me and domineer over me as if I was a small boy? It's highly insulting. We've fed you for nothing, and given you drink, and done our best to please you. Our women do your washing and get the food ready for you also for nothing. You can kill me this moment, on the spot, but with you around life has become one long burden. And yet we mustn't give you just cabbage soup, you've always got to have meat in it. You're always demanding that I should supply you with vodka. . . . When those uninvited guests came into the yard I gave you warning, and it didn't take me long to guess that they weren't merchants, and I turned my back on them and told them: 'God be with you! Take the calf for nothing if you wish, only clear out!' But you, my good sirs . . . But what's the good of talking to you?" He waved his hand hopelessly and leaned against the doorpost, hiding his face in his hands.

With the strange equanimity which had long since taken charge of him, Polovtsiev said in a toneless voice: "After all, I think the old man's right, Mr. Lyatievsky. It did seem like a showdown at first, but now I think we'd better clear out of here before it's too late. What do you think?"

"We must clear out this very day," Lyatievsky said resolutely, cautiously lowering the machine gun onto the disordered bed.

"But how about the liaisons?"

"We'll discuss that afterwards." The Pole nodded towards Yakov Lukich. Turning back to him, he said sharply: "Stop playing the old woman, Lukich. Tell us what you talked about with the merchants. Did they pay you the money in full? Are they coming back here?"

Yakov Lukich sobbed like a child, blew his nose into the hem of his unbelted shirt, wiped his beard, eyes, and whiskers with

his palm, and briefly, without looking at them, repeated his conversation with the visitors, mentioning the drover's suspicious behaviour and not forgetting to add that they would be coming back in the evening to seal the bargain with a drink.

When they heard that, the two conspirators exchanged glances.

"Very pleasant!" Lyatievsky said with a nervous smile. "You couldn't have thought of anything more clever, inviting them here. You're devilishly stupid, you hopeless idiot."

"I didn't invite them; they insisted on inviting themselves, and they did their best to come straight into the house without waiting. I had all my work cut out to persuade them to leave it till the evening. And as for you, your excellencies, or whatever your titles may be, you're making a mistake in calling me an idiot. What the devil—may the Lord forgive me—should I invite them into the house for while you're around? To make sure that both you and I lose our heads?" His moist eyes glittered unpleasantly as he ended with unconcealed malevolence: "Down to 1917 you officer gentlemen thought you were the only intelligent people around, and that the soldiers and simple Cossacks had all got holes where their brains should be. The Reds have taught you and taught you, but it's clear you haven't learnt anything. All your knowledge and fine living has gone to the devil."

Polovtsiev winked at Lyatievsky. Biting his lips, the Pole silently turned to the curtained window. But Polovtsiev went up to Lukich, laid his hand on his shoulder, and gave him a conciliatory smile. "You seem very quick to get worked up over trifles, Lukich. Does a man never say things in hot blood? Don't be too hard on us. You're right in one respect: those men who bought your calf are no more cattle collectors than I am a bishop. They're both Cheka men. Lyatievsky recognized one of them personally. D'you see the point? They're looking for us, that's clear, but so far they're only searching blindly, and that's why they're pretending to be cattle collectors. Well, then: before dinner-time Lyatievsky and I must get away from here, each on his own. You go and keep your merchants occupied for a couple of hours, or more if you like, how you like and with what you like. You can drive them to visit acquaintances somewhere, to some of our own people who're at home, drink vodka with them and

talk, but God forbid that you and your host should get drunk and let your tongues wag. If I find you've done that I'll kill both of you. Remember! And while you're keeping them busy with drinks, we'll quietly make our way along the ravine that runs from behind your yard into the steppe, and then they can whistle for us! Tell your son to conceal my sword, the machine gun and its discs, and our two rifles in the dung-fuel store."

"They can hide your rifle, but mine will go with me," Lyatievsky interjected.

Polovtsiev glanced at him but made no comment, and went on: "Have all this property well wrapped in canvas and carry it quietly into the shed; but do make sure no one sees you. Whatever happens, don't dare to hide anything in the house. I have one other request, or rather, order: Take over any packets which will come for me and put them under the threshing stone lying by the granary. We'll come and collect them by night from time to time. D'you follow what I'm saying?"

"Yes, very good!" Yakov Lukich whispered.

"Well, get to work; and don't lose sight of those damned merchants. Get them as far away from here as possible; within two hours we shan't be here. You can invite them home for the evening. Shift the camp beds from this room to the loft, and give the room an airing. To prevent them from being suspicious, put some old lumber in here, and then, if they ask, show them all over the house. They'll certainly want to have a good look all over your place under various pretexts. We'll stay away for a week, then we'll come back. Don't throw up the food we've had from you in our faces. You'll be paid back with interest for all you've given us and all you've spent on us as soon as our cause is victorious. We've got to come back here because I shall start the rising in this sector, here in Gremyachy. And the time is now very near," he ended solemnly. He gave Yakov Lukich a brief hug with both arms. "Now go, old man, and God be your aid."

The moment Ostrovnov had closed the door behind him Polovtsiev sat down at the table and asked:

"Where have you met that Cheka man before? Are you sure you're not mistaken?"

Lyatievsky shifted a stool across to the table, leaned over to Polovtsiev, and, perhaps for the first time in all their acquaintance, said without sarcasm or jest: "Jesu Maria! How could I be mistaken? I shall remember that man to the end of my life. Did you notice the scar on his cheek? I gave him that: I slashed him with a dagger when they picked me up. And this left eye of mine he knocked out during my interrogation. Did you notice what mutton fists he's got? That was four years ago, in Krasnodar. I was betrayed by a woman; she's dead now, glory to the Eternal! That was while I was still in the inner prison, but her guilt had already been proved. She gave up the ghost two days after my escape. She was a very young and beautiful Cossack bitch, a Kuban Cossack woman or, to be more exact, a Kuban bitch. I'll tell you all about it. . . . You don't know how I escaped from prison, do you?" He smiled with self-satisfaction and rubbed his small, dry hands together. "They'd have shot me in any case. I had nothing to lose, so I took a desperate risk and even resorted to a dirty trick. . . . So long as I was giving the investigators trouble and pretending to be only a pawn, they kept me in strict isolation. At last I decided on one final way out. I gave away a Cossack who came from the village of Koronovsky. He was in our organization, but he was the last link in the chain; he could only give away three of his fellows in the district; he didn't know a single one of our people. I thought it over and argued this way: 'Supposing they shoot or eliminate some who are far more important to the organization than these four animals?' I must tell you I was quite an important link in the Kuban organization. You can judge of my importance and the value of my work by the fact that since 1922 I've crossed the frontier five times and I've had five meetings with Kutepov in Paris. So I gave away those four supers, and by doing so I softened up the investigator, and he gave me permission to walk in the inner yard together with the other prisoners. I had no time to waste. You'll understand why. While exercising with a crowd of Kuban scum, all of them destined to death, during my very first turn round the yard that evening I saw a ladder running from the yard to a hayloft. Evidently it had only recently been put up. It was the time of the haymow, and the G.P.U. men were bringing in hay for their horses during the day. I walked

round the ring once more, my hands behind my back as ordered. But when I went past the third time I calmly walked up to the ladder and began to climb up it as though I were in a circus arena, not taking one look back. I kept my hands behind me all the time. My calculations were sound, Mr. Polovtsiev, psychologically sound. The guards were flabbergasted at my crazy audacity, and they let me climb up eight rungs or more before they said anything. Then one of them shouted desperately: 'Halt!' just as I started to run up the ladder two rungs at a time; I stooped down and leaped onto the roof like a goat. Ragged rifle fire, shouting, cursing! In two bounds I was at the edge of the roof, and from there I took one jump down into the alley. By morning I was safely hidden in Maikop. The name of that hero who knocked out my eye is Khizhnak. You saw him just now, a Stone Age Scythian woman in trousers! And would you really want me to let him get away alive? Don't worry, he'll lose the sight of both eyes in exchange for my one eye which he knocked out. Two eyes for an eye!"

"You're crazy," Polovtsiev exclaimed furiously. "D'you want to ruin everything just to have your personal revenge?"

"Don't get so worked up. I shan't kill Khizhnak and his friend here: I'll get them somewhere well outside the village. I'll stage a highway robbery, and that'll fix them. I'll take their money too. They've not done well with their trading, so they're pretty poor merchants. You can have your rifle hidden, but I'm taking mine with me under my coat. Don't try to reason me out of it. D'you hear? I'm not changing my mind. I'll go off first; you come later. We'll meet after sunset on Saturday in the forest near Tubyanskoe, at the spring where we first met. So long for now, and for God's sake don't be annoyed with me, Mr. Polovtsiev. We've just about had as much as our nerves will stand here, and I must admit I haven't always behaved decently to you."

"That's enough. Men in our position can get along without kind words," Polovtsiev muttered, a little embarrassed. None the less he embraced Lyatievsky, and pressed his lips in a fatherly fashion to the Pole's high, white forehead.

Lyatievsky was deeply moved by this unexpected demonstration of comradely feeling. But he preferred to conceal his emotion; standing and holding the door handle, with his back

to the other man, he said: "I'll take Maxim Kharitonov of Tubyan-skoe with me. He has a rifle, and he's a man you can rely on in times of difficulty. I take it you'll have no objection?"

Polovtsiev paused before answering. "Kharitonov served in my company as sergeant. You've made a sound choice. Take him. He's a fine shot, or at least he was. I understand how you feel. Do as you say, only on no account must it be done close to Gremy-achy, nor in a village, only out on the open steppe. . . ."

"Very good! So long."

"I wish you success."

Lyatievsky went into the passage, flung an old peasant coat belonging to Ostrovnov round his shoulders, and looked through the crack of the door into the deserted alley. A minute later he strode leisurely across the yard, with his carbine pressed close to his left side, and vanished as leisurely round the corner of the shed. But as soon as he jumped down into the ravine he was transformed: he took off the coat and put it on with his arms in the sleeves, released the rifle safety catch and held the weapon at the trail, and stole up the ravine with a crouching, stealthy step, like an animal, looking around him keenly, listening to every rustle, and occasionally glancing back at the village below half hidden in the lilac haze of the morning.

Two days later, on Friday morning, on the high road between the villages of Tubyanskoe and Voiskovoi, at a spot where it runs some sixty yards from the head of the Klenovsky ravine, two cattle collectors and one of their draught horses were shot dead. The driver, a Cossack from the village of Tubyanskoe, cut the traces of the second horse, leaped onto its bare back, and galloped to the village Soviet of Voiskovoi to report what had happened.

The local militia-man, the Soviet chairman, and the Cossack driver drove to the scene of the shooting, and established the following facts: bandits hiding in the forest had fired about ten shots from rifles. The sturdy, broad-shouldered drover had been killed by the very first shot. He had fallen face downward from the drozhki with a bullet through his heart. The stocky collector had shouted madly to his driver: "Whip them up!" had torn the

knout from the Cossack's hand and swung it at the offside horse.
But the lash had never reached the animal: a second shot had
brought the merchant down in the drozhki. The bullet had entered his head just above the left ear. The horses had torn
away, and the dead man had fallen out of the drozhki some
twenty yards farther on. Several more shots had been fired from
two rifles at once. The nearside horse had been shot through the
head as it galloped, breaking the centre shaft and turning the
drozhki over. The driver had cut the traces of the surviving horse
and had galloped off at top speed. Several shots had been sent
after him, but evidently more in order to frighten him than to
hit him, for he said they whistled high above his head.

Both the dead men had had their pockets rifled. No documents whatever were found on them. The merchant's document
case was found lying in the wayside grass, empty. The drover
had been turned over on his back while the bandits searched
him, and had had his left eye gouged out with a kick from a boot
heel, judging by the imprint on the skin.

The village Soviet chairman, an old and experienced Cossack
who had come through two wars, told the militia-man: "Look,
Luka Nazarich, some snake has even insulted the dead! Had he
crossed his road, or what? Or quarrelled over a woman, perhaps?
Ordinary bandits don't behave like beasts." Trying to avoid
looking at the swollen, livid eye-socket, at the cold, gelid bloody
mess oozing over the cheek, he covered the dead man's face with
his handkerchief. As he straightened up, he sighed: "There
are desperate men about. I should say it was wild men tracked
down these merchants and robbed them of more than a thousand. . . . Curse them! What vultures have flown up to get
their money?"

The day the news of Khizhnak's and Boiko-Glukhov's murder
reached Gremyachy, Nagulnov, finding himself alone for a minute or two with Davidov in the collective-farm office, asked
him: "D'you see, Siemion, where things are getting to?"

"I see just as well as you do. Polovtsiev or some of his sub-
ordinates had their hand in this."

"That goes without saying. The one thing I don't understand

is how they could have discovered who these two were. That's
the problem. And who could have done it?"

"That's a question which won't be settled by you or me. That's
an equation with two unknown quantities, and you and I aren't
strong in arithmetic and algebra. Don't you agree?"

Nagulnov sat for some time without speaking, his legs crossed,
staring meditatively at the toe of his dusty boot. Then he said:
"One of the two unknown quantities I do know. . . ."

"Then what is it?"

"Why, that a wolf never kills close to his lair. . . ."

"And what do you deduce from that?"

"That the murderers came from some distance, not from places
so close as Tubyanskoe or Voiskovoi. That's definite."

"From Shakhti or Rostov, do you think?"

"Not necessarily. But maybe from our village. What do you
think?"

"That's possible," Davidov assented, after a moment's thought.
"But in that case what do you suggest, Makar?"

"I think we Communists must keep our eyes skinned. We must
sleep less at night and must wander about the village, very
quietly, not letting ourselves be seen, but keeping a sharp look-
out. We may even have the luck to fall in with Polovtsiev or
some other suspicious stranger. Wolves go hunting at night. . . ."

"Are you comparing us with wolves?" Davidov smiled thinly.

But Nagulnov gave him no answering smile: knitting his bushy
brows, he said: "They're the wolves, we're the hunters. Can't
you see that?"

"You needn't lose your temper. I agree with you, that's a fact.
Let's call a meeting of all our Communists at once."

"Not at once, but a little later, when people are going to bed."

"That's sensible too," Davidov agreed. "But we mustn't patrol
the village: that would only alarm the villagers. We must set
ambushes."

"But where are we to set them? Suggest a suitable spot! That's
useless. It was easy enough for me to lie in wait for Timoshka:
he had only Lushka to go to, no other road was open to him. But
where can we set a trap for these scum? The world is wide, and
there are lots of houses in our village; you can't set a watch over
every one of them."

"There's no need for that, in any case."

"How are you going to select your houses, then?"

"We'll find out who the collectors bought cattle from and keep a watch only on those houses. Our dead comrades spent most of their time calling on people they suspected, and bought cattle chiefly from them. I think the bandits will make their way back to one of these people. D'you follow my reasoning?"

"You're a man of ideas!" Nagulnov said with conviction in his voice. "At times you think up some very useful ideas indeed."

Chapter 27

Polovtsiev and Lyatievsky returned to Ostrovnov's house, as arranged. They arrived at dawn, just half an hour after Razmiotnov, who had been keeping watch on the house from the neighbouring orchard, gave a last yawn, scrambled to his feet, and quietly went home, ruminating as he went: "Siemion thinks up some devilish fine ideas. Four days now we've been lurking in other people's yards like horse thieves, or just ordinary thieves, for that matter. We hide, we get no sleep all night, and it's all for nothing. Where are these bandits? We're watching our own shadows. I must get a move on, or some woman will be getting up early to milk her cow and will see me, and then the story will go all round the village like a wave along the river: 'Razmiotnov was kicked out at dawn. She must have been a wild woman that slept with him and warmed him, seeing he woke up only as light was coming!' And then the tongues will wag, and my authority will be undermined. We must put an end to this business. Let the G.P.U. hunt the bandits: there's no point in our taking on jobs that rightly belong to Cheka-men. Here I've spent all night in an orchard, all but stared my eyes out of my head, and what sort of work shall I be fit for today? They'll be saying again: 'He's been having his fun all night, the devil, and now he's yawning like a dog by the wall.' And that'll undermine my authority too. . . ."

Troubled with doubts, weary after his sleepless night, almost convinced that all this watching was pointless, he stole into his yard, and ran into his mother at the door. "It's me, Mother," he said in some embarrassment, trying to slip past her into the house.

But the old woman barred his way, and commented sternly: "I can see it's you; I'm not blind. But, son Andrei, isn't it time you gave up your wild life and stopped dragging around night after night? You're not all that young, you're long past marrying age, isn't it time you had more shame in front of your mother and the people too? Get married and stop it at once, you've had enough!"

"Shall I get married at once, then, or wait till the sun's up?" he asked in a filthy temper.

"Let the sun rise and set three times, but get married on the fourth day; I shan't hurry you," she said, parrying the unpleasant joke quite seriously. "Have pity on my old age. It's hard for me with all the troubles of my age to milk the cow, and cook, and wash for you, and tend the garden, and do everything on the farm. Why can't you see that, my son? You never lift a finger to do anything at home. What sort of help are you to me? You eat and you go off to your office like any lodger, just as if you were a stranger in the house. Only the pigeons give you any anxiety: you fuss over them like a kid. Is that a man's business? You should have some shame in front of people, to go amusing yourself with children's amusements. If Niura didn't help me I'd have had to take to my bed long since. But you're always out, and you never see how she, the darling girl, runs along to us every God's day to do all sorts of jobs, milking the cow, hoeing and watering the garden, and helping in all sorts of ways. She's such a kindly girl, such a good girl, you'd have to search all the district to find another like her. She gazes into your eyes, but you don't see it, you're blinded by your nights out. But where does the devil take you to? You just look at yourself: you're covered with burrs like a homeless dog. Bend your head down, my everlasting sorrow! Now, where have they been rolling you, torturing you?"

She laid her hand on his shoulder and gently pressed on it,

making him stoop. When he bent his head she pulled a clump of tightly clinging burrs out of his greying head.

He straightened up and smiled, gazing straight into her squeamish frowning face. "Don't think badly of me, Mother. It wasn't pleasure but necessity that sent me rolling among the burrs. At the moment it's all too much for you to understand, but you will when the time comes for me to tell you. But as for getting married, the time you've set, three days, is too long; as sure as tomorrow I'll bring Niura home to you. Only, do remember, Mother, it's you who's choosing her as your daughter-in-law, and you must get on well with her, so that there's no scandal between the two of you. I can live in harmony even with three women under one roof; you know I'm easy-going enough so long as I'm left alone. But now let me come in; I'll go and have an hour or two's sleep before going to work."

The old woman stepped aside, crossing herself. "Well, praise be, the Lord's brought you to have pity on my old age. Go, my dear, go, my little son; get some sleep and I'll fry some pancakes for your breakfast. And I've collected a little clotted cream for you. I just don't know what more to do for you in exchange for such joyful news." Andrei had gone in and closed the door behind him when she said as softly as if he were still standing beside her: "After all, you're the only one I've got left in all the wide world." And she broke into a quiet weeping.

At that same hour, at daybreak, several men lay down to sleep. Besides Andrei Razmiotnov there were Davidov, who had sat all night by a shed in Atamanchukov's yard, Nagulnov, who had kept an unblinking watch over Bannik's house, and Polovtsiev and Lyatievsky, who slipped safely through the cordon into Ostrovnov's house.

Andrei Razmiotnov was the first of them all to wake up. He shaved his cheeks till they were blue, washed his head, put on a clean shirt and the cloth trousers he had inherited by direct inheritance from Marina Poyarkova's dead husband, spat copiously on his leg-boots, then thoroughly cleaned them with a scrap of cloth torn from an old service overcoat. He got himself ready thoughtfully, without unnecessary haste.

His mother guessed what all these preparations were for, but

she asked no questions, afraid of disturbing her son's solemn mood by some imprudent remark. She only gave him an occasional glance and fussed around the stove more than usual. They ate their breakfast in silence.

"Don't expect me back before evening, Mother," he warned her in an official tone.

"God be your aid!" she wished him.

"He'll help if you wait long enough," he answered sceptically.

He was businesslike about his matchmaking and, unlike Davidov, spent only ten minutes over it. But when he entered the house of Niura's parents he had regard to the proprieties: he sat for a minute or two smoking silently, then exchanged a few words with her father concerning the harvest prospects and the weather. Then he announced outright as though it were something arranged and settled long since: "I shall be taking Niura from you tomorrow."

Her father was not lacking in his own peculiar brand of wit, and he asked: "Where to? To run messages for the village Soviet?"

"Worse. As my wife."

"That's for her to decide. . . ."

Razmiotnov turned to the blushing girl, and asked without even the ghost of a smile on his usually humorous features: "Agreed?"

"I've been agreed for five years," she answered without hesitation, keeping her bold, round, and adoring eyes fixed on his face.

"Well, that finishes the conversation," he said with satisfaction.

The parents wanted to observe the ancient customs and put up some show of opposition. But Andrei lit another cigarette and put his foot down firmly.

"I shan't try to extract any dowry or anything else out of you, and what could you get out of me? Tobacco smoke? Get the girl ready. We'll drive to the district today to register the marriage, and we'll be back this evening. Tomorrow we'll celebrate the wedding, and that'll be that."

"What are you in such a burning hurry for?" her mother asked in a vexed tone.

But he looked at her coldly, and answered: "I was burned

right out twelve years ago, burned out and reduced to ash. But I'm in a hurry because the harvest's all ready for reaping, and at home, as you know, my old mother is in retirement. So let's agree on this: I'll bring vodka back from the district, but not more than ten litres. You get some eats ready to go with the vodka, and invite the guests. On my side there'll only be three: Mother, Davidov, and Shaly."

"But how about Nagulnov?" his future father-in-law asked interestedly.

"He's fallen ill," Andrei said craftily, feeling perfectly sure that Makar would not turn up at the wedding in any case.

"Shall we slaughter a lamb, Andrei Stepanich?"

"That's your business; only remember we shan't be making over-merry. I mustn't. I'd be sacked from my position, and the Party sentence might be so hot that I'd be blowing for a good twelve months on the fingers that had held the glass." Turning to his bride, he winked impudently, but his smile was not very generous. "I'll be back in half an hour, and you put on your finest things meantime, Niura. You're not marrying any ordinary individual, you're marrying the chairman of the village Soviet."

It was a sad little wedding, without singing, without dancing, without the often rather free and sometimes quite indecent merry joking and good wishes that are customary at Cossack weddings. Razmiotnov set the tone: he was altogether too serious, restrained, and sober. He took hardly any part in the conversation, but sat silent, and when the tipsy guests shouted "bitter" from time to time, it was almost as though he forced himself to turn to his ruddy-cheeked wife, as though he kissed her cold lips only reluctantly. And his eyes, usually so vivid, gazed not at his young bride, not at the guests, but with a far-away look, as though into a very distant and mournful past.

Chapter 28

In Gremyachy Log and above it life passed on with the same age-old, majestic, unhurried tread; the clouds, edged with frosty white, still floated over the village in their seasons; their colour and hues would change from time to time, passing from a deep bluish-black, thunderous in their portent, to a colourless grey; at times, as they burned dimly or brightly at the setting of the sun, they presaged wind for the coming day, and then the women and children in the farmyards of Gremyachy Log heard from the masters of the house, or those who were preparing to be the masters, the calm, curt phrase, irreproachable in its tone of age-old conviction: "Why, what's the good of loading a wagon, or stacking in such weather?" One of the older members of the family or possibly a neighbour would slowly respond: "Of course you can't. It would all be blown away." And in such seasons of violent eastern wind above and enforced human idleness below, in all the three hundred farmyards of the village someone would begin one and the same story of a certain villager, Ivan Ivano-vich Degtariov, long since dead, who once, long, long ago, thought he would bring home the grain from the fields to his threshing floor when an east wind was blowing. But, seeing the wind sweeping the bundled sheaves of ripe wheat off his wagons, despairing of this struggle with the elements, he raised an enor-mous load of wheat on his three-pronged pitchfork and, gazing eastward and addressing the wind, roared furiously: "Come on, then, carry this away too, since you're so strong. Carry it away, damn you!" Turning a wagon laden with wheat over on its side, cursing ruthlessly, he had driven home with empty wagons.

So life passed on in Gremyachy Log, never accelerating its deliberate pace; but every day and every night brought its own great and little joys, sorrows, agitations, and more or less perma-nent troubles to every one of the three hundred houses. At day-break one Monday Agei's long years of service as the village drover came to an end in the pasture. He ran to head off a play-ful young cow in her first calf and drive her back to the herd. But

he had not run far at his aged trot when he suddenly stopped, pressed the knout to his heart, swayed where he stood for a minute or two, treading with bent legs, and then, staggering as though drunk, dropping his knout, went back slowly and uncertainly. Beskhlebnov's daughter-in-law, who had just driven up her cow to join the herd, ran to him, caught hold of his chilling hands, and, hardly able to get her breath, breathing hotly into the old man's eyes, asked him:

"Daddy, are you feeling bad, my dear?" Then she cried out: "Oh, my dear, what can I do to help you?"

Hardly able to move his stiffening tongue, Agei got out the words: "My little darling, don't be afraid. . . . Put your arms under mine and support me, or I'll drop. . . ."

And he did fall, first on his right knee, then rolling over sideways. And he died. Just like that. And at noonday, almost at the same hour, two young collective-farm women gave birth. One had a very difficult travail. Davidov had to send urgently to Voiskovoi for the local quack, despatching the first wagon that happened to come along empty. He had only just returned from Agei's home and had said a last good-bye to the old drover when the young collective farmer Mikhei Kuznetsov ran into his office. Standing at the door, pale and agitated, he cried:

"Dear Comrade Davidov, for Christ's sake help me. My wife's been in labour for over twenty-four hours and she simply can't manage to drop the child. And I've got two children besides, and I can't stand seeing her suffer. Help me with horses, we must fetch a doctor; our women don't seem able to help her at all."

"Come on!" Davidov said, and hurried into the yard.

But Shchukar had driven out to the steppe to get hay, and all the horses were in use.

"Let's go along to your house, and we'll send the first cart we come across to Voiskovoi. You go back to your wife, and I'll get hold of one somehow at the gate and send it off."

Davidov knew very well that it was not regarded as proper for a man to be close to a spot where a woman was in labour, but he walked up and down outside the low wattle fence of Kuznetsov's

house, taking great strides, turning his gaze from one end of the deserted street to the other, listening to the woman's hollow groans and protracted shrieks and himself moaning quietly with pain over this mother's sufferings and swearing in his juiciest sailor language under his breath. When he saw a brigade water-cart driven by the sixteen-year-old Adrei Akimov jogging quietly along the street, he ran up like a boy to cut him off, with a great effort pushed the full water-barrel off its cradle, and panted out the words:

"Listen, boy! A woman's having trouble here. You've got good horses; drive as fast as you can to Voiskovoi and bring back the doctor dead or alive. Drive the horses hard: I'll take the responsibility, that's a fact."

The sultry noonday silence was broken by another quivering scream, muffled and low, from the suffering woman. Davidov stared into the lad's eyes and asked: "Did you hear that? Now, off with you."

Standing bolt upright on the wagon frame, the lad gave Davidov a brief glance, a grown man's glance. "I get it, Daddy Siemion, and don't worry about the horses." He sent them off at a tearing gallop, standing on the wagon, whistling dashingly and saucily waving his knout.

Staring at the dust flying up from the wheels, Davidov hopelessly waved his hand, then went back to the collective-farm office. As he went he heard the woman's wild cry yet again, frowned as though with severe pain, and muttered in a tone of annoyance when he had gone a little way: "Fine idea! Thinks she'll have a baby and doesn't know how to do it properly, that's a fact."

Before he had had time to deal with certain current matters in the office a young lad, the son of the old collective farmer Abramov, came in with an embarrassed air and, shifting from foot to foot, said shyly: "Comrade Davidov, we're having a wedding at our place today, and all our family invite you to it. It'll not be quite right if you don't sit down at the table with us."

That was the last straw: Davidov jumped up from the table and exclaimed: "Has everybody in the village gone mad? A birth, a death, and a marriage all in the one day! Are you all in a conspiracy, or what?" Laughing inwardly at his own vehemence,

he asked more calmly: "And what the devil are you in such a hurry for? You could have had the wedding in the autumn. Autumn's the proper time to celebrate weddings. . . ."

Fidgeting as though standing on hot coals, the lad replied: "The matter doesn't allow of waiting till the autumn. . . ."

"What matter?"

"Well, you ought to know without my having to say it, Comrade Davidov. . . ."

"Ah! So that's it! My son, it's always advisable to think over such matters in advance," Davidov admonished him. He had to smile as he thought: "It's hardly for me to lecture him, and hardly for him to listen." Maintaining an impressive silence for a moment or two, he added: "Well, all right; off with you. I'll drop in this evening for a few minutes; we'll all come along. Have you spoken to Nagulnov and Razmiotnov?"

"I've already invited them."

"Then all three of us will come and spend an hour or so with you. Don't be offended if we don't have much to drink; this isn't the time for it. And now off you go; I wish you happiness. Though we'll wish you that when we arrive. Is she pretty big already?"

"Not all that much, but you can see . . ."

"Well, it's always better when it can be seen," Davidov said again in a rather edifying tone, and he smiled once more, conscious of the note of hypocrisy in his remarks.

Just as he was signing a report an hour later Mikhei Kuznetsov rushed in beaming with happiness and, throwing his arms round Davidov, informed him in a burst of emotion: "Christ save you, Chairman! Andrei brought the doctor just in time; my wife was all but dead. But with his help she's shelled out such a son for me, he's as big as a young calf, you can't hold him in your arms. The doctor says he shouldn't be as big as all that. But what I think is, whether he should or shouldn't, there's a boy in the family now. Will you be the godfather, Comrade Davidov?"

Rubbing his forehead slowly, Davidov answered: "Yes, I'll be godfather. I'm terribly glad everything's turned out all right for your wife. See Ostrovnov tomorrow for anything you need at home. I'll give him instructions, that's a fact. And as for the child not coming as it should, that's nothing to worry about; remem-

ber, boys rarely come as they should, not real boys!" And this
time he didn't even smile: he was quite unconscious that he had
adopted the same edifying tone which had made him smile a
little earlier.

Evidently the sailor lad was growing sentimental, when another
man's joy and the happy outcome of maternal labour brought
tears to his eyes. And, feeling those tears, he covered them with
his broad hand and ended rather roughly: "You go back home
now; your wife's waiting for you. If you want anything come and
see me. But now clear off, I've got a lot to do; there's enough on
my plate without you, get that?"

Late the same afternoon an extraordinary happening took
place in Gremyachy, though hardly anyone noticed it. Just before seven o'clock an elegant-looking drozhki rolled up to
Ostrovnov's house. It was drawn by a pair of good horses. At
the wicket gate a short man in a linen jacket and similar
breeches got out. He brushed the dust off the lapels of his coat
with an elderly fastidiousness, and confidently walked on to the
veranda where Yakov Lukich, alarmed at this new arrival, was
waiting for him. Revealing his tobacco-stained teeth, he gripped
Lukich's elbow with his small, dry hand, and asked with a
friendly smile:

"Is Alexander Anisimovich at home? I can see you're the master
of the house. Are you Yakov Lukich?"

Judging by the man's bearing, sensing with the instinct of a
former army man that this visitor was a high authority, Yakov
Lukich submissively clicked the heels of his patched shoes and
answered hurriedly: "Your high excellency! So it's you? My God,
how they've been waiting for you!"

"Take me to them."

With quite unnatural haste Yakov Lukich obediently threw
open the door to Polovtsiev's and Lyatievsky's room. "Alexander Anisimovich," he reported. "Forgive me for not announcing
him in advance, but a very dear visitor has arrived to see you."

The stranger strode into the room and threw his arms wide
open with a threatrical gesture. "Greetings, my dear hermits.
Can we talk aloud here?"

Polovtsiev was sitting at the table and Lyatievsky was loung-

ing carelessly on the bed, as usual; they both sprang up as though they had been ordered to attention.

The stranger embraced Polovtsiev and pressed Lyatievsky to himself with his left arm, saying: "Please sit down, gentlemen. I am Colonel Sedoi, the person who has been sending you your instructions. Today, by the will of fate, I am the agronomist of the regional agricultural department. As you can see I've come here on a visit of inspection. I haven't much time. I must briefly. put the position before you." He again invited the officers to sit down and, displaying his stained teeth in a smile, continued with an exaggerated air of friendliness: "You're having a very miserable life I should think: you don't even seem to have anything to offer your guest. But we're not here to discuss entertainment now, I shall have my dinner elsewhere. Please ask my coachman to come in, and take steps to ensure that we are secure by posting someone to keep watch at least."

Polovtsiev obediently hurried to the door; but the colonel's well-built, handsome-looking coachman was already coming in. He held out his hand to Polovtsiev and said:

"Good morning, Captain. Russian tradition says it's bad to greet one another over a threshold." Turning to the colonel, he asked respectfully: "Do you allow me to be present? I've arranged for a watch to be kept."

Sedoi was still smiling at Polovtsiev and Lyatievsky with his deep-set grey eyes. "Let me introduce Cavalry Captain Kazantsev to you, gentlemen," he said. "Captain Kazantsev, you know our hosts. Now, gentlemen, to business. We'll sit down at your bachelor table."

Polovtsiev asked nervously: "Colonel, won't you let us give you some refreshment? Whatever we've got, though it won't be much."

Sedoi curtly answered: "Thank you, but there's no need. Let's get down to business at once, my time's very short. Bring out the maps, Captain."

Kazantsev drew a five-mile-to-the-inch map of the Azov and Black Sea area out of his jacket inner pocket, spread it out on the table, and all four men bent over it.

Sedoi took a blue pencil out of his pocket, tapped it on the

table, and said: "My name, as you can guess, is not Sedoi.
It's Nikolsky, Staff Colonel in the Imperial Army. This map is a
general one, but you don't need one with more detail for military
operations. Now for your task: you have about two hundred
active bayonets or sabres. Having disposed of the local Communists, but avoiding petty and protracted conflicts at all costs,
you are to march by forced marches, cutting communications as
you go, to the Soviet farm 'Red Dawn.' There you will do whatever is necessary, and as a result you will acquire some forty
rifles with appropriate stores of ammunition. And, above all,
retaining all the hand and tripod machine guns in your possession
and acquiring some thirty trucks in the Soviet farm, you move on
by forced marches to Millerovo. One other main thing: you see
how many main tasks I'm setting you: you, Captain Polovtsiev—
and this is my strict command—will have to launch a surprise
attack on the regiment which is quartered in the town of Millerovo and not give it any chance to deploy; you must smash it at
once, disarm it, seize its arms and equipment, and collect any
Red Army men who will join you. Then, travelling on the trucks,
you will set out in the direction of Rostov. I sketch this task only
in general outline, but much depends on it. If, contrary to
expectations, you meet with resistance on the way to Millerovo,
make a detour round the town and move on to Kamensk by this
route." With his blue pencil he sluggishly drew a straight line
across the map. "In Kamensk I shall meet you with my detachment, Captain."

He sat thinking for a moment, then added:

"It is possible that you will be supported from the north by
Lieutenant-Colonel Savvataev. But don't rely on that too much,
and act independently. One thing you must understand: very
much depends on the success of your operation. I refer to your
disarming of the regiment in Millerovo and your exploitation of
its fire power. It has a battery in any case, and that would help us
a great deal. From Kamensk we shall open the fight for Rostov,
assuming that forces will come to our support from the Kuban
and the Terek, where we have the help of the Allies, while we
already hold the power in the south. I ask you to bear in mind,
gentlemen, that the operation as we have worked it out has its
risks, but there is no other way. If we don't exploit the possi-

bility which history affords us in the year 1930 you can say good-bye to the empire and we go over to petty terrorist activities. That's all I have to say. We can have a brief word from you, Captain Polovtsiev. But take one circumstance into account: I have still to drive to the village Soviet, let them know of my visit, and then go on to the district. I am, so to speak, an official person, an agronomist attached to the Agricultural Department, so let us have your remarks briefly."

Without looking at Nikolsky, Polovtsiev said gruffly: "Colonel, you have set me a general task, but you haven't supplied any definite details. I can take the Soviet farm; but I have always assumed that our next step would be to raise the Cossacks. But you're sending me to engage in a fight with a regular Red Army regiment. Doesn't it occur to you that that is hopeless, given the possibilities and forces at my disposal? And if even one Red battalion comes out to meet me on my way, you're sentencing me to certain destruction."

Knocking his knuckles on the table, Colonel Nikolsky smiled wryly. "I think it was a mistake ever to raise you to the rank of Captain. If you vacillate at a difficult moment and don't believe in the success of the enterprise we've planned, you're not worth a fig as an officer of the Russian army. You're not taking it into your head to be clever and putting forward your own, independent plan, are you? How do you wish me to understand your remarks? Will you act, or have we got to remove you?"

Polovtsiev rose to his feet. Bending his bullet head, he quietly answered: "Very well, I'll act, Colonel. Only . . . only, if the operation fails, I shall not be responsible, but you."

"Oh, that's not your concern, Captain," Nikolsky said with a cheerless smile. He stood up, and Captain Kazantsev got up too. Putting one arm around Polovtsiev, the Colonel said: "Courage, and yet more courage! That's what is lacking in the officers' corps of the fine old Imperial Army. You became teachers in secondary schools, or settled in agriculture. But the traditions, the glorious traditions of the Russian army: have you forgotten them? However, I'll say no more. Only start to act as those who are thinking for you have commanded, and then . . . and then . . . the appetite comes with eating. I hope to see you, Captain, a Major-General before you're finished, in Novorossisk, say, or

even in Moscow. Judging by your unsociable air you're capable
of a great deal. And now to our meeting in Kamensk. My last
word to you is: the order for simultaneous activity wherever we
have our centres of resistance will be issued separately, you understand that, don't you? Good-bye till we meet in Kamensk."

Polovtsiev embraced his visitors with no warmth whatever,
opened the door of the room, and met the gaze of Yakov Lukich,
who was standing shivering in the passage. When the two had
gone, Polovtsiev did not sit so much as drop down on to the bed.
After some time he asked Lyatievsky, who was sitting huddled
with his back against the windows: "Did you ever see such a
beetle?"

Lyatievsky waved his hand contemptuously. "Jesu-Maria,
what else did you expect of the Russian soldiery? You should
rather ask me, Mr. Polovtsiev, what the devil I ever got involved
with you for?"

Yet one more tragic incident occurred that day: Trofim the goat
was drowned in a well. Restless by nature, often wandering
about the village all night, evidently he ran into a pack of homeless dogs, and they chased him, forcing him to leap across a well,
close to the collective-farm office. Shchukar, with carelessness of
age, had left off the well cover the previous evening, and when
the terrified goat attempted to leap, his hoofs must have caught
on the edge, and he fell in.

When, next evening, Shchukar returned from the steppe with
a load of hay, he went to water his stallions and let down the
bucket. But he felt it dragging over some soft obstacle. Despite
all his manoeuvring with the well rope he completely failed to
draw up any water. Then, struck by a terrible surmise, he looked
round the yard in the hope of seeing his everlasting enemy. But
Trofim was not to be seen. He went hurriedly to the hayloft,
then trotted to the gate: but there was no sign of Trofim. Shedding miserable tears, he walked into the office and dropped on to
the bench in front of Davidov. "Well, Siemion, we've lived to see
a new sorrow: it looks like our Trofim drowned in the well.
Come and help us get him out."

"Are you sorry, then?" Davidov asked with a smile. "You were always asking us to slaughter the goat."

"I've asked all sorts of things," Shchukar burst out angrily. "But you didn't slaughter him, and thank God for that. But now how can I live without him? He kept me in fear every day of the week. I never parted with my knout from morn till evening: it was my one defence against him. But now what sort of life will I have? It'll be one long, flat, boring time. I might as well throw myself head downward into a well. . . . Were we friends in the least? Not at all. I fought many a battle with him. Sometimes I'd catch the accursed beast and hold him by the horns and say: 'Trofim, you son of this and that, you're no longer a young goat, where d'you get all your ill nature from. Where d'you get so much spunk that you don't leave me at peace for one moment? You're always watching out to catch me in the rear or the side.' But he'd stare at me like a standing spectre, and there wouldn't be the least spark of humanity in his eyes. I'd bring my knout down across his back and shout after him: 'Run, you triply damned, you old defiler! No one can ever get any satisfaction out of you.' But the son of a devil, he'd rear up with his backside, run a dozen or so paces away from me, and begin to nibble the grass for want of anything better to do, as though he was hungry. But he'd squint at me with his goggling eyes and he was obviously scheming to cut me off again. It wasn't life, it was fun we had with him. For it was quite impossible for me to come to any agreement with such a stupid idiot, or, to put it simply, such a fool. But now he's drowned and I'm sorry for him, and I'm a beggar. . . ." He snivelled miserably and wiped his streaming eyes with the sleeve of his dirty cotton shirt.

They obtained a grapnel from the next yard, and hauled the thoroughly steeped goat out of the well.

"And now what do we do next?" Davidov asked.

Still snivelling and wiping his bleary eyes, Shchukar answered: "You go and attend to your state business, Siemion, and I'll bury him myself. That's not a job for you youngsters, that's for an old man to do. I'll do him proud, the old villain, and then cry a little over his mournful end. Christ save you for helping to haul him out: I couldn't have managed it myself. He must

weigh at least a hundred pounds, the horned gelding. He grew fat on free vittles, and that's why he got drowned, the fool; if he'd been lighter he'd have jumped across the well like any little kid. Those dogs must have worried him a lot for him to fly over the well like a mad thing. But, Siemion, give me enough to get a quarter litre of vodka for my sorrow, and I'll remember him in the hayloft this evening. There's no point in my going home to the old woman; what good would come of it if I did? It would only mean the break-up of all my nervous system. And another battle. And at my time of life I get no pleasure out of that. But I'll have a little drink quietly, and remember the dead, and have a good sleep, that's a fact."

Trying to avoid smiling, Davidov gave the old man a ten-kopek piece, and put his arms round his scraggy shoulders. "Don't grieve over him too much, Daddy. We can always buy you a new goat."

Mournfully shaking his head, Shchukar replied: "You couldn't buy another goat like that at any price. There never has been another goat like that in all the world. And my grief will remain with me." He wandered off to get a spade, his shoulders bowed, the picture of misery, yet touchingly absurd in his sorrow.

And that was the last incident in a day filled with great and petty events.

Chapter 29

After supper Davidov went to his room. He had just sat down at the table to look through some newspapers when he heard a quiet knock on the window frame. He opened the window, and saw Nagulnov. Standing with one foot on the wall ledge, Makar said in an undertone:

"Get ready for business. Let me in; I'll climb through the window and tell you all about it." His swarthy face was pale, and had a set expression. He threw his leg lightly over the sill, climbed in, and sat down on a stool. Banging his fist on his knee, he said:

"I warned you, Siemion; it's just as I said. I've seen one at last. I've been lying a good two hours close by Ostrovnov's house, and I saw a rather short fellow come up cautiously, and stand listening. It must be one of those we're after. . . . I was a bit late in getting to my hiding place, it was already getting dark. I was late because I'd been out in the fields. So who knows whether he was the first? Come on now, we'll pick up Razmiotnov on the way. There's no point in wasting time. We'll catch them there with Lukich, red-handed. Or at any rate we'll get this one."

Davidov slipped his hand under the pillow of his bed and took out his pistol. "But how shall we set about it?" he asked. "Let's talk that over here before we start."

Lighting a cigarette, Nagulnov smiled almost imperceptibly. "I know what to do from past experience. So listen: this stocky fellow didn't knock at the door but at the window, just like I did just now. Yakov Lukich has a best room with one small window opening on to the yard. This bandit knocked at the window—I couldn't make out whether he was wearing a peasant coat or a raincoat because it was too dark—someone, either Lukich or his son, opened the door the least bit, and this fellow went in. But as he went up the steps he gave one look back, and when he went in he looked round again. I was lying behind the fence and saw it all. You know, Siemion, respectable people don't go about like that, showing such wolfish anxiety. This is what I suggest: you and I will knock at the door, and Andrei will slip in from the yard to stand by the window. We'll see who opens to us. I remember the door to the best room is the first on the right as you go in. If it's fastened we'll have to break it open. You and I will go in, and if anyone jumps through the window, Andrei will catch him. We'll take these nocturnal visitors alive; it'll all be quite simple. I shall break open the door, you'll stand right behind me, and if there's any trouble, shoot into the room without any further palaver, aiming at the least sound."

Makar looked into Davidov's eyes with his own slightly narrowed eyes, and a smile again flickered over his lips.

"You keep that little toy of yours in your hands, and check the clip and make sure there's a cartridge ready for firing before we leave here. We'll go out through the window, and close the shutter behind us."

He adjusted the strap round his tunic, threw his cigarette on the floor, stared at the toes of his dusty boots, and smiled yet again.

"Through these filthy reptiles I've been rolling in the dust like a puppy. I had to lie flat as best I could while waiting for these dear visitors. Well, one's turned up at last. I've got a feeling there may be two or three, but not more. There can't be a whole platoon of them quartered on Lukich, can there?"

Davidov spun the cartridge chamber, slipped a cartridge into the drum, thrust the pistol into his jacket pocket, and said: "You seem very cheerful today, Makar. You've only been sitting here five minutes and you've already smiled three times."

"We're going to a cheerful job, Siemion. That's why I'm smiling."

They climbed through the window, closed it, then folded back the shutter, and stood still for a moment. Though the night was warm, a refreshing breeze came up from the stream. All the village was asleep; the peaceable labours of the day were ended. A calf bleated somewhere; dogs barked at the other end of the village; not for off a stupid cock crowed before its time. Without exchanging a word, Nagulnov and Davidov strode to Razmiotnov's house. Makar knocked very quietly on the window with his bent forefinger. When, a moment or two later, he saw Andrei's face glimmering through the pane, he beckoned to him and showed him his pistol.

Davidov heard Razmiotnov say quietly but seriously: "I see, I'll be out quick."

He appeared on the veranda almost at once. As he closed the door behind him be called back angrily into the house: "Must you carry on like that, Niura? I've been called to the village Soviet on business. You know very well they don't send for me to go out on a spree. Get to sleep and stop your sighing. I'll soon be back."

Outside, they stood with their heads close together. Andrei asked in a delighted tone: "Have you caught them, then?"

In a hoarse whisper Nagulnov told him what he had seen. Then all three stole off and silently entered Yakov Lukich's yard. Razmiotnov squatted down at the warm base of the wall with his

back leaning against it. He laid his pistol barrel carefully across his knees; he was anxious to avoid any unnecessary strain in his right wrist.

Nagulnov led the way up the steps, went to the door, and rattled the latch. It was very quiet in Ostrovnov's yard and house. But this ominous silence did not last long; Lukich's voice sounded from inside, unexpectedly loud.

"What evil spirit is that wandering about at night?"

"Excuse me, Lukich, for knocking so late," Makar replied. "I've got some business to settle with you: you and I have to drive to the Soviet farm at once. It's a matter of urgency." There was a moment or two of uncertain silence. Then Nagulnov demanded impatiently: "Well, what's the matter with you? Open the door."

"Dear Comrade Nagulnov, you're such a late visitor . . . in the dark . . . and our bolts . . . it's difficult to find them . . . come in."

The solid iron bolt was shot back with a crash, and the door was opened the merest fraction.

With all his great strength Nagulnov charged the door open with his left shoulder, sent Yakov Lukich flying back against the wall, and strode into the passage, calling over his shoulder to Davidov: "Give him one if he makes trouble."

His nostrils caught the warm smell of the living room and of freshly ground corn. But he had no time to sort out these smells or his sensations. Holding his pistol in his right hand, with his left he swiftly groped for the doorpost of the best room and sent the door flying open with one kick. "Now, then, who's in here? I'll shoot."

But he had no time to shoot: his shout was followed immediately by the cracking explosion of a hand grenade flung right at the door, and then, sounding sinister in the nocturnal silence, a hand machine gun stuttered. There was the jangle of a window frame being knocked out, a single shot outside, a cry. . . .

Sprayed and mutilated by the grenade fragments, Nagulnov died on the spot. But as Davidov rushed into the room he managed to fire twice into the darkness before he was caught in the hail of machine-gun bullets.

He lost consciousness at once and fell backward, flinging his

head back in agony; in his left hand he clutched a rough splinter
shot off the doorpost by a bullet.

From that moment a fearful struggle for life was fought out in
his broad chest, which was holed in four places. Stumbling in
the dark, but striving their utmost to avoid shaking him, his
friends silently carried him home in their arms. For more than
sixteen hours his terrible wrestle with death went on as he lay
unconscious.

The district surgeon, a young man serious beyond his years,
arrived at dawn, his carriage drawn by horses lathered with
foam. He spent not more than ten minutes in the room where
Davidov was lying; during those ten minutes the Gremyachy
Communists and the many non-Party collective farmers who
loved their chairman, waiting tensely silent in the kitchen, heard
only a muffled, choking groan, as though in his sleep. The doctor
entered the kitchen, wiping his hands on a towel, his sleeves
rolled back; he looked pale but outwardly calm, as he answered
the mute question.

"Not a hope. I can't do anything here. But he's amazingly
tenacious of life. Don't shift him from where he is now, he
mustn't be touched at all. If there's any ice in the village . . .
though it doesn't really matter. But someone should be with him
all the time."

Razmiotnov and Maidannikov had come out of the bedroom
with him. Andrei's lips were quivering; his vaguely staring eyes
wandered round the kitchen without seeing anyone. Maidannikov came out with head bent; the veins in his temples were
swollen fearfully, and two deep, perpendicular furrows above the
bridge of his nose were as red as scars. Everybody, with the
exception of Maidannikov, went out into the yard and departed
in various directions. Razmiotnov leaned his chest against the
wicket gate with his head hanging, his shoulders heaving; when
old Shaly reached the wattle fence he shook the crooked oak
tether post in a blind, senseless frenzy; Diemka Ushakov pressed
himself almost flat against the granary wall like a naughty
schoolboy, dug his finger nails into the rain-soaked plaster, and
made no attempt to wipe away the tears rolling down his cheeks.

Each one was suffering the loss of his friends in his own way, but the one terrible, manly grief was common to them all.

Davidov died during the following night. Before his death he recovered consciousness. Glancing at Shchukar sitting and sobbing at the bed head, he said: "What are you crying for, old man?" But a crimson foam at once bubbled and gushed up from his throat. He only made a few convulsive attempts to swallow, let his white hand fall on the pillow, and was hardly able to finish the sentence: "There's no need . . ." He even tried to smile.

Then with a prolonged groan his body painfully straightened out, and he said no more.

And now the Don nightingales had sung their last song for those dear friends of mine, Siemion Davidov and Makar Nagulnov; the ripened wheat had whispered its last farewell to them; the nameless little stream flowing down from the head of the Gremyachy Ravine had tinkled its last melody over the stones for them. And that is all.

Two months passed. The white, autumnally packed clouds still floated in the lofty zenith above Gremyachy Log; the leaves of the poplars, faded with the burning summer, were streaked with gold along the Gremyachy stream; the water in the stream was translucent and icy. But, fostered by the meagre autumnal sun, a fragile, pale-green grass sprang up on the graves of Davidov and Nagulnov, who had been buried on the village square, not far from the school. And there was even some unknown steppe flower belatedly trying to establish its miserable life, huddling against the palisades of the fence round the graves. But three sunflower shoots, sprouting not far from the graves after the August rains, had succeeded in growing at least four inches high, and swayed gently whenever the wind blew low over the square.

Much water had flowed down the Gremyachy stream during those two months. Many changes had occurred in the village. After the burial of his friends old Shchukar had obviously gone downhill and was changed almost beyond recognition: he had grown unsociable, taciturn, still more lachrymose. After the funeral he lay in bed at home for days without stirring, and

when he did get up his old woman noticed with alarm that his mouth was twisted a little and the left side of his face was crooked.

"Why, what's happened to you?" she exclaimed in fright, clapping her hands.

Stammering a little, but calmly enough the old man answered, as he wiped away the spittle dribbling from the left corner of his mouth: "Nothing particularly. Two such fine youngsters have fallen, and it's long since time I was resting there. Is that clear?"

As he slowly made his way to the table, it transpired that he was dragging his left leg. When he rolled a cigarette he had difficulty in raising his left arm. "Damn it, I must have had a stroke, old girl. I see I'm not the same as I was," he said, staring in astonishment at his refractory arm.

After a week he grew a little better: his step was more confident; he could control his left hand without much effort. But he flatly refused to work any more as a coachman. He walked into the collective-farm office and informed the new chairman, Kondrat Maidannikov: "I'm through with driving about, dear Kondrat. It'll be too much for me to manage the stallions."

"Razmiotnov and I have already been thinking about you, Daddy," Maidannikov answered. "Supposing you take over the night watchman's job at the village store? We'll fix you up with a warm hut for the winter; we'll put an iron stove in it and make it warm for you, and we'll have a sheepskin coat made for you by the time winter comes, and an overcoat and felt boots. You'll get your wages, and it'll be light work. And, best of all, you'll have something to occupy you. Well, what d'you think?"

"Christ save you, that's just the right job for me. Thank you for not forgetting the old man. It's the very devil; I hardly ever did sleep at night, and now I don't at all. I'm grieving over the boys, Kondrat, my dear, and sleep's begun to leave me altogether. Well, I'll go and say good-bye to my stallions, and then get home. Who are you handing them over to?"

"Old Beskhlebnov."

"He's a tough old man; but as for me, I'm gone all to seed. Makar and Davidov have bowled me over, they've robbed me of my life. . . . With them around I might have lived on for another year or two; but without them I've grown weary of wandering

about the world," he said mournfully, wiping his eyes with the crown of his old peaked cap.

He started work as watchman that very night.

Davidov and Nagulnov's graves, surrounded by a low fence, were not far from the village store, almost opposite it. And the next day, armed with an ax and saw, old Shchukar fixed up a small bench by the fence. And there he spent his nights.

"I'm drawn more and more to my dear ones," he told Razmiotnov. "It'll be more cheerful for them lying there when I'm around, and I'll find the nights shorter and more friendly when I'm by them. I've never had any children, Andrei, but now it's just as though I'd lost two sons at once. And my damnable heart gives me twinges day and night, I never have any peace from it."

But Razmiotnov, who was now the Party secretary, shared his fears with Maidannikov. "Kondrat, have you noticed how terribly old our Daddy Shchukar has gone of late? He's sunk in grief for the lads and he's nothing like his former self. I'm sure the old fellow will be dead before long. His head shakes and his hands are going black. By God, he'll bring sorrow on us. We've grown so used to the old crackpot that there'll be an empty place in the village when he's gone."

The days grew shorter, the air more translucent. The wind no longer blew the bitter scent of wormwood from the steppe to the graves, but the smell of newly threshed straw from the threshing floors outside the village.

Old Shchukar was cheerful enough while the corn was being threshed; the winnow rattled away till late in the evening on the threshing floors; the stone rollers clumped hollowly over the beaten earth; human voices called encouragement; and horses snorted. But then the village grew very quiet. The nights were longer and darker, and now other voices sounded in the night: the groan of a crane in the slaty black vault of the sky, the mournful calls of the barnacles, the quiet honk of geese and the whistle of ducks' wings.

"The birds are setting out for the warm countries," the old man sighed in his lonely vigil, listening to the sounds dropping in a challenge from high above.

One evening, when it was quite dark, a woman wrapped in a

black kerchief came quietly up to Shchukar and stood there without speaking.

"Who is that God has brought?" the old man asked, vainly trying to identify the stranger.

"It's me, Daddy. Varia. . . ."

Shchukar rose from the bench as nimbly as his age would allow him. "My little darling, so you've come back after all. I was beginning to think you'd forgotten us. . . . Ah, droopy Varia, the way you and I have been orphaned! Come, my dear, come to the little wicket here; this is his grave, this side. . . . You just stay with him while I go and take a look at the store and check the padlocks. I'm working here as watchman; it's enough for my old age. . . . Quite enough, my dear, oh my dear. . . ."

He hurriedly hobbled off across the square, and did not return for a good hour. Varia was still on her knees at the head of Davidov's grave; but, hearing Shchukar's discreet cough, she got up and came out through the gate, swaying, resting her hands fearfully on the fence. She stood thus without speaking for a time. The old man, too, was silent. Then she said quietly:

"Thank you, Daddy, for letting me stay here with him, alone. . . ."

"There's nothing to thank me for. What are you going to do now, my dear?"

"I've come back for good. I arrived this morning, but I came here so late because I didn't want people to see . . ."

"But how about your studies?"

"I've given them up. My people can't manage without me."

"As I see it, our Siemion would not be pleased."

"But what else am I to do, dear Daddy?" Her voice shook.

"I'm not your councillor, my dear; think it out for yourself. Only don't offend him; you see, he did love you, that's a fact."

She turned swiftly and ran off across the square; she lacked the strength to stop and say good-bye to the old man.

But the groaning and calling of the cranes sounded in the impenetrably black sky till dawn came; and, till dawn, old Shchukar sat huddled on the bench, sighing, crossing himself, and crying.

Slowly, day after day, the counter-revolutionary conspiracy and

the rising which was being organized in the Don lands were unmasked and rendered impotent.

The third day after Davidov's death, members of the regional G.P.U. arrived in the village from Rostov. They at once recognized the man Razmiotnov had shot in Ostrovnov's yard as someone they had been after for a considerable time: a former lieutenant in the White Volunteer Army named Lyatievsky.

Three weeks later, in a Soviet farm not far from Tashkent, a nondescript-looking man in civilian clothes went up to the elderly book-keeper Kalishnikov, who had recently started to work there. Leaning across the table, he said quietly: "You've fixed yourself up in a comfortable little job, Mr. Polovtsiev, haven't you? . . . Steady now. . . . We'll go outside for a moment. . . . You lead the way."

Outside was another civilian, with hair greying at the temples. He was not so irreproachably polite and self-controlled as his younger comrade. When he saw Polovtsiev he stepped forward, blinking rapidly and turning pale with hate, and said: "You reptile! You'd crawled a long way. . . . So you thought you could hide away from us here, in this warren? You wait: I'll talk to you in Rostov. You'll do a dance or two for me before you die."

"Oh, how terrible! How you frighten me! I'm trembling all over like an aspen, I'm trembling with terror!" Polovtsiev said ironically, stopping to light a cheap cigarette. But from under his brows he looked up at the Cheka-man with sneering, hateful eyes.

They searched him on the spot. As he turned round and round obediently, he remarked: "Listen, you needn't take all this unnecessary trouble. I haven't any weapon on me: why should I bring it here? I've hidden my Mauser in my room. Come along."

On the way to his room he talked calmly and with deliberation, turning to the Cheka-man. "What do you think you can frighten me with? You're too naïve! With tortures? That won't come off: I'm ready for anything and can stand anything. And, besides, there's no point in torturing me, because I shall tell you all I know, not hiding anything and not trying to pull the wool over your eyes. I give you my word of honour as an officer. You can't kill me twice, and I've long been ready for death. We've lost,

and so life has come to be meaningless for me. I'm not talking for
the sake of talking, I'm no poseur and no fop, I face the truth,
and it's bitter for all of us. I believe above all in honouring my
debts: you've lost, so you pay. And I'm ready to pay for losing
with my life. I swear by God I don't find that terrible."

"Come down off your stilts and shut up, and leave it to us to
settle accounts," the man he had addressed this bombastic speech
to advised him.

They found nothing compromising except the Mauser when
they searched his room. There was not one document in his
plywood trunk. But on the table all the twenty-five volumes of
the works of Lenin were set out in order.

"Do those belong to you?" they asked him.

"Yes."

"And what did you have them for?"

He smiled wryly. "In order to beat your enemy you need to
know his weapons."

He kept his word: during his interrogation in Rostov he
betrayed Colonel Sedoi-Nikolsky and Captain Kazantsev, and
indicated from memory all the Cossacks who had been linked in
his organization in Gremyachy Log and the neighbouring villages.
Nikolsky betrayed the others.

A wave of arrests rolled through the Azov-Black Sea area.
More than six hundred Cossack rank-and-file members of the
conspiracy, including Ostrovnov and his son, were condemned
by special commission to various terms of imprisonment. Only
those who had taken direct part in terroristic activities were
shot. Polovtsiev, Nikolsky, Kazantsev, Lieutenant-Colonel Savvataev of the Stalingrad region, and two of his assistants, and
furthermore, nine White Guard generals and officers who had
been living in Moscow under pseudonyms, were sentenced to
death. Among the nine arrested in Moscow and around it was
one man who was not unknown in the Denikin army circles, a
Cossack lieutenant-general who was the head of the conspiracy
and was in regular contact with emigré organizations abroad.
Only four of the central organizing group managed to escape
arrest in Moscow and make their way abroad by devious routes.

So ended that desperate, historically foredoomed attempt to

organize a counter-revolutionary rising in southern Russia against the Soviet regime.

A few days after Varia Kharlamova had returned to the village, Andrei Razmiotnov came back from a trip he had made to the town of Shakhti. He had gone there at Maidannikov's request to buy a locomotive for the collective farm. They sat late in the evening in the collective-farm office, together with Ivan Naidionov, the secretary of the Young Communist group which had been started in Gremyachy. Razmiotnov reported in detail on his journey and the purchase, and then asked:

"I hear Varia Kharlamova's come back; she's given up her studies and has been to see Dubtsiev to ask him to take her back in his brigade. Is that correct?"

"Yes," Maidannikov sighed. "Her mother and the children have got to live somehow, haven't they? So she's left the agricultural school. But she's a capable girl."

Evidently Razmiotnov had thought it all out beforehand, and now spoke in perfect confidence that the others would agree to what he had to say.

"She's the fiancée of our dead comrade Siemion. She's got to go on studying. That's what he wanted. And that's what has got to be. Let's send for her to come here tomorrow, have a talk with her, and send her back to the school. And we'll take care of her family in the collective farm. Seeing as our dead comrade Davidov is no longer with us, it's up to us to take on the job of looking after his family. Any objections?"

Maidannikov nodded without speaking, but the fiery Ivan Maidionov squeezed Andrei's hand and exclaimed: "You're a great guy, Daddy Andrei."

Then Razmiotnov suddenly remembered something. "Oh yes, and I forgot to tell you, boys. Who d'you think I met in the street at Shakhti? You'll never guess. Lushka Nagulnova! I saw a rather fat woman coming along, and at her side a rather fat man, going bald. I took a glance at her and was struck: was it she, or wasn't it? She'd got a fat muzzle, her little eyes were sunk in folds of fat, and you'd need three arms to embrace her. But I could

tell by her walk it was her. I go up to her and speak to her,
asking: 'Is it really you, Lukeria?' But she answers: 'I don't know
you, citizen.' I laugh and say: 'You've soon forgotten your fellow
villagers. You are Lushka Nagulnova, aren't you?' And she pouts
her lips town fashion and says: 'My name was Nagulnova once,
and was Lushka to you once; but now I'm Lukeria Nikitichna
Sviridova, and this is my husband, a mining engineer. Let me
introduce you.' Well, I shook hands with the engineer, and he
stared at me as if I was the devil, as though he wished to know
why I was talking like that to his wife. Then they turned round
and walked off. Both of them fat, and very clearly satisfied with
themselves. But I couldn't help thinking: 'Well, but women are
strong creatures. It's not surprising Makar was against them all
his life. She's hardly had time to bury two, Timoshka and Makar,
when she's caught a third. But what I'd like to know isn't so
much how she caught him, but when she managed to get all
that fat?' That's what I wondered as I stood in the street. And I
felt quite sad at heart. I felt a touch of regret for the old Lushka,
young, smart with her tongue, and beautiful. But now you might
almost say I'd seen her in a dream a long, long time ago, once
upon a time, so to speak, but never lived with her in the same
village." He sighed. "Well, that's our life, boys; that's the way
things go. And sometimes they take a turn that you could never
think of for yourselves. Well, coming?"

They went out. Far beyond the Don heavy thunder clouds
were gathering and lightning rent the sky; they could just hear
the distant roll of thunder.

"I'm surprised the storms are so late this year," Maidannikov
said. "Let's stand and admire the performance for a minute or
two."

"You can if you want to. I'm off," Razmiotnov said. He wished
his comrades a good night, and ran youthfully down the steps.

But he did not go home. He strode out of the village, stood
for a moment or two, then made his way deliberately to the
cemetery, taking a wide circle round the mournfully glimmering
crosses, the graves, the half-demolished stone wall. He had come
to the spot where he wished to be. He took off his cap, stroked
his greying hair above his forehead with his right hand, and said
softly as he gazed down at a sunken grave: "I don't look after

your last home at all well, Yevdokia. . . ." He bent down, picked up a dry clod of clay, rubbed it into dust between his hands, and added in a thick undertone. "And yet I love you even now, my never to be forgotten one, the only one in my life. . . . You see, I've never any time. . . . We rarely see each other. . . . If you're able to, forgive me for all the evil I did you. . . . For all the ways in which I have done you wrong, you . . . the dead. . . ."

He stood there a long time with bared head, as though listening and waiting for an answer. He stood without stirring, his back bowed like an old man's. Beyond the Don, sheet lightning flickered white over the sky; and now Razmiotnov's stern, joyless eyes gazed not downward, not at the sunken edge of his wife's grave, but out to where above the invisible thread of the horizon half the sky lit up suddenly with a lurid light. Awakening all sleeping nature, majestic and vehement as in the heat of mid-summer, the last thunder of the year rolled overhead.

MIKHAIL SHOLOKHOV was born in 1905 in a village in the Don region, of a family that had been living there for many generations. His parents were poor, but they managed to send him to school in Moscow. At the age of fifteen he returned to his native village, where he became a schoolteacher, then a statistician, a food inspector, and half a dozen other things. He and his father were the only men in the town, and there, in those bloody years 1920-3, he saw with his own eyes what civil war meant.

He began writing when he was eighteen years old. Today he is one of the most popular writers in the Soviet Union—literally millions of copies of his works have been sold. But though his vast royalties would permit him to live luxuriously in one of the large cities, he prefers to live with his wife in the town of his forefathers near the Don. He has a small farm, with a few head of cattle, and he enjoys working on it. His leisure he spends hunting and fishing.

Regarded as a Soviet national hero, Sholokhov has nonetheless continually asserted his independence of the official Communist viewpoint in his writings and in his often blunt challenges to the Soviet's literary dictators. Thus, he was one of the few writers in Russia to defend Boris Pasternak during the controversy over the publication of *Dr. Zhivago*.

Mr. Sholokhov is now at work on a cycle of novels entitled *They Fought for Their Country* which will tell the story of the Don country and its people during World War II.

A NOTE ON THE TYPE

THE TEXT of this book is set in CALEDONIA, a face designed by W. A. Dwiggins. It belongs to the family of printing types called "modern face" by printers—a term used to mark the change in style of type-letters that occurred about 1800. Caledonia borders on the general design of Scotch Modern, but is more freely drawn than that letter.

The book was composed, printed, and bound by H. Wolff, New York. Paper manufactured by S. D. Warren Co., Boston.

M Abr

1961

1st Swern d. op